*B*rand had one of the best bodies she'd ever seen not on a movie screen.

A body she could imagine wrapping herself around all too vividly. She could taste the salt of his skin, feel his muscles moving under her exploring hands…

And as she stood there trying desperately not to drool onto the scallops, he finished pulling the shirt off, tossed it aside with a flourish, and winked at her.

Be still my beating heart.

"I thought…the apron…" she said weakly.

He grinned and tied on an apron emblazoned with a bunch of grapes. It said "Pinch Me, Squeeze Me, Make Me Wine."

Over a shirt, it would have looked adorable. Over bare skin, it was devastating. Pure sex.

OUT OF THE
frying pan

a hollywood spice novel

sophie
mouette

LKP
LITTLE KISSES
PRESS

OUT OF THE FRYING PAN

Sophie Mouette

Print edition published 2014 by Little Kisses Press

ISBN-13: 978-0615938462 (trade paperback)
ISBN-10: 0615938469 (trade paperback)

Inquiries should be addressed to
Little Kisses Press
littlekissespress@gmail.com
http://www.littlekissespress.com

Cover image © inarik / Bigstockphoto.com
Cover design by Allyson Longueira
Little Kisses Press logo by Dayle Dermatis

For Ken & Jeff,
who add sizzle and spice to my life.

OUT OF THE
frying pan

Chapter 1

That morning, Chloe's horoscope had said "avoid false turns."

If only she'd heeded that advice. It was just that she'd never put much stock in astrology, and only started reading the horoscope page when she'd moved to Los Angeles a month ago, adrift and starting a new life across the country with nothing much to do in the morning but read every inch of the *LA Times*, starting with the food section and ending with the horoscopes.

She hadn't expected it to be so hard, the move and all. In Boston, she'd had a fabulous job as the sous-chef at an acclaimed restaurant.

What she hadn't known until she'd gotten here was that acclaimed restaurants in Boston were sneered at by acclaimed restaurants in LA. Who knew that LA restaurants looked down their long noses and sniffed at Boston restaurants, then turned dismissively away, making snide comments under their breaths?

Which is why she'd taken this temp job helping cater for the American Action Movie Awards, or AAMies. It was beneath her talent and skill, but it would help pay the rent—and rent in LA was outlandish.

But everything was going horribly wrong.

First of all, she'd been late. Very late. Boston traffic was bad, but it didn't hold a candle to the southern California freeways.

She'd had to show her ID and pass to five different security checkpoint guards, and then she'd gotten turned around and almost missed the door to the kitchen.

Only to learn that she'd been hired as a waitress.

There had to be a mistake. She was a *chef*, dammit. Trained at Culinary Institute of America. Paid her dues at Printemps and Harvest before working for Maurice.

She was not, by any stretch of the imagination, a goddamn waitress.

Chloe wanted to storm out. She *almost* stormed out.

Almost.

But she had no money, and no real job.

And Luanna was counting on her to pay her half of the rent. Because if she didn't, they'd be out on the street. That meant Evenrude, Luanna's Welsh corgi wouldn't get fed, or even have a home. When Chloe imagined those big, liquid brown eyes staring up at her, she caved. She pushed aside her pride (it pushed back, but in the end, she muscled it into submission), grabbed hold of her responsibilities with both hands, gritted her teeth, and said,

"Right. Waitress. Where do I change?"

She repeated the directions under her breath. "Down the hall, past the dining room, across the lobby, behind the staging area, the door's on your left. No, on the right. It's not marked, but it's just past the Steven Seagal display."

Getting across the lobby entailed going through two more security checkpoints, one at either end, and at the first one she'd forgotten where she'd shoved her ID once she thought she was free and clear, and in the lobby she thought she'd spotted The Rock, so she was admittedly flustered.

And she didn't even *like* The Rock that much.

So where was the staging area?

"Excuse me," a voice said. "Do you need any help?"

"I'm looking for the staging area," she said as she turned.

If she hadn't been so frazzled and late and miffed, she would've taken more time than just *Huh, he's really cute!* But all she processed was a killer pair of bedroom eyes behind a cute pair of little wire-rimmed glasses as he said, "I think it's that way, but I'm not sure—let me ask."

He headed back towards the lobby, and Chloe felt bad but she just didn't have time to wait. She went in the direction he suggested, and hallelujah! found the Steven Seagal cardboard cutout surrounded by posters from *Marked for Death* and *Out of Reach* and *Under Siege* (*1, 2,* and *3*). She pushed open the first door on her left. It was heavier than she expected, and she stumbled in.

No, she stumbled *out*. She was outside.

On the freaking red carpet.

Red was all she saw before the flashbulbs started going off, at which point just about all she could see was yellow and white glowing blobs. She'd been blinded. She'd never see again.

Chloe whirled. The door, swinging shut on its well-oiled hinges, was almost closed. She lunged.

There was no handle. It was an out-only door.

Her fingers scrabbled for a handhold, to just catch the very crack of space before the door—

—shut with an utter, resounding finality.

Shit. Oh holy shit on a stick.

Surely there was another door. She scanned the wall, left and right, back and forth. Nothing. Nada.

She turned back around, frantically seeking an exit. Running right along in front of her like the damn Yellow Brick Road was the red carpet. There were stars on it—not The Rock, or even Vin Diesel, although that woman there could have been Angelina Jolie's stunt double—as well as the press—she was sure that lady there was from VH-1's *Hottest Entertainment News.*

Just beyond the carpet was a rope barrier and a buttload of paparazzi, all with cameras and booms and mics and equipment she couldn't recognize and didn't want to, and where the hell was she going to go?

Okay. She couldn't go left, in the direction the stars were headed. That would send her through the front door, and she didn't have the creds to get through the front door. So she'd go right, and find the street where they were all coming from, and then she'd get her bearings…

Who was she kidding? She didn't know the damn Hollywood streets without a Thomas Guide or a cheap GPS.

Still, it was better than no plan at all.

She took a step forwards, and lights exploded in her face.

"Wait, no, I'm not famous—"

They couldn't hear her. She was on the red carpet, and thus they had to capture her for tonight's television recap and tomorrow's website and next week's *US Weekly*.

And that's when she saw the security team advancing, looking as menacing as rent-a-cops could.

Rent-a-cops with tazers, she saw, and gulped.

"Hey," a deep voice said. It didn't sound menacing, thank goodness.

She turned.

He was tall, broad-shouldered, and his tuxedo jacket had obviously been tailor-made for him because nothing off the rack would have contained those bulging biceps and sculpted pecs.

He looked a little familiar.

"Who are you?" he asked.

His brown eyes were kind, and somehow they reminded Chloe of Evenrude, and something broke inside of her and she started to babble.

"I'm one of the caterers." Okay, technically not true, but she *ought* to be one of the caterers, dammit. "I got lost, and I came out the wrong door, and it closed behind me and doesn't open from the outside. I'm really, really lost."

He laughed, a rumbling chuckle that triggered some memory for her. "Yes, you really, really are." He glanced over his shoulder. "They don't look too happy," he said of the guards.

"Please don't let them arrest me," she said in a teeny-tiny voice that made her cringe, but she couldn't help it. That was the way it came out when she was in a panic.

"Okay, Miss Pretty Caterer," he said. He held out his arm. When she didn't respond—she was still gaping in dread—he gently took her hand and tucked it into the crook of his arm, and started back down the red carpet at a leisurely pace, smiling and waving at the photographers.

Out of the corner of her eye, Chloe saw the guards stop, confer quickly, and then turn away.

She wilted, relieved. It was all going to be okay.

"Ray!" a reporter cooed. "Where's Sandrine? Who's the lovely lady you're escorting tonight?"

Ray. Suddenly it all crashed down, complete with a roaring in her ears. She was on the arm of Ray Stark, who was expected to win the Best Action Actor AAMie for his role in *Rode Hard and Put Away Wet* (although Jackie Chan was considered a close contender for his latest kung-fu flick).

Of course he looked familiar. He looked just a little bit like Brad Pitt (if Brad Pitt were bald and three inches taller and beefier), which all the media capitalized on.

And *Rode Hard had* been an awfully fun movie.

"Just a new friend," Ray told the reporter. "Sandrine's still resting her foot—the temporary cast doesn't go with any of her evening gowns."

"Ray!" another reporter called. "What's her name?"

Ray glanced down at Chloe.

"Chloe Montiero," she whispered.

"Chloe Montiero," he told the reporter.

"And where did you meet her?"

"It's a long story," he said, flashing that twinkling grin that made the ladies swoon and had put him in *People* magazine's Most Beautiful People issue (although he hadn't made the cover, sadly). "Let's just say we sort of ran into each other."

A microphone was shoved into Chloe's face, a very bright light hovering over it. She could feel the heat pouring out of bulb. Dizzied, she tried to step back, but the crowd had gotten too thick.

"Chloe, that's an unusual choice for the red carpet," the interviewer said. "Who are you wearing?"

"I—uh—" She was wearing a strappy little turquoise dress, one of Luanna's creations. It had been so hot today that she hadn't wanted to put on more. The little sandals were off-brand, although she'd been vain enough to go with spiky heels to add to her height, figuring she'd change into flat shoes right before she got to work.

Thank the gods she wasn't wearing her chef's whites already. Nobody would have believed she belonged there. The tote bag—thank goodness a cute bohemian-chic one embroidered with shisha mirrors—containing her comfy shoes was bad enough.

"Luanna Devenaux," she said to fill the silence.

"So how did you and Ray…"

Inexplicably, Ray saved the day again. "I'm sorry we don't have more time to talk, but I need to get inside. Don't want to miss those exquisite hors d'oeuvres they always serve." He smiled that dazzling smile again, and steered Chloe in the direction they needed to go. It was all she could do to keep herself from stumbling, the after-effects of the flashbulbs still causing spots in front of her eyes.

Inside it was just as cacophonous as outside, but in a different way. Whereas outside there had been a lot of shouting to get the stars' attention, inside it was just crowded and busy, the normal sounds trapped and bounced back off the walls and ceiling. Harried PAs tried to direct the flow of people, but everyone seemed to have their own agenda of where to go and what they wanted.

"Well, this is where I get off the train," Ray said. "I gotta go in and make sure I haven't forgotten anybody in my acceptance speech, just in case." He patted his chest, where he had apparently tucked the speech.

"Good luck," Chloe said. "I mean, break a leg. Is that what I'm supposed to say? I hope you win. I loved *Rode Hard*."

Jesus, could she *ever* stop babbling?

"Good luck to you, too, Miss Pretty Caterer," he said, a smile crossing his face and making him look far less menacing than he did on screen when he was beating the bad guys all the way to hell and back. "Go make some of those fabulous hors d'oeuvres."

He put an arm around her, leaned down, and kissed her cheek. Just barely brushed against her skin, a touch that was obviously brotherly as opposed to flirtatious or sexual. (Brotherly she knew, having an abundance of big brothers.)

Then he was gone, lost in the crowd of people except for the fact that he was one of the tallest among them. Chloe watched him go, still reeling, until someone bumped into her. She opened her mouth to bitch, but thankfully no words came out before she realized that the offender was Kit Harding, star of the *Amazon* series of films.

You don't piss off a six-foot-tall woman with gladiator arms who could wipe the floor with Jennifer Garner's Elektra. You just don't.

"Sorry, my fault," she mumbled and squeezed her way through the crowd until she found a wall to press herself against.

Right. She just had to find her way back to the Steven Seagal exhibit and figure out where she'd gone wrong. They wouldn't've needed any servers yet, and even if they did, she could slip in and grab a tray from some overworked waiter and everything would be fine.

Taking a deep breath, she pushed away from the wall.

"Hey, aren't you Ray Stark's date?" A reporter shoved a microphone in her face.

Shit. There was no way she could go out there in a waitress uniform and not get attacked by a camera.

Self-preservation won over rent money. Chloe ducked under the man's outstretched arm and fled, right out the door she'd first entered not half an hour before.

*

Chloe woke when a violent shaking nearly tumbled her out of bed.

Earthquake!?

Her heart thudding as hard and painfully as her head, she ripped the sleep mask off her eyes. She squinted in the bright sunlight pouring in her window that made her head throb worse.

Luanna had been out when she'd gotten home last night, and she'd fixed a miserable (but creative) dinner while sipping Trader Joe's Two-buck Chuck, and she didn't remember much more than that.

Well, okay, she remembered being concerned that Evenrude had split into three corgis, and she'd wondered whether she needed glasses, which she couldn't afford anyway.

Now there was a blurry blob blocking some of the light. Was their apartment haunted? Did those crumbling Art Deco features and once-fancy molding mask a sordid and horrifying tale of murder and revenge?

At least the shaking had stopped. If it had been an earthquake, it was over now. She braced herself in case there was an aftershock and she'd have to fling herself at the nearest doorway. (She wasn't sure why you were supposed to do that—the doorframe was just as creaky as the rest of the place—but that's what everybody said.)

The blurry blob in front of her shifted into semi-focus of a dark outline of Luanna.

Oh good. She didn't need glasses.

Then her morning took a sudden downturn as her best friend demanded, "What the hell have you done?"

Chapter 2

*E*venrude put a paw over her eyes when Luanna showed Chloe the online gossip page.

"I swear, nothing happened," Chloe repeated for the millionth time, or at least the nth time in the span it took her to get out of bed, escape to the bathroom to pee, splash cold water on her face, pop some much-needed Advil, and pull her hair up with a tortoiseshell butterfly clip because the feel of anything on her neck right now made her want to scream, and never mind that her hair was barely chin-length.

During all that, she'd carefully explained to Luanna how the evening had gone. Late arrival, wrong turn, red carpet, saved by a polite Ray, and retreat. The end.

"That's not what everybody else is saying," Luanna said.

Everybody else?

Which is when Luanna showed her the website.

Her stomach churned, but not from the effects of last night's wine.

RAY DUMPS SANDRINE FOR MYSTERY DATE?

Ray Stark showed up at the AAMies—where he went on to win Best Action Actor for his role in *Rode Hard*—with Chloe Montero, whom he introduced deliberately vaguely as "a new friend."

Montero.

"*Filho da puta.* Can't they even spell it right?" she muttered.

> The two were seen in an intimate embrace just inside the Shrine Auditorium, but Ms. Montero appears to have left soon thereafter and was not seen in the audience when Stark collected his Best Action Actor statue.
>
> Stark's long-time girlfriend, Sandrine Moss, was not present at the ceremony. When asked, Stark said she was resting.
>
> Ms. Moss has been recovering from a foot injury, which she suffered on the set of her last movie, the soon-to-be-released *Soul's Road.*
>
> Stark and Ms. Moss's relationship seemed rocky in its early years, but Stark recently moved into Ms. Moss's Bel Air estate and the couple seemed to be content. Stark's mystery date may be a sign that cracks are beginning to show.
>
> Ms. Moss's agent said her client had no comment at this time.

Accompanying the article was a picture of them on the red carpet, her hand tucked protectively in the crook of his arm.

Then, worse—far, far worse—a picture of him kissing her.

"Ray Stark kissed you!" Luanna's voice went up to a register that made the gorgeous but very old stained glass in the window rattle in its loose lead panes.

"Just on the cheek."

"It doesn't look that way to me."

And it didn't. The angle the photographer had found made the innocent, brotherly peck look steamy. Ray's head blocked hers just enough that it looked as though he was meeting her head-on, lip-to-lip. The casual arm he had around her had mutated into a groping hug that seemed to be pulling her against him.

"What are you going to do?" Luanna whispered.

"First, I'm going to sit down and put my head between my knees." Chloe did exactly that. Evenrude jumped up on the sofa next to her and lay down with a sigh.

"Here." Luanna reappeared with a tumbler of cold orange juice.

Chloe grabbed the glass with both hands and guzzled the juice like it was the first thing she'd had to drink after being trapped on *Survivor*. It felt like that, anyway.

It didn't ease the pounding in her skull, but it was still good.

That was when the phone started to ring. And ring. And ring…

*

Her horoscope that morning read, "Remember: The truth shall set you free."

That wouldn't be so hard. She already intended to tell nothing but the truth. Her mama had raised her to be an honest girl (with a healthy dollop of politeness—white lies were okay if they were employed to keep someone's feelings from getting hurt).

So when Luanna politely began to dissuade the third reporter who called, Chloe reached out for the phone. "Let me clear this up," she told her friend. "Once and for all. I'll get it over with, and then everybody will go away and it'll all be a bad memory, like that recipe I tried with catfish, molé sauce, and brie."

"Chloe Montiero," she said into the phone. "How may I help you?"

Her mama had also taught her that politeness, even feigned, was a virtue.

"Chloe, this is Grace Templeton with VH-1's *Hottest Entertainment News*. I'd like to ask you a few questions about your relationship with Ray Stark."

"Oh, we don't have a relationship."

"So it was a first date?"

"No, no, you've got it all wrong. It wasn't a date. I was there to cater—"

Okay, she'd accidentally been sent there to be a waitress. Which reminded her, she had to call MerryTemps and complain. Yes, she'd checked the box that said "food service experience," but she'd written right next to it that she meant cooking. Couldn't they read?

"To cater to Ray's needs?" Grace Templeton, girl reporter, asked.

"Good lord, no! I'm a *chef*."

"And that's how you know Ray?"

How much did she want to say? Getting locked outside the venue was pretty embarrassing. It shouldn't affect her ability to get a job or anything…but then again, if a potential employer heard about this, maybe they'd think she was flaky or something.

So much for falling off anybody's radar.

"In a manner of speaking, yes," she said. It wasn't a lie. She'd been there to cook, and that's how she'd run into Ray. No need to tell them about the getting-lost part, or the getting-locked-out part, and certainly not about the waitressing part. That was to keep her own feelings from getting hurt.

The cell phone buzzed in her hand, and she checked the display. Crap, it was her mother. It wasn't that she didn't want to talk to her mother; it was just that her mother would panic if Chloe didn't answer the phone. Because Chloe lived in Los Angeles now, and everyone knew Los Angeles was full of kooky people who would kidnap you and get you hooked on drugs and the next thing you knew you were a dried-up former porn star and current junkie starting the cycle all over again by preying on innocent newcomers.

She wasn't sure which part her mother was most concerned about, and she didn't dare ask. The bottom line was, if she didn't answer her phone, the downward spiral must already have begun.

"I'm sorry, Grace, but I have another call coming in," she said. "I hope I've cleared everything up. Thank you."

"Thank *you*." Grace sounded burblingly happy.

Chloe hung up and answered her mother's call. "Morning, Mama."

"Sweetie! Pumpkin! Chloe-pie! What's all this about you marrying some actor?"

Luanna handed her a fresh glass of orange juice and mouthed that she was going out for Krispy Kremes.

It was going to be a long morning.

*

Brand's phone sang the original *Star Trek* theme. Without taking his eyes from the thirty-inch flat-panel monitor that displayed the CGI magic he was creating, he answered.

"Brand? It's Olive."

His sister's personal assistant. Uh oh. She never called unless there was a problem with Sandrine that only he could handle. He sat up, dropping his feet to the floor, and glanced around. It was lunchtime, so half of his team members were gone and the other half were at their work stations in the open floor plan, slices of celebratory pizza in their left hands while with their rights they continued clicking and typing.

Joe had stopped in mid-chew to zoom in on some detail. Brand hoped he wouldn't drip cheese on his track pad.

He probably wouldn't be disturbed. He reached out and eased his office door closed.

"What's wrong?" he asked.

"Did you hear what happened last night?"

Last night his team had won a Best Special Effects AAMie for *Jane Austen in Space*, and there had been much carousing. His sister's beau, Ray Stark, had won the coveted Best Actor award, but by the time Brand had stumbled home, it had been too late for congratulations.

"I'm afraid to ask."

"Apparently some woman got lost and ended up on the red carpet, and Ray took pity on her. Next thing you know, there's a pap shot that makes it look like he's kissing her, and then Perez Hilton reported his usual half-correct info, and now VH-1…oh, it's probably already on YouTube."

Brand had already been accessing the gossip site, so he opened a new window and did the keyword search Olive suggested.

The boringly pretty VH-1 reporter said, "The mystery woman spotted with Ray Stark has identified herself as his personal chef. Given that Ray has taken up housekeeping with his girlfriend, starlet Sandrine Moss, it stands to reason that Chloe Montiero is cooking for both of them. It's still not clear what she was doing on the red carpet with Ray, but we can only guess that Sandrine's notoriously fussy eating habits have rubbed off on the action star."

Brand groaned. Sands had fired her latest in a long string of chefs last week, and thanks to the stories in the cooking community about her notoriously picky tastes, she hadn't found a replacement. That some woman was claiming to be the replacement was very, very bad.

Then the woman in question's face flashed up on the screen, a shot from the red carpet, and Brand's stomach dropped faster than Gandalf tumbling after the Balrog.

He knew that woman. She'd asked him for directions at the AAMies, and—it appeared now—he'd sent her the wrong way.

The camera pulled back. Her hand was tucked in Ray's arm, and Ray looked his usual easy-going self. The woman looked terrified and vaguely ill, but her chin was up, as if she were telling herself that she would get through this somehow, probably by sheer force of will.

He respected that, even as he wanted to reach through the computer screen and pluck her out of there and Make It All Go Away.

(And, he had to admit, he also wanted to pluck her out of there to find out if her curves really were as luscious as that flirty little green sundress indicated. He was, after all, a guy. And she was tempting and adorable and spunky.)

The new view was accompanied by voice-over of another conversation with her. She said, "…to cater—I'm a chef."

"And that's how you know Ray?" the VH-1 reporter's voice asked.

"—yes."

He cradled his forehead in his hand, shaking his head. Typical press and their soundbites. It was clear there had been much more to the conversation. Clear to anyone with half a brain, that was. The rest of the tabloid media, and a good portion of America, would take it at face value.

"Has Sands seen this?" he asked Olive.

"Not yet, but—"

In the background came a furious shriek. It almost sounded like one of the peacocks on the estate, but Brand knew better.

"She's seen it now," Olive said. "I'd better go. Ray and I will handle her. If not, I'll call you if you need to come home."

Brand opened his organization software and stared at the long list of things he had to do: mockups for the new movie, two employee reviews, check some dailies, and, oh, follow up on a slew of phone calls thanks to their AAMie. By all rights, he couldn't—as much as he wanted to—leave to go take care of his sister.

Responsibility tugged him in both directions.

He had to stay. But he was unable to resist doing a quick search for more clips and photos of the hapless but striking Chloe Montiero.

*

Chloe ignored the incessant ringing of her phone for several hours, through various relatives, Boston and Culinary Institute friends, and a couple of members of the press (including one fashion writer trying to find out more about Luanna).

She ignored them long enough to take Evenrude for a long walk to the farmer's market on the other side of town, where she looked longingly at beautiful produce and instead splurged on one 75-cent bunch of epazote to dress up tonight's Cheap Dinner Special of rice and black beans.

She ignored them long enough to get the already-cooked beans reheating with epazote and chilies.

She ignored them long enough to decide that a dollop of Trader Joe's Two-buck Chuck red would make the mixture taste better, and that since it was open, a drink was a reasonable investment in her obvious future career as an unemployed alcoholic.

Just as the first sips of the rough-but-fruity red were hitting—the alcohol hadn't taken effect but the idea of alcohol was already starting to relax her—the phone rang again.

"Go away!" she yelled, startling the drowsing Evenrude into a barking frenzy. "Just go away."

A crisp, professional voice came through the answering machine. "Hello. This is Olive Welsh, Sandrine Moss's personal assistant, calling for Chloe Montiero."

At least Chloe figured it had to be "Olive." The woman pronounced it Ah-*leave*, accent on the last syllable, so it took a few seconds to process.

At any other moment, Chloe would have been inclined to giggle. This was not one of those moments. This was one of those moments that made her inclined to throw up.

Chapter 3

Chloe froze, tumbler of wine halfway to her lips, Evenrude running in circles between her and the phone and yipping.

"Ms. Moss wishes to speak to Ms. Montiero immediately. Please contact…"

Chloe tripped over the dog, banged her elbow on the doorjamb, and splashed some wine onto the already nasty carpet, but got to the phone before Ah-leave hung up. She set the glass down on the rickety plywood bookcase that doubled as a phone stand, took a deep breath, and picked up.

Maybe this would be her chance to set things right once and for all. If Sandrine Moss went to the press with the real story, they'd listen to her, right? Right?

Chloe didn't get a chance to say much beyond, "Hello, this is Chloe Montiero," before Olive/Ah-leave started in.

"Ah, hello, Ms. Montiero. I'm so glad I've caught you at home."

Olive's silky voice left it unclear whether she was actually glad or not. She was, after all, just doing her job, Chloe figured.

"Chloe," Olive went on. "May I call you Chloe?" She didn't give Chloe time to respond. "As you're no doubt aware, recent circumstances have brought your name and Ms. Moss's into close proximity. I fear Ms. Moss is…concerned by this. She's not pleased with the concept of someone claiming to be her chef when in fact this is untrue."

Chloe's stomach dropped to somewhere in the vicinity of the garage-level trash room of the apartment building. So much for the real story. She was going to be sued. Sued by someone who appeared on the cover of *US Weekly* on a regular basis. Which meant, obviously, that Chloe would lose.

Instead of preparing succulent lobster dishes for adoring diners, she'd be helping out on her brother's lobster fishing boat in Rhode Island.

"Ms. Welsh, please, this has all been a terrible misunderstanding—"

"Ah, yes," Olive continued smoothly. "Ms. Moss has been dissuaded from taking any immediate cease-and-desist action until she speaks with you personally. I've penciled you in for eight forty-five tomorrow morning. If you've got a pen, I can give you directions here from Panorama City." She said "Panorama City" with the kind of tone people normally used for "dog poo" or "rotten meat."

Chloe couldn't take it anymore. Her legs gave way, and she found herself sitting on the world's scariest carpet, leaning against the rickety bookcase.

Evenrude flopped down on her back and shot all four paws in the air, secure in the prospect of a belly rub.

You can't always get what you want.

"Hold on!" Chloe clutched the receiver. "Tomorrow morning. I'm not sure—"

"Don't tell me you have to check your calendar." Olive/Ah-leeve's voice managed to be professional and sarcastic all at once. "What could you possibly have to do tomorrow morning that would be more important than sorting this issue out?"

And avoid getting sued was an unspoken, but clearly implied, addition.

"Of course," Chloe said weakly. "Since you put it that way, eight forty-five is fine."

It wasn't as though she had anything planned other than walking the dog, scanning the want ads and job boards, and sending out résumés.

Somehow, that didn't have the same weight as convincing Sandrine Moss not to sue her for...for whatever legal grounds the actress had to sue. Slander or libel or falsely impersonating a personal chef or whatever.

Chloe closed her eyes and took a long, deep breath. If Sandrine did sue, she'd get a 2003 Mini Cooper with way too many miles on it and no air conditioning, and a framed degree from the Culinary Institute of America. So fine, let her sue.

"Excellent," Ah-leave said. "Here are the directions. Oh, and Ms. Montiero? May I say it might behoove you to be forthcoming about your culinary experience."

*

"You know what they say about not looking gift horses in the mouth?"

Chloe had gotten that far on her horoscope at 6:50 a.m., just before she completely panicked about the time. She ran downstairs, clutching an avocado sandwich in one hand (they were eating a lot of avocados these days, since one of Luanna's co-workers had trees in his backyard and shared his wealth) and a messenger bag in the other. The *Times* remained on the kitchen counter for later.

Luanna had loaned her a soft, lipstick-red chiffon blouse, fitted under the bust and pleated from bust to waist, bowing to the '40s but very modern, which went perfectly with her cream-colored silk suit.

"It's the prototype of one of my designs for Luscious," Luanna said, "and it hasn't been released yet. Red's supposed to be a money-drawing color—at least if you're Chinese, which you're not, but still, a billion Chinese people can't all be wrong—so maybe it'll bring you good luck."

Chloe decided not to point out that many Chinese people were poor as dirt, because the blouse did transform the plain suit into something chic and special, and the shade of red complemented her olive complexion.

After her experience trying to get to the AAMies on time, she was leaving with lots of time to spare. Or, if LA traffic followed its usual gridlock, she was going to squeak in just in time. Twenty miles could easily take her an hour and a half.

And she'd thought Boston traffic was bad.

She swung by the nearest Coffee Bean and Tea Leaf for a double espresso extra-large please-God-help-me-wake-up special, jiggling nervously when it took the barista more than a minute to pull the drink together. She had to *go*. She couldn't be late.

Heaven forbid if she was late! Sandrine would sic the dogs on her or something. She probably had Dobermans. Big, mean ones.

She set the cardboard cup between her thighs—the next time she could afford to buy a car, the number two thing it had to have was a cup holder (the number one thing being air conditioning)—and navigated the palm-lined streets to the freeway.

Then some bastard in the next lane driving a gargantuan black gas-guzzling SUV and talking on his cell phone realized that he, too, needed to take the same freeway on-ramp that she was entering. *That she was already entering.* Without even deigning to glance down at her, he one-handedly jerked his steering wheel, sending his behemoth of a vehicle barreling at her.

Chloe swerved to avoid being crushed, leaning on her horn. Without missing a beat—without, apparently, pausing in the phone conversation that took all of his attention because obviously none was on, oh, say, *driving*—the driver of the SUV of Doom flipped her off and floored it, accelerating away from her.

For a moment, Chloe thought she'd peed herself.

Then she looked down and saw that the plastic cover of the coffee cup had popped off while she was attempting to avert certain fiery death.

She wailed "Shiiiiiiiit!" once, then switched to Portuguese out of habit. A long, expressive series of invectives.

The lone flimsy napkin from Coffee Bean and Tea Leaf, along with one of the three copies of her résumé, mopped up the worst of the hot liquid, but there was no way around it.

She was going to meet Sandrine Moss with a huge coffee stain on her cream-colored slacks.

*

Twenty miles did not, in fact, take an hour and a half. Nor even an hour.

It took approximately thirty-seven-and-a-half minutes from her door to the curlicued metal security gates that crossed the entrance of Sandrine's driveway.

Now she really wished she'd brought the *Times*.

She ate the rest of her avocado sandwich, washing it down with the remains of the now-lukewarm coffee. All told, she'd only spilled about ten percent of it, but it had been a super ultra venti, which meant that losing ten percent still meant she had a pint and a half of coffee to enjoy on her drive.

Well, at least it would keep her awake.

That still didn't mean she could press the call button and ask to be let onto Sandrine's estate. She was hideously early, and although that wasn't as bad as being late, it would hardly be appreciated.

She rummaged in the backseat and pulled out one of the old newspapers she'd tossed in the back for when Evenrude went for a ride. Damn, she'd already done the crossword....

Chloe woke with a start. Oh God, how long had she been asleep? She fumbled to twist her watch upright on her wrist, then sagged with relief. Eight thirty-five. She still had ten minutes.

As she un-slumped herself, however, another reason for panic surfaced.

The mega-mega-sized coffee hadn't put enough of a dent in her fatigue, maybe, but it sure had done wonders on her bladder.

She chewed her lower lip, a prickle of perspiration at her brow. The last portion of her drive had been through the long, winding, tree-shaded canyons of the so-upscale-it-put-sheiks-to-shame neighborhood, where the driveways (no self-respecting house would be visible from the street) seemed to be miles apart.

There was no way, unless instantaneous transportation systems were invented in the next few seconds, that she could get all the way out to a public restroom and back in ten minutes.

She examined the bushes lining the gateway with a calculating eye. If she could find Kleenex in the glove box...

No. No, a thousand times no. The last thing she needed was to be caught peeing in Sandrine Moss's shrubbery. There were probably a thousand paparazzi lurking around in their own claimed shrubbery, waiting for a juicy snap of the starlet.

She'd just have to wait it out.

It was, no doubt, going to be the longest ten—no, wait, nine now—minutes of her life.

She drummed her fingers on the steering wheel. Thought about that game where you shoved as many Saltines in your mouth as you could and then tried to whistle.

Seven and a half minutes. It was the coffee shop's fault. She should sue. It was Los Angeles; surely she'd win. They'd call it the Caffeine Defense. Like the Twinkie Defense, only with more twitching.

Four minutes and fifteen seconds. Why did she have to be a girl? Why couldn't she have been born a boy like her brothers, and been able to make use of that empty water bottle in the backseat?

She thought about her brothers. Didn't Craig used to have a poster of Sandrine in his bedroom? Or was that Casey? Either way, they'd all hoot and holler when she told them the story of meeting Sandrine.

Three minutes. Fine. Being a little early was a virtue, right?

She eased the car forwards and reached out the window to press the intercom button.

"Yes?" The voice came through the low hum of a connection.

"Hi, yes, this is Chloe Montiero, and I have an eight four—"

The hum ended abruptly.

"—ty five appointment—"

The iron gates slid open, soundless on their well-oiled tracks.

"—with Sandrine Moss," Chloe finished lamely.

She'd seen pictures here and there—probably nomads in the Kalahari had too—but they hadn't really conveyed just how big and grandiose the estate was.

It was like Versailles in Beverly Hills.

To the left, the lawn sloped up to a broad, elaborately tiled patio the size of the front yard of the house she'd grown up in, with a cabana next to it that looked like it belonged in the Arabian Nights. An achingly blue kidney-shaped pool was the focal point.

Or, it would have been, if it weren't for the Pool Boy of the Gods.

He was skimming the pool with a net on a long pole. She caught a glimpse of reddish brown hair, a little too long and curling at the ends.

Sunglasses, de rigueur. A very bare, very nice chest angling down to a narrow waist and hips. His jeans rode low on those hips.

Then the main house loomed into view, and distracted her even from Yummy Pool Boy.

About the size of a city block to her dazzled eyes, the place was so white it gleamed in the morning sun. It was vaguely Mediterranean in style, although not any one part of the Mediterranean. A little Spanish. A little Italian. Even a little French—the round turrets reminded her of the chateaux she'd snuck away to see during her internship in France. Moorish archways. Lots and lots of windows. Tiled terracotta roofs. A bronze fountain in the shape of a mermaid, gently burbling water in the middle of a tiny garden set in the middle of the circular driveway. Archways with statues in them.

The scary part was that Sandrine was a star, but not one of the highest paid ones. This meant that, say, Tom Cruise or Julia Roberts probably had even more lavish homes.

What the hell was a coffee-stained girl from Galilee, Rhode Island, doing in a place like this?

A coffee-stained girl from Galilee, Rhode Island, with a degree from the best culinary school in the country, an apprenticeship in Paris, and fabulous restaurant experience. She sat up a little straighter in her seat, albeit wincing as she did. A girl who had come to Los Angeles on purpose, to make her career. And what she was doing here might even involve her résumé—not her stained suit.

But above all, a girl who really, really needed to pee.

With all the cool she could muster under the circumstances, she eased out of the car, holding her messenger bag in front of her to mask the obvious.

A short, black, forty-something woman was waiting for her on the broad, shallow marble steps. In another context, a different outfit, she might have looked dumpy—a little plump, not especially pretty—but between an expensive-looking haircut and an artfully unmatched "suit" that hinted at cleavage without showing any and accented shapely calves while downplaying a fireplug middle, the effect was more *very professional*.

Certainly no stains on her outfit. She appeared not to notice Chloe's state, though, as she extended a hand. "I'm Olive Welsh."

Hearing her in person, Chloe picked up the slight French accent that probably explained the pronunciation of the name.

"Delighted to meet you, Ms. Montiero."

Delighted? Maybe, maybe not.

"Follow me, please. Ms. Moss is waiting for you."

She seemed less sarcastic in person. Extremely brisk and efficient, but that was softened with a pleasant smile.

No, Olive wouldn't look dumpy, even in a Walmart sweat suit. Or rather, she would, but you'd be too busy being organized by her to notice.

"Um, Olive?"

The woman turned, finely plucked eyebrows raised.

"Could you please direct me to the restroom first?" She thought quickly. "So I can freshen up?"

"Of course."

Olive pointed her to the appropriate door (there were many more choices than the fabled three).

After she'd saved herself from certain ruin, Chloe washed her hands and tried not to be overawed by the bathroom, which was larger than her bedroom. To think this was really a powder room, with just a sink and a toilet.

She dried her hands on a towel with a higher thread count than the sheets the President slept on, and returned to her guide.

They ended up in a courtyard area, the kind of "outdoor room" Maurice used to sigh that he wanted for the restaurant, but couldn't really pull off in the Boston climate, where it was either too cold, too hot, or too wet almost all the time.

Chloe was vaguely aware that it was lovely, but she wasn't paying much attention to anything but the slender figure sitting at a mosaic patio table in a shade-dappled corner.

Sandrine Moss.

Chapter 4

She'd been prepared for Sandrine to be less spectacular-looking in the flesh. No one could really look as good as Sandrine did in the movies, not even Sandrine.

And she didn't.

Not quite.

But even in a floaty peasant skirt in shades of green and blue and a deliberately rumpled sleeveless white linen blouse, with a plain thong sandal on one foot and a cast on the other, Sandrine looked inhumanly good. The famous red curls were pulled back in an artfully casual way that, if a normal woman attempted it, would look like a dust mop attached to the back of her head. (All right, maybe it looked a bit like that on Sandrine, too, but the hair itself was so gorgeous that she could pull it off.)

Her bone structure was just as extraordinary as it looked in pictures, even if the skin over it didn't actually have that unreal brushed-silk texture. Behind small glasses with tortoiseshell frames, her eyes weren't quite as startlingly turquoise as they were on screen, but they were definitely closer to turquoise than human eyes normally were.

Chloe's tongue cleaved to the dry roof of her mouth. Of course. *Now* things would go dry.

"So you're the caterer," Sandrine said without preamble, setting down the script she'd been holding. "Chef. Waitress-for-hire. Whatever. Well, that settles one niggling worry: you're *so* not having an affair with Ray. I had just this tiny bit of concern, because every once in a while the media gets something right. But not this time."

Chloe's tongue freed itself.

She promptly bit it so she didn't snap out any of the five or six bitchy responses that came to mind. Okay, there was no way on earth Ray would want someone like her when he had Sandrine—but there was no need to rub a girl's nose in it.

Sandrine must have seen the urge pass over her face, though. "It's not a looks thing. Remember, I did see pictures of you. Way too many of them. You're cute enough in a low-maintenance East Coast way, and Ray wouldn't be the first actor who decided he wanted a vacation with someone outside the business. No, it's a body language thing. I can just tell you're not sleeping with him. You're not guilty or defiant enough."

"What I am," Chloe said, as politely as she could (her mother would have been proud of her), "is confused."

"I can see that," Sandrine took off her glasses and wiped them on her shirt, just like a mere mortal, then put them back on. "You're out of your depth, aren't you? Way out of your depth. I thought when Ray told me what happened that you'd set something up to get attention, and then deliberately lied to the press, but now I think you're just clueless."

Chloe considered being insulted.

Then she conceded Sandrine was, in fact, right. "Of course I am, when it comes to things like this. I'm a chef. From Boston. The only time I ever talked to the press before was to give a recipe to the *Globe's* food writer. Come to think of it, she misquoted me, too."

A hint of a smile crossed Sandrine's lips. Chloe relaxed, just a fraction. It was a good sign that Sandrine might have a bit of a sense of humor.

"Sit down," Sandrine said.

It was less an invitation than an order, but Chloe knew better than to do anything but sit. At least it gave her the opportunity to set her bag on the floor instead of clutching it over her crotch; the table hid the view of the stain from Sandrine.

"Olive did a little poking around for me. You were supposed to be a waitress that night. Where do you get off saying you were my personal chef? I was just going to sue your ass from here to next Tuesday, but Ray and Brand convinced me to talk to you first. So. Talk."

Yowch. From light humor to claws-out in the blink of an eye. Chloe felt out of her depth.

"I'm sorry," she said, guessing that starting out with groveling would be a good plan. "I didn't say that I was your personal chef, but I was mis-quoted about that, too. I said I was a chef, and I guess the press assumed..." She trailed off. Sandrine was just staring at her, those turquoise eyes narrowed in contemplation.

"You really are new here," Sandrine murmured, shaking her head. She looked down at a piece of paper on the table. "MerryTemps sent a copy of your résumé. You interned with Gerard DesJardins in Paris? Is that the res-taurant DesJardins?" Her voice rose, as if she were impressed despite herself.

Completely unsure of where *this* was going, Chloe nodded.

"Love him. Ray flew me to Paris on Valentine's weekend just to have dinner there. I cannot wait until he opens in LA this fall."

No point in telling Sandrine that what she'd done for Monsieur DesJardins was chop vegetables endlessly, usually while he criticized her lack of speed and precision. She'd spent a lot of her free time during that internship wandering along the banks of the Seine and enjoying the beau-tiful architecture through a veil of frustrated tears.

And occasionally kicking light poles while pretending they were Monsieur DesJardins' shins.

Sandrine glanced down at the resume. "And Printemps on Nantucket. I adore that place! When we filmed *Princess of Nowhere*, I ate there all the time. It was *the* place to be, of course, so thank goodness the food was good."

Of course. Chloe wasn't surprised that Sandrine really chose her res-taurants by where she'd best be photographed. She wasn't sure how to respond, so she just said, "I was just interned for one summer while I was at the Culinary Institute."

"Still. There was some grilled fish, I can't remember what it was—you know the recipe?"

Now she was on comfortable ground! "It was grilled skate, and the recipe's dead simple. The secret's in the seasoned avocado oil you brush it with." *I cannot believe I'm talking food with Sandrine Moss!*

She realized a moment later that Sandrine's eyes had glazed over after she'd said "dead simple." Sandrine didn't give a flying rat's ass what the recipe was, just if Chloe knew how to make it.

Dammit. She'd done that before: got all enthusiastic about foodie stuff only to realize the people around her had wandered off in search of a conversation they actually cared about. It was the curse of her obsession.

Way to go. Way to make nice with the lady who's on the verge of suing you.

Thankfully Olive chose that moment to arrive with a tray of what smelled like peppermint tea (thank goodness it wasn't a caffeinated option, because that was the *last* thing she needed) and a plate of something. Scones of some kind.

Olive poured them tea, and Sandrine waved a hand to indicate that Chloe should take a scone. She wasn't really hungry—her stomach was still too fluttery—but she figured that saying no would just provoke the actress.

She broke off a small bit, popped it in her mouth—and nearly choked.

Since when did they make scones of sawdust?

Whole-grain was all very well, but this took the concept a bit too far! Either it was a cruel joke or the latest food-fad-gone-horribly-wrong, but either way, there was no power on heaven or earth that could make Chloe finish it.

"So, what did you think of the scone?"

The question threw Chloe. It was definitely a trick question…but what kind of a trick? Sandrine's impassive expression gave her no hints. "Different. Definitely different."

"Ghastly, you mean."

Chloe nodded, relieved to be honest.

"I'm not eating white flour right now. That was a mixture of spelt and millet that my last chef tried. Part of the reason he's past-tense. Could you do better?"

"Oat flour and rice flour," she said promptly. "That would be lighter. If you're just off white flour and aren't allergic to wheat, whole wheat pastry flour mixed with oat flour would give a lovely texture. It wouldn't taste like a traditional scone, but it would taste good. And unless there's some reason not to, scones just need currants."

Crap, she was babbling again.

Apparently Sandrine had tuned back in for the last thing, though.

"I don't like currants. Maybe dried cranberries. But anyway, you're hired."

Chloe blinked several times before saying, "Excuse me?"

"You're hired."

"For what?" she said, still blinking like an owl awakened in the daytime.

"Listen, everyone thinks you're my personal chef, and you have the right credentials, and the fact is, I need a chef. You might as well have the job. Six-month contract to start. Live here... Well, not here, but in one of the outbuildings. Olive will sort it out. Oh, hi, darling!"

Ray had just wandered out into the courtyard, wearing nothing but a pair of yoga pants that draped on what Chloe had to think of as brawny thighs.

Chloe tried not to stare, but dammit, she was only human. Ray's muscles-on-muscles build wasn't really her thing, but taking an up-close look at a world-famous movie star was a bit too much temptation to resist.

Ray seemed oblivious to her presence, let alone her stare, padding over in his bare feet and giving Sandrine the kind of kiss that made Chloe wonder how the actress could have possibly been worried that Ray was straying.

When he finally looked up, his huge brown eyes finally seemed to focus on her. "Well, hello, Miss Pretty Caterer. It's nice to see you again. How are you?"

"Fine, thanks," Chloe managed. "And thank you again for rescuing me. I'm sorry for all the fallout afterwards."

He looked at Sandrine. "Is everything okay?"

Chloe remembered Sandrine saying that Ray and someone else whose name already escaped her had convinced her to talk to Chloe before suing her.

"She's going to be our new chef," Sandrine said quickly.

She was? She hadn't agreed—

"Don't want to interrupt. I'm off for a swim with Brand." He smiled, a sweet, doting smile that wasn't in keeping with his tough-guy persona, but very much in keeping with the little bit she'd seen of his character the other night, and started to wander off. Then he turned back, looking at Chloe. "Nice blouse. Luscious Couture?"

Stunned, she nodded. "My roommate Luanna works for them. It's one of her designs."

"Lucky girl," Ray said, grinning—his smile really was adorable—then wandered off.

"Luscious…best casual clothes ever!" Sandrine tagged on. "You must see about snagging yourself some more samples. That suit, even if the coffee stain ever comes out, is just too…"

Damn. So the stain wasn't hidden under the table. Chloe smoothed her napkin over her lap. "Too Boston?"

"I was going to say 'boring,' but Boston covers it. Anyway, can you start tonight, or will you need a day to get moved in? Tomorrow we'll be out all day anyway—live feed for the *Today* show about the new movie, and you can only imagine how early that starts, so they'll feed us some ghastly breakfast on the set, and more interviews after that, plus a party in the evening—but I'd kill for a decent dinner at home tonight. To celebrate getting this damn cast off this afternoon."

"Wait a second!" Chloe gripped the edge of the table, because if she didn't, she'd fall over, given the way her head was spinning. This was moving way too fast. She took a deep breath. It didn't help much, but it was all she had.

"Sandrine, I appreciate the offer, I really do. But I haven't said yes. I need a little time to think about it. Please believe me, it's a great honor to be asked, but until the fiasco with that stupid reporter yesterday, I'd never even considered being a personal chef. I've always worked in restaurants.

I love working in restaurants. I hope to open my own someday, and this would be…"

She wanted to say "a detour," but sensed Sandrine wouldn't take that well.

"…a big change for me. Could I have a day or two to think about whether it's a direction I want to take? And maybe a few more details about what the job entails?"

Such as the salary? And what did she mean by six months?

Sandrine leaned forwards and smiled. It wasn't the charming smile famous from *Princess of Nowhere* and *Love in a Bubble*—more like the one she used as the assassin in *Silk and Suede*. Chloe shivered.

"I think you've misunderstood," Sandrine said, and her voice was as steely as the smile. "You embarrassed me and Ray the other night, got some ugly rumors started about our relationship being on the rocks, and a simple retraction won't do anything to stop the gossip. It's just not as interesting as the idea of Ray screwing around with a mystery woman. Nobody's going to believe you were just misquoted about working for me. So the only solution is to make sure you actually *are* working for me."

"It was an accident! I just…"

"I know what happened. You made a mistake and then you panicked, and without meaning to, you screwed up my life and Ray's. And yours, I suppose. You seem like a perfectly decent person," and here Sandrine seemed to step back a notch on the really scary tone, "but that only helps so much. Ray didn't mean to make things worse, either, but sometimes he's just too nice for his own good. The fact remains: I need you to come work for me. I need a chef, you need a job, and it's the best possible way to get the press to leave us all alone."

"I'm really not sure…" It was all happening so fast!

Back to the evil smile. Fuck.

"Let me make this clear," Sandrine said. "You have two choices. One: You take the job, and everything's fine. Two: You don't take the job, and I make sure you'll never work in this town—not even as a waitress with MerryTemps. In fact, I'll blacken your name so much you'll be lucky to get a job at a diner in Podunk, Iowa."

She sat back and paused to let that sink in. When the panic and confusion Chloe was feeling made it to her face, Sandrine continued.

"Prospective employers won't like to hear that you lied about being my personal chef because you wanted to cover up how you're stalking my boyfriend. And that's what they'll hear if I'm forced to take my story to the media."

"But that's not true!" Her wail sounded pathetic to her own ears, and must sound even worse to Sandrine, but she didn't know how else to respond.

This kind of thing wouldn't have happened if she'd gone to the vo-tech school in Kingston and taken over her uncle's clam shack like he'd wanted. Sure, she'd be bored witless, but right now bored sounded pretty good.

"Sweetie, 'true' doesn't matter. It's a juicy story, and if you've learned one thing in the last few days, it's that the media would rather get a juicy story than the truth." There was a note in Sandrine's voice that Chloe couldn't quite place, a sort of world-weary regret that didn't really fit with her behavior.

"So, what'll be, Chloe: a good job that isn't exactly what you were looking for, or no job in your field ever again?"

Chapter 5

*B*rand had seen the somewhat world-weary green Mini Cooper pootle up the driveway, but he'd assumed it was a delivery of some sort.

Then he finished with his morning swim and the little car was easing its way back down the drive. He fumbled for his glasses on the deck chair, peered down the sloping, manicured lawn (no grass blade longer than an inch).

"Who's that, do you know?" he asked Ray, who'd joined him in the pool for laps.

Ray paused in the act of running the towel over his bald head. "Oh," he said. "That was probably Miss Pretty Caterer."

"That's right, the party tomor—uh oh." Brand's mind reeled from the resounding thump of the cosmic two-by-four. "You don't mean the one from the AAMies?"

Ray pulled his yoga pants over his massive thighs. "One and the same. Sandrine wanted to meet her."

"The fact that she's able to drive away is a good sign," Brand said.

Then again, Sands still had the cast on her foot—Chloe would've been able to outrun her.

"They seemed to be getting along fine," Ray said. "They were eating those awful scones Raoul made before he quit. She says her roommate works for Luscious Couture."

Ray had a habit of jumping topics like a kangaroo on crack, so Brand just ignored the non sequitur.

This still didn't bode well. He'd gotten stuck at work late yesterday, so he hadn't had the chance to talk to Sands directly about the red-carpet brouhaha. He'd texted her, though, gently advising her not to sue the poor woman or do anything hasty. Because Olive hadn't called him back, he'd assumed (still feeling guilty that he hadn't been there) that things had been smoothed over.

Apparently not. *Hiring* Chloe pretty much fell into the category of "hasty."

He was torn. He needed to shower and get in to work. He also needed to talk to his sister and make sure she hadn't thoughtlessly dug herself into a hole he'd have trouble getting her out of.

Compromise: he'd shower here in the pool's cabana—nearly a guesthouse in its own right, with several changing rooms, each with shower, toilet, and sink; a spacious sitting room with a sweet TV and stereo set-up; and a wet bar—go talk to Sands, and be air-dried off before he got back to his place to get dressed.

He showered in record time, then made a detour in the kitchen of the main house to make a pot of Moroccan mint tea. If there was anything that could coax Sands out of a bad mood, it was Moroccan mint tea. And chocolate, except she went through great swaths of time when chocolate was the work of the Devil.

Calories. Fat. Antichrist. In Sands's mind, it made sense.

He walked out onto the patio and found her studying a script. "Hey, Sands. Thought you might like some tea."

"Oh Brand, you're such a dear!" She took a sip of the steaming tea, sighed with pleasure. "Thank you. You read my mind." Then she blinked. "So did Olive, come to think of it. Must be a mint tea kind of day."

She was good about thanking him for the little things, most of the time. The big things... Well, he figured she honestly didn't notice, the way Parisians didn't notice the Eiffel Tower or locals didn't notice the Hollywood sign. Just part of the scenery.

Fact was, their mother had fed her mint tea whenever Sandrine needed calming, and he'd picked up the habit, and taught Olive the trick. Smart, savvy Olive had known to serve it when Chloe Montiero was coming.

Olive probably deserved a raise. If only he could afford to give her one. Maybe flowers. And a really, really nice card.

"So," he said, because he was possibly the only person in her life who could approach a delicate subject head on, "Chloe Montiero."

"Hm?" Her reply was distracted; she was already back into the script. As flaky as she could be at other times, there was a side to Sandrine Moss that only other professionals—and her brother—knew. "I've taken care of that, sweetie," she said.

"Do I have to hide a body for you? Is this why you were talking about putting in a new swimming pool?" Big Brother Weapon #1: Make her laugh, even if it was at him and his poor attempt at humor.

It worked: She laughed. "Goodness, no! I hired her as my chef. That's what everyone believes, so why not make it official? She had brilliant ideas about how to make those abysmal scones palatable, so how could I not hire her?"

In Sands's head, that was logic. It was no surprise to him that she and Ray were perfect for each other.

"So, you're not concerned that anything untoward was happening between her and Ray?" he asked, choosing his words carefully.

Now her smile faltered. "I don't know. I don't think so. The thing is, even if Ray were cheating on me, he wouldn't bring her to the AAMies. He's not dumb. But something's up with him lately. He's being strange, kind of secretive. Not about this."

Having dated more than one high-strung model in his day, Brand was not inexperienced with gorgeous but completely insecure women.

"Trust me. A man who's cheating might be able to look his girlfriend in the eye, but not his girlfriend's big brother. It's just a guy thing. Part of the code."

"But he's been weird lately," she insisted, setting her teacup down with a rattle. "I can't put a finger on it, but he seems different ever since I got back from shooting *Soul's Road*. Haven't you noticed? Clingy, but kind of distant at the same time."

Brand mentally counted to five. "He's probably been nervous about the AAMies and didn't want to admit it. And he's been worried about you.

He was a wreck when you were in Tunisia and hurt and he couldn't get away to take care of you, and I'm sure he wasn't happy having to leave you home last night—he knew you'd been looking forward to being there."

Then again, that described himself. Except for being nervous about the AAMies. He really hadn't thought much about that.

The tense lines of Sands's body visibly relaxed. "And he's Ray, so it's not like he'd actually *say* any of this, just get all quiet and weird. You're right. You're absolutely right."

Brand tapped a forefinger against the teacup he hadn't drunk from. The Chloe Montiero crisis might be solved for now—although having her around might cause a different crisis altogether, that being a crisis in his pants—but the Ray thing was something different entirely.

He supposed he'd have to pay more attention. He'd been so wrapped up in the latest film that he'd probably missed obvious clues.

"By the way, I almost forgot," Sands said. "Can you tend bar for me tomorrow night? The new girl will handle the food, so I fired the caterer, which means…"

"I've got it covered," he said. Okay, he'd had plans to take his crew out to dinner at The Magic Shop to celebrate their AAMie, but that could wait.

Plus there would be hot women at the party.

Problem was, the only woman at the party he was already thinking about was, as Ray described her, "Miss Pretty Caterer."

There was no way in hell he could tell Sandrine *that.*

*

They packed into the night, Chloe driving back and forth to Sandrine's estate with her tiny car stuffed to the gills while Luanna canvassed the liquor stores and kept on filling boxes. Olive had given them the code to the estate's security gate and directed Chloe to the guest house.

Chloe had at least convinced Sandrine that she couldn't make dinner before she moved, and Sandrine had accepted having her there by the next morning.

When the beleaguered Mini's Check Engine light came on during the last run, she realized she should've insisted on a clause in her contract that

Sandrine pay for a moving company for them. Oh well. Twenty-twenty hindsight. At least with both her and Luanna working, they should be able to get the poor thing fixed.

"Okay, I understand about you getting the job," Luanna had said when Chloe explained the need for speed-packing. "But how do I fit in?"

"I said you couldn't afford the apartment on your own, and Ray knew you worked at Luscious," Chloe said.

"How did he know that?"

"Damned if I know. Then Olive said that the fashion press would eat the story up: Star helps talented young designer, yadda yadda. She said Sandrine's publicist might be able to get a *Vogue* article from it—even the international editions."

Luanna's shriek rattled the dodgy, blurred glass of the bathroom mirror. "I might be mentioned in *Vogue*?!"

"Not to rain on your fashion parade, but Sandrine's only thought was that she might get Luscious samples from you," Chloe said. "I believe her exact words were 'even if you can afford to buy anything you want, there are few finer words in the English language than *free chic clothes*.'"

"I can totally live with that," Luanna said. "Sandrine Moss being spotted in the latest Luscious creation will do wonders for us. I think I could get forgiven for taking today off, even."

The first thing Chloe looked at in the guest house was the kitchen. It was small—guests weren't likely to be cooking gourmet meals—but impeccably clean and modern and comfortable. Then she walked into the living room. She chucked off her shoes and dug her toes into the plush, non-scary, hunter green Berber carpet and made happy noises usually reserved for more intimate moments.

Her bedroom was small, too, but the mattress was new and firm and tempting, the cool zillion-thread-count sheets a delicious shade of pale sea blue. Chloe had let herself sit on it briefly, but hadn't dared lie down for fear she'd pass out before they were done.

The sky was just lightening when they brought the last load in, caravanning in their respective cars. Luanna promptly retreated to her bedroom and collapsed, fully clothed, on top of the covers, since she couldn't take any more time off of work and needed a few hours' sleep before she went in.

Evenrude had slept through much of the moving process, but had been delighted to stick her head out the car window, ears flapping in the soft LA night air. Once in the guest house, she'd sniffed every nook and cranny of the space. Then she joined Luanna, flopping down on the bed with a weary, put-upon sigh, because that had been *really tiring*.

Chloe unpacked her kitchen things carefully into a pantry with roll-out shelves before exhaustion threatened to overwhelm her.

"Bed" sounded like a really nifty concept.

But first, a soothing shower to wipe away the sweat, grime, and residual stress of turning her life upside-down in less than twenty-four hours.

Half an hour later, wrapped in a luxurious, snow-white bath sheet, a matching towel around her head, she left the steaming bathroom.

"Darling!" Sandrine swept into the guesthouse as if she owned the place.

Which, in fact, she did. Still, it was disconcerting to have a relative stranger come bursting into your home. Chloe suspected locking the door would have little effect.

She clutched the edges of the towel together and said, "Um. Hi, Sandrine."

"So good to see you're settling in. Anyway, I'm dashing off to the *Today* shoot, but Olive will give you all the details you need about the party tonight. It'll be smallish, only about a hundred people. Hundred-fifty, tops. Don't worry about getting a bartender; that's handled."

Her head whirling from more than exhaustion, Chloe managed to squeak out "Wait. The party…I…?" She remembered Sandrine mentioning going to a party.

Sandrine *had* said *going* to a party, right?

"For Ray winning the AAMie," she said as if it were the most obvious thing on earth. "Once I hired you, I fired the outside caterer, of *course*." Sandrine beamed a smile brighter than the sunrise outside. "I'm delighted to be able to show off my new personal chef. Anyway, must dash. Ta-rah!"

In a swirl of peach silk and a mist of floral perfume that Chloe vaguely remembered reading was custom-blended for her, Sandrine was gone.

Chloe sat down hard on the sofa.
She had to cater a party.
An AAMie celebration party.
Tonight.
For more than a hundred people.
And she hadn't slept in days.

Chapter 6

*C*lothed, and awake only by virtue of the terror that coursed adrenaline through her veins, Chloe made her way across the manicured grounds to Sandrine's mansion. A maid directed her to the kitchen.

Chloe walked in and near to fainted.

The kitchen was as big as the apartment she and Luanna had just vacated. Rose-colored marble covered the flat surfaces, and gleaming copper pots hung from a rack above a center island the size of Oahu, which boasted a prep sink and indoor grill. Chloe's mouth watered at the top-of-the-line appliances—a silver industrial KitchenAid mixer, a Braun coffeemaker that would serve a small army, a huge Viking professional range and an extra wall oven—and a set of Wüsthof-Trident knives. (She still swore by her Henckels, but it was nice to know she didn't have to bring her own set over here.)

Beech wood cabinets gleamed, and the refrigerator and freezer, both vast, were tastefully tucked behind matching wood doors. Chloe wandered, trailing her fingertips on the cool marble, the silky wood, the lovely implements of cooking perfection.

A copy of the *LA Times* sat on the counter. Out of habit, she turned to the horoscope, read the words, "Enjoy life's little surprises."

Snorted and shoved the paper into a recycling bin concealed (the door discreetly labeled with an engraved brass plate) in the center island.

"Finding everything okay?"

The voice made her shriek and jump, feeling outrageously guilty for trespassing even though she was really supposed to be here.

Dressed in a sage green linen pantsuit and heels, her hair impeccable, Olive looked to be the epitome of calm and organization. Chloe wanted to fling herself into Olive's arms and soak up that aura. But armed with an iPhone and an iPad, a Bluetooth headset in her ear, Olive also looked far from comforting.

"So, Sandrine broke the news to you about the party tonight?" Olive asked.

"How long have you known about it?" Chloe asked.

Olive pursed her lips. "On one hand, Sandrine only confirmed the decision about the caterer this morning. On the other hand, I wasn't entirely surprised."

Judging from Olive's expression, this sort of thing was just part of life with Sandrine.

"I've e-mailed you a list of good wholesale places that deliver," Olive continued, sliding a credit card across the counter to her. "We use them regularly; just give them my name and they'll accept the card. Same for the catering supply shops."

Chloe grabbed the credit card and clutched it like a lifeline. "We're not talking about a full sit-down meal, are we?"

Olive shook her head. "Just hors d'oeuvres, finger foods."

"Does she have any preferences?" Chloe asked helplessly. "Likes, dislikes? Allergies?"

The look Olive gave her held a hint of something akin to pity. "No allergies," she said. "Her preferences are…variable. I'd suggest going with your specialties." Olive smiled. "Money's not an object. The best advice I can give you is to have fun."

Fun. As if pulling a cocktail party for a hundred and fifty people out of her ass could be considered anywhere in the realm of "fun."

But if there was one thing Chloe understood, it was a challenge. She took a deep breath and re-secured her hair in its clip. She could do this. It wasn't going to be easy, but she could do it.

Or die trying.

*

Brand hesitated at the kitchen door. He needed to check the contents of the cavernous back-up liquor cabinet, but really, what he needed to do was apologize to Chloe for giving her bad directions at the AAMies and throwing her life into chaos. Just a second to collect his thoughts—and okay, to enjoy the view before she ripped his eyes out so he'd never get to enjoy any view again.

Chloe was talking to herself.

"At least the artichokes are great this time of year," she said, scribbling on a pad. "Lemons. Can't have too many lemons. How's the olive oil supply?" She put down the pen, darted to the pantry. "All good. Just need to worry about fresh foods."

Most creative types talked to themselves. He and his colleagues all did it sometimes—not to mention swearing at and/or cajoling the computer. Sandrine did it all the time, too, either because she was trying to capture a character's voice or because she'd forgotten she was alone in the room.

Ray, as far as Brand knew, didn't talk to himself. Ray was blessedly low in the creative-angst department.

Yeah, it was perfectly normal, but it didn't bode well for a conversation.

Not to mention that she must be crazy-busy. Even if she'd known about the party yesterday, which Brand doubted, it wasn't like she'd had time to plan. And Olive had already told him that her early morning calls to staffing agencies had turned up no one who could support Chloe in the kitchen.

He should go.

She looked into the refrigerator and let out a few words in a language he didn't recognize. They almost had to be curses.

Yes, definitely time to go. He could check on the booze situation later. Or hell, just order whatever wasn't on the bar already. It wasn't like Sandrine couldn't afford it.

But damn, Chloe was cute, even with her hair in a haphazard ponytail and chef's whites concealing her tasty curves.

Actually, the chef's whites, though they weren't figure-flattering, complemented her olive skin and dark hair. And he could imagine the curves. Brand could create all the 3-D details of an imaginary spaceship. He could certainly visualize all the warm, lush, distracting, real details of Chloe's body, including the very private ones he could only hope he'd be lucky enough to see someday.

For all she was muttering and moving at the speed of light, Chloe seemed comfortable in the huge kitchen. Her forehead was screwed up as she rummaged around and made lists, but she didn't have that deer-in-the-headlights look he'd seen in the damn video clips. Busy and a bit harried here, but in control.

She opened a cupboard, took out a jar. Did a gleeful jig. "Capers! That takes care of what to do with the artichokes. Why are people always impressed when you put capers on something?"

"We don't know what they are, so they sound exotic. What *is* a caper, anyway?" It seemed as good a conversation opener as any, seeing he'd always vaguely wondered.

"Pickled seed pod of a plant native to the Mediterranean." Then it seemed to sink in that someone else was in the room. (She couldn't be much less like Sandrine, but that bit seemed familiar.) Chloe turned around and smiled. "Oh, hi. What can I do for you? I'm Chloe, the new chef."

Good news: she wasn't leaping over the kitchen island, grabbing one of the dangerously sharp chef's knives on the way, to attack him for the bad directions.

Bad news: she didn't seem to recognize him in his natural jeans-and-T-shirt state instead of suited up and groomed to something close to Sandrine's specifications.

On second thought, that *was* good news, even if it was more flattering when a hot woman remembered you. He could get to know her and then tell her about his contribution to the fiasco at the AAMies. Or not. Maybe it just wouldn't be important. "Brand. I'm tending bar tonight. Is there anything I should know? Any special requests?"

It occurred to him after the words came out that maybe he should explain who he was.

On the other hand, maybe starting off on neutral ground was better. "Sandrine's brother" sounded a lot less friendly than "Brand the bartender," especially since she was probably directing some of those foreign curses at his sister. Work up to all the complications of his role on the estate slowly.

Then again, she probably already knew. It was no secret that Sandrine had a brother, that his name was Brand, and that he had frequently been seen with her at public appearances before her relationship with Ray got serious.

"Just keep them happy," Chloe said, extending her hand.

A small hand, but strong. It fit well into his. He had to remind himself to let go of it. "Will do. Do you need help with anything?"

She smiled again. Her lips were full, deep rose, sensual-looking. The kind of mouth that inspired wicked thoughts, thoughts that were going to make his jeans uncomfortable if he wasn't careful. He looked into her eyes instead, glad the kitchen island was between them in case his body was showing its appreciation a little too eagerly.

"Thanks for the offer, but no, I'm all set," she said. "Didn't I see you cleaning the pool yesterday? Do you need coffee before you go? I have a pot going."

"I help out when I can," he said. "And I'd love some coffee."

He'd had some already—coffee was one of the few things he always had on hand in the guest house he called home—but more coffee was never a bad thing, and it was an excuse to chat with Chloe.

"No, don't worry about getting it for me," he added when she turned, away from the island where she'd been laying out ingredients. "You're busy. Big party and everything." He hoped, a little too late, that she wouldn't think it was weird he was comfortable rummaging for a coffee cup in Sandrine and Ray's kitchen. Then again, she was so new to Hollywood that everything must seem odd.

Not that it got any less strange when you'd been here awhile. You just learned to accept the weirdness.

"Thanks," Chloe said. "I'm glad somebody knows where things are. The kitchen's well-stocked, but planning a menu would be easier if my cookbooks were unpacked."

"There's a computer behind that panel." Brand pointed. "Would that be helpful?"

"Brilliant! Thank God for technology. I can do one order over the phone while I'm typing in the other. Once I look up a few recipes, that is."

She headed over to the computer-concealing panel, which opened with a recessed handle so discreet you might miss it at first glance. Slipped her fingers into the cleverly concealed opening and pulled.

Failed.

"It sticks sometimes." Brand remembered the chef-before-last complaining about that. He thought it had been fixed and made a mental note to take care of it. Sure, they had handymen on call, but all it needed was a little WD-40. "Here, let me."

"I can..." She banged on it a few times, cursed again in that language that wasn't Spanish or Italian. "Okay, fine." She stepped aside, but glared at him as she did.

"For some reason, if you push on the left top while you're using the handle, it helps."

"Thanks." She glared again.

Oh well. Stress made people get grumpy about the dumbest things, and this situation had to be stressful. Anything involving Sandrine had the potential to be stressful, and Chloe had been dumped right into the middle of it.

She fired up the computer and grabbed her pad from the counter. "Okay, I've got some ideas for a menu, but it's all basic stuff. Tasty but typical. I need a few things that stand out. Something daring. Something different."

Brand wasn't sure if she was being conversational or thinking out loud at him instead of at the wall, but he felt like he should answer. "Deep fried butter?"

She turned the glared back on him. For someone with eyes the color of melted chocolate and a face that looked more suited to laughing, she glared like a pro. "Leave the food up to me. You deal with the bar. Everything will be better that way."

Stressed woman with a big knife…time to leave while he still had all his body parts. "Sorry, my bad. I'll get back to the liquor inventory."

She nodded, went back to her list-making.

Brand tried not to stare at her too much. Even from the back, she looked bristly. But hot nevertheless.

Just about when he admitted to himself that he couldn't stretch out his time in the kitchen any longer—he'd finagled the day off by dint of working ridiculously late, but had to at least check his emails and see what fires needed putting out—Chloe exclaimed, "Clam cakes! That's it!"

Brand applauded. He wasn't sure what a clam cake was, but it sounded tasty. And she sounded happy and relieved, which was all good.

"Great idea!" he said, "Okay, I'm off now. Catch you later."

She was so engrossed she barely looked up.

*

Clam cakes. Why hadn't she thought of them right away?

Fresh, hot clam cakes, doughy and deep fried and delicious—the taste of summer to someone raised in a fishing town on the Rhode Island shore. She'd have to tinker with the family recipe a bit: increase the proportion of clams to batter, come up with a spicy, sophisticated sauce.

Was she insane? Who in the world would serve clam cakes—basically seafood donuts—to a bunch of skinny movie people?

She would, damn it.

Because as soon as one person tried them and exclaimed in glee (which they would), they'd be a hit. Sure, not everyone would like them, but they'd definitely get people talking.

And because she could make clam cakes without actually engaging her brain—they were one of the first things she'd ever cooked professionally. Sure, it was at Uncle Carmine's clam shack, but she'd been only in junior high the first time she made a batch of clam cakes for eager tourists, and the Shore Shack had the best damn clam cakes on the Rhode Island coast, and she knew the recipe by heart.

And besides, it was summer and she hadn't been near a beach yet, and she doubted she could get a clam cake out here if she did. She was a little homesick, and there was nothing like sharing the taste of home to get that under control.

If nothing else, the hot bartender would like them. He'd applauded the thought. Or maybe he'd just applauded her enthusiasm, but it had been awfully cute, and a little positive feedback was just what she needed.

Maybe, just maybe, this would work.

Chapter 7

Ten a.m. So far so good. Everything was ordered and several deliveries had arrived with the speed that only great wealth could call forth, so the first dishes were underway. She might just survive.

Over the din of the mixer, she heard her cell phone ring. (Blondie's "Eat to the Beat," of course.) She grabbed it, hoping chocolate and butter wouldn't gum up the keys too much (and if it did, that it wouldn't invalidate the warranty).

"Chloe. Olive. The delivery from Giordano's just arrived. They're coming up to the side entrance."

Crap. Perfect timing. Wiping her hand on a towel (high quality, pristine linen, of course), she glanced around the vast kitchen. Nothing would burn, boil over, or explode in the next few minutes. Just to be safe, she eased down the heat under one pot and glanced in one of the three ovens at the mini-quiches cooking there before she dashed down the hallway.

She reached for the doorknob, then leapt back as the door swung inwards, narrowly missing clocking her on the nose.

It wasn't the delivery guy from Giordano's, but a now-familiar figure backing through the entrance, manhandling a dolly stacked with liquor boxes over the sill.

She was focused enough to appreciate the nice, formfitting black tank top that showed off his biceps.

So Brand the Yummy Pool Boy-slash-Bartender ran errands, too. Good to know.

He turned and saw her.

"Hello again," he said. He pushed his sunglasses up onto his head, and she saw that his smile was reflected in his eyes, which were blue like the Mediterranean. Or Sandrine's pool. How had she not noticed those gorgeous eyes before? Oh, because she was losing her mind. "How are the crab cakes coming?"

"Clam cakes," she said. "They have to be done last, because they're best when they're hot out of the fryer."

"Got it. You're the expert. By the way…"

"Yes?"

He reached out and stroke her cheek with a long-fingered hand. Chloe's stomach fluttered. In fact, she felt a pang a little lower, too. It had been far too long since she'd been touched by a man, much less gotten happily naked and rolled around with one on a cool manicured lawn before slithering into the outdoor Jacuzzi and…

His next words popped the soap-bubble of her erotic fantasy.

"Do you know you have flour on your nose?"

She shrugged, hoping it helped hide the sudden hunger. She could imagine letting him know all about how hot he made her at the right place and time, but this was so not the right place and time.

"Hey, the booze aspect of this bash is under control with this delivery. Can I lend a hand?"

Her knee-jerk reaction was to growl territorially at him. The kitchen was her arena. Brand was, as they said back home, wicked cute, but she didn't need him underfoot, tripping her up while trying to help. She could handle this on her own, damn it. Sandrine had entrusted the job to her and she'd do it. (Never mind Sandrine probably didn't have a clue how much work a simple party for one hundred and fifty people involved. Or that Olive had tried to find her proper help.)

Then she thought about the pots on the stove and the mini quiches in the oven, and she took a deep breath, forcing herself to be realistic. Any help she could get would be a life saver.

Even if it stung to admit it.

"Actually, yes," she said. "Giordano's is here to make a delivery—can you get everything to the kitchen for me?"

"Not a problem," he said with a grin. "I'm authorized to sign for deliveries."

"That's great." Only when she said it did she realize how true it was; the cliché about a weight being lifted was kind of accurate. Whee.

Which is probably why the next words that came out of her mouth, completely unbidden, were, "Then, if you've got the time, stick around. I can probably find something for you to do."

"I only do survival cooking," he warned, "but I clean up pretty well."

I bet you do. Two images sprang into her mind in rapid succession: Brand all dressed up and Brand all undressed in the shower.

A primal part of her suggested creative ways for Brand to lend a hand to any number of interesting and long-neglected places. It wouldn't help her get the food prepped, but her body chimed in loudly that a few orgasms, or even some simple old-fashioned smooching, would go a long way towards relieving stress.

Chloe forced herself to think about less attractive things, such as filleting fish. Naked-Brand thoughts would be too, too distracting when she was dealing with sharp knives and open flames.

She glanced around the kitchen. It might look organized to someone who wasn't a professional chef, but it was just this side of disaster by her standards. Taking a deep breath, she forced herself to be realistic.

By the time he arrived with the delivery, his sunglasses exchanged for regular ones, she had her brain back on work and had figured out how to make use of him in a decidedly non-salacious way.

"How about dealing with the dishes in the sink?" she said. "Then I'll get you started rinsing the tomatoes and fruit. But not the artichokes—that's a job for a professional."

He laughed. "I am a professional," he said. "Just not a kitchen professional."

She rolled her eyes. "Just get to work!" He was bringing out all sorts of flirty urges, not to mention downright naughty ones, but as tempting as he was, right now she was juggling too many things to add sexy innuendo and playfulness to the list.

She smiled in a way she hoped conveyed a promise to flirt when she had the spare brain cells and got back to her mixer.

They quickly settled into a rhythm. After a mangled attempt at chopping celery, Brand conceded that his survival-cooking skills weren't up to what she'd need. But he was great at washing vegetables, cleaning knives, wiping up spills and a dozen other dumb little things that saved her time. And thankfully he took orders without argument.

Not to mention that he was easy on the eyes and good company, even when she was too busy to chat with him except about the task at hand.

Which she was most of the time. With Brand's unskilled but eager assistance, she only needed to do four things at once instead of six or seven. It was enough to give her hope, but still, she could use a trained sous-chef or three of Brand. (Identical triplet Brands? She filed the scrummy image away for a time she could truly appreciate it. Preferably after she unpacked her vibrator.)

After about an hour of running as fast as she could with Brand cleaning up behind her, Olive called again. "Got you some help," she said, sounding almost as breathless as Chloe felt before.

"Who? How?" Relieved as she was, she couldn't gather enough wits to say anything more coherent; one of her dishes was at a critical point and she was trying to make sure it didn't scorch while she listened.

"Short version of a long story: someone who's on the board of Hollywood Saves the Mustangs with Ray sent over some kid she knows who's supposedly a cook."

"Is he?"

"Do you care at this point?"

"Not so much, if he knows which end of a knife to hold."

"Good," Olive said. "Because he's already here. And Valerie Turner is just not someone you say no to."

Chloe had a flash of horror at the thought of someone who could intimidate Olive.

About five minutes later, Chloe was shaking the hand of a young man with spiky dyed-blond hair and barbed-wire tattoos wrapping his biceps. "Lance Boudreaux," he said. "Mrs. Turner's assistant called me and said Mrs. Turner had heard from Ray Stark that you might need help. And I am so here for you. Ray Stark, man! My friends'll never believe this."

She introduced Brand. Lance shook his hand, but it was clear Brand didn't register since he was neither a chef nor a celebrity.

For all she was lusting after Brand with what few brain cells she could spare, Chloe had to admit Lance was cute. Too young, but cute.

The important question, though, was could he cook?

Only one way to find out.

"Why don't you start by chopping the shallots over there and adding them to the reduced Cabernet demiglaze on the stove?" She gestured vaguely to a pile of vegetation that included shallots, scallions, and three kinds of onions.

He unerringly pulled the shallots from the confused pile of produce. "How fine do you want them?" he asked, reaching for the proper knife.

He knew a shallot from a scallion and a chef's knife from boning knife. He'd do.

"So what next?" Lance asked, as he stirred the shallots into the sauce. "You've only got me until five because I need to go to work at my other job, which isn't nearly this cool, but hey, I gotta pay the rent. So take advantage of me while you can."

It was a measure of Chloe's exhaustion that she didn't realize until it was too late for a witty comeback that Lance had been grinning evilly as he said it, attempting to flirt with her.

It was only after she'd gotten Lance settled that she realized Brand had been trying to get her attention for several minutes. "Sorry," she said, although she was too elated over the sous-chef who fell like manna from heaven to say it with much conviction. "Too much going on."

"I see how it is," Brand said, barely restraining a chuckle. "You don't need me anymore. I'm just…" he fake-sobbed theatrically "…forgotten."

"Oh, please!" She considered snapping at him with the towel, since this time he actually deserved it, but decided it might set a bad example for Lance. "You've been a huge help. I couldn't have gotten this far without you. But I feel bad having you stuck in here doing my grunt work all day. He's getting paid for it. You're…" She hesitated, realizing that he probably was getting paid—and that Sandrine probably thought he was doing something else, like cleaning the pool or polishing the billiard balls or whatever else he did on the estate. "You're incredibly sweet, but this isn't your job. Why don't you take a break and we'll catch up later?"

She hoped she managed to get the right flirty inflection in those last words, even through her haze of fatigue.

She'd definitely like to catch up with the man later—preferably at a time when she could concentrate on getting to know him and not on six gazillion culinary details.

*

The one thing she hadn't reckoned on was that this meticulously equipped kitchen wouldn't have a deep fryer. Of course it didn't. Sandrine's lean build and Ray's amazingly cut body didn't suggest a weakness for late-night French fry fiestas.

Luckily there were several deep, heavy pots available, but that trick reminded her why she didn't make clam cakes, or anything else deep-fried, at home. It was messy.

Very messy.

As in "Thank God that Sandrine had a cleaning staff" messy, with oil spattering on the counters, the stovetop, the floor, and all over her.

She'd also reckoned without the fact that, while clam cakes were dead easy, they were so last-minute as to be crazy-making. It hadn't been much of a problem at the Shore Shack, where they were the only things on the menu with tricky timing and the kitchen was fully staffed.

But now, between finishing them up and making sure everything else was plated and ready for the servers, she felt like she was in a lost episode of *I Love Lucy*. Everything was moving too fast, and Lance, who had been a huge help, had had to run off to his real restaurant job, and there was no way…

Suddenly a tray of hot mini chocolate cakes disappeared out of her hands.

And into the hands of Brand. "I can put these on the serving trays for you," he said. "And if you have a list of what needs to be on the buffet when the guests arrive, I'll start herding the servers for you."

"Thanks, but I can handle it." She could, couldn't she? She'd been in chaotic kitchens before.

On the other hand, it was the first time she'd been completely alone in the chaotic kitchen. Okay, not counting the first dinner party she and Luanna had thrown in Boston, but that had only involved three courses and six guests, and dammit, she knew where everything in that kitchen *was*. Even when she'd been in charge, she'd had staff to whom she could delegate.

He smiled. "There's not much for me to do until the guests show up. I can take some of the non-cooking stuff off your hands so you can concentrate on what needs your attention. Like—" he pointed to the pot of bubbling oil "—that. It looks dangerous."

"It's all right. I…"

"Hey, I know you could do it alone. I also know you'd normally have either more help or more prep time for a party this size. I can take on some of the dumb stuff you shouldn't have to worry about anyway."

She instinctively opened her mouth to argue. Then Brand smiled again, and this time the smile was so dazzling her resolve to go it alone weakened, if only so she could keep him in the kitchen longer and look at him when she had a spare second.

*

When Start Time Minus Ten Minutes arrived, Brand was still in the kitchen. "Get out!" Chloe urged, smacking him lightly on the butt to herd him. She probably shouldn't have—getting fired for sexual harassment would *not* help her career one iota—but how could she resist such a cute butt? "Don't you need to get a shirt and tie on or something?"

He glanced at the clock on the stove. "Oh, shit!"

"What?"

"I left that stuff in the gatehouse to keep it clean and I don't have time to run back there. I can probably get a tie, but Ray's shirts'll never fit me."

Chloe looked up from the tray of scallops she was garnishing. Her one unoccupied brain cell registered it as a bit odd that the pool boy/bartender would even think about borrowing a shirt from Ray...

And then promptly became distracted by the fascinating image of Ray stripping off his shirt to give to Brand. Now that was something women (not to mention her brother Carl) would pay good money to see. Ray wasn't really her type, but the muscles were impressive. And Brand—Brand was definitely her type.

"Best I can do for you is a clean apron. Back there, I think." She pointed with her elbow towards a small closet. "Or maybe it's the other closet..."

"I think I know." She heard him rummaging a bit. When she looked up again, he was pulling his tank top over his head.

Chloe froze, a curl of lemon peel in her hand, staring at the show.

Chapter 8

She'd gotten a distant glimpse of his chest by the pool, but not like this. Not with the unexpected intimacy of him undressing making the already great view even hotter. Sure, her brain knew it was a matter of necessity, but her hormones were getting ready to strip off his jeans along with the shirt, and then get to work on anything he might be wearing underneath.

Either he was taking that tank top off a little more slowly than was strictly necessary or she was so turned on she was altering time. She was registering details a little bit at a time as they were revealed, a glorious tease.

Tight abs, not overly defined, but defined enough to show he took good care of himself. Strong-looking but lean, not cut and bulked up like Ray, and she definitely liked lean better. (Ray looked like an attractive alien—humans just weren't built like that). He had a light dusting of reddish-brown fuzz, enough to look very male without being furry. Just the right degree of tan, too—not the office pallor she was still used to from growing up in the Northeast, but not baked.

In short, Brand had one of the best bodies she'd ever seen *not* on a movie screen. A body she could imagine wrapping herself around all too vividly. She could taste the salt of his skin, feel his muscles moving under her exploring hands…

And as she stood there trying desperately not to drool onto the scallops, he finished pulling the shirt off, tossed it aside with a flourish, and winked at her.

Be still my beating heart.

"I thought…the apron…" she said weakly.

He grinned and tied on an apron emblazoned with a bunch of grapes. It said "Pinch Me, Squeeze Me, Make Me Wine."

Over a shirt, it would have looked adorable. Over bare skin, it was devastating. Pure sex.

"Gotta go!"

"Thanks so much, Brand!" she called as he fled towards his post.

She wasn't sure if she were more sorry or relieved to see him go. On one hand, his cheerful company had probably saved her sanity.

On the other hand, having him around the kitchen dressed (or undressed) like that would rob her of the sanity he'd saved. Tackling him on the floor would be a poor idea.

Which might not have stopped her if she'd actually had time.

The next she saw of him (when she did a pass through a herd of gorgeously dressed guests to see what might need replenishing—she was gratified to see the clam cakes could use a refill) he'd found a bow tie, which looked extraordinarily rakish against bare skin, and he was being flirted with by three women who, if they hadn't been in *Playboy* yet, would be soon.

And she couldn't blame them one bit. If she had time, she'd be body-checking her way to the front of the line.

Unfortunately, (a) she couldn't compete with the *Playboy* types, and (b) she had to make more clam cakes.

*

It was over.

Was it really over?

Chloe staggered into the living room and ascertained that yes, there was nary a guest to be seen. If any were still lingering, they were in private places she didn't want to know about, and she didn't need to deal with them. The place was a wreck, a disaster area, littered with wine glasses and crumpled cocktail napkins. She had no idea if she'd be expected to clean up, or if there were staff for that sort of thing.

Right now, she couldn't fathom picking up one sauce-smeared plate. Her feet were killing her, and she tugged off her shoes, not caring if Sandrine came sweeping in and saw her chef barefoot.

"You look like you need a drink."

It was Brand the Scrummy Pool Guy and Amazing Fill-In Bartender, and he was holding out a flute of champagne. Chloe considered dropping to one knee and proposing to him, but she settled for accepting the glass and rewarding him with the biggest smile she could muster out of her exhausted facial muscles. "You are a god," she told him with utter sincerity.

The champagne was top of the line, cold and crisp and simply gorgeous, and she hoped that whimper she knew she just made hadn't really been audible.

"Whoa, I was going to suggest a toast to celebrate your first success at catering a Sandrine Moss party," he said.

Whoopsie. She peered at the expensive Waterford glass in her hand. Yep, she'd knocked back the entire contents (and damn, but it had been exquisite, and she'd deserved it). "Sorry! Guess you'll have to give me a refill."

She followed him to the bar, staying a few steps behind to better admire his ass in those tight jeans and the play of muscle in his naked back. He filled her glass and topped off his own, holding it up.

"To Chloe, for grace under fire."

"To Brand, for…kick-ass bartending and obedient kitchen help." She couldn't really say *for being terrific eye-candy*, could she?

They clinked glasses. This one went down as smoothly as the last one. *Damn* but that was *good* champagne.

Amazing champagne and an amazingly hot co-worker? With perks like those, maybe this gig wouldn't be so bad.

Chloe hopped up onto a stool, swinging her legs and curling and flexing her aching toes. She leaned on the cherrywood bar. "So, how exactly did you get this gig?"

"Bartending?" Brand refilled her glass and topped off his own.

"Mm-hmm." It fleetingly occurred to Chloe that she couldn't remember the last time she'd eaten except for a few taste-tests. There was a plate with a scattering of Thai rolls on the bar, and she popped one in her mouth, savoring the flavors of mint, basil, and plump shrimp. Yeah, baby, she'd done a kick-ass job herself.

"Sands needed me," Brand said, moving around the bar and propping a hip on the barstool next to her.

Huh. He hadn't called her Sandrine. Was "Sands" a pet name? Was there illicit stuff going on that Chloe really didn't need to know about?

A crush on Sandrine's secret boy-toy would absolutely get her fired. Damn. Maybe she should have let Lance flirt with her after all.

No, she liked this one a lot better.

Brand's expressive mouth curved in a wry smile, and Chloe felt another part of her insides melt, just a little.

"Eh, story of my life," he said. "I'm more interested in you, though. How'd you end up here?"

Chloe didn't mean to go into detail, but the fact that she hadn't slept in several days and worked like crazy and now was drinking really fine champagne all conspired against her. A section of her brain calmly pointed all that out while her mouth independently rambled on.

She paused for breath in the middle of a completely silly story about her oldest brother, Curt, and how he was training his toddler son to "take care of Aunt Chloe," trying to regain control of her urge to fill in the entire story of her life in the next five minutes to this man with the gorgeous blue-green eyes who actually seemed to be listening.

"Sounds like you've got a great family," Brand said softly. "On the other hand, I can see why you needed to get away."

"Yeah, I love 'em and I miss 'em a lot, but they're so...sooo..."

So, what? The right word for what they were "so" lingered on the tip of her tongue, something that would impress him with her wit, but it was long gone. Hell. "Anyway, thanks for listening. And thanks for being a lifesaver tonight. I could just kiss you."

Then her eyes focused through a lens of champagne. Brand's mouth looked as rich and tempting as melted organic dark chocolate. Then there was the rest of him, which looked like the rest of the decadent dish. He'd taken the apron off as they chatted, and incredibly sexy as that had been, his bare chest was a thousand times better. If she could put him on a dessert cart, she'd be on the cover of *Bon Appètit* in a heartbeat. Or maybe *Cosmo*.

If she could put him on a dessert cart, they could get some momentum going and neck in every room in the house that didn't have stairs. Whee.

"I could just kiss you," she repeated and watched for a response.

A half-grin, a little challenging cock of the head, a shift forward.

And as if that wasn't clear enough, he said, "So why don't you already?"

The stools were so close together she just had to slide a little to wrap her arms around his trim, strong body, lean in, press her mouth to his.

For a fraction of a second, it seemed like this might stay a semi-innocent smooch—just flirting, maybe testing the waters for later.

Then something went *click* in her brain and any feeble thoughts of common sense washed away on a flood of arousal and Dom Pérignon.

He tasted of champagne, and mint and basil from the Thai wraps, and a hint of clam cakes and spicy sauce. He smelled…well, to be honest, he smelled like party and sweat, but it was good sweat, the warm, clean kind. The heat of his hard body, the softness of his red-brown hair, the strength of his arms as they wrapped around her, all sent flutters between her legs.

And when she experimentally flicked her tongue against his lips they opened for her. Their tongues met. She snuggled closer, trying to get as much contact as possible, and her stool rocked dangerously. Brand scooped her up, and, by means she only found important because they made his muscles shift in the most wonderful ways against her, they found themselves half on the bar, pressed against each other.

Most of her was exhausted, but parts woke up and insisted on attention. Her nipples swelled and ached as she rubbed against his bare chest. Her red shirt felt like it might catch on fire, and that was fine with her because it would be out of the way then, not standing between her and Brand.

His hands cupped her ass and as she shifted to enjoy the sensation, she realized she was drenched.

She wrapped one leg around his hips, pulled him even closer, bringing his package into teasing proximity to her throbbing sex. It wasn't enough, not by a long shot, not through two sets of clothes, but it would have to do until she was willing to let go long enough to get undressed.

Hard. He was as hard as she was melting, and he groaned into her mouth, cupped her closer, worked her against him.

Waves of sensation shot through her body, and she clenched around a nothing that she wished was the hard cock hidden behind Brand's zipper. Not quite an orgasm, it pushed her higher instead of taking the edge off.

"Need you," Brand breathed, and she nodded her agreement. Okay, it was crazy fast. Not the way she usually behaved. The lustful woman in her had usually deferred to the sensible small-town girl from a traditional Portuguese Catholic family.

But what the hell, she was in Hollywood now. Mom and Aunt Rosa were on the other side of the damn country. They didn't have spies all the way out here. They'd never know.

And if she'd met someone like Brand when she was still in New England, she would have gotten over her inhibitions a lot faster.

One last brain cell chimed in to suggest that they might want to continue things somewhere other than their mutual employer's living room. Brand, though, didn't seem to be in any hurry to leave. In fact, he was working her top up, nudging her bra out of the way. Her eager nipples sprang free, and he bent to capture one in his mouth.

"Just a taste," he said, his mouth full of breast.

It took Sandrine's clear, high voice to shatter the moment.

"What exactly do you think you're doing with my brother?"

Chapter 9

Chloe and Brand leapt apart and slid off the bar, knocking over a pile of cocktail napkins and sending them fluttering to the floor in the process. As Chloe tried, not quite successfully, to right her shirt and bra, she looked from Sandrine to Brand.

Except she barely glanced at Sandrine because she was just too scared to find out she'd been sacked for indiscretion after only one day on the job.

"Your brother?" she squeaked, her voice almost lost over the pounding of her heart. (And of other bits—panic and embarrassment hadn't quite conquered her raging hormones.) Then, realizing as she said it that she sounded like a complete idiot, "You're her *brother*?"

He pushed his glasses up his nose and nodded. He had the good graces to look sheepish.

Great. From triumph to getting canned in one kiss. That had to be some sort of record. And okay, it had been a little more than a kiss, and astoundingly erotic, but probably not worth her job.

Even if it got her in some record book.

Probably, although her nipples and her pussy insisted on offering a different—less practical, but more entertaining—opinion.

Her temper surged briefly. What the hell had he been thinking, not saying he was the boss's brother? Shouldn't she be mad at him?

Her body argued against it. Who cared whose brother he was when he was damn hot? And wouldn't a real dog pretend to be related to someone famous, instead of brushing it over?

She decided she'd worry about whether or not to be mad once she appeased Sandrine.

But how could she have not noticed? Same cheekbones, same shape to the eyes, although his were a different amazing shade of blue from Sandrine's, same basic coloring. Sandrine's copper hair easily could have started out the same reddish-brown as her brother's, or even come from the same gene pool without too much hairdresser intervention.

Same full, sensuous mouth, even, although God knew she hadn't gotten the urge to kiss Sandrine.

And yet, how the hell was she supposed to know that Sandrine even had a brother—let alone that he'd be tending Sandrine's bar and cleaning her pool instead of enjoying the rewards of being rich and famous by proxy, and mouthwateringly gorgeous in his own right? It wasn't like it had ever come up on *Entertainment Tonight*.

At least as far as she knew. She hadn't paid all that much attention to Sandrine's private life before she'd stumbled out onto the red carpet and everything had gone to hell in a proverbial handbasket.

"I'm sorry." She slid off the counter, tugging down her shirt. "I…" And then she stopped, because she had absolutely no idea how to apologize for making out with a superstar's brother. Especially without making it sound like she regretted the making-out part, which she didn't.

Brand stepped between her and his sister. "Sands, she had no idea. She thought I was the bartender."

Sandrine clenched her fists as though she was restraining the urge to smack someone. "Even better, Brand. You made a pass at her under false pretenses. Didn't you think that might get her pissed off? You're not usually an asshole. Why start now, when I finally get a good chef—a chef I'd like to keep a while this time, thank you. She hasn't even been here a full day and you're sexually harassing her?" She rolled her eyes. "Men!"

"Sands, it's not like that." He stepped closer, put a placating hand on her arm, but she jerked it away.

"Can you say 'lawsuit,' Brand? More negative publicity is the last thing…"

Still clutching at the edges of her shirt, Chloe made herself speak up. "That's not what happened." Her voice squeaked again, and she wished for Sandrine's perfect control over her speech—the hateful woman could bitch out her brother and not sound like a harpy. Like a crazy psycho woman, maybe, but a crazy psycho woman with a beautiful, well-modulated voice. "If anything, I was harassing him, although I don't think it's technically harassment if he says it's okay and enjoys it. But I kissed him, not the other way around. So if you're going to yell at anyone, it should be me."

"I assumed you knew who I was," Brand said. "My fault: I should have told you. You probably wouldn't have…"

"I still would have wanted to," she admitted, looking at the hottie she'd never see again because his sister (his sister!) was about to fire her ass, "but I probably wouldn't have. Not without talking a lot more first and making sure it wouldn't be a problem." Technically that was true—she wasn't in the habit of crawling all over men she'd barely met—although the quick hits of champagne had probably had just a little to do with how she'd reacted to him.

How much champagne had she had, anyway?

The problem was that now she felt guilty as hell, not for kissing him, but for getting him bitched out by Sandrine Moss, which she wouldn't wish on her worst enemy.

She turned back to Sandrine. "I'm really sorry. I didn't mean to cause trouble with your brother, who is a really great guy and you shouldn't be mad at him. Or at me, either, because I wasn't trying to…glom onto your brother because he was your brother or something tacky like that. I thought I was just kissing a cute bartender. And he's a fantastic bartender, by the way," she added. Not that it probably mattered to Sandrine, but she wanted to say it anyway, let Sandrine know he wasn't a goof-off.

"Well, good for you!" Sandrine chuckled, a rich, throaty laugh that suggested she'd had plenty of champagne herself, along with maybe just a few mojitos.

They both stared at Sandrine, who now looked much calmer.

"Hey, you worked hard today," she said. "You pulled off a fabulous party that's going to have people talking about the food tomorrow instead of who wore what and who's sleeping with whom. So you ended up in a clinch with a good-looking guy—and even if he is my big brother, I have to admit Brand *is* cute. These things happen. And this time I have no doubt you're telling the truth, because you seem to be the queen of stumbling into weird situations and my brother…well, he's a guy." She shrugged, smiling a little sheepishly and looking even more obviously like Brand with that expression. Now she seemed like a perfectly normal (if gorgeous and very, very expensively dressed) person who'd just caught her brother and an acquaintance in a semi-undressed clinch, overreacted from embarrassment, and was now putting things into perspective.

The fact that she'd probably rehearsed it at some point didn't make it any less effective.

It was as if Sandrine were suddenly playing a different character, a good-humored, reasonable one instead of a psycho starlet from hell.

Chloe could live with that.

"I just don't want any drama," Sandrine added. "Not for my brother—" she pecked him on the cheek "—and not for my fabulous new chef." To Chloe's amazement, she gave Chloe a peck on the cheek, too, wafting perfume and mojito in her general direction. "So if you hook up and it all goes horribly wrong, I will simply have to kick at least one of you from here to next Tuesday. Capisce?"

Brand gaped at his sister like she'd grown a second head. Chloe figured her own expression must be just as confused and goofy.

"Oh good," Sandrine bubbled, "there's an open bottle of champagne and some of the chocolate tart things left. I knew I'd come in here for a reason! Well, that and to tell Chloe what a wonderful job she did tonight. The guests were raving, darling. Just raving. Even that insane Valerie Turner stopped talking about conservation and fund-raising long enough to say how wonderful the food was, and Chloe, trust me, that's nothing short of a miracle. People hand her checks just to make her shut the hell up."

Snatching the bottle Brand had set on the counter and popping a tart into her mouth, Sandrine swept out of the living room, leaving Chloe and Brand gaping in her wake.

"I've known her since the day she was born," Brand murmured, "but I'll never understand her."

What Chloe meant to say was, "Then I have no hope." What actually came out was lost in a massive yawn that made her lower jaw pop alarmingly.

"Sorry," she managed to get out, her voice muffled behind her hand. "Not the company. I like the company."

And how. Despite the utter insanity of being caught half-naked by your boss—with your boss's brother—said boss's brother still looked damn tasty. For some other time, sometime when she had the brain cells to figure out if it was a good idea or not.

Her body, running on exhaustion as it was, insisted that it was a great idea, the best she'd had in a long time, and that there was no time like the present to act on it.

"Want to go find someplace more private?" He held out his arm like a courtly gentleman.

"I'm not sure that's such a good idea..."

"Listen, I'm sorry I didn't tell you, but I figured you probably knew. Plus it was so nice being just me for a little while, playing bartender and sous-chef, not Sandrine Moss's brother."

"It's all right," she said automatically.

"Let's do the introduction properly this time. Hi, I'm Brand Mossiman—Sandrine Moss's big brother. It's Brandon on the birth certificate, but Sandrine insists on calling me Brand, and I've pretty much given up and accepted it. I'd like a chance to prove I'm not a jerk who uses a fake identity to pick up girls."

She thought as best she could through the haze of fatigue and champagne and realized she wasn't upset. "I totally understand. Remember, I'm the one who moved across the country so I could stop being the Montiero boys' kid sister, and they're not even famous. And...well, you're fun, I'm single, and I'd love to pick up where we left off. But I don't want to cause more trouble between you and Sandrine—or for me, for that matter—and I don't know which was real, the exploding part or the laughing-it-off part."

Brand laughed, the way people laugh when something's more weird than funny. "They both were. Sands has a quick temper, but it blows over just as quickly."

She yawned again, so hard that suddenly she was sure Brand could see her tonsils, and she snapped her mouth shut. "God, I'm not sure I can stay awake much longer. It's all caught up with me all of a sudden." She rubbed her eyes, looked at her shoes dubiously. The idea of putting them back on sounded like torture. She'd just go barefoot and hope the peacocks she'd glimpsed earlier didn't poop everywhere like geese did.

"It's been a long day."

"More like a long few days. I know there's a bed waiting for me. I just hope I can find it. The guest house, that is. I'm pretty sure I can find the bed once I get there."

"I'll walk you there—and take a rain check on anything else until you're awake enough to enjoy it."

"I'll hold you to it." She was proud that she maintained the flirtatious grin for all of three seconds before spoiling it with yet another jaw-stretching yawn.

She experienced the trek across the estate in a blur of alcohol and weariness, although she vaguely appreciated the cool grass against her aching feet and the distant, liquid burbling of fountains.

The kiss Brand gave her at the door woke up parts of her, if not her brain. He cradled her face in his hands, his thumbs stroking her jaw as he bent towards her. At first his lips brushed against hers gently, but she moaned, and he caught his breath, and his mouth came down on hers hard.

When he pulled away, they were both gasping for air.

Luanna chose that moment to open the door, wrapped in a rose bathrobe, hair wild, eyes blurred. "Chloe, who's the hunk?"

"Brand, Luanna. Bartender, roommate. Roommate who loves me very much so she's going back inside now."

Luanna retreated.

Brand kissed Chloe once more, lingeringly.

"Sweet dreams, Chloe," he said, in a voice that was just the tiniest bit strained, and then he was gone.

Chapter 10

$\mathcal{B}$rand didn't even bother turning on the lights. Between the Bose stereo, the various computers, and the USB-powered glow-in-the-dark lightsaber (from a friend who'd gotten a job at Industrial Light and Magic), the living room/dining room/office of the guest house glowed enough to get around and he didn't really feel like bright lights. He clicked a few buttons, letting the music software on his computer do its job and randomly select something from the collection.

The punk-gypsy sounds of Gogol Bordello filled the little house, singing something surrealistic in heavy Eastern European accents. It was sexy and angry and strange, and that suited his mood perfectly.

Damn.

Damn his aching cock.

Damn his sister and her bad timing.

And damn himself for being too greedy too soon. If he'd scooped Chloe up and gotten her back here before things got to the naked-flesh stage, they could be fooling around right now and Sands never would have known. (Or, more likely, Chloe might have passed out on him as soon as she'd gotten horizontal, but there was always morning.) And if he'd been more upfront about who he was in the first place...

Chloe wouldn't have gotten near him. Sandrine had her scared half to death.

Chloe and about half of Hollywood.

Which, as far as Brand was concerned, was hilarious. Despite her temper, Sands was harmless. Talked a good game, but almost never carried through on her threats. Holding a grudge required an attention span, and unless it was related to acting, she didn't have one.

Granted, tonight had been weird, even by the generous standard of weird he applied to his crazy-genius sister. But she'd been twitchier than usual ever since she got back from Tunisia. She'd feel better once she started working again. When Sands was hard at work, she was sane: focused and happy and relatively calm. Relaxing was what did her in. Always had, even when she was a kid.

And getting her busy and thus calmed down would give Chloe a chance to settle in and relax—and for him to get to know her.

And to cash in that rain check, because letting her go to her bed alone tonight had been damn hard.

Which was another weird thing about the night. Several women had flirted heavily over the course of the party, and two had slipped him phone numbers. Actresses, women who, like Sands, had taken their natural good looks and honed them into deadly weapons of man-slaying. Cleavage to die for (and it might be the best that money could buy, but it *looked* real enough to fool his gonads). Exquisite faces with impeccable makeup. Great clothes that showed off perfect bodies.

And sure, he'd enjoyed the attention. Who wouldn't? His sister's circle of friends included some of the hottest women in Hollywood. Not that they wanted an actual relationship with a mere CGI specialist, but in the past, a few had been all for a short, sex-drenched fling. He didn't like to think of himself as shallow—not full-time, anyway—but straightforwardly shallow could be fun sometimes, and who was he to say no to the latest model-turned-starlet?

Only tonight he had. (Okay, he'd tucked the numbers into his back pocket out of habit, but he knew he'd never call.)

Because sexy as she was, and she certainly was, Natalia or whatever her name was didn't intrigue him the way the way Chloe did. Chloe reminded him of the girls he'd known at Cornell: smart and cute and basically unadorned and utterly herself. Real curves, including a real little belly. Real hair. Just enough makeup to highlight things. He even liked her accent—not Boston Brahmin, but something gritty and working-class, with broad A's that slipped in when she wasn't paying attention.

Maybe he'd finally overdosed on Hollywood or something, but from the first time he'd seen Chloe in those stupid tabloid pictures, he'd liked her. Never mind she'd apparently been kissing Ray.

Yeah, that had raised his brotherly hackles, but he'd also thought that if it turned out Ray was a dog, he was at least a dog with taste. Actually seeing her in the flesh, in less-than-pristine chef's whites, her hair in a messy ponytail and a streak of flour across one olive cheek, had distracted him to the point he'd almost lost control of the booze-dolly.

And when she kissed him, he had lost it. Lost control, lost common sense. (Not that she'd minded. From the way she'd been rubbing up against his cock and moaning, her common sense had pretty much evaporated, too.)

Sweet lips that tasted of champagne and spice, and an eager, curvy little female body that seemed to want him as much as he wanted her would do that to a guy. But starting to undress her on his sister's bar? That was teenage stuff. And someone else's teenage stuff at that—he'd never been that dumb. (Sands had the dumb-stunts department covered; his job as the sensible older brother had always been cleaning up her messes.)

Thinking about the on-the-bar adventure with Chloe made his cock ache and insist on attention. Damn. He should have sweet-talked his way into the guest house...

No, he was too much of a gentleman for that. He cursed himself for it, but it was true. She'd been tipsy, on both alcohol and exhaustion, and he didn't take advantage of that.

That didn't mean, however, he couldn't think about what could have happened—what would, with any luck, happen sometime soon.

So easy to picture Chloe sprawled naked on his bed, her mocha-tipped nipples puffy and slick with his spit, her legs spread, showing how much she wanted him. Fat, juicy labia, dark and swollen and shiny with her juices and… would she be waxed bare? No, just tidied up, he guessed, with a tangle of unruly dark curls that signaled to a guy like mistletoe at Christmas: Kiss under here.

And he would. Oh yeah, he would.

Brand flopped down on the black leather couch (his sister, or rather his sister's decorator, had winced at it in the Art Deco gatehouse, but it was comfortable and stood up to a single guy's life of late-night snacking and impromptu masturbation), unzipped his fly, eased out his straining cock.

The hell with that. He raised his hips so he could strip out of the jeans and underwear completely, and sighed at the freedom.

His hand worked up and down in the familiar pattern as he fantasized.

Chloe would taste sweet and rich and smoky, and she'd roll her hips, rising to meet his lips and tongue. Pretty soon she'd start begging for his cock, and he'd want to give it to her, but he'd make himself be patient because he knew it would be worth it in the end. And he'd enjoy it too, enjoy making her squirm and mewl and plead, enjoy feeling her getting wetter and juicier. Enjoy her moans when he slipped two fingers inside her, and the way she'd contract around his fingers and shudder, going rigid and then limp as the orgasm passed through her.

The first orgasm. He'd want to give her a couple before he entered her, but would he have the patience?

He'd like to think so, but he knew his cock would have other ideas. Chloe wasn't the type to simply lie there and take. No, she'd be playing with him, her small but strong hands stroking him, fondling his balls. Maybe she'd work them into a sixty-nine. He already knew her mouth was delicious, and on his cock…

Oh God. He pictured that full, sensual mouth devouring his cock as he licked and suckled her towards orgasm, and his cock surged.

Images exploded in his head, an erotic kaleidoscope: Chloe coming; Chloe sucking him; Chloe on the bar, her breasts bare and tempting;

Chloe dipped in chocolate. Chloe taking him inside her tight, hot depths and meeting his thrusts, crying out under him. Or maybe from behind. She had an adorable ass and he'd be able to reach around to her clit and keep her primed as they fucked.

His belly twitched. His balls drew tight. He was close, so close, and he'd like to draw it out longer, enjoy the sensations, but he was going to…

Screams that sounded like tortured children split the warm night air, effectively destroying the moment.

He grabbed a nearby pair of sweatpants—jeans would take too long—and yanked them on. Glanced around for a flashlight, couldn't remember where it was, grabbed the lightsaber instead—it was charged enough to provide light for a while. Feeling like an underdressed Jedi, he raced out into the night.

*

Forget the rousing success of the party. Sandrine was going to kill her.

She was going to skip the firing and the career ruining, and go straight to killing.

"Evenrude!" Chloe raced across the lawn after the escapee dog. Earlier she'd appreciated the cool grass. Now it felt unpleasantly wet and cold beneath her feet.

It would have shocked her awake and sober if the screams hadn't done that already.

She'd been so tired, her eyeballs throbbed. So tired that even the residual arousal wasn't tempting enough to do something about. She seemed to be moving through frozen molasses, because the clock assured her she'd been home for half an hour or so, but she'd just managed to gulp down some water, brush her teeth, and change into her PJs—of course it took a while longer because she had to find both the toothbrush and the PJs, and her comfy cotton jersey ones were nowhere to be found so she was in something much prettier, but less practical. She was on the verge of collapsing, thanking the powers that be that Olive had told her Sandrine wouldn't want anything before a lunch/brunch/whatever around two o'clock, when Evenrude had padded up to her.

Evenrude, with her big piteous brown eyes that plainly said, "Hey, lady, I gotta pee."

When Evenrude had to pee, the world was wise to facilitate.

Chloe had made her way to the front door, stubbing her toe in the unfamiliar cottage only once. Damn. No leash in sight. At the apartment, they'd had a hook by the front door. She didn't even know if Luanna had found the leash in the mayhem.

Well, Evenrude, being of stout body and unimaginative mind, was unlikely to go far. She'd do her business locally, and Chloe would make a point of cleaning up the yard tomorrow.

So she'd opened the door.

Evenrude had stepped out and paused on the stoop, nose to the breeze, stout body quivering.

Then, with a low woof, she'd taken off into the darkness.

Crap. Chloe hadn't even considered whether Sandrine had dogs, or exotic big cats, or even a llama farm. But Evenrude was harmless. And afraid of cats, to the extent that she'd run away if she scented one.

Then Chloe heard the unearthly scream, and she'd raced out into the night.

Chapter 11

Obviously, Evenrude had morphed into Cujo and attacked a guest (or, worse, Sandrine herself, because Chloe wouldn't put it past Sandrine to wander her own estate in the wee hours of the morning like some tipsy Gothic heroine).

"Evenrude!" She stumbled, caught herself before she fell. Thankfully there were little solar-powered lanterns sunk into the ground to keep her from pitching into the pool or discovering a cactus garden with her bare feet.

A flashlight would've been awfully nice, though.

And a map.

Especially since there did seem to be a cactus garden.

And a looming mass of hedge that might just be a hedge maze—now wouldn't that have been a pretty thing to stumble into?

She heard a familiar whine. To her relief, it sounded nearby.

She slowed to a walk, trying to place which direction the sound had come from. "Evenrude?"

"Who the hell is Evenrude?"

Chloe screamed.

The owner of the deep male voice yelped. She turned and saw a looming figure, illuminated by a strange glowing…sword? She'd thought her night couldn't possibly get any stranger. Apparently she'd been wrong.

"Well," Brand said, "at least I know it wasn't you screaming before."

"You scared the hell out of me!" Chloe pressed a hand to her chest, convinced that her thudding heart couldn't take the strain.

Both from fear and the fact that Brand, brandishing a lightsaber or not, was gorgeously shirtless, and his sweatpants were rather, um, revealing of his condition.

A bark of curiosity to their left, followed by another shriek.

They both ran.

A waist-high stone wall surrounded the tennis courts, and on the wall perched two affronted-looking peacocks. Chloe sagged with relief. No humans had been maimed or ravaged or terrified. She didn't know how highly Sandrine prized her peacocks, but at least they seemed to be unharmed.

Chloe sighed. "Oh, Evenrude."

Evenrude, at the foot of the wall, swung her head around to acknowledge Chloe, then went back to gazing at the peacocks, her tail wagging so hard her butt was wobbling.

"Does your dog make a habit of treeing birds?" Brand asked.

"She wasn't hunting them," Chloe said indignantly. "She was trying to make friends with them."

The fact that she'd just gone from being exasperated with Evenrude to defending her was not lost on Chloe.

"I don't think the peacocks are feeling the same level of gregariousness," Brand said. He crouched down. "Hey, pup."

Evenrude momentarily abandoned her antisocial new friends for a newer and more responsive potential acquaintance, and showed her adoration by burrowing her face in Brand's crotch.

Thankfully she had dodgy aim, and shoved her snout beneath the most sensitive areas.

"Evenrude!" Chloe grabbed at the dog's collar.

"It's okay," Brand said, holding out his hand for Evenrude to sniff. "You should reserve your friend-making for daylight hours," he added, scritching Evenrude behind the ears and making her moan with ecstasy.

Chloe instantly felt jealous.

"Time to get you home," she said, tugging at the dog's collar again.

The minute Brand stood and Chloe let go of the collar, though, Evenrude turned and snuffled by the wall. The peacocks had long since vanished during the distraction, but Evenrude was showing signs of that she had some bloodhound in her.

Brand handed her a long string. She nearly dropped it when she realized it was the cord to his sweatpants.

"Thank God for elastic," he said. "You can return it tomorrow."

"Thanks." Chloe tied one end to Evenrude's collar and made a loop at the other end for her hand.

She looked around. "Oh, crap."

"What's wrong?" Brand asked.

"I have no idea where I am."

He grinned and crooked his arm in that same gallant gesture he'd used before. "I'd be happy to escort you," he said.

"My Jedi knight in shining...sweatpants. With a magic sword and everything." She managed to purr suggestively on *magic sword*, because really, you just had to make a joke of it.

"My damsel in incredibly sexy scraps of lace."

In...what? Very, very belatedly, Chloe remembered what she'd been wearing when she raced out of the house.

She couldn't help looking down, just to confirm her worst fears.

She'd had those dreams about being naked in public, and she'd never much liked them. Exhibitionism wasn't her thing, despite her flagrant display on the bar in the middle of Sandrine Moss's living room.

The scraps of lace—and silk, she wanted to protest—were a pale mint green, and seemed to glow in the moonlight. Although she was semi-decently covered, the camisole and tap pants, cut high on the thigh, clung to her curves. And despite the fact that it wasn't at all chilly out, her nipples were at full alert, and no flimsy layer of silk was going to hide *that*.

"Well," she said. "Well." She tucked her hand in the curve of his elbow. The warm flesh of his inner arm made her fingers tingle. "What *does* one wear to a dog chase? I'm not up on the proper Hollywood etiquette there."

He laughed, and bantered back, "Well, first you need your lightsaber. Once you have that, the rest is optional."

She looked him up and down, lingering on the bare chest, the treasure trail leading down to the intriguing tent in the front of his sweats—and still coming back to the damn glowing sword. Some things you just couldn't ignore, even if you wanted to.

"Okay," she finally said. "I'm not sure I *want* to know, but I *need* to know. Was that a present from George Lucas or something, or are you that much of a geek?"

Brand roared with laughter. "Neither. Okay, I *am* a geek, but I don't always carry a lightsaber. Only when I can't find the flashlight and I think someone may be in trouble out in the dark."

"But why do you…oh, never mind." One of her brothers had a friend who was such a huge Star Wars fan he drove up to Boston in costume to be part of "Imperial Storm Troopers Local #46" or something like that. (They did charity appearances.) Brand didn't seem anything like Tommy, who was thirty and still lived in an apartment over his mom's garage, but there was no cosmic law that said some geeks couldn't clean up really well.

"I do CGI special effects, and one of the guys I used to work with got a job at Industrial Light and Magic and got this for me. It's a real prop from one of the movies, just a little…doctored."

Okay, maybe Chloe was just a little bit of a geek herself, because her immediate reaction was, "Cool! Special effects? What have you worked on?"

It was nice, if a bit staggering, to learn he had a real job as opposed to being his sister's pool boy and occasional bartender.

Still chatting, they reached the patio in front of the guesthouse. Suddenly, in the darkness together, at what she realized was a moment of decision, special effects seemed much less interesting.

Brand turned and rested his hands on her hips, but not before he started at her ribcage and slowly drew them down. Her skin tingled at the contact.

She'd turned him away once before.

"Chloe Montiero," he said, pressing his lips to the crown of her head, ruffling her hair. "You are going to be the death of me."

She couldn't do it again.

"If you're going to die, you should do it with a smile on your face," she said. She pulled back so she could look at him. "Come inside with me."

He searched her face. "Are you sure?"

"Absolutely. Sober, and sure. We know the rules: no drama. I'm good with that. Let's just enjoy tonight, and each other. No promises, no expectations in the morning."

She sounded like most men's fantasy, she knew. Her brothers would lock her up and toss the key in the middle of the Atlantic if they heard her right now. But her brothers were three thousand miles away, and she was horny, and Brand was hot and sexy and sweet; she deserved this after the week she'd had.

She just hoped to hell she remembered where she'd packed the condoms.

They stumbled through the door, half-wrapped around each other, lust robbing Chloe of what little coordination had been spared by utter, boneless exhaustion. Without Brand's arms around her, she would have fallen. But the carpet was soft, she thought dreamily, and if Brand fell with her, it would all be all right.

"Everything okay?" Luanna called sleepily from her bedroom.

"Fine," Chloe said.

"'kay, good. I heard a scream, but I fig'red it was just you with that hunky bartender guy."

Chloe made a mental note to poison Luanna's morning coffee. "Go back to sleep."

"'kay." A rustle of bedcovers, and then soft snoring.

"'Hunky bartender guy,' hmm?" Brand said.

Chloe was glad for the darkness hiding her flaming cheeks. "Hey, she saw your ass and came to her own conclusions."

"And what conclusions did you come to?"

She slipped a hand down his back and over the fine, firm curve of his mouthwatering ass, and squeezed gently. "I would think that was obvious."

She wanted him. Bad.

*

Brand felt dizzy with desire. He suspected it might have something to do with the fact that all of his blood was in his crotch. Either that or the perfume Chloe wore was downright hypnotic.

She turned on a bedside light, adding a warm, golden glow to the room. "Sorry about the mess."

As if he would have noticed an elephant in the room, what with Chloe standing there, all highlights and shadows and curves, and those delectable nipples pressing against the silky fabric of her camisole, a hint of dark areole visible through the pale fabric.

For chrissakes, the poor woman had just moved in yesterday, and had spent the day cooking. He didn't expect her to have the place unpacked and pristine.

But he understood that she was a little nervous, a little self-conscious.

"I'll give you a few minutes… I need to hit the bathroom," he said.

Fact was, he did have to pee, provided he could calm things down enough southwards to do the deed. He stood in front of the toilet, trying to ignore the underwear randomly tossed on the floor—he definitely recognized that bra—and the perfume bottle that smelled like Chloe, trying to forget the sight of her in those scraps of a nightie, all long legs and upturned breasts, trying to think of software coding and script blocking and shooting schedules.

Afterwards, when he was washing his hands, he allowed himself to imagine her getting ready for him, maybe putting out some toys or lube, or just arranging the pillows in anticipation of a long night of raucous sex.

The last thing he expected, when he got back to her room, was to find himself poised on the edge of indecision.

Because Chloe had fallen asleep.

Chapter 12

Chloe had obviously stretched out on the covers to be provocative, but somewhere between provocative and unconscious, she'd rolled onto her side, tucking one hand under her pillow.

She looked utterly desirable.

And utterly untouchable.

Brand couldn't claim to be perfect. He certainly wasn't a cad, and he tried to be gentlemanly, but he was only human. He'd done a few things he wasn't proud of, sure.

But he drew the line at seducing women who weren't awake enough to be a part of the process.

He dragged a hand through his hair. He also apparently drew the line at waking up a poor woman who hadn't slept in days, no matter how delectable she was and how interested she'd been in him before she'd succumbed to exhaustion.

Fact was, he liked Chloe. He hadn't known her for long, but what he'd seen so far, he was pretty damn interested in. She'd pulled off an incredible array of food for a party on amazingly short notice, and then she'd stood up to Sandrine, something few people did and lived to tell the tale. Then she'd chased her silly dog out into the night, just to make sure everything was okay.

Somehow, she'd done all that without having a meltdown or hissy fit. The few grumpy moments had been minor.

Quite the capable, level-headed woman.

Gorgeous, too. And incredibly sexy.

Brand contemplated that tempting, sleeping form, and weighed it against the silent, lonely walk back to the gatehouse.

He might be gentlemanly enough not to push the sex issue, but damned if he wanted to sleep alone. He just wanted to curl up with her, drift off to sleep listening to her breathing.

But if he curled up next to her, he was just going to lie awake and, well, throb. He seriously doubted he could be that close to her and think about anything else but what he'd like to do to her, in great detail. Mentally reviewing software code wasn't going to help, nor was reciting baseball stats or mulling over the restoration of Sandrine's Bentley.

All that said, he didn't want her to wake up later and think he'd ditched her. Women could be funny like that, and although he had the sense that Chloe would handle it better than most, he didn't want to bail on her—again.

He found a quilt, possibly handmade, hanging half out of a box, and spread it over her.

That gave him the idea.

There were boxes all over the guest house, some opened and half-emptied, others still hastily sealed. He remembered her saying that she and Luanna had been up all night packing and moving. It must have taken a million trips in that little car of hers.

Sandrine would have paid for the move without a second thought, but Chloe probably hadn't even thought of that.

She was in this predicament because of him. The least he could do was help her out.

He started in the living room. There was already a media center, and he found a few boxes of books, CDs, and DVDs. He wondered whether Chloe or Luanna was the fan of foreign films. He wasn't sure where to put knickknacks, so he set them in empty spaces on shelves and on side tables.

The kitchen was a little easier. Food and cookware went in the cabinets. The magnet in the shape of Rhode Island that simply said "Unwind" went on the fridge. (He'd have to remind her of that philosophy.)

Of course, it all would have been easier if the boxes were properly labeled. Many weren't at all, unless you counted the logos for Stoli and Captain Morgan. Some of their belongings had just been tossed into garbage bags—thankfully he looked before he tossed out one full of clothes and extra rolls of toilet paper.

He remembered her saying they hadn't moved to LA that long ago, so it made sense that they'd re-used their boxes. Everything was a jumble anyway—hats mixed with a dog leash and sewing supplies and random electronics charging cords and a couple of mismatched socks.

The box in the entryway marked "Cookbooks" seemed suspiciously light, but when he set it on the coffee table and opened it, in fact there were several cookbooks on top. He stacked them on the table to transfer later. Reached back in.

And came up with a double handful of flirty lace and silk.

Under normal circumstances, he would have immediately dropped them and closed the box back up. Problem was, when he saw what was also in the box, every muscle in his body went into immediate rigor mortis.

Except for his penis, which surged to life again.

He was no stranger to sex toys. It was the mental image of Chloe pleasuring herself with the nubbly, curved, fuchsia vibrator that caused his brain to misfire.

Which was when a steely voice behind him said, "What kind of pervert *are* you?!"

*

Chloe had startled into consciousness on a wave of panic. The room was lighter than it should be. What time was it? Olive had told her she didn't need to worry about breakfast, but she'd be expected to make a light lunch. Given Sandrine's fondness for springing things on her, that could mean a light lunch for twenty. She'd set her alarm...at least, she was pretty sure she had.

She'd been kind of tipsy.

And then she'd been kind of distracted....

Crap, *what time was it?*

She tried to roll over to see the clock—and found herself looking out her open door to the living room at an extremely nice specimen of male ass covered by stretched sweatpant cotton as he leaned over.

Brand, her still sleepy mind identified.

There were far worse ways to wake up, although it took her a second to figure out how he'd gotten there and what had happened the night before.

Or more to the point, what *hadn't* happened. Dammit.

How in the world had she fallen asleep on such an incredibly sexy guy? Okay, she knew how: no sleep for forty-eight hours and an insanely busy day, topped off by guzzling champagne. It made sense, but that didn't mean she wasn't sorry about it.

She could have lain there for some time, just admiring the view, but she was still kind of nervous about the time. Plus she had to pee.

And if, on her way to the bathroom, she found an excuse to goose that delectable butt, who could blame her?

She solved problem #1 by focusing on the clock. Six forty-two a.m. How could Southern California be so impossibly bright at that hour? But at least she wasn't late for anything.

She slipped out of bed, wrapping the quilt around her against the cottage's air conditioning, which seemed to be working very well indeed. No more relying on cheap fans, hooray!

She was right behind him, fingers curved and ready to goose, when she saw what he was holding. What was he doing pawing through her boxes—much less *that* box? She didn't have a problem with men seeing her in lingerie, or with toys, but this was a little early in the relationship.

"What kind of pervert *are* you?!"

As if released from a spell, he dropped her red silk teddy back in the box. He turned, pushing up his glasses. At least he had the presence of mind to look abashed. "I was helping you unpack."

"Excuse me?" She'd expected some lame excuse—but this just made no sense.

"You fell asleep," he said, deftly folding the flaps of the box together. "I didn't want to just disappear on you, and if I was here I figured I might as well be useful." He picked up the box and carried it past her into the bedroom. "In my defense," he added, "this box is marked 'Cookbooks.'"

Clearly, she was hallucinating. What had been in that champagne, anyway? "You went through all our stuff?" she asked.

"I *unpacked* it," he repeated, as if it were the most normal thing in the world, like "use the freshest ingredients" or "always whip egg whites in a pristine bowl." He went on, "I know you'll need to rearrange some of it, but it's in the right rooms, at least."

Aaaaand there it was. Hunky Pool Boy's Fatal Flaw.

She'd known he wouldn't be perfect—nobody was—but did he have to be A Fixer?

Chloe considered herself pretty damn lucky where boyfriends were concerned. She'd never dated a gambler, a cheater, a dickhead who didn't respect women, or a sports nut who insisted on wearing war paint and screaming at the TV. By comparison, a fixer wasn't all that bad. Some women even *liked* fixers, liked having someone in their lives who took care of things. Chloe could understand that sometimes, a fixer's attentiveness was kinda romantic.

She didn't find it romantic, though. She didn't even like it. And this was *her* relationship.

Well, not a relationship yet, if ever, but she'd had a really good feeling about Brand up 'til now.

Inner Chloe wanted to stamp her foot and pout.

Outer Chloe took a deep breath and questioned whether she might be overreacting due to exhaustion and post-stress loopiness, and accepted that this might not be the best time to address the problem.

She didn't realize how badly she'd been scowling until Brand spoke again, his brow furrowed. "Okay, I see I've upset you. I'm not sure what I did, but I'm sorry." He sat on the bed and held out his hands. "Let's talk about it."

"No."

Now his brows shot up. "No?"

"I have to pee," she said, and with her head held high, she retreated to the bathroom with as much dignity as the dragging quilt allowed her.

What was it with this place and her having to pee?

She exchanged the quilt for a robe hanging on the back of the bathroom door, did her business.

She took a deep breath, then released it on a very quiet string of Portuguese curses. Unleashing the curses on a relative stranger—especially when the relative stranger was her boss's brother—was *not* a wise idea.

Brother. Pretend he's one of your brothers.

Ew. That was the last thing she wanted to do with someone who made her nerve endings sizzle, with whom she'd shared such a thrilling-down-to-her-toes kiss.

But she knew from experience how to deal with brothers and anger. An only girl in a family of five older brothers had to learn that early. Especially with brothers like hers.

She marched back out, held up a forestalling hand before he could speak.

"Okay," she said, projecting calm and soothing into her voice. "Here's the thing. I'm still behind on sleep, I'm still really stressed, and I have to make lunch for your sister. I don't like to run away from a disagreement, but I'm not in the right place to discuss this rationally now. Can we table it for later?"

Behind those cute glasses, his sea-blue eyes narrowed. Not as malleable as her brothers, then. Good to know for future encounters.

"Maybe that would be best," he agreed, although his voice didn't quite indicate complete acquiescence.

"Exactly." It also helped to make them feel like you were agreeing with their idea, even if it was your idea first. "It would be best if you left right now so I can get dressed and get to work." She clutched her robe tighter to reinforce her point. The fact that she didn't have to go to work for a couple of hours didn't matter. *He* wouldn't necessarily know that, and it was the best excuse she could come up with under the circumstances.

He placed his hands on the bed, levered himself to standing. "I'll see you later, then."

The second he was gone, Chloe flopped down on the bed. This was the last thing she needed: a new—and impossibly sexy—complication.

A bleary-eyed Luanna stumbled from her own room into the hallway. "Did I hear voices? Why is your lingerie out? Did I miss a party? Damn. Who was here?"

"Trouble," Chloe said. "A big hot mess of trouble."

Chapter 13

Chloe walked into the mansion's kitchen and staggered back a step, wondering if the strong scent of lemon cleaner had just bleached her brain.

The kitchen wasn't just clean—it was as if a nightmare impromptu party had never happened. The night before, she'd tidied up some, wiping down counters and putting dishes in the sink. Now all the appliances gleamed and the pots and pans had been put back in their cabinets or hung on the rack over the center island.

"House elves?" she wondered aloud.

"Cleaning service on speed dial."

Chloe jumped when Olive's precise voice sounded behind her.

Olive made her feel guilty for no reason at all. Well, there was the whole necking-at-the-bar-with-Brand thing, which Sandrine easily could have told Olive.

Chloe was pretty sure she was more scared of Sandrine than Olive, but Olive was terrifying by proxy.

The older woman wore another impeccable outfit, this time in a plum shade that gave a glow to her dark skin. She set a basket of lemons, limes, and avocados, probably from the trees outside, on the counter.

How could she look so unruffled when she dealt with Sandrine every day? Maybe she was a robot. Or a cyborg. Chloe could never remember which was which.

"You did a fine job, last night," Olive said. She kept her usual formality, but Chloe was sure she heard a note of admiration in the other woman's voice. "You really kept a cool head. Sandrine was impressed, and it's hard to impress Sandrine."

And with that, Compliment Time was over and they got down to the business of the day's menus and the schedule for the next few days.

No more parties were planned (or even hinted at being planned), hallelujah. Chloe wasn't responsible for breakfast—Sandrine usually just had tea and toast and fruit, so all Chloe had to do was make sure fresh fruit was sliced and waiting in the fridge. If Sandrine was filming, she wouldn't be home during the day, but since she wasn't working in the next week, Chloe would be expected to prepare lunch.

Chloe was just grateful that Olive had shared with her a Google calendar that spelled out exactly what was expected for the week, because her head was already spinning.

But as soon as Olive was gone and Chloe had the kitchen to herself, she found her center again. Kitchens were her sanctuary. Here, she was in control; she knew what she was doing and how to do it well.

So she was better prepared for a certain visitor wandering in.

Sandrine had made happy noises over lunch (salad platter with three-beet caviar and a beautiful fresh goat cheese from Sonoma), which had left Chloe feeling confident and happy, humming to herself as she prepped dinner. There was some fantastic fresh ahi in the fridge just crying out to be grilled with a wasabi glaze and served with bruschetta (on whole-wheat bread, which wasn't quite the same, but would have to do).

Brand was wearing a simple blue collared golf shirt with a movie studio logo on the left breast.

Inner Chloe and Outer Chloe swapped roles. Inner Chloe purred *yum*. Outer Chloe noticed Brand was wearing Vans with retro spaceships on them, and decided to make it a learning experience.

"Good," she said, pointing her knife at his feet. "Bare feet aren't allowed in my kitchen."

"*Your* kitchen?" Brand asked with a raise of brows.

"When I'm working, no matter where it is, it's my kitchen and I'm in charge." She reached for a clove of garlic, already peeled, and went to work on it. The knife blade glinted in the sunlight that came through the high windows, and hopefully looked menacing enough to emphasize her point.

He wasn't saying anything. Maybe he knew better than to bring up the subject of his perverted pawings while she was holding a sharp weapon.

Of course, right then a timer dinged, and she wiped her hands on a dish towel before flipping the tuna in its marinade.

When she turned back, Brand had picked up the knife and was about to finish off the garlic clove.

Argh!

"Hey!" Chloe reached for the knife.

"I'm just trying to help," Brand said. A furrow appeared on his forehead, just about the bridge of his little glasses.

"I don't *need* any help." Chloe gently hip-checked him to move him away from the cutting board, even though what she really wanted to do was drop-kick him halfway down the driveway.

And it was a long driveway.

Something flashed into her mind, a hint from years of dealing with the brother contingent: Sometimes guys needed things spelled out that seemed obvious to her.

"Yesterday I really needed another pair of hands and I appreciate you helped out," she said, choosing her words carefully, and keeping her eye on the garlic and sharp implement, because safety first. "But that was a special case. The rest of the time, this is my territory. If I ever need a bartender, I'll ask you." She glanced up and made herself smile, because she didn't want to come off as mean. Even if she felt mean at the moment, she couldn't help liking—or at least lusting after—the guy. "Otherwise, stay out of my way and no one will get hurt."

He held up his hands. "Ooookay." Out of the corner of her eye, she saw him settle onto one of the barstools on the other side of the island.

She still felt unsettled. Dammit. She'd won the battle, but they still had boundary issues to discuss.

She scraped herbs and onions and garlic into a ceramic bowl, where they'd shortly become salad dressing, still aware of Brand's presence, of his gaze, like a physical touch. She put down the knife and cutting board, wiped her hands again, and came around the island. He turned, and she found herself standing between his knees, a mirror position of how'd they'd been last night at the bar.

Mmm, supplied Inner Chloe.

"Hey," he said before she could speak. "I'm sorry about this morning. Starting a new job is hard enough without moving at the same time. Not to mention getting used to my sister, who's not exactly your typical boss. I figured if I could get a few things put away it would be one less thing for you to deal with. I swear I wasn't perving over your panties and…" He turned surprisingly red. "Okay, I was a little. Visual imagination, you know. I was expecting cookbooks, though, I swear. I was just trying to help."

"In a heavy-handed way," she said, totally thrown off balance. She'd come over to apologize for overreacting, and he'd gazumped her? If she wasn't the teensiest bit impressed, she might have been irked.

And she was still irked because he kept using the "trying to help" excuse. People had been beating her on the head with that one on her for her whole life, and it never got less annoying.

"Uh…guilty as charged," he admitted. "You said something about liking things just so. I can respect that. I'm sorry I overdid it. Not to mention that I looked like a perv." He grinned a little. Obviously, despite the apologies, he was enjoying a few fascinating mental images.

Which, despite her still being irked, was flattering. She was more than a little interested in finding out what those images were, to see if she could re-create them at some point.

Brand might be interfering, but he was still pushing her happy buttons.

Sigh. He seemed to get how he'd stepped over the line and that would do for now. They'd resolved the immediate issue and could go from there. Maybe he wasn't truly A Fixer.

Now it was her turn to say a few things. "I'm sorry I called you a perv. And that I snapped at you when you picked up the knife just now."

He rubbed his hands lightly up and down her arms, and even that soft touch made her body wake up again, her girly parts perking up hopefully. Hello, sex soon, please?

The fact that he could distract her from cooking was quite astonishing. She'd once broken up with a guy simply because he found her chef's hat sexy and kept trying to have his way with her in the middle of her sauce Béarnaise.

"I'm sorry, too," Brand said. "I was just trying to help."

Oh, he just *had* to say it and ruin the moment.

She gritted her teeth to keep herself from snapping "but I don't *need* help!" *again.* How could she get him to understand that the Mr. Helpful routine, which no doubt endeared him to a lot of people, was guaranteed to make her want to go all stabby on him with a good kitchen knife?

"I understand that," she said, "and thank you. But it's my job, and it's important that I—"

"You know what?" Brand said. "I obviously need to stop talking, because I keep putting my foot in it. So I'm going to do something else with my mouth."

He slid his hands up to her shoulders, pulled her closer, and laid his mouth on hers.

Given the kisses they'd shared before, she would've expected this one to start from where the others had left off: confident, bold, claiming. But instead, the kiss was almost tentative…checking to see if all was forgiven for now, if this contact was welcomed.

And that was what made her bones melt.

She let him stay tentative for a moment longer. She was probably torturing him, tormenting him by not giving him the answer he hoped for, but…

She wanted to think *he deserved it.*

But all thought rapidly fled, and she relented, because what she wanted more than anything was to be kissed. To kiss him.

She wanted more.

A small part of her brain reminded her that this could only go so far— she was, after all, in the middle of making dinner, and she was pretty sure Sandrine wanted her meal on time and wouldn't accept "I was boinking your brother on the kitchen island" as an acceptable excuse for the food being late.

As much as Chloe's body clamored for it, there would be no boinking at the current time.

Kissing was still awfully fun, though.

She took a step forwards, leaning into him with mouth and body. His fingers flexed against her shoulders as he relaxed, no doubt relieved she wasn't going to brain him with a saucepan.

Then he yanked her even closer still, parting her lips to find her tongue with his. They fell on each other like starving people on a...she couldn't finish the simile because her body short-circuited her brain.

Over the odor of onions and garlic, she smelled his soap or after-shave, something musky and understated. Her hormones reacted to the scent-memory, and heat pooled in her groin.

She wanted his hands on her breasts, his mouth there again, too, moving down to...

Odor of onions and garlic. Her wonky brain circled back around to that, reminding her that she was supposed to be making dinner for a woman who could send her packing back to Rhode Island on a whim. And "late dinner" was a pretty strong motive for a whim.

Or something like that.

As she started to pull away, so did Brand, as if picking up on a subtle signal. Despite the soft moan of regret she failed to muffle, she appreciated his understanding. You had to respect a guy who got the concept of when to nudge a little farther and when to ease off.

"Dinner," she managed. "As in, I need to finish it and get it to your sister. But we're not done here."

She meant with the talking, with the sorting out of things.

Brand grinned cheekily. "Oh, you've got that right. We're not even close to done."

She smacked him lightly on the arm. "Stop that. I meant—"

She didn't have time to finish, because just then Luanna burst into the kitchen and said, "I'm *starving*. What's for dinner?"

Chapter 14

*C*hloe sighed and stepped away from Brand. The action allowed her brain to clear, to snap back into focus on the task at hand. "Once I finish the fish and bruschetta for Sandrine and Ray, I'll use the extra tomatoes and onions to make an arrabbiata sauce for pasta for the rest of us."

"Sounds great. Anything I can do to help?"

Ah, she'd trained Luanna well: Her friend knew to ask first. "No, I've got it covered."

"Okey-doke." Luanna found a bottle of water in the fridge and then plopped down next to Brand. Chloe sighed again, this time appreciating her friend even more. Chloe slid each piece of fish onto a plate and put a piece of toasted whole wheat French bread next to it, covering the bread with bruschetta and sprinkling a little on the fish itself.

"Wow, something smells great." The new arrival was Ray, freshly showered and smelling of some sort of manly soap.

The kitchen was starting to feel like Grand Central Station, but that was fine with Chloe. Big family; used to kitchen traffic. In some ways, she liked it—as long as everyone kept out of her way.

"Oh, hi!" Ray said to Luanna. "I wanted to talk to you. Nice shirt, by the way. Good color for you."

"Me?" Luanna said, her water bottle halfway to her mouth.

"Yeah." Ray eased his bulk onto the stool next to her. His shoulders were so broad that his arm brushed against hers. "That robe you were wearing this morning was really pretty."

Chloe and Luanna had managed a few minutes of girl time over coffee on the cottage patio that morning before Luanna had to leave for work. Apparently it had also been Ray's jogging time, and he'd waved on his way by.

"Uh," Luanna said. "Thank you?"

Chloe frowned. What a weird thing for him to notice, much less say. Okay, yes, that shade of deep rose-pink *was* a great color for Luanna and it *was* a pretty robe, but he shouldn't be complimenting Luanna like that, should he? Or was this yet another bizarre Hollywood social norm she hadn't learned yet?

Nothing, she decided, was normal in Hollywood.

She glanced at Brand. He was leaning his elbows on the island in a deceptively casual pose, his face showing nothing, but she could see that his head was tilted towards the pair as he took everything in.

"Is it designer? Where'd you get it?" Ray asked.

"It's La Perla. I found it at a consignment store in Boston, still in its original gift box...a real bargain." Luanna said. "Why?" She'd seemed relaxed while talking about clothes, her favorite subject, but suddenly sounded a little suspicious.

Which made sense to Chloe, because there was something just slightly off here...even for Hollywood.

"Ah, oh, I just thought...maybe I'll get one for Sandrine, she looks really good in that color." He seemed to realize he sounded about as convincing as Lizzie Borden insisting she hadn't whacked her parents, because he quickly added, "So how did you get into designing clothing?"

Luanna had a very strange look on her face, one that Chloe, from years of experience, recognized as *I have no clue what's going on, so I'm going to start babbling while I try to figure it out.*

"I grew up in a town in Louisiana so small it didn't even have a Walmart—not that Walmart is haute couture. My grand-mère taught me to sew when I was about five, then one of our elderly neighbors died and there was an estate sale. Turned out she'd been a missionary in the Far East and her attic was crammed with silk. I was doomed."

"Nice kind of doom." Ray smiled. His smile was really sweet, and he looked as if listening to Luanna talk about her career genuinely fascinated him. (Well, he *was* an actor, even if he was better known for his impressive muscles and his grace than his emotional range.) "So how's a small-town girl finding LA?"

She shrugged. "I've lived in cities before…but LA is different. Exciting and overwhelming. I still can't believe I'm here, and by 'here' I mean in LA at all, let alone living *here*."

Another charming smile. "Hey, sometimes I'm convinced I'm going to wake up and I'll be back in my home town, getting up to go check on the cows."

"So you really were a farm boy from the Midwest?" Luanna asked, and Chloe wondered just when her friend had had time to research their landlords. "That's not just publicity?"

Chloe saw Ray shook his head, but didn't really listen to the response. Dinner was ready, and she was ready to spring into action.

Chloe knew from Olive that she was expected to serve the food so Sandrine could ask her any questions about ingredients or preparation. A little unusual, but she figured she could handle it.

"I'm all set," she said, half hating to interrupt, half wanting to get away from still more encroaching weirdness.

"That's my cue," Brand said. "I've got to get moving. I'm treating my crew to dinner. Worked from home today, but now I've got to go." When he rounded the island, Chloe heard the alarm go off: *whoop, whoop, intruder alert*. But then he took her face in his hands and kissed her so soundly her toes tingled. "Remember," he said, his voice husky, "we're not done yet." Then he was gone.

"Wow," Ray said.

"Wow," Luanna said.

"Wow," Chloe agreed. She cleared her throat, looked at the tray of food, tried to process what she was supposed to do with it. "What about drinks, Ray?"

"I'll get 'em," Ray said, moving around the island. She stiffened again, but it was, after all, half his house, and it was faster for him to get the drinks that to explain what they wanted. She paid attention, though, for next time.

The fridge hummed and ice rattled into glasses. He poured iced tea into both, and Chloe noticed the glass pitcher was almost empty.

"Leave that out; I'll make more tea," she said.

"Great, thanks," he said, smiling at her again.

She took a deep breath and picked up the plates, aware of Ray following her out of the kitchen with the drinks.

She didn't know what she was more nervous about: Sandrine's reaction to the food, or having to explain whatever was or wasn't going on with Brand to Luanna, because she didn't know yet herself.

*

To her relief, Sandrine had seemed pleased with dinner. Chloe fled back to the kitchen and gratefully made the pasta, because she'd been starving, too, and tucking into a bowl of pasta had sounded almost as good as sex.

Almost.

At the same time, she'd told Luanna the story of Evenrude's rebuffed romance with the peacocks, the failed attempt at sex thanks to her ignominious narcoleptic fit, and Brand being caught red-handed with her lingerie, to the point that they were laughing so hard they cried. Because the Brand/lingerie thing was pretty damn funny, now that she had distance.

Now she also had distance to think through what she had to say to Brand to make things right.

Making things right, after all, was her specialty.

Hadn't her horoscope said something about that?

*

Pleasantly cool water. Warm sun. The soothing repetition of swimming laps. Usually the combination put Brand into a trance, letting him put aside anything that was bugging him, sometimes letting him come up with a solution that never would have occurred to him otherwise.

This time, though, no amount of swimming seemed to get his brain either to stop or to work better.

It had been two days since he'd seen Chloe, or anyone else on the estate, for that matter, except this morning when the peacocks had been inexplicably camped out in front of the garage door behind which he'd parked, and he'd had to shoo them away without making them shriek in indignation.

Winning the AAMie meant his special effects design team was suddenly in high demand, so he'd spent stupid amounts of time in meetings with higher-ups, reviewing offers, and trying to hammer out possible schedules.

He could only imagine that Ray's agent was fielding the same kind of calls.

What was up with Ray? Brand's brain rolled right back to the problem he'd been unable to shake.

First the incident with Chloe at the AAMies. Brand had been happy to write that off as one of Ray being too small-town nice for his own good, which was pretty normal for him—the big guy had once completely freaked out the landscaping crew by deciding to help them with something, just because it looked like they could use another set of hands. Besides, it was obvious nothing had happened with Chloe.

But this interest in Luanna? Asking where she got her bathrobe? Not the most graceful conversation opener—it really made you wonder what he might have said if Brand and Chloe hadn't been around.

It just didn't make any sense.

He reached the end of the pool, executed a neat flip turn, started another lap.

Not that Brand saw anything strange about being interested in a blond bombshell type with a cute Louisiana drawl—for someone who wasn't involved with Sandrine.

But Ray *was* involved with Sandrine. Involved with Brand's little sister, who didn't love easily or talk easily about it when she did.

She loved Ray, though. Maybe she'd didn't say it, not to him, maybe not even to Ray, but Brand could tell.

If Ray hurt her, Brand would have to kill him.

Another lap.

Okay, maybe not kill as in *kill*, but…something. Something violent and big-brotherly.

The fact that Ray was a gazillion times bigger than him and trained in martial arts was a problem, granted.

Was Ray coming on to Luanna? Or had he really just thought the robe was something Sandrine would like? In which case, he must be pretty unobservant; Sandrine hadn't worn pink since she was old enough to realize it clashed with her hair. Even Brand knew that, and he wasn't exactly Mr. Fashion Guy. Then again, neither was Ray.

Weird. Just weird.

Almost as weird as Chloe being so edgy at him in the kitchen…it just didn't seem like her. During the party, despite the mayhem, she'd seemed so on top of things, so able to keep her cool.

Another lap.

And that's when the Swim Effect hit him, and suddenly things began to become more clear, at least where Chloe was concerned.

A chef was a sort of artist. She was probably as serious about her work in her way as Sandrine was in hers. And that meant that sometimes she'd be so engrossed that she might as well be on another planet and would do things that might not make sense to people who weren't on that planet.

She wasn't being weird, not if you looked at it that way. She was just intense and focused.

And if she was that intense about her work, she might be just as intense about her fun. The way she kissed like she was shutting out the rest of the world certainly suggested that.

Which was a hot, hot thought. He'd love to be the subject of all that intense focus, to have Chloe pay as much attention to his body as she did to whatever she was cooking. If he could just get her back to the kissing, instead of the working and snapping, they might get somewhere.

Like to bed. Or the pool house. Or the center of the hedge maze. Or one of the estate's several hot tubs. Hell, a Super Eight motel in the Central Valley would be fine as long as she was there and they were both naked.

Yeah, no problem with Chloe. Ray was another story, one that would bear watching.

But he'd rather watch Chloe.

After five more laps, Brand pulled himself out of the pool.

And found Chloe standing there.

Boo-yah.

She wore a one-piece suit in a shimmery copper that set off her cream-and-honey skin and her dark eyes. She'd tied a paisley-patterned sarong around her waist, brown and tan and shot through with sparkly copper threads, and she wore flat slip-on sandals.

She had cute toes.

He shook his head. Her suit looked practical rather than decorative, the type of suit a girl would wear to really swim, rather than lounge in the shallow end of the pool or splash in ocean waves that didn't reach past her thighs. He appreciated that.

Bottom line? She looked good enough to eat.

That is, except for the expression on her face, which was somewhere between repentant and grim. Uh-oh.

Then the expression changed to a flirty one. He liked that a lot better.

Chapter 15

*I*t was another blisteringly hot Southern California day. Palm-tree-lined beaches, her ass. Los Angeles was a desert, plain and simple and saliva-suckingly arid.

Chloe's horoscope for the day had read simply, "Keep your cool." But it just wasn't possible.

Despite the air conditioning in the main house, she'd been sweating by the time she'd clocked out. Sandrine and Ray were away for the next couple of days, so after breakfast making, breakfast cleanup, lunch prep, lunch making, and lunch cleanup, all Chloe had had left to do was plan meals for the next week and make lists and order the food and…

You know. Little stuff like that.

Now, though, she was free. Free! And that pool with its elaborate cobalt-and-crimson Moorish tiling had been calling her name all day.

She'd dashed back to the cottage—which meant she'd had to down a gallon of water to make up for what she'd sweated out on the way over—made sure Evenrude had enough water, and thrown on a suit and cover-up.

And returned to the pool area to find a mostly naked, completely sexy Brand there.

She'd seen wet, après-swim men a gazillion times before—she was from a tiny coastal state, after all. But Brand…

…Brand made her breath hitch and her knees go weak.

His skin glistening with water, his wet, bright blue swim trunks clinging enticingly to his…assets in a way that was somehow sexier than stark naked. She couldn't stop staring. The sun rainbowed off the water droplets clinging to him, and he looked like Apollo risen from the ocean.

Apollo? Or was it Poseidon? Some Greek god anyway, all sleek and elemental and jaw-droppingly delectable. There was probably a statue on the estate somewhere, quite possibly with water spouting out of its head.

A drop of water traced its way down his left nipple. She followed its movement down, down, down to the treasure-trail smattering of hair that pointed into the waistband of his trunks, let her mind do the rest.

Brand snagged a towel off a lounge chair, dried his face, and slipped on his glasses.

"Oh, good," he said. "I've been wanting to talk to you." He looked serious.

Oh, good? That didn't sound good. That sounded like oh, *bad*.

Maybe he'd had a girlfriend all along. Maybe he'd run off with that girlfriend to Vegas and eloped and that's why Chloe hadn't seen him for a few days. Maybe he had a terminal illness. Maybe Sandrine had changed her mind about being cool with them being together. Not that they *were* together, but still. Potentially being together.

Or was "potentially" even still on the table?

"I have a proposal for you."

He…what?

"I think we should start over. Clean slate. Put all the crazy weirdness and misunderstandings behind us."

She took a step back, she was so startled. Not startled, exactly. Just so surprised by the unexpectedness of his words that her brain had to reboot.

His hand flashed out, catching her arm, and she *eeped* because she realized she'd come *thisclose* to toppling into the pool. She slid carefully away from the edge.

"Thank you," she said. "And I…I think that's an excellent idea."

"Good." He smiled, his brown eyes warm, and she felt a rush of delight shiver through her. "So let's make it official. Chloe Montiero, will you go out on a date with me? A proper date, so we can get to know each other?"

Now she stepped forwards, confident. "Brand Mossiman, I would very much like to go out on a proper date with you."

"Excellent," he said. He stepped forwards, too, meeting her in the middle. Pulled her close.

Kissed her.

She felt like she was falling, falling, not into the pool but into him. His skin was damp and cool, and those enticing water droplets didn't feel quite so enticing shocking her overheated skin. She shivered, and yet, it was a good shiver in the end. He tasted and smelled of chlorine. The smell wasn't bad—clean and somehow comforting—but it wasn't her favorite flavor.

But underneath that he tasted like Brand, although even her highly developed palate couldn't quite narrow down what Brand tasted like, and she could feel the heat of his body, his strength, his sheer deliciousness.

She threw her arms around him and clung for dear life.

Kissed him until her head spun so hard her brains fell into her panties and she didn't care about professionalism or much of anything else.

Kissed him until the wet spot in her bathing suit felt as big as, and certainly warmer than, the one his wet trunks were making on the front of her sarong. Until the trunks had a tree-trunk. Until she dug her fingers into his buns to pull him closer, and he slipped his cool hands around her waist, and the ends of her loosely knotted sarong slipped apart, the fabric fluttering apart but not to the ground because it was trapped between them.

That jarred her back to reality—the reality that included being outside in a place where Sandrine, Ray, Olive, or any of the staff might appear at any moment.

"Here we go again," she said with a chuckle, easing away reluctantly and snatching at the paisley fabric before it fluttered its way into the pool.

"Can't seem to keep my hands off you."

"Can't seem to keep my clothes on around you." She clutched at the sarong.

Some of the blood returned to her brain, and she remembered that there were probably things she should talk to Brand about.

But not right now.

"A date." She blew out a breath. "Right."

"It's what, about five? Get in a nice swim, and meet me at the garage at seven. Wear jeans and low-heeled shoes that cover your ankles—hiking boots if you have them."

He brushed his lips against hers once more—light and quick, but it still left her breathless and tingly in all the right parts. Once he was out of sight, Chloe dropped her sarong and finally let herself topple sideways into the pool, giggling as she sank under the blissfully cool water.

Chapter 16

Chloe leaned against the side of the open garage door and said, "Nice bike."

She was trying to sound all casual and blasé, but inside she was squeeing, because she was looking in Sandrine Moss's fabled garage. She wasn't a huge car buff herself, but she could appreciate the classic lines, polished metal, and enormous amount of money that had gone into amassing the collection.

Plus she figured her brothers were going to grill her for details.

There was the much-talked about Bentley, the classic Mustang, and the...whatever the rest of those pretty shiny beasts were.

Besides, she really *was* distracted by Brand's motorcycle. (Yes, Brand, too. But honestly, his motorcycle was *sweet*.)

It was an older bike, restored, she could tell that much. Painted black with white piping, it had two small saddlebags in the back and a decent fairing. She appreciated the back rest added to the pillion seat.

"Thanks," Brand said, and she saw the flush of pride in his grin. "Nineteen-seventy-six BMW R60/6. I finished restoring her last year. I spend so much time doing virtual design that I need a hands-on hobby. It's a whole different experience being able to touch and feel the project."

He glanced up from programming the GPS—a strangely incongruous device against the lines of the classic bike—and grinned again. This time the grin, lascivious and arriving on the heels of "touch and feel," made her whole body suffuse with erotic heat.

Now, no longer distracted by the bike, he apparently saw her for the first time. His eyebrows raised above his wire-rimmed glasses as he took her in. "Wow. Well done."

She'd forced her curls into a short, messy French braid—it had helped that her hair was still wet from her swim and subsequent shower. She didn't have her riding gear from back east, but the jeans were better than bare skin, and she had in fact crammed sturdy boots in her Mini when she moved to California. Now, she'd also grabbed a long-sleeved denim shirt, just in case.

Of course, *just in case* wasn't good enough; if he didn't hand her a proper helmet, decent jacket, and gloves, she wasn't getting on the back of *anything*.

The pavement didn't get appreciably softer on the head in hot weather, and she'd rather suffer through sweat than road rash.

Her turn to grin. "I had a suspicion you were referring to a bike when you asked me on this date." She appreciated that he'd noticed, and complimented her, that she'd put two-and-two together. "So, where are we going?"

"That's a surprise. I'll have her ready in a minute."

"Is it okay if I look around? Or does Sandrine have a laser grid protecting the cars?"

Brand snorted. "As long as you don't smudge the wax job or, God forbid, scratch the paint, Sands won't even notice."

"Really? I thought these cars were her pride and joy." She leaned over to look at the soft leather seats in the Mustang, her hands firmly clasped behind her back.

She might trip and fall into one of the cars, but she was *not* going to accidentally touch one. He *said* Sandrine wouldn't notice....

Brand sat back on his heels; she felt him watching her. "Only when she's in them and people are cooing over them," he said. "She doesn't care about the cars themselves, just the attention they bring. Which she didn't realize until after I'd restored the E-Type Jag over there."

Chloe turned. "You did the work on all these, too?"

He lifted one shoulder in a casual shrug. "Back when we had no money, I bought a clunker and figured out how to make it run, and found out I enjoyed it. So when Sands hit it big, she bought me the Jaguar to thank me for taking care of her for so long. It just went on from there. I fix 'em up and she drives 'em around."

Chloe wondered if she should be irked that Sandrine didn't publicly acknowledge her brother's amazing work, but given the affection she heard in Brand's voice, he was apparently fine with it.

She didn't have time to ponder it further, because then Brand was handing her a proper motorcycle jacket and gloves and helmet, and she was making a wisecrack about having gear in all sizes for all his girl-friends, and he was laughing and trying to buckle her helmet on.

Even though she liked the feel of his hands on her, she gently moved them away and buckled her own damn helmet. But she was laughing with him.

Damn. She already had it bad.

Getting on the bike was a little less successful—it was taller than she was used to, and she was the exact opposite of tall, so it took her three tries to balance on the foot peg and get her other leg thrown over the seat.

Brand chose a fun, squiggly canyon road to get them to Sunset Boulevard, which he then took all the way to the beach, eschewing the faster (maybe) but boring 405 freeway. Brand handled the motorcycle with confidence and skill, assessing the traffic flow and avoiding the crazy drivers who weaved in and out even though it didn't get them any farther ahead. The road crested, then dipped towards the ocean, and the air grad-ually cooled as they approached the water.

She felt the tension in her shoulders gradually dissipate, too. She hadn't realized how good it would feel to be away from the estate until it actually happened. Now she felt less like Harried Chef to a Fruit Bat Starlet and more like The Real Chloe again.

They reached Pacific Coast Highway—the famed Highway 1—and Brand turned right, up the coast.

He was almost too careful, she mused as he navigated a turn. She sensed he wanted to open the bike up, have some fun, but he was restraining himself. Aw. That was kind of cute.

The sun was sinking towards the horizon, turning the ocean into a sparkling shimmer too bright to look at directly. Actual sunset would be in about half an hour, she guessed as he pulled in to a public parking lot.

Brand slid off the bike, and she looked down.

Way down. Gulped. Damn, this bike really *was* tall.

Really tall.

Once in college, she'd gotten drunk and crashed in a friend's dorm room, and the friend had had a loft bed, and Chloe'd woken up and had to pee, and looking down from that bed to the chair had been like looking down from the observation deck at the top of the Hancock Tower.

This was kinda like that, only without the room spins.

Thankfully, Brand was a true gentleman. He held out his hand, and thus steadied, she was able to swing one leg over and then slide to the ground. Not lifting her off the bike, just offering a helping hand.

He was such a gentleman, he didn't even comment on it.

"Have you been to the beach much since you got to California?" Brand asked as he locked her helmet to the bike.

"The first thing Luanna and I did when we got here was stick our toes in the Pacific," she said. "It was a *lot* colder than home! In the movies, everyone is swimming in it. Holy crap! We went to the Santa Monica Pier once, too. Also cold. But otherwise, I've been too busy job hunting."

"Good," he said, taking her hand. "That means I get to be part of your first real experience."

They'd stowed their boots in the saddlebags and rolled up their jeans. The sand was warm beneath Chloe's bare feet, and Brand's hand was warm in hers.

"Okay," Brand said. "First date questions, one for one. I'll go first."

"Hey, how come you get to go first?" Chloe asked.

"I asked you on the date."

She pondered that. "That's reasonable. Shoot."

"I know you stumbled into working for my sister—pretty much literally. So what's your dream job?"

It was out of the blue, but luckily, it was a question she could answer easily, because it was one she'd thought about a lot. "Someday I'd like to own my restaurant. But that's in the future. I have a lot to learn about the business side of running a restaurant. So my dream job now is to be the second or third in command at a great, well-run restaurant so I could suck the owner's and business manager's brains while continuing to hone my cooking skills."

Brad applauded. "You think strategically. I like that in a woman. Also, you said suck." He slipped into the inevitable Beavis and Butthead imitation. "So what kind of restaurant?"

"One where I use my grandmother's amazing Portuguese recipes for inspiration but isn't a 'Portuguese restaurant.'" She did the air quotes. "Okay, my turn: Do you hit on all of Sandrine's chefs?"

He roared with laughter. "Cutting right to the chase, are we? You'll be happy to know you're the first. Honestly, most of them haven't stayed around long enough for me to get to know them. Of the last few…Raoul was gay, Miranda was in her fifties—although she was well preserved, I'll give her that—and Sands made Ginnifer cry and quit on her very first day. You may be already setting a record. Which brings me to my next question: Why did you become a chef?"

She didn't need a degree in psychiatry to know the answer to that, so she told him the story. The youngest child in a large family, and the only girl to boot, her desire to take care of people was practically handed to her at birth. Her brothers tried to take care of her, and she responded by handing them warm cookies straight out of the oven by the time she was six years old. Nothing pleased her more than watching her parents, siblings, cousins, aunts, and uncles all crammed around tables in her parents' dining room enjoying a warm and satisfying meal that she'd created.

Part of the dream of owning her own restaurant was of having a break in the flurry of dinner prep to look through the doorway from the kitchen and see diners tucking into her preparations, happy and content and relishing the food before them.

"And now you're stuck with Sandrine," Brand commented, squeezing her hand.

It was sort of another question, but she didn't mind. "It's a detour on the road to my dream, sure, but that doesn't mean I won't get the same satisfaction out of preparing a meal that would make Sandrine, Ray, and any of their guests feel just as happy and content. I hadn't found a job yet anyway, and I can shove most of my salary into savings since I don't have major living expenses. Speaking of which, why do you live in the gatehouse?"

He laughed again. "Once you see it, you'll understand. The place is sweet!" Then he sobered. "How much do you know about Sandrine's life?"

"Not much more than the bio on Wikipedia," Chloe admitted. She'd wanted to do more research, but just hadn't had the time. "I've seen most of her movies, though—although I know that's not the real Sandrine."

"We were just a normal family, normal kids growing up in suburban Denver, when Sands decided to audition as a lark for an indie movie that won all kinds of awards at Sundance."

"*Antigone's Mirror.*" Chloe looked out at the streaks of sunlight across the vast Pacific. Squeezed her toes in the sand.

He nodded, took a deep breath. "Long story short, everything changed. She was thirteen and suddenly thrust into this crazy world none of us were prepared for. And then our parents died, and I just kept on taking care of her."

"You're older?"

"By three years. She didn't have anyone else—all we had was each other, really. We're each other's link with that former life, with family. She has Ray now, though, which helps. But she likes having me around, and I don't really mind. The gatehouse really is great." He smiled, and Chloe guessed he was trying to lighten the mood. "Besides, it gives me a chance to play bartender and meet the cute new chef."

Chloe wondered what it would be like to lose her parents young, and to not have a passel of brothers and aunts and uncles and cousins to help fill the unfillable void, and failed. It was just too alien for her.

At the same time, though, it was an interesting insight into Sandrine. Now she felt a little guilty for mentally referring to Sandrine as a fruit bat.

Just a little.

He must have seen her frown, because he stopped walking, swung around to face her. "Sorry," he said. "Didn't mean to bring things down."

"Just don't tell me we have to start over *again*," Chloe said.

He smiled. "No, I think we're doing just fine." Still holding both of her hands, he leaned down and kissed her.

She had to hand it to him: He was doing pretty damn well on the perfect first date front. On the beach with the setting sun, water lapping at their ankles, and a romantic kiss to seal the deal.

Because as much as the kiss made her toes curl, digging into the cool, wet sand, it wasn't like the mad full-on passionate kisses they'd shared previously. It went back to square one. A "hi, I like you, and I'd like to kiss you if that's all right" kind of kiss.

And as much as she wanted to leap up and wrap her legs around his waist and go for serious tonsil-hockey, she let him set the pace. She'd agreed to a reboot first date.

Later, though, she intended to break all the rules she had about what she didn't do on a first date. Whether he liked it or not.

She was pretty sure he was going to like it an awful lot.

Brand seemed to like the toned-down version well enough to repeat the experiment with a little more oomph a few minutes later. He didn't exactly tackle her on the sand (which was probably not a bad thing, fun as it might have been, because she knew from teenage experience that sand got *everywhere*, even if you were fully dressed) but the way he moved against her, the way one hand clutched her butt and the other tangled in her hair, let her know he was considering it.

As they pulled apart, Brand asked, "Hungry?"

"Why yes, and you look good enough to eat." She went to kiss him again.

Her stomach chose that exact moment to growl that it wanted proper food. They stepped apart, both chuckling. "You look good enough to eat, too," he said, "but I don't want to take off chunks. There's a great taco stand not far from here. You up for it?"

Chloe felt a grin splitting her face. "And how! Do you know how refreshing it is that you want to take me to a taco stand? Real local food instead of something fancy schmancy you think will impress the chef."

He took her hand. "The tacos will impress you. Trust me."

And they did, perfectly seasoned and fresh and just spicy enough.

Although—Chloe could barely admit it to her foodie self—right now she could've eaten a Big Mac and almost enjoyed it in the current company.

They laughed on the way back to the bike, and their hands bumped as they both reached for her helmet buckle.

"I've got it, thanks," she said, tempering her words with a smile. If he tried a third time, they'd have words. She swung her leg over the seat—it took only two tries this time, yay for success!— and settled down, then added, "By the way, are you going to ride like my grandmother again?"

He twisted around to stare at her. "Excuse me?"

"Five brothers," she reminded him. "The bike was technically Craig's, but everybody got their mitts on it at one time or another, including me. Don't tell my mother that, though. All I'm saying is, you don't have to hold back on account of me."

Behind his helmet, she saw his grin. "Mind if we take the long way home?"

Part of her wanted to say *no, go straight home so I can jump your bones.* But it *was* a beautiful night, and who said a motorcycle ride couldn't be foreplay?

This time they did cut up Sunset to the 405, so Brand could get a little speed up. When he twisted the throttle and the BMW jumped, Chloe felt a thrill right in the pit of her stomach.

They got off at Mulholland, and did a twisty-turny ride along it, then south on Laurel Canyon, then back on Sunset to loop around home. Chloe clutched Brand's jacket, not because she was scared, but because there was nothing more exhilarating than pressing yourself against the back of a rider as you swooped and dipped through the curves.

They roared into the carport behind her cottage. Chloe noted with relief that the Mini wasn't there. She wasn't in the mood for explaining anything to Luanna. Or for keeping quiet when she came.

Not that she was assuming anything.

Oh, who was she kidding? Of course she was.

"Whoo!" she exclaimed, pulling off her helmet. "I'd forgotten how much fun that was!" Then she had an evil, fun, hot thought. "You know what else I'd forgotten?" She leaned over the bike, grabbed an end of the cover Brand was stretching across it, and said, "That motorcycles are like giant vibrators. At least, if you're riding with the right person."

Chapter 17

She blushed as she said it, ducking down to hook the cover to the foot peg so she could hide her blush. It was *so* not her style to say things like that. To think them, sure, but not to say them *out loud*.

But Brand was the perfect combination of super hot and…well, comfortable wasn't a sexy word or she'd say comfortable. She felt she could say something a little outrageous and he'd take it in the right spirit.

Which, judging from the speed at which he abandoned the cover and shot around the bike, hauled her upright, and started kissing her, he did.

This time, she didn't worry about proper first date protocol. She'd already blown it with that remark.

And hell, they'd both known that, although they wanted a chance to talk and get to know each other better, it was going to end like this.

In a clinch, lips to lips, body to body, touching each other frantically.

Stumbling in the door like a couple of drunks because they didn't want to let go of each other.

Tearing off clothing as fast as they could, Chloe cursing that you just couldn't wear something easy-access for a motorcycle ride.

Tasting every inch of skin revealed as clothes went flying.

They were down to underwear and had stopped there for a while, tangled together on the remarkably comfy couch, to kiss and caress and tease and generally enjoy being half-naked together before they went to the bedroom and got all the way naked.

On the floor, Brand's jeans started buzzing.

The sound only seeped through the hormones flooding Chloe's brain because it sounded like a vibrator, and right now she had vibrators on the brain. Possibly because it had been so long since she'd had sex that involved a real boyfriend, not a battery-operated one, that she was subconsciously confused, though delighted, by being this aroused when it didn't involve one of her reliable (but not so much on the kissing) silicone friends.

The sound wasn't coming from a vibrator, in fact, but from his phone. She figured he'd ignore it, and went on licking his nipple, which he seemed to like a lot. Sure, he was a responsible guy and everything, but sex was sex.

Instead, with a groan of frustration, he rolled off the couch, grabbed his jeans, and checked the number. "Gotta get this—sorry!" he said, and answered, sounding far more polite than he probably felt, "Hi, Sands."

As he said that, he used his free hand to reach between Chloe's legs and start stroking, through her rapidly dampening red satin tanga panties (hey, it was a date—even if a girl couldn't dress up too much for a bike ride, she put on nice undies).

"Pooh?" he said. "No, I haven't seen him."

He sighed and shook his head as Sandrine obviously wailed.

"Calm down, Sands. Pooh can't have gone far. You had him when you got back from Tunisia. I remember seeing him then."

Sandrine said something that made him nod, even though Sandrine couldn't possibly see him.

"Did you pack yourself or have Olive do it?" A deep breath. "Olive wouldn't have forgotten Pooh. Check the front pocket of the big suitcase."

He stood, withdrawing that wonderfully teasing hand as he did, and started to pace.

Chloe's body started to pout, and Chloe let her face reflect it. Dammit, her first non-self-induced orgasm in way too long had been in sight. So close…

"Not a genius—just being logical," she overheard. "You'll do brilliantly. You always do. Now practice your lines on Pooh for a while, then have fun with Ray and your friends. Good night, Sands."

He hung up. "And now I'm turning the phone off," he said.

"She interrupted your date to find a stuffed animal?"

"Not just any stuffed animal. Her lucky Pooh." He sat down on the couch. Chloe's body perked up again and demanded he pick up where he left off. But Chloe's brain needed a little more explanation before she could jump back into the game.

"Her lucky Pooh? Sandrine's a little old to call her big brother so he can help find her stuffie, isn't she?"

"Normally." He sighed and kissed her. The kiss was almost enough to make her forget her annoyance—but not enough to completely dim her curiosity. Just how much of a fruit bat *was* her employer? She stopped feeling bad about mentally referring to Sandrine as a fruit bat.

"Pooh's special," Brand went on. "Mom made him for Sandrine when she was, like, three. When Sandrine's stressed, even now, she wants her Pooh. If having that ratty stuffed animal is what it takes to help her focus so she'll be the genius—the crazy genius—we know she is, I'm glad to help."

"She could have picked a better time to freak out. I thought you were going to have to find her and make some mint tea."

He laughed, and try as she might, Chloe couldn't find any bitterness or resentment in the laugh. "She could have picked a worse one. Like ten minutes from now, when we'll be in the bedroom and I'll be having my wicked way with you."

For a second, Chloe's mind flooded with snarky comments about whether he could stop rescuing his sister long enough to fit in some nookie.

Then he pressed his face between her legs and breathed.

Just breathed.

And the heat of his breath through her damp panties was enough to chase the snarky right out of her mind.

And when he kissed her, still through her panties, the capacity for rational thought followed the snarky bits of her brain to some nice vacation spot.

Except for that one, truly annoying, responsible part of her brain, which reminded her that Luanna had probably left a note somewhere about where she was and when she'd be back, but Chloe didn't want to stop to look for it, so they should probably head to the bedroom so Luanna didn't walk in on them.

She babbled something to that effect and thank the gods in the heavens, Brand understood her. They stumbled, half-clinging to each other still, and landed on the bed.

Her lips and tongue tingled and Brand's mouth moved against hers.

Her skin caught fire against his.

Her nipples pebbled and clamored for attention, and she realized she was moving like a happy cat, rubbing her chest against Brand's hard one to enjoy the feel of hot man through the thin satin of her bra. His skin was like silk, sueded silk. Heat spiraled outwards from her breasts, making her breath catch in her throat as they kissed.

And that was nothing compared to what was going on between her legs.

When he'd shifted underneath her and then pulled her down, she'd ended up more or less on top of him. Her body had decided to finish the pleasant job and actually straddle him—apparently without her mind getting involved, because she wasn't quite sure how she'd gotten there.

Not that she was complaining.

With their height difference, she couldn't rest squarely on his cock and still kiss him the way she wanted to, but she could feel the head underneath her, brushing against her still panty-protected pussy as if questing for entrance, and his muscular lower belly and her clit were getting to know each other very well.

The sensations were dizzying. Their tongues were dancing, and his hands were roaming up and down her body, sending sparks behind them, and he smelled like sex incarnate, and she had managed to unearth the condoms (miracle of miracles—she still hadn't found her pot holders or *The Joy of Cooking*) before they'd headed out, just in case, and they were right on the bedside table.

Without breaking the kiss, she groped with one hand for them. Premature, perhaps, but she doubted they'd want to let go once things went a little farther.

Inevitably, her keys and a plastic cup of water crashed to the floor in the wake of her questing hand. She jumped and, for a millisecond, lost track of what she was doing.

Brand started rolling his hips in the most interesting way, though, and she focused again on what really mattered. She'd find the keys later and there hadn't been much water left in the cup. At least there probably weren't dust bunnies under the bed.

If there were dust bunnies, they were probably sneaking out to enjoy the view, because Brand had moved so he could peel off his briefs, which were some dark color, black or evergreen or navy or something. She had more important things to admire.

She wanted at least two pairs of eyes and three sets of hands to appreciate the feast of naked Brand. But she had make do with one pair of each, so she was touching him everywhere she possibly could, rubbing against him, trying to take all he had to offer, his taste and smell and texture and sheer masculine beauty. Hot skin, soft hair, hard muscles, harder cock.

Her silky little bits of underwear felt like a chastity belt or a nun's habit, enveloping her, shutting out sensation. "It's not fair," Chloe said, a bit breathlessly. "You're already naked. Not that I'm complaining about that, but…"

Brand laughed throatily. "But you'd like to be, too. I'm looking forwards to seeing you naked, trust me, but I'm having fun teasing." He raised his head to close his lips around one nipple. The fabric diffused the heat and moisture of his mouth, changing the sensation without making it weaker. His fingers played at the other nipple, plucking and pinching it until it, too, stood at attention. Then he pulled back, blew tantalizingly on the damp satin. She shivered, and when he turned his oral attention to the other one, she shivered again.

Okay, so the underwear had something to say for it. But she still felt overdressed.

She raised her hips for a second, pulled aside the crotch of the panties. Pressed her wetness against Brand.

Rolled her hips like he had earlier.

In response, he bit down gently, deliciously, on her nipple. The act sent a line of fire down to her groin.

She raked down his chest with her nails—not hard, just enough to make him shudder. "I want to be naked," she said again.

He grinned his concession. "Sit up for a second."

His hands skimmed her body before he plucked open her bra and slid it down her arms.

With each bit of skin he bared, she felt her arousal grow. And once her breasts were bare and he'd spent a little breathless time stroking and caressing and generally exploring them to the point that she was mewling, he rolled her over (in a laughing, awkward tangle of arms and legs that knocked a pillow off the bed but got them where he wanted them, with her on her back) and helped her pull the panties off. He made this a tantalizing ceremony, pulling them off slowly, making her feel the passage of the fabric as they moved down her legs.

And then he kissed his way back up.

It seemed excruciatingly slow, torturous, but her skin tingled wherever his lips brushed. Instep. Ankle. Calf. Thigh. A lot of time on her sensitive inner thighs, until Chloe was ready to scream from a mixture of pleasure and frustration.

And then, leisurely, deliciously, he worked his way to where she needed him.

Warm lips on a hot, swollen clit.

Swirling tongue, drawing out waves of sensation. She danced on the edge of the precipice, buried her fingers in his thick hair, not to control, but to connect. His tongue lapped, teased, as his lips suckled, and she felt herself starting to fall.

A groan escaped her.

And then first one, then two fingers penetrated her slick, sensitized folds, found the most sensitive spot in that sensitive place.

There was nothing but Brand—Brand's mouth, Brand's hand, the heat of Brand's glorious body, Brand's distinctive musk that she was sure she'd recognize blindfolded.

Nothing but Brand and shattering pleasure.

She arched, cried out, beat on the mattress so she didn't beat on him.

Not that she thought that would stop him. He was unrelenting, pushing her to another peak, another shattering fall.

And when she thought she couldn't take any more, he stopped—but just long enough to deal with a condom. She tried to help, but her fine-motor coordination seemed to be shot, and it just seemed like a better bet to flop back onto the bed in what she dimly hoped was an enticing position.

Without falling asleep this time. Oh no, there was no chance in hell of that. She might have had the exquisite luxury of two orgasms already, but she was far from through.

She needed to feel him inside of her.

He positioned himself between her legs, stroked the head of his sheathed cock against her eager pussy lips. "Again with the teasing?" she managed to squeak out.

"Just wanted to make sure you were ready for me."

He raised himself up on his forearms, cockhead still nudging her opening and making her head swim, and gazed down at her like the god of sex come to pay her a visit. His smile, half cocky and half tender and all melting, just added to the effect.

"If I get much more ready," she managed—just barely—to say, "my brain will melt."

She wiggled her hips in encouragement, ran her hands down the sleek corded muscles of his back, and gripped his firm ass. Sweet. It felt like a little bit of heaven in her hands. "Now," she demanded. Her "please" was no less imperative.

And somewhat to her surprise, Brand complied.

Chapter 18

She expected to be teased more with a gradual entry, one millimeter at a time, and prepared to be driven to a sobbing frenzy of pleasure and frustration.

Instead, he buried his length inside her in one smooth stroke, making her realize just how wet she must be. Making her cry out in wordless, startled joy.

Heaven.

Like they'd been born to fit together.

It just didn't get much better than this.

Except that Brand began to move, each long stroke seeming to awaken her inner walls a little more, to find new pleasurable places inside her. She began to move with him, under him, in a fierce yet unhurried rhythm she never could have caught if she had to think about it, but luckily seemed to come by instinct.

And it got better.

Astronomically better.

Astronomical as in she was rocketing into space before she knew it, traveling among the stars on the power provided by Brand's fucking.

Maybe it had just been too damn long since she'd had anything inside her that wasn't battery-operated and/or made of silicone.

Or Brand was simply very good at this.

Or maybe it was something more profound than that going on.

Something to consider when her brain resolidified.

Because considering anything except her body and Brand's body and the amazing way they worked together was way beyond anything she could handle at the moment.

Her hands clenched convulsively, driving her fingernails into his sweet ass, as a wave of orgasm overtook her. She could feel her abs rippling, feel herself clamping down on Brand's cock. His hips snapped faster, pounding into her, pushing her to call his name and convulse again as she drowned in something sweet and hot as a Chinese chili sauce.

"Chloe, I can't…"

Brand couldn't focus enough to finish the sentence but she guessed what he meant, so she groaned, "Yes, Brand…now!"

He reared up and froze above her, his face locked in a rictus that looked like agony as much as ecstasy, his lips pulled back in a silent scream, the cords of his neck and shoulders standing out in relief. Sweat beaded on his muscular torso.

Chloe thought (to the extent she was thinking much of anything other than "Oh my God!" at that moment) that she'd never seen anything so beautiful.

As he went boneless, he managed to catch just enough of his weight that he didn't crush her.

And then he did crush her—with a resounding kiss that made her realize she wasn't as sated as she would have thought, not from the way it made her jump.

Hmm, was Brand one of those rare guys who could make a quick comeback? She'd be delighted to find out.

Brand disengaged from the kiss slowly, nipping at her lower lip and nuzzling her cheek. "Mmm," he said. He shifted his weight, reached across her. The movement made his still-semi-hard cock hit some lovely spots deep inside of her, and she smiled.

He pushed up his little wire-framed glasses and smiled back at her. "That's better," he said. He brushed a lock of hair back from her forehead.

Before he could say anything else, "Eat to the Beat" trilled through the cottage, and Brand chuckled. "How appropriate," he said, but the end of the words hitched as she eased herself away from him.

Chloe staggered to the living room, where she'd left her purse with the phone, flipped it open just in time to catch Olive.

"Sandrine just called," Olive said. Her calm, professional voice held an undertone of tension. "She and Ray decided to come home early from their trip. The good news is she says the food at the resort can't compare to yours. The bad news is she'll be home on time for brunch."

"No problem." Brunch was still hours off. She could worry about it in the morning.

"For her and Ray and twenty of their closest friends," Olive continued, strained patience in her voice.

Chloe closed her eyes. An omelet bar, where everyone could pick their ingredients and she'd whip up fluffy omelets to order. That always went over well. Paired with muffins and fresh fruit and that yummy chicken/apricot/gouda sausage and... "Okay," she said.

"Just no eggs," Olive said.

What? "What?"

"Sandrine has apparently just made the connection between adorable fluffy chicks and eggs. So no eggs, and nothing that contains eggs."

No eggs. No omelets, quiches, frittatas, or any large number of baked goods. She wouldn't use Egg Beaters, either. Those were just gross.

"Okay," Chloe tried to say again. Nothing came out. She cleared her throat, squeaked the word.

"And snacks ready when they all arrive at about 5 a.m.," Olive said. "I'm e-mailing you everyone else's dietary restrictions right now."

Theoretically she could wait until 4 a.m. and whip something together, but she was too much of a professional for that. Dammit.

So much for exploring Brand's powers of recuperation.

Dammit!

*

Brunch had been a success, but Chloe hadn't had any time to bask in her glory, because a light supper for Sandrine, Ray, and only two other couples was expected in a few hours.

Of course.

"Something barbeque-y, but light," since they were hanging out by the pool. So nothing fatty like ribs…and one person was vegetarian, one was vegan, one was lactose intolerant, and one had a shuddering distaste for mushrooms.

She was chunking vegetables for kebabs (some without mushrooms) when Brand sauntered in. Her stomach did a delighted little flip-flop when she saw him, but she kept her face composed. One romp in the hay didn't mean she could presume anything.

Although her body was all for repeating the romping experience.

"Hey," he said.

"Hey, yourself," she said, flashing him a smile.

"Anything I can do to help?"

At least he asked. "Nope. But thanks." She meant it.

He slid onto a barstool on the other side of the island, rested his forearms on the granite counter. Aware he was watching her, she concentrated on the wicked-sharp knife in her hand, because one flustered slip and the vegetables would not be technically vegetarian anymore.

"Let me know when you have a sec," Brand said.

"Okay." She finished with the zucchini and onions, washed her hands. "What can I do for you?"

"I need your help with something."

She'd assumed he wanted to talk (oh please, not a "it was nice but that's all it was" speech, pretty please), so this was a little weird. Did he just want a bottle of water out of the fridge but was giving her a hard time because the fridge was on the forbidden side of the island?

She rounded the counter. He was wearing black jeans and a T-shirt with some computer logo on it, which she didn't recognize and didn't care about because the tee was fitted and showed off his lean muscles, yum.

When she got to him, he stood. Resting his hands on her waist, he drew her forwards one more step. He bent his head, and Chloe had just enough time to think *Oh, goody!* before their lips met.

The kiss was long, slow, sensual. Unhurried, as if he had all the time in the world…and quite honestly, Chloe was willing to give it to him. Nothing was on the stove to burn; she could indulge.

Good thing, because her brain had turned to oatmeal. The micro-wave-minute kind, not the good kind.

His lips were warm, and she melted into the kiss. His tongue stroked her the way his hands had the night before, and her body responded to the memory. Her breath released on a soft moan as warmth pooled in her groin.

Finally he released her, but not before he caught her lower lip between his teeth and gave it a gentle tug, a gesture that had her reaching out blindly to find something to steady herself before her legs gave out and she slowly collapsed onto the floor, because that would be a signal for Sandrine to walk in and fire her for inappropriate floor-sitting or some-thing. She found the countertop, grabbed hold, the granite cool beneath her fingers.

"There." Brand smiled. "Much better."

"Uh huh," Chloe agreed, unable to form actual words. He'd barely touched her—his hands had never left her waist—and yet she was all a-quiver.

It was *awesome*. That was the only reaction her mushy brain could give her.

He nudged her gently. "You should probably get back to work."

"Oh. Oh! Right."

As tingly as her body was, her sense of responsibility kicked back into force. She had a job to do, and she was going to do it damn well.

She hadn't picked the knife back up yet when Olive came in.

Guilt frissoned through Chloe, as if she'd been caught necking by her high school locker. Silly—she was an adult and so was Brand, and it wasn't Olive's place to approve or disapprove unless Chloe's work was being neg-atively affected by her canoodling with the boss's brother.

Sandrine had made it clear she didn't have a problem with potential canoodling, so there.

Then again, Chloe had already witnessed Sandrine's moods turning on a dime...

But if Olive noticed, or had an opinion, her face and demeanor didn't reveal anything.

"Oh, hello, Brand," she said. "I didn't expect to see you here. Thank you for dealing with the Pooh situation last night." She turned to Chloe. "Nice job this morning. If you've got a moment, I wanted to go over this week's schedule—although I know you've learned that 'schedule' is a relative term sometimes around here."

Olive didn't crack a smile as she said it, so Chloe still didn't know whether the world's most efficient assistant was joking or not.

She glanced around the kitchen. The free-range low-sodium turkey hot dogs, tofu dogs, and whole-wheat buns were ready to go outside, but she needed to assemble condiments. The veggies needed to be slid onto skewers, and she needed to slice the strawberries to go with the blueberries over the sorbet...

"Keep working," Olive said, because obviously Olive missed nothing. Which meant if she saw that Chloe's mouth was kiss-swollen and she looked a little flushed, Olive was also very, very good at hiding her thoughts. "Just stop me if you have questions, and of course of the schedule is on Google Docs."

In the end, the discussion didn't take long, although Chloe was glad for the electronic copy of the schedule because her head was whirling a little. Even with crazy-efficient Olive at her side, Sandrine had to be pretty savvy to keep up with all of the commitments that came with being one of the world's most sought-after actresses.

Unfortunately, it was only after Olive left that Chloe realized she *did* have a question: How was she supposed to get all this food out to the cabana?

"There's a serving cart," Brand said. "I'll get it."

She hated herself for it, but she felt her shoulders tense and creep up towards her ears as he slid down from the barstool. She stretched her neck left, then right, taking slow breaths. Fact was, she didn't know where the cart was—she simply hadn't had time to explore every nook and cranny and cabinet. The cart, she saw, was stored in an alcove next to the wine room, and she hadn't been to the wine room because Brand had handled the booze the other night.

"Thank you," she said as he wheeled it halfway past the end of the island. She pulled it the rest of the way around and started piling on plates and bowls and the little cooler that held the sorbet and fruit.

A thought struck her. "Um, have you had dinner?" she asked Brand. "When I get back, I could whip something up—if it's okay for me to do personal cooking in here. It never occurred to me to ask the other night."

"One," he said, "yes, you may cook in here; all her other chefs have. Two, I haven't had dinner. But, three…" and he grinned a slow, lazy smile accompanied by a hungry look in his eyes "…when you get back, what I want to eat is something else entirely."

He leaned on the island and added, his voice throaty and sexy, "I want to taste you all over, Chloe."

Gulp. The way he murmured it, the illicit promise in his eyes, and suddenly her sex felt heavy, swollen.

She was going to be aware of that with every step she took out to the pool and back. The bastard.

But she wasn't angry. Just…needy.

It was going to be a long walk.

"Maybe," she called on the way out, "we should head back to your place instead for dinner. Might be safer. You do have food, right?"

Chapter 19

The pool and spa were a Moorish fairy tale, the cabana sporting minarets and lavishly tiled inside with the same brightly patterned blues and reds and yellows as the watery areas themselves.

The outdoor kitchen by the cabana was bigger and nicer than the one in the apartment Chloe and Luanna had just vacated—hell, it was almost bigger than the entire apartment: gleaming stainless steel appliances and a granite prep space, not to mention a regular fridge and a wine fridge and a brick fireplace-thingie with a rotisserie large enough to roast, if not an ox, then at least a lamb or a suckling pig. (A rotisserie on the grill, she couldn't help thinking, would be much more practical—but this looked far cooler. It also didn't look like it had ever been used, a sad lack that she'd have to remedy.)

Chloe handed off the hot dogs and buns to Ray and started arranging the condiments on the counter.

"Thank you, sweetie," Sandrine chirruped from beneath her giant floppy hat and enormous sunglasses that would put the Olsen twins to shame. Chloe jumped. She still wasn't used to having Sandrine speak to her—she was still sure an axe was going to fall.

"This is my new chef," Sandrine added for the benefit of the others.

"Chloe's doing a great job," Ray added, beaming at her. She realized Sandrine had sort of trailed off, no doubt having forgotten Chloe's name.

The way Ray phrased it was smoothly done—he didn't make it obvious that he was reminding Sandrine.

Ray was a genuinely nice guy, and she liked how he took care of Sandrine even if she couldn't entirely understand why anyone should need that level of care. But it was nice to see they were honestly in love, especially with all the awful gossip-show stories about phony Hollywood relationships.

Ray leaned over and gave Sandrine a kiss. Just a quick peck, but somehow it carried all the weight of what they might want to be doing if they'd been alone.

Or maybe Chloe's mind was just in the gutter. Good thing she had a hot date lined up.

*

They finished the last of the fried egg, Manchego, and tomato sandwiches Chloe had thrown together with what she could find in Brand's tidy, but rather barren kitchen. Some impromptu guacamole lingered in the dip bowl. "That was amazing," Brand said. "So simple, and yet so tasty."

"It wasn't much. Maybe we should have stayed in the main house, where I had access to more ingredients...except I would have felt weird about all the making out we did while I was trying to make the guac, because it would be like fooling around at work. But now I feel weird I didn't make something fancier for our first meal alone together."

Brand laughed. "I already know you're a kitchen goddess. I'm just amazed you even want to cook for fun after doing it for your job all day."

Chloe shrugged. How could she explain it? "Cooking helps when my head's on fire," she ventured.

"Now where did I put that fire extinguisher?" Brand pretended to rummage around for it under the sink and to her astonishment actually found one, which he brandished at her.

"Don't you dare, Brand!" She threw a dishrag, slightly stained with tomato juice, at Brand. "I'm entitled to my head being on fire. I've been blackmailed into a job, moved, catered a lavish Hollywood party with less than twelve hours' notice, *and* had amazing sex with my batty boss's brother. Okay, I have no complaints about that part, but it does add to the surreality." She hesitated. "Surrealness? Something like that. A lot's happening at once, and a lot of it's good, but it's all unexpected—and oh, my God, my brain hurts."

"You should be sainted," Brand agreed, his voice and face solemn, his eyes laughing.

"Or at least drink mojitos."

"Mojitos later. I have a better idea for now." He set the fire extinguisher down and crossed the room to her.

Although *stalked* might have been a more accurate word.

Even in the small space of the guest-house kitchen, he managed to captivate her with the way he moved. She couldn't say what he was doing that made a simple walk look so sensual. It wasn't like Carl's boyfriend showing off his tango moves or like Ray being both tough and graceful doing martial arts. It was just hot.

Or maybe it was just that Brand was hot.

Yeah, that was it. Brand was hot. Anything else would be over-analyzing, and she didn't feel like analyzing right now because Brand had finished his stalk across the room and drawn her into the kind of kiss that would make a romance novelist swoon with envy.

His lips were soft at first, caressing and tender, his tongue teasing at hers and then retreating. But he pulled her in close with a strength that told her he was holding back with great difficulty, trying to take it slow.

He'd already shown he could be incredibly patient and controlled, and sometimes that could be wonderful.

But right now she didn't want to be patient and controlled. She wanted something spicier than any salsa she'd ever made, richer than a perfectly ripe avocado or a lovely flan, and she wanted it now, or maybe five minutes ago.

Okay, five hours ago.

Okay, as soon as they'd finished the first time, but who was counting?

As they kissed, Brand's hands glided under her tank top and raised it slowly, making the motion a caress. Her nipples, already tight and eager, ached as the fabric glided over them, ached some more as Brand dipped his head to lick first one nipple, then the other. She arched against him, fingers tangling in his hair.

A delicious tension spread from her breasts to meet the equally delicious tension creating happy butterflies in her tummy and a low, rhythmic throb in her pussy.

How fortunate she was wearing a skirt. That made things so much easier.

They had to break contact long enough for him to finish pulling her tank top over her head. It was the kind with the built-in bra, which she'd chosen partly because even with the best air conditioning on earth—which it was possible Sandrine had—a kitchen in warm weather tended to get hot, and she wanted the bare minimum under her whites while still being able to do a quick change before serving dinner.

But face it, mostly she'd picked it because she hoped she and Brand would end up ripping each other's clothes off at some point during the day, and the fewer clothes to rip, the better.

She took advantage of the break to separate Brand from his shirt. Then she took a few minutes to explore every inch of his torso she could get at, drinking in his scent, kissing, licking, reveling in the sound of Brand's accelerated breathing.

When he clearly couldn't take it any longer, Brand lifted her onto the counter, raised her skirt, and wriggled her panties off fast enough to make her head spin. Not that it wasn't spinning a bit already, what with the way all the blood was rushing to her clit.

His hands gripped her thighs—not too hard, but hard enough to let her feel his strength—and some primitive part of Chloe wished he was gripping just a little harder, so he'd leave finger-bruises on the insides of her thighs, something she could enjoy looking at for the next few days. Her cotton skirt felt soft and sensual as silk where it brushed her heated skin. The granite countertop was cool and slick on her bare ass.

She'd always figured if she ended up in this position she'd be too busy worrying about disinfecting the countertop afterwards to enjoy what was going on, but bleach was the furthest thing from her mind. (It probably helped that while Brand was nowhere near the slobby-single-guy stereo-type, the counter hadn't been cleaned to professional-kitchen standard to start with.)

Brand's tongue was doing things that were probably illegal in seven Bible Belt states and Utah. The musky smell of lust mingled with the scent of the food she'd cooked, making the whole thing that much more deli-cious. Chloe's hands tangled in Brand's hair, pulling him exactly where she needed him. Her body quivered with need, trembling and clenching.

Time lost its meaning. She could have been on the brink of orgasm for mere, shimmering seconds or hovered there for hours while her body decided between enjoying the delirious ride a little while longer and pushing to explosion.

But the orgasm still took her by surprise with its sheer power. She cried out, grinding against Brand's mouth and her body filled with can-died-habañero sweet heat. Her body arched convulsively, and her brain slipped its tracks and went careening off on its own.

Brand stopped licking just before the pleasure became so strong it was almost too much. She would have slid off the counter in a boneless heap, but he stood and caught her, pulled her into his arms.

When she could remember her own name, two things struck her with roughly equal force.

One was that the wonderfully hard cock pushing against her deserved attention, as did all the rest of Brand.

The other, springing from years of culinary training, not to mention lessons from her mother and grandparents, was really not something she wanted to think about at the moment.

But Monsieur DesJardins would cross the Atlantic and box her ears, and her instructors at the Culinary Institute would somehow find out about it and join him. Not to mention that her grandmother would rise from the grave and haunt her.

Reluctantly, she slipped out of Brand's arms.

"Hey, where do you think you're going?"

"To wipe out the frying pan."

Brand shook his head. "You are too much!"

"It's cast iron and has cheese melted onto it." She grabbed paper towels and a big blue box of Morton salt—you couldn't use any other abrasive without destroying the seasoning. "It'll take just a few minutes to clean now, but if I leave it too long, I might need to reseason it and that's a pain. It might even rust."

He followed her the few steps to where she worked and put one hand on her butt. Serious as she was about wanting to get the pan clean, she appreciated the continued contact, because moving away from him had been a wrench. "Could it really rust in such a short time?"

She turned and kissed him. "Who said anything about a short time, Brand? Once I get you into bed, we're not leaving it until morning."

And they didn't.

Chapter 20

Two weeks later, dreamy and thinking about the previous night with Brand while keeping an eye on dinner, Chloe didn't even bother to jump at her employer's unexpected visit, though it took all of Chloe's good efforts to keep from rapping the star's knuckles with a wooden spoon when Sandrine lifted a lid from a saucepan on the stove and peered underneath.

"Are you sure this is okay?" she asked, staring at the shrimp risotto as if it might bite.

"The shrimp is utterly fresh. And wild caught, not farm-raised, so it's also environmentally friendly," Chloe said, smiling to hide the grimace of fury. As if she'd allow anything else in her kitchen. Growing up with her family, Chloe knew seafood like she knew Brand's body.

Well, like she wanted to know Brand's body: in excruciating detail. Repeatedly.

"Huh." Sandrine put the lid down. "You might want to double-check. I don't think this is on the approved list."

"Approved list?"

"For The Zone Diet," Sandrine said patiently.

"The Zone…"

"Mm-hm. My zones are all out of whack or something."

Thank God for the computer in the kitchen, because Chloe hadn't the foggiest idea what The Zone Diet entailed. Turned out it wasn't the shrimp that was the problem, but the rice: no carbs allowed (and Sandrine had just started eating them again recently!) She had managed to re-do or re-use some of what she'd planned for the meal, and gotten it on the table only twenty minutes late, a problem she'd mitigated by sending out pan-seared scallops early as an appetizer.

And at least she and Luanna would enjoy the risotto.

Chloe knew she'd survive the rest of her involuntary servitude, but she might make like Uncle Pete and start screaming for no apparent reason before she did.

*

When Brand popped into the kitchen the next night, Chloe allowed herself a few seconds to vent. "And I'm going to be making about a million mini-meals a day," Chloe explained to Brand. "Apparently, the Zone Diet calls for eating every few hours whether you're hungry or not, and Sandrine couldn't possibly be expected eat *packaged* Zone bars."

He snorted. "No. Of course not."

"I can't blame her for that," Chloe added thoughtfully. "If I were a rich movie star with a personal chef, I wouldn't eat some packaged crap that tastes like cardboard and wood shavings and may be made of them. But it's why you've hardly seen me this week. I'm so glad she's going out tonight."

"So, since you're free, do you want to see where the magic happens?" Brand asked with a twinkle in his blue eyes.

"Is that code? Because if it is, we've already done it in your bedroom, and we're not doing it here as long as your sister and Ray are home, because Ray's going to be popping down for his snack any minute. Tempting as that gleaming expanse of counter is."

Chloe grinned. She couldn't help grinning. Being around Brand had that effect on her.

That and a few more intimate effects. Her pulse was already speeding up at the thought of Brand's particular form of "magic," and she figured if the conversation continued in a flirty vein, she'd start in with the perky nipples, rising humidity in her panties, and irresistible desire to rub up again him like an overly friendly cat.

An overly friendly cat in heat, to be more precise. "But the answer's still yes. Even if you need to work on your code so the average five-year-old doesn't know you're talking about S-E-X."

"The kitchen counter's tempting—although I'd probably go for the multi-head shower if we were going to do something naughty here—but I actually wasn't thinking about sex this time." He laughed. "Okay, I was thinking about it a little because (a) I'm a guy, and (b) I'm around you, but I wasn't talking about it. I was wondering if you'd like to see where I work. I forgot a flash drive I'll need over the weekend, so you might as well come with me and get the grand tour. And since it looks like we'll both be working a lot this weekend, we might as well steal some private time after you've fed Ray." He dropped his voice to a conspirator's whisper. "I can even show you a few top-secret bits of the project we're working on."

"Oooh, does any of it involve really hot actors naked? Hugh Jackman, maybe? Or that dude who played Thor?"

He gave her a playful smack on the butt. (She'd figured it might happen so she'd set her knife down before she'd made the naked-actor crack.) She yelped. The conversation degenerated into a playful scuffle for a few seconds, resolved, not that it really needed to be resolved, with a quick, but devastating, kiss.

They kept the kiss quick, despite the obvious temptation to do otherwise, out of habit. Chloe felt totally at ease in the kitchen by now, but it was still her workplace, and they'd yet to figure out the Ms. Manners protocol—was there even one?—for dating your boss's brother (or your sister's employee, from Brand's point of view) when both of you lived on the boss's property—lived with the boss, for all practical purposes.

Sandrine had no reason to wander into the kitchen right now, when she was supposed to be primping to go to whatever glittery, star-studded and paparazzi-tempting event she was attending tonight, but lacking a logical reason didn't seem to keep Sandrine from doing things.

It probably wouldn't bother Sandrine to catch them smooching, unless it interfered with them jumping to her bidding (Chloe figured that as an employee, it was her job to jump, although Brand could really afford to let his kid sister wait once in a while; she had staff, after all), but it would still leave everyone involved a little pink and flustered.

Oddly, the thought of Ray catching them canoodling seemed much less embarrassing, but Ray Was Not Sandrine. Which was a good thing, because Ray in a designer miniskirt would make old ladies faint and children cry. Something about the baldness.

"Joking aside, that sounds like fun, if you can wait a little while." Chloe said, pushing him away reluctantly but firmly so she could finish what she was doing. (A burger, fries, and broccoli-jicama slaw for Ray, who often liked to eat before going to parties so he could focus on something other than trying to glean enough calories to sustain life from the trendy hors d'oeuvres.)

"Every minute without you will seem like an eternity," Brand said, managing to out-melodrama his sister in a tongue-in-cheek way. "But if we sneak in when most people are gone, it'll be easier—and we can go for a midnight motorcycle ride afterward."

"Or just come home," Chloe said. "I have taco fixings and then you could ravage me on *my* kitchen counter. Or the shower. Or at your place leaning on the pool table—I don't think we've done it there yet. Or even in the bedroom, just for a change."

*

Brand made a great show of "sneaking" as he let them into the Renegade Effects and Design building with his pass key—a show that was totally blown when the security guard greeted him with a friendly, "Hey Brand, what brings you here so late on a Friday?"

"I have a hot date with some evil aliens this weekend and I forgot some files I needed."

The guard smiled. "Your friend doesn't look like an evil alien. No ray gun, no green skin, nothing."

Chloe decided to play along, and called upon the knowledge gleaned from her brothers (all right, she had her own share of science fiction geekiness, but most of hers involved movies that boasted both fun special effects and sexy heroes, or books that mixed adventures in other worlds with a touch of romance).

"Actually, I'm like the alien from *Species*," she said. "I look like a cute, harmless woman, but as soon as I get Brand alone, I'm going to pounce on him and devour him."

Oops, was that her outside voice? That came out just a bit suggestive. Maybe more than a bit, judging from Brand's expression and the security guard's ill-suppressed chuckle.

"So not going there," the guard sputtered out.

"I won't tell HR on you if you do," Chloe said. "Come on, I set myself up for that one fair and square. Would it help if I said 'turn into a fierce thing with fangs and armor plating and tentacles and then pounce on Brand'?"

"Maybe we better change the subject," Brand said, putting his arm around Chloe, which probably made it clear that any naughty speculations the guard was having were justified. "Did your boyfriend get that problem with his green card cleared up?"

The smile on the guard's face changed from teasing to something a lot more heartfelt. "Thank God, yes. Someone checked the wrong box when Li first came here as a kid, and no one noticed until he applied for that last job. Pretty simple to fix once we found the right people to talk to, but what a nightmare."

Brand bumped fists with him. "Glad to hear."

"And now to get those files I needed—and to show Chloe here the mysteries of Renegade."

"That was really nice," Chloe said when the elevator doors closed.

"What?" Brand sounded genuinely surprised.

"Remembering that guy was dealing with something nasty and asking about it. It's not like you see the night security guards all the time."

"More than I'd like, sometimes. But a couple of weeks ago I'd worked late and said hi to Paul as I was leaving. He's a real friendly, happy dude, but he seemed down that night and I asked if he was okay and got an earful."

She grinned puckishly. "Be honest. Did you think about hiring them a lawyer or something? Because I probably would have. And then I'd remember I couldn't pay a decent lawyer but I'd still think about it…."

"I thought about it for about thirty seconds, but that would have been weird since I don't know him all that well, so I just listened. Sometimes it's the most useful thing to do."

Several ideas flitted through Chloe's brain, none fully formed. Some of these half-thoughts pointed out she should remember this conversation when Brand did something would-be helpful that annoyed her.

Maybe it wasn't that he thought she was like his sister and too flaky/girly/something to take care of herself. He just liked to help people where he could, and she could appreciate that. If she'd known that guy, she'd have been on the Internet looking for information he and his boyfriend had probably already found, just because she felt bad for them.

Some of the other half-thoughts were more along the lines of "Brand should remember that listening *is* being useful when he's dealing with me." Problem solving was a wonderful impulse, really it was, but she could generally solve her own problems, thankyouverymuch—simply having another person to bounce ideas off was all she often needed, and sometimes Luanna wasn't the right person.

Then the elevator doors parted and all the half-baked thoughts, positive and negative, fled Chloe's mind as she experienced a geekgasm.

Little green men and tentacled monsters galore. A huge ray gun thingie displayed on one wall that looked like the one Ray had used in *Monument* and might well have been. Adorable mock-ups of the puglike "good guy" aliens in Regency clothing that had featured so prominently in *Jane Austen in Space* (which Chloe had thought were the best part of an otherwise awkward movie even before she found out Brand had worked on them).

And on Brand's desk, an autographed picture of Hugh Jackman saying, "Brand and team, thanks for making us superheroes look good."

That was before Brand showed her the deleted scene from *Jane Austen in Space* in which the Pugsly prince attempts to seduce our heroine—very politely in proper Regency fashion until he started humping her leg. The scene had never been finished—for good reason, they agreed—but it was fun to see the disconnected parts: the half-completed animation and the actress responding, first with flattered politeness and then with disgust, to something that wasn't in the scene. Sure, it might end up on the special features in the DVD release, but seeing it on Brand's ginormous work computer, with his personal commentary about creating the Pugslies, was a lot more interesting.

Especially since they started out in two chairs, but before long she ended up on his lap with him delivering the commentary directly in her ear in a delicious, sexy whisper, in between kissing said ear and nibbling her neck. Hot kisses became punctuation. Brand's hands strayed from the keyboard and up her shirt.

Before Chloe's brain managed to shut down except for the important job of registering yummy sensations, she managed to choke out, "Uh, Brand. Your office has windows."

Although the rest of his team worked at stations in an open floor plan—better for collaborative efforts—Brand had his own office, but the walls facing the work stations were glass.

"We're the only ones here. Well, us and Paul, but he stays out front." Still, he slipped his hands from under her shirt. "On the other hand, I'm not the only team member who shows up at weird hours sometimes. Damn open layout anyway. Great for collaboration, not so great for fooling around in the office."

Then he smiled so broadly the skin around his eyes crinkled. "On the *other* other hand, I've always wanted to make out in the screening room. And I can show you the prelims for my evil aliens on a bigger screen."

"So you weren't kidding about the evil aliens?"

"Alan Rickman's voicing the Rugulator leader. Should be great. Unfortunately for now," he added, "you'll have to make do with Jordan from Concept saying cheesy lines in his best Alan Rickman voice so we can get an idea of how the aliens' mouths move when they're talking. I warn you, his best Alan Rickman voice sucks and we haven't bothered to sync the voice up perfectly."

"I doubt," Chloe purred confidently, wiggling on his lap in a far more sex-kittenesque way than she'd have thought possible during her long pre-Brand "focus on the career" dry spell, "that we'll be listening for too long."

The screening room had comfy leather chairs and a big, sturdy walnut table.

Chloe paid attention to the aliens onscreen just long enough to determine that (a) they looked pretty cool, though Brand's team had its work cut out for it, getting something that looked like an evil six-legged, four-handed anthropomorphic rhino to move like a mammal, not an insect, and (b) Jordan from the concept team wouldn't be giving up CGI for voice acting anytime soon.

Then Brand's hands were moving over her body and Brand's lips were on hers and she decided the rhinolike aliens could invade Hollywood right now and she wouldn't especially care.

She had a fleeting memory of meaning to ask him about the difference between a robot and a cyborg, but then his hand went *there* and all thoughts were gone.

*

Chloe eased her way onto the courtyard patio where she had first met Sandrine. This time, she was laden with a simple yet stunning (if she said so herself) meal of salmon sprinkled with macadamia nuts, steamed snow peas and pea-vine tendrils (so pretty!), and a berry compote.

The sun, half-set, left the sky streaked with color. Pierced-metal Moroccan-style patio lights provided illumination for the script Sandrine was reading, which she now set on a stack of reference books on the chair next to her. Chloe hadn't seen her all week without the script in her hand, or some book that appeared to be background material related to the script. (Chloe had been impressed both by her dedication and by how calm and focused she seemed when wrapped up in work.)

Ray was away that night; Chloe assumed he had some work commitment.

She presented supper with a flourish.

Sandrine stared at the plate, and poked suspiciously at the salmon and vegetables.

"No butter," Chloe promised. "I used cumin, turmeric, pepper, and just a dash of extra-virgin olive oil, and I tasted it, and it's really good."

"I can't eat this," Sandrine said.

Chapter 21

*F*or a moment Chloe thought they were having an earthquake, because she swore the floor tilted. Or maybe it had been caused by the blood suddenly draining from her face. "What?"

"I'm doing the Raw Foods Diet," Sandrine said. "Didn't Olive tell you?"

Chloe's voice was very small. "No."

"Oh. I thought I told her. Anyway, it's all the rage now. Everyone who's anyone is on it. Haven't you read this week's *Us*?"

"Just a few speed bumps to negotiate," her horoscope had said. More like a gaping chasm that had swallowed the damn road.

She soon learned why Ray hadn't joined Sandrine for dinner that night. When she got back to the kitchen, she found him there, looking in the pantry. He jumped when she walked in, and if he could've squeezed his broad frame into the cabinet, he would have hidden there.

"Oh, I thought it might be Sandrine," he said. "You've got to help me." His voice dropped to a whisper. "Could you make me some real food, please? Just grill me a steak or something. Anything cooked that's not a vegetable. You have to help me. She's threatening kale smoothies."

*

Over the next week, Chloe discovered Ray hadn't been kidding about kale smoothies. Or spinach and strawberry smoothies. Or...shudder...

seaweed, blueberry, and soy milk smoothies. Chloe thought she'd gotten used to Sandrine's food whims, but the raw foods diet was going to kill her. She was a chef, dammit. She was supposed to *cook*, and she couldn't *cook* when a diet called for only *raw* foods. If she had to chop another carrot, she thought she was going to shove it up…

She took a deep, calming breath, and reminded herself that Sandrine was her employer, and this was just another phase, and hopefully it would be over in another week or so.

She could handle it. She always did. She was determined to weather any crisis or challenge Sandrine threw at her.

After all, she had only four months, three weeks, and six days to go to fulfill her contract…

So it was a relief one Friday night when both Sandrine and Ray had left for a weekend at a spa in Santa Barbara (Chloe allowed herself one brief indulgent "let some *other* chef deal with her" thought), and she could relax and not worry about what would be sprung on her next. Despite the fact that her horoscope had talked about putting the pieces together.

Chloe and Luanna relaxed on the cottage patio, savoring a bottle of really nice Chablis that Luanna had won in a raffle at work. At some point, Chloe thought lazily, she'd have to get up and make them something for dinner.

Something really simple. Like sandwiches. She pursed her lips, trying to remember if they had the ingredients for homemade mayonnaise.

"It's just plumb crazy," Luanna said.

"What is?" Chloe asked.

"Everything. All of this." Luanna waved her hand to encompass the estate. "You dating Sandrine Moss's *brother*. And I expect—*expect*—Ray Stark, *the* Ray Stark, to go jogging by at any moment and wave and shout "Nice shirt.""

"You and Ray seem to be getting along well," Chloe commented.

"Honey, I'm from the South. We get along with everyone—until they cross us, of course. That's what we have shotguns for."

"Well, just be careful," Chloe said. "Sandrine is very protective. If she thinks you're after Ray, she will cut you like a bitch."

Luanna laughed. "Oh, Sandrine's just a sweetie."

Chloe paused, glass halfway to her mouth, and stared. "Are we talking about the same Sandrine? The one who said if I didn't come work for her, I'd never cook in this town again? Who said that very tired cliché and made it sound like a *real threat*?"

"Pfft." Luanna waved her hand dismissively. She reached for her wine, but instead of taking a sip, stared into the glass.

Chloe knew her well enough to know when she was trying to figure out something difficult to say. "What's wrong? Is it about Brand and me?"

"Oh goodness, no!" Luanna laughed, took her sip, set her glass carefully back down. "No, it's…" She looked past Chloe and her green eyes widened. "Is that Brand? In your car?"

Chloe turned in her seat to watch Brand ease the Mini into the parking spot next to the cottage. "Yep. The check engine light has been on since we moved here—as you well know—and he said he could fix it."

"You let him fix your car?" Luanna's voice rose at the end of the sentence. "Just *let* him?"

"It's his hobby," Chloe said. "He thinks it's fun. Look, I know if Craig or Corey had done it, it would've annoyed the snot out of me. But Brand offered rather than just going ahead and doing it, which I appreciated. And honestly, I don't know if I could've afforded the work, not with trying to pay down the credit card from when I was out of work. And if he enjoyed himself, it's not really just helping."

"That's a lot of justification," Luanna said.

"I've been practicing."

Brand came around the side of the cottage then, carrying several plastic bags. The scents of cilantro and galangal wafted through the air.

"Just in case you hadn't eaten yet," he said, "I brought Thai."

Chloe narrowed her eyes. Okay, maybe *that* was too much like taking care of her. Couldn't he have called and asked?

But the fact was, she really was hungry, and it was nice to have another night off. Give her a few minutes and she could probably get it justified away.

So she rose, kissed him, and asked him if he'd like some wine.

"Actually, if you've got beer…" And then he offered to get it.

"No," she said firmly, and went inside and gathered a beer and plates and forks and napkins.

There. That felt better.

Once they'd finished eating, Chloe made coffee, and they continued relaxing. Pulling her chain to its greatest length, Evenrude stared into the deepening shadows, occasionally letting out a low whine from deep in her throat.

"Unrequited love is a bitch," Chloe commented.

"The peacocks just aren't coming around to her way of thinking, are they?" Brand asked. He threaded his fingers loosely through Chloe's, a sweetly intimate gesture.

"Speaking of that," Luanna said. Then she stopped. "No, never mind."

"What's wrong?" Chloe asked, concerned.

"It's silly," her friend said. "I'm over-thinking things."

"No, tell me," Chloe said, in a voice that brooked no argument. She would never let Luanna face a problem on her own—she'd been waiting to ask about Luanna's earlier comment, anyway.

"Well, it's Ray."

"Ray? What about him?" Brand let go of Chloe's hand and sat up straighter.

Luanna twirled her wine glass, staring into it. "It's probably nothing. I just…he seems to hang around an awful lot. I know he's between movies, and it's his house, too, but he's stopped by several times, like he's finding excuses to talk to me."

"You think he's crushing on you or something?" Chloe asked.

"I don't know." Luanna gave a helpless shrug. "On one hand, he's going out of his way to talk to me, but on the other, it's not like he's made even a hint of a move. He's kind of like a puppy dog, just following me around sometimes."

Evenrude looked back at her and wagged her tail, then resumed her hopeful gaze into the night.

"That doesn't make sense," Brand said. "He loves Sandrine. He's utterly devoted to her. It's obvious. You have to really love Sandrine to put up with her bullsh…eccentricities."

Chloe refrained from pointing out that she didn't love Sandrine and she put up with more than most people ever would. Ever.

"That's why I didn't want to say anything," Luanna said. "It's been entirely innocent. I would've thought if he was going to make a pass at me, he'd have done *something* by now. Not that I want him to," she added hastily. "I'm totally not interested. He's hot, but he's taken, end of story."

"Plus you don't want Sandrine mad at you," Chloe said. "Trust me. I know."

Brand reached out and squeezed her hand in sympathy.

"It's not like Ray to be shy," he said. "For all he's a nice geeky farm boy, he knows how to go out and get what he wants. He wouldn't have gotten as far as he has otherwise. So if he was after you, Luanna, you'd know it. All I have to say is, it's a good thing he isn't."

"Otherwise you'd have to stab him with your lightsaber," Chloe said.

Luanna looked at both of them. "Is that a euphemism I'd rather not know about?"

Chloe giggled. The wine was really good, but she didn't want to overdo it. She had plans for Brand tonight—plans that didn't involve her passing out from exhaustion or tipsiness.

"So he's just hanging out 'cause he's a nice guy?" Luanna asked.

"What does he talk to you about?" Brand asked.

"My work, mostly. He seems really interested in clothing design and fashion." As the words left Luanna's mouth, her eyes widened.

It was Chloe's turn to sit up straight, as a sudden realization sobered her. Oh, *those* pieces to be put together. "When I interviewed with Sandrine, he asked me who made my blouse—it was one of yours, Luanna, the red Luscious Couture one."

"And then he asked me about my robe," Luanna said slowly, "and when he came by last week, he wanted to know if I still had any of that silk I'd gotten in that estate sale in Louisiana."

"He also seems really interested in my cooking," Chloe said. "I thought he was just being nice, but…"

"Hold on," Brand said. "Are you saying Ray's *gay*?"

"Now that you say it out loud…" Chloe said.

"He does kinda act that way sometimes," Luanna said. "I just didn't think about it because he's so very...buff."

"So's Carl, and he's a commercial fisherman," Chloe pointed out.

"He's not as buff as Ray," Luanna argued.

"I'm going to have to kill him," Brand said.

"Who, Carl?" Luanna said. "Don't kill Carl. He's a sweetie, and he's got great fashion sense."

"You are not allowed to kill my brother," Chloe said. "What's he ever done to you? He hasn't called you about me, has he? That would be just like him. Mom and Dad always make him check up on my boyfriends."

"If Carl hasn't called yet," Luanna said, "does that mean Brand's not officially your boyfriend? Or were you finally smart enough not to tell your parents?"

"Don't change the subject," Chloe said. Brand stood. "Where are you going?" she asked.

"To kill Ray."

She leapt up and grabbed his arm. "What are you talking about?"

"He's going to break my sister's heart, and I'd rather have her mourn over his dead body than suffer the humiliation of being left for another man."

"Sit. Down." Chloe said.

Evenrude, at the end of her chain, sat.

Brand ran a hand through his hair, tousling it further, as if considering. He finally sat, but on the very edge of the seat, his body tense.

"Thank you," Chloe said. "Now, let's review. You said Ray is devoted to Sandrine, right?"

Brand nodded.

"Then there are several possibilities. One is that he isn't gay, and we're just reading something weird into all of this. The other is that he *is* gay, in which case, he either doesn't know it, or he's not willing to come out. It's very possible that even if he *is* gay and knows it, he loves Sandrine enough that he doesn't want to hurt her."

"It won't work out, though," Brand said.

"No, it probably won't," Chloe admitted. "But we could still be jumping the gun. We don't even know if he's gay. Or maybe he's bi and he's happy with Sandrine but just has this…other side."

"That could work out fine, as long as Sandrine knows," Luanna said. "Then they could stealthily check out hot guys together or something." The other two stared at her. "What? We all enjoy a good view, even if we're not going to do anything about it. It might be kind of fun to compare notes with your sweetie."

Chloe rolled her eyes.

Brand stood again. "I'll go ask him."

Chloe grabbed his shirt sleeve and used all her weight to drag him back down. "He's not home, remember? They won't be back until Sunday night." She was expected to have some snacks ready for them when they arrived. She had no idea what new fad food Sandrine would have glommed on to at the spa. Ray, on the other hand, would be willing to give up his AAMie for protein. "Besides, I should be the one to talk to him."

"She's my sister."

"And my brother is gay, and I was there when all hell broke loose when he came out," Chloe said. "I've been through this. I have a pretty good idea of what he'll be going through, even if he hasn't figured it out yet."

"It's my responsibility," Brand insisted.

"Maybe I should talk to him," Luanna said. "He seems to like me an awful lot."

"No," Chloe and Brand said simultaneously.

Luanna pouted into her wine, but Chloe knew she wasn't really upset. Truth be told, she kind of did want Luanna as backup, just in case, because Ray might in fact feel more comfortable with her.

Then again, Chloe had a distinct knack for getting people to open up to her. She wasn't sure how she did it, but sometimes complete strangers on the bus ended up telling her about their marital problems or their phobia of fuzzy bear-claw slippers or how their kids just didn't listen to them.

"He's more likely to talk to me than to you," Chloe said. "Especially if you're going to confront him all macho and aggressive."

"Ray knows all about macho and aggressive," Brand said.

"If he *is* gay, he's not going to want to talk to you," Chloe argued.

"Because I'm a guy? Why? Are you insinuating he wouldn't find me attractive?"

"Well, you might *not* be his type, even if I think he'd be crazy not to be after that sweet ass of yours," Chloe said. "But no, that's not my point at all. You're Sandrine's brother. If he has a secret and he's keeping it from Sandrine, he's not going to tell you."

"I could get him drunk," Brand suggested.

Chloe gritted her teeth. She understood his need to protect Sandrine, but he just wasn't listening to reason.

"How about this?" Luanna said. "Let's give it a little while, and really keep an eye on him. We might be way off base. If we're looking for signs, we'll either see them or not."

"Makes sense," Brand said, and Chloe nodded.

"If it does look like he is," Luanna continued, "then Chloe's right, she's really awesome at talking to people and getting them to tell her stuff. Ray's been chatting with both of us, and he's likely to feel more comfortable with her than you, Brand."

"Thank you," Chloe said primly.

Brand opened his mouth, but Luanna held up a hand to forestall him.

"Plus she does have the experience with her brother. But, if Chloe isn't successful at getting the truth out of him, we'll send you in, Brand."

"To get him drunk, not to beat him up," Chloe said. "'Cause I hate to say it, but you'd lose."

"I'm considering being offended by that," Brand said. "Anyway, if he *is* keeping a secret that will hurt Sandrine, I do plan to get involved."

"Fair enough," Luanna said. She sipped her wine. "And if you both fail, then I get a shot at him."

Chapter 22

As it turned out, Chloe didn't get a chance to approach Ray for several days, even after he and Sandrine got back from the spa. As she'd feared, Sandrine came back with all sorts of ideas of food Chloe should make. Thankfully, Olive had already contacted the spa and gotten some of the recipes on Sandrine's behalf. Chloe didn't relish the idea of using someone else's creations, but she figured out some ways to modify them or take a riff on them, and for a while Sandrine seemed appeased.

But Ray had some promotional work to do for his upcoming film, *Eyes in the Ice*, so he was gone a lot. She ran into him a few times in passing (once, he told her that her shoes were divine), and saw him jogging in the distance most days, but they were never alone for any length of time, certainly not long enough for her to sit him down and broach a delicate subject.

It gave her time to consider just how to approach the issue, though. She thought about her interactions with Ray so far. He was a genuinely nice guy, surprisingly gentle (compared to his characters in his action films), pretty easy-going, and a lot smarter than people assumed based on his massive build and the often-inarticulate heroes he played. He probably wouldn't react well to being sat down for a serious discussion—it would more than likely scare him and make him defensive.

On the other hand, it wasn't as if she could just casually toss out "So, Ray, do you have anything in common with Neil Patrick Harris and Rupert Everett and Richard Chamberlain?" or "Hey, Ray, don't you think Brand has the most grabbable butt?"

She was formulating some sort of opening gambit that involved her brother when Sandrine threw another monkey wrench into the works.

Lance Boudreaux.

Apparently, unlike Chloe, Lance's big dream was to be a chef to the stars. He didn't like authority, although he was suffering through his apprenticeship at Rossiya in relative silence. Which translated to, he got a lot of warnings, but he hadn't been fired—yet.

Chloe had been so impressed with his help at Sandrine's party that she'd sent a note to his patron, Valerie Turner, praising both his cool head and his cooking skills. She just hadn't expected Valerie to tell Sandrine, and Sandrine to then get it into her head that Lance could come and help Chloe out a couple of times a week, to get more experience.

The first day he showed up, he was glowing and practically bouncing with pleasure, making him look even younger than he already did—which basically meant high school.

When her horoscope had said something about wisdom from babes, she'd joked with Brand that Sandrine would have one of her rare moments when the genius showed through the ditz. She never imagined that someone who might be below the legal drinking age would be involved.

Okay, so maybe the other definition of *babe* fit, too. Definitely cute, but in a slightly scary way.

Made even scarier by the fact that the first words out of Lance's mouth were, "I love you."

Chloe boggled.

"No, not like that...although hey, if you ever get a night off when you're not doing anything..." He waggled his eyebrows in what he obviously thought was a sexy manner, and cocked his hips in a way that actually would have been sexy if he hadn't spoiled the effect by *talking* beforehand.

Trouble to go…with a side of fries. Her brothers would use him for lobster bait if they knew he'd gotten anywhere near her (except for Carl, who'd probably hit on him if he didn't already have a boyfriend).

"Sexy bad boy" wasn't Chloe's preferred flavor—at least not his style of bad boy (she preferred dashing rakes to junior hellions, thank you), but if you liked that sort of thing, he'd be the sort of thing you really, really liked.

She couldn't help wondering if it was the sort of thing the mysterious Mrs. Turner liked. It would explain a lot.

"But seriously, this is so fu…I mean this is great. One afternoon cooking for Ray Stark and Sandrine was like…dude, dream come true. And now I'm actually working for the stars and I'm just out of school." He grinned broadly and repeated, "Dream come true."

More like a nightmare, but he'd figure that out soon enough.

And she still couldn't figure out how someone who knew Ray would also know this kid, who knew his way around the kitchen but was definitely a little rough around the edges.

"It's just crazy, you know," he continued, even as he took over boning the black bass—exactly what Chloe was about to ask him to do— unprompted. "When I moved to LA, Mrs. Turner—she's a board member at this place I used to work—said she'd help me get started. But I didn't think she'd actually do it, you know. I mean, I'm just a cook. Not a chef yet, like you, just a cook. And I knew she was rich and famous, but I didn't know she was like 'knows Ray Stark' rich and famous. This is so fucking… sorry…really awesome."

"Shut up and filet," she said, but she said it with a smile that was more like gritting her teeth. He was doing a terrific job with the bass, his hands deft at the delicate work.

Despite her family's seafood-oriented heritage, or maybe because of it, boning fish was a task Chloe hated.

And she'd been about to ask him, anyway. He was just proving he was really *good* kitchen help, the kind who read a chef's body language and knew what needed to be done, meaning she could spend less time supervising and more time cooking. Right?

She let go a breath she hadn't been aware she was holding.

The distraction of the fish kept Lance quiet for about thirty seconds. Then he piped up again. "So, does Ray like…practice his martial arts here? 'Cause I saw on *Entertainment Tonight* that he practices outdoors and I would be so into getting to watch that. If he wouldn't mind, that is," he added, suddenly polite and almost humble.

And just to get him to shut up, Chloe conceded that yes, Ray did…but only very early in the morning, before Lance would ever be at the estate.

"I could, like, come and make breakfast," he volunteered, practically salivating. "You could sleep in and everything."

*

"So now *he's* following *Ray* around like a puppy dog," Chloe concluded the story, then kissed Brand's nose. They were snuggled in Brand's bed. They'd eaten way too much popcorn watching *Star Riders*, which he'd done the special effects for, and it was making them as sluggish as pythons who'd swallowed small elephants. Still, Brand was enjoying the feel of Chloe's compact curves snuggled against him and was hoping that maybe, just maybe, they'd both manage to stay awake long enough to do more than cuddle.

"How's Ray reacting to that?" Brand asked.

"He's like a mother hen with a chick. He's trying to talk Lance into getting into movies, but I think Lance is as crazy about food as I am. Lance is loving the attention, though."

Brand raised an eyebrow. "Sounds like our boy has a bit of a crush on Ray." What he worried, of course, was that the crushing—or worse—might be mutual.

He'd barely met Lance, but he remembered young and brash and pretty good-looking…the guy equivalent of the Central Casting barely legal, bubblegum-popping White Trash Homewrecker. Probably perfect material for turning you into a cheater, assuming you were a guy who was into other guys.

Chloe cracked up. "No way! It's all very manly. He's starstruck, that's all."

"You sure?" Anyway, couldn't a starstruck bad boy with tattoos turn someone's head if he wanted to? Even Ray's. Maybe especially Ray's. And then Brand would have two people he needed to kill.

Two people who could probably kill him first, just to make matters interesting.

After all, chefs knew how to use knives.

More laughter. "He is so not gay." A thoughtful pause. "I suppose he could be bi, but he's definitely into women. Note the plural. I've seen him hitting on Sandrine's yoga instructor and the delivery girl from Kuan's Produce. Who I think took him up on it. He even flirts with Olive."

"That settles it. He's gay. Olive is much too scary to flirt with if you actually mean it."

Chloe rolled over, settled herself more comfortably on his chest, trailed her hand idly down his thigh. "Let me put this another way. After he kind of suggested that he and I should...well, I was going to say go on a date, but I don't think he meant date as in *date*, more like date as in *screw like lust-crazed weasels*...and I said *no* firmly enough he believed me, he started telling me about the three girls he's seeing. Showed me pictures, even. All Asian American and two of the three are black belts or something, so I'm really glad I wasn't available and interested. If I had been, I'd probably be getting my butt kicked by the Bad-Ass Asian Chick Posse."

He was so distracted by her cute rambling that the first part of what she said took another moment to penetrate his brain. "What?" He reared up so quickly that Chloe rolled off his chest. She laughed and smacked his shoulder. "He made a pass at you? I'm going to kill..."

"Brand, you're not allowed to kill my sous-chef. Or beat him up. Or anything."

He interrupted his rant for a kiss before continuing, "You never let me have any fun. First I can't kill Carl. Or Ray, at least not yet. Now I can't kill Lance. And I mean, I understand about your brother and everything, but what's Lance to you?"

She sighed and drummed her fingers on his thigh. His inner thigh. Very near to more critical and sensitive areas. If it was supposed to distract him, it was working. "Lance is useful."

He mock-pouted to cover a sudden and, he knew, utterly stupid, urge to scowl for real. He'd love to be useful to Chloe somehow, but he couldn't seem to manage it. Not even to talk to Ray, which was really his job as the pseudo brother-in-law.

Sure, it was a dumbass thing to stress about, since Chloe's competence was one of the things he really liked about her. And taking care of Sandrine was a full-time job in its own right, so he should be grateful Chloe didn't require more of the same. But still, it would be nice to feel useful.

Needed, even, as he sensed Kitchen Boy Wonder was, whether Chloe would admit it or not.

"If he's useful, what am I?"

Chloe grinned evilly. "Useful *and* decorative. And a hell of a lot of fun."

The hand that had been toying with his inner thigh purposefully slid up and to the right.

Okay, it might not have been exactly what he had in mind for *useful* and *needed*.

On the other hand, he wasn't about to complain.

Especially since, before long, the verbal center of his brain decided to shut down because all his blood was rushing elsewhere and he couldn't have voiced a complaint even if he'd been stupid enough to want to.

*

Catching up with Ray was easier said than done while he was up to his eyebrows (which were damn high off the ground) in promo. He wasn't home a lot, and he blocked out his minimal free time (on the constantly updated schedules Olive kept on the Google calendar) as "Sandrine." Even if the topic wasn't such a sensitive one, Chloe knew better than interrupt that time, not if she valued her neck.

After a week, though, Chloe got lucky. Ray wasn't rushing off somewhere to be interviewed by someone, and had blocked out a couple of hours in the early afternoon to lift weights in the mansion's exercise room.

An exercise room, Chloe was willing to bet, that would make most ritzy gyms green with envy at its high-end equipment. That was simply Sandrine's style.

Chloe still hadn't had a chance to explore the vast building in full. She was pretty sure it didn't have a gift-wrapping room like the Spelling estate, but there was a screening room and a greenhouse with carnivorous plants and of course a wine cellar big enough to house a family of four if it had a bathroom, too.

If she timed it so she got to the exercise room towards the end of Ray's workout, it would be the most natural thing in the world to start chatting. And he was probably comfortable in that space, like she was in the kitchen, which might make the weird conversation a little easier.

Perfect.

So Chloe put on yoga pants and a T-shirt, tied a bandanna around her forehead, and bit the bullet. She hated gyms. She'd had bad experiences with school gym class. Rope climbing, her ass. She'd never forget clinging there, terrified, everyone staring at her...and she'd been only three feet off the ground.

Any mention of dodge ball was strictly verboten.

But she had a mission, a duty, and if this was what she had to do, then by God she was going do it.

She marched into the room with Darth Vader's theme resounding in her head, and managed to stop herself just short of saluting.

"Well, hey there," Ray said, grinning in a way that made her feel truly welcome. "Haven't seen you in here before."

He wore a pair of faded red sweatpants and a black sleeveless cotton shirt, enhancing a body that made men envious and women swoon worldwide. But to her, he was just Ray—helpful, kind, friendly Ray, who just might be poised to throw everyone's lives into turmoil. Major action movie star with a fresh new gleaming AAMie on the mantel, maybe, but he was still Ray.

And she needed to talk to him about a rather delicate subject.

"I'm turning over a new exercise leaf," she lied. She flexed her biceps.

He laughed, not unkindly. "Yeah, you could use a little work there. Don't forget to stretch out first, so you don't pull a muscle."

She went over to a bar on the mirrored wall and did some pliés, the only thing she could remember from the horror that had been ballet lessons in first grade. She propped one heel up on the bar and tried to bend over her leg, lost her balance, and nearly fell. Okay, not that. She might be precise and graceful in the kitchen, but here she was a total klutz.

She managed to finish stretching without actually injuring herself or anyone around her, and moved to the free weights stacked on low racks along the side wall. Twenty pounds. That didn't look so bad. She picked up the round metal disc. Holy crap. She staggered backwards, belatedly realizing she didn't know what to do with it now that she was holding it.

"Here, let me." Ray relieved her of the weight, which she was sure had increased in volume. Or maybe gravity had grown stronger. She still wanted to insist that she could do it. But the fact that she staggered again when he took the weight away from her kept her mouth shut.

"Okay, you've got to start with lighter weights," he said. "Otherwise you're going to injure yourself." As he set the weight down, his bicep flexed, and the resulting bulge made it look like he was hiding a small ferret in his upper arm.

"That would be bad," she agreed.

"Here we go." He picked up two small dumbbells in one hand as if they were made out of paper and handed them to her. She took one, and caught herself before she dropped it. She peered suspiciously at the number on each disc. Two pounds. Each.

He showed her how to curl one, then the other, and suggested she do eight with each arm, rest for a moment, and try for eight more.

She looked in the mirror to check her form. Hey, this wasn't so hard after all. Maybe she'd keep up with it. Brand would like it if she were a little more toned, a little sleeker, right? Then she could race him in the pool. Winner gets to have his or her way with the loser. She grinned. That sounded like a really fun game.

Movement in the mirror caught her eye. She looked over. Ray was doing squats with what looked like every weight in the room, save her little piddly four-pounds-total, on the bar across his shoulders.

His back was to the mirror, his eyes focused on some middle distance between the far wall and a spot two inches in front of his eyes. The motion of his exercise tugged at his sweatpants, which were already somewhat strained by the girth of his thighs. A gap appeared between the waistband and the bottom of his fitted tee.

Chloe froze, one weight curled up, the other hanging at her side. Her jaw dropped.

Ray was very clearly wearing a fire-engine red pair of women's lace panties.

Everything clicked into place. He'd been hanging out with Luanna not because he was interested in her, and not because he wanted to be her, or even date the same people she dated.

He wanted to *dress* like her.

The comments about Luanna's robe, about Chloe's blouse and shoes. How could they have been so blind?

Well, as Luanna had said, Ray was just so *buff*. It would take a healthier imagination than Chloe's to come up with the visualization of him in lingerie.

Or a skirt and bustier. With heels. And stockings. Oh good lord in heaven. That was just a mental picture that made her brain spitzen-sparken like a science-fiction robot with its arm in the wrong light socket.

Think, think. She had to re-examine her entire plan of attack, her entire conversation strategy.

Ray glanced over at her, and she quickly started doing the curls again, praying he hadn't seen her staring.

Her horoscope that morning had said something about taking the bull by the horns, which was somehow appropriate given Ray's size. She waited until he'd set the barbell on a stand before she went ahead and blurted the only thing she could come up with.

"So, Ray, how long have you been a cross-dresser?"

Chapter 23

*R*ay froze. A flicker of something like fear crossed his strong features before a mask dropped into place. He was a better actor than people gave him credit for, but she'd still seen his initial panicked reaction.

Her heart went out to him. She set the weights down on the padded floor with a *clunk* and stepped to his side.

"Oh Ray, it's okay." She threw her arms around him. She couldn't exactly hug him properly—the circumference of his chest rivaled a centuries-old redwood—but she could certainly give him a comforting squeeze.

He didn't say anything. She craned her neck to look up at him. He had an expression like a deer in headlights. Well, more like a moose in headlights. A very burly moose. In women's underwear.

No, that was just wrong.

"Ray, really, it's okay. I have a friend in Boston who's a cross-dresser. A drag queen, actually."

"Chloe." Ray disengaged from her and set her a pace back. "Do you think the public will accept the hero of *Rode Hard* in a new role as a freakin' *drag queen*?"

"It didn't hurt Hugo Weaving's career, did it?" Chloe pointed out. "*The Lord of the Rings* was *huge*."

Ray sighed. "He played an elf. And not even a cool elf. Elrond was a much better character in the books, but in the movies he's…well, bitchy."

She decided it wasn't the moment to mention that Carl had dubbed Hugo's character "The Queen of Elfland." Instead, she regrouped. "I'm totally not saying you should take a cross-dressing role. I'm just saying that there's nothing wrong with your personal preference."

He stared at her. "Are you serious?"

She sat down on a bench, and he followed suit, dropping down opposite her. "It's not anyone else's business, what you do in the privacy of your own home," she said. "Cross-dressing certainly isn't in the mainstream, but it's not that unusual, either. There's a lot more that's weirder. Not that I'm saying this is weird," she added hastily. "Just less common than…some other things."

"So it really doesn't bother you?" he asked. "Shock you?"

She reached out and patted his hand. "Not at all. We were worried that you were gay, so this is actually kind of a relief."

Whoopsie. He looked horrified. "'We' who?"

"Luanna and I," she said. Technically it wasn't untrue. She just didn't add Brand to the list. That might freak Ray out right now. "We kind of compared notes, and realized you were asking us about clothing and stuff. I'm sorry we were so off base. I've got to admit, it was hard to believe you were gay."

"But wearing women's underwear isn't hard to believe?" He was staring at her as if she'd grown a second head.

She shrugged. "Like I said, it's not *that* unusual. My friend Johnny back in Boston is a respected and successful lawyer. It's not anyone's business unless he chooses to share it with them."

"I…you're the only other person who knows," Ray said.

She closed her hand over his and squeezed. "I'm sorry I was so nosy."

"No. No, it's okay," he said. "I'm kind of relieved, really." He sounded a little surprised. "I really appreciate how accepting you are about it. I didn't think anyone would be."

"Honey, I'm from Boston—Hollywood has nothin' on us," she said, laughing. "I have to admit I've never really talked to Johnny about it, asked him if he knows why it's his thing."

And so Ray poured his heart out to her, telling her how he was entirely heterosexual and had no interest in men—not that there was anything wrong with that, he quickly added—but it was just kind of that he liked the sensual feel of women's clothing. The silks and satins. Skirts flowing around your legs, stockings hugging your legs.

He'd always loved petting women's clothing while women were in them—what guy didn't, right?—and gradually that had grown into curiosity about what it might be like to wear them, too. The clothes, not the women.

He liked the primping and pampering, too. The spa had been heaven, even if all he'd gotten was a massage and mud bath. Sure, on a movie set, men wore makeup, too, and he liked that sensation.

His confession poured out of him like a champagne fountain at a million-dollar wedding, and Chloe held his hand and stayed with him all the way through it, nodding and cooing words of reassurance.

It turned out that he was fairly new to the realization himself, coming to it during a role where he'd played a spy who had to disguise himself as a woman for a sting. The spy character had been macho enough that the disguise hadn't affected his masculinity, and it had worked well for light comedy effect.

Ray had tried to take the dress home as a "souvenir," but wardrobe had whisked it away too quickly. He still had the pumps, though, buried deep in his closet.

He'd been too concerned about anyone finding out to do something like get information on the Internet, much less find online shops that catered to "larger" sizes. He was certainly too recognizable to be able to be able to walk into a physical store—it wasn't like he could throw on a baseball cap and sunglasses and be instantly incognito. He just didn't blend in.

Chloe glanced at the clock on the wall and blanched. If she didn't start dinner oh, about five minutes ago, it would be late, and Sandrine didn't take well to "late." Maybe she could whip up some chilled gazpacho or some kind of appetizer for a starter to give herself some time leeway.

This was actually going pretty well, and she didn't want to walk away, which might cause him to shut down and retreat. He really needed someone he could confide in, and that someone was now her.

"Ray, honey," she said. "I've got to start dinner. Why don't you come with me? I'll make us some tea and we can talk more."

She could see the hesitation in his eyes, torn between wanting to continue to pour his heart out and still being a little wary.

"It'll be fine," she said. "No pressure. We're just chatting."

"Okay, I'll meet you down there," he said.

She'd taken to keeping a spare change of clothes in the little bathroom off the kitchen; she was pretty much the only one who used the room anyway, since the mansion had something like fifty bathrooms. Okay, that was an exaggeration. Thirty. Twenty-five, tops.

The water was boiling for tea and she was chopping the vegetables for the soup when he came in, showered and dressed in clean clothes—she forced herself not to wonder what he had on underneath them—and settled onto one of the bar stools. She was grateful for the time alone, because it had given her the opportunity to think. She always thought better in the kitchen, surrounded by comforting things, her hands moving in familiar patterns.

She gave him peppermint tea and ginger–lemon crème cookies, let him talk for a few more minutes, then leaned on the granite-topped island across from him.

"You said I'm the only other person who knows," she said.

He nodded around a mouthful of cookie.

"So, you haven't talked to Sandrine about it?"

He shook his head, his eyes downcast.

She cradled her own mug of tea between her hands, glad for its warmth even on this hot summer afternoon. "Ray, you know you have to tell her."

His face crumpled.

She went around the counter and hugged him again. "It's okay, honey. I know it's scary."

"I love her so much, Chloe," he admitted, and she could see it in his eyes, hear it in his voice. She felt a pang deep in her stomach. God but she'd love to hear someone say it like that about her. She wanted to hear it in her own voice when she said it about someone else.

Now, where had that come from? She was doing just fine on her own. Oh, she still wanted a husband and kids—lots of kids, in fact, because she loved her family, loved the chaos and the closeness and the warmth. She wanted to take care of her brood, have a house with a big kitchen where everybody gathered to eat and laugh and bond. But that was all slated for later in her life. She wanted—needed—her career, too, and it had to come first. Romance wasn't on the schedule just yet.

But what about Brand? an evil little voice whispered in her head.

Brand wasn't a romance. Brand was a fling.

All right, more than a fling, but less than a full-scale romance. She liked Brand. She liked him a lot. He was fun and intelligent and kind, and she respected how much he cared for his sister despite everything she did. He was definitely more than just someone to have sex with (although the sex was really, really good. Incredibly, mind-alteringly good. Scarily good.).

Right now, though, she didn't have time for anything more than hot sex and good company. She was on a short-term contract here, and after that, her life would be up in the air again. She had to get through the six months, which was now down to four months and.... Huh. She couldn't remember exactly how many days it was right now.

Anyway, then she had to find a way to interest someone in Los Angeles enough to hire her. Or maybe she'd have to go somewhere else. San Francisco, maybe, or Austin, Texas. She'd heard good things about Austin.

That would take her farther away from Brand, the persistent little voice pointed out.

Now was *not* the time to think about that. She had to deal with the crisis at hand, help the man in front of her.

And make dinner for the World's Most Finicky Eater.

Thank goodness for shrimp. Tasty, low-fat (so they were approved on almost all of Sandrine's bizarre diets. Even the raw foods one, come to think of it, even though Sandrine didn't much like them raw) and best of all, quick to cook. A little garlic, some hot pepper flakes, some extra-virgin olive oil, splash of wine, five minutes in the skillet and you're good to go. With rice…no, bulgur, because rice wasn't on this week's weird diet. Better get that soaking.

"Sandrine loves you, too, Ray," she said.

"Yeah, I know…I know she does," he said. "But I don't know how she'll take something like this. I *hate* keeping a secret from her—I'm all torn up about it, Chloe. I just don't know how to tell her, how to explain it to her. I don't know if she'll be able to handle it.

"I'm afraid I'll lose her."

Yoiks. Chloe set the package of bulgur down as gingerly as if it was made of crystal.

Chloe understood his fear. Sandrine might love him, but she was… delicate. Even Brand said he tried not to upset her.

A cross-dressing boyfriend probably didn't fit in with any role she'd done, or any classic movie she could think of. It was going to be entirely out of the realm of her experience and knowledge, and Sandrine was likely to be just unstable enough to lose it.

Sandrine needed to trust people. Other than Brand, Ray, and Olive, she was surrounded by people who wanted things from her—award-winning acting, an autograph, a smile for the camera. If she found out she couldn't trust Ray, she'd be shattered.

More shattered, Chloe truly believed, than if she learned what Ray's secret was.

"I don't know Sandrine as well as you do," she said slowly, "but I think she'd feel worse knowing you had a secret, that you were keeping something from her."

He shifted, uncomfortable. "I don't know about that."

"She's got a good imagination," Chloe said. "If she thinks you're hiding something, she's going to build it up in her mind until it's far worse than this. Hell, she even briefly thought you were after me, and that was just from a couple of rumors at the AAMies.

"Sandrine's been through a lot in her life. She doesn't have a lot of people she can trust. If you betray her trust…"

"Yeah, you're right about that," he said. "It took her a long time to tell me she loved me. She's really cautious about opening up." He sighed with a sound like a geyser erupting. "You're right. Of course you're right. But I just don't know *how*."

Chloe sprinkled some finely chopped basil on the gazpacho, and finally got the hot water over the bulgur. "You know," she said. "Part of it might be because *you're* not comfortable with it yet. You're still learning to understand what you're feeling—you can't be expected to explain it to someone else who's going to have a hard time understanding it."

"I'm confused as hell," he admitted.

"You did a decent job explaining it to me," she said, "but I already had some understanding and background. I think you have a pretty good sense of *why*, but you're still uncomfortable that you feel that way."

He nodded. His huge hands dwarfed his tea mug as he took a drink.

"If you can get more comfortable with it, accept that it's who you are, then I think you might find it easier to tell Sandrine about it." She smiled reassuringly.

"But how do I do that?" he asked.

"I'll pick up some information for you, and also give Johnny a call and see if he'll be willing to talk to you," she said. "You can use my cell phone so there's no chance of someone finding out. We'll see if we can't get you a few more things to try wearing, too."

"You're just amazing, Chloe," he said, shaking his head. "I can't believe how lucky I was to run into you on the red carpet."

Luck wasn't the word she'd have used—that event had been the beginning of her tumble down the rabbit hole into this utter craziness.

But still, she smiled. She was glad she could be here to help Ray.

Plus if it hadn't all happened, she never would have met Brand.

Chapter 24

*I*t was only around 9 o'clock by the time she staggered out of the main house, but she felt like she'd been up for three days again, and not for anything resembling a fun reason.

She'd blanked out how drained she'd been by all the drama when Carl came out, and Ray's situation…well, different presentation, but same basic ingredients, and *identity crisis* and *imploding families* always caused heartburn, no matter how you seasoned them or dished them up.

And this, of all nights, was not the night to find out that Sandrine had decided to give up all seafood because of something Valerie Turner said about overfishing (and that Sandrine, apparently, had completely misunderstood, but Chloe wasn't about to try to explain it). Pulling a different spa-diet-approved entrée out of thin air after trying to counsel her boss's boyfriend through coming out as a cross-dresser…shouldn't she be able to file for worker's comp or something? Maybe sue for hostile working conditions?

Plus, her arms ached.

That had to be psychological, from feeling like she was supporting Ray (who was a pretty heavy weight, after all) or something. She couldn't be in that bad shape, could she? Sure, she didn't work out, but cooking was pretty physical. All those heavy pots to haul around. And turkeys. Turkeys weighed a lot more than four pounds.

Part of her wanted nothing more than to crawl back to the cottage, grab some chocolate, and shut her bedroom door. Maybe allow Evenrude in, but no one else. Evenrude didn't demand much other than scritches and pats, and she could handle that.

Probably. With her luck, Evenrude would insist to be taken out so she could continue wooing the peacocks, secure in her belief that any day now they would succumb to her incredible doggy charm.

Then again, Brand would want to know how the conversation with Ray had gone. Needed to know, even. He'd be relieved to know Ray wasn't gay. Okay, the truth would probably hurt his head a lot, but at least he'd know Ray loved Sandrine and wasn't cheating on her or planning to leave. He was just a little…different.

Besides, a sly voice pointed out, after a day like this, she deserved to be cuddled.

Pampered, even. Have someone else bring her the chocolate, and maybe a drink to go with it.

She told the sly voice to shut the hell up. She needed to tell Brand what was going on, and the pleasure of his company was just a bonus. It had nothing to do with her feeling like the mental and emotional equivalent of overcooked pasta.

In a word: limp.

*

"You look like you could use a drink," Brand said when he opened the gatehouse door. "Or a hug. Or both."

"Start with the drink. Your hugs are too distracting." Once he folded her in his arms, she might not be able to let go again, and not in the fun, sexy sense. Limpets weren't sexy.

The Cabernet, rich and fruity and hinting of leather, helped restore a little of her mental energy. So did telling the story. The new no-seafood policy made Brand sigh and shake his head. The rest…well, he looked confused.

Couldn't blame him for that. So was she.

"So he likes to wear women's clothes. He doesn't want a sex change, right?"

Hmm, that was a concern she hadn't thought of, but she thought back over what Ray had had to say and was able to say, "No. He's a guy. A straight guy, and happy to be one. Not a woman trapped in a man's body."

"Damn good thing, considering the body he's got. Think about it. On second thought, don't."

Oh, yeah. Ray in a dress but not trying to look like a woman was an odd enough mental image. Ray actually trying to pass as... Heads had exploded over less bizarre thoughts.

Brand blinked, looking thoughtful. "Okay, I don't claim to get it, but I guess it's in the weird-but-harmless category. I mean, *Three Musketeers*, right? Big heroic guys used to wear silk and velvet and lace. And it wasn't all that long ago that a woman wearing jeans was pretty unthinkable. So it's just fashion," he concluded, as if saying it would make it that simple, "not some fetish."

Chloe wasn't sure she could reassure him on that point. When did sensual segue into kinky anyway? (And was it any of her business, as long as kids or small fuzzy animals weren't involved and everyone participating had fun?) But she could, and did, safely assure him that Ray adored Sandrine and wasn't going anywhere.

As she alternately sipped and talked, Brand walked around behind her and started rubbing her shoulders. At first, it was lovely and soothing.

Then he applied a little more pressure. She winced and barely stifled a yelp.

"Little tense?"

"I had to catch Ray in the gym, so I worked out with weights for the first time in..." Well, the first time ever, but that sounded lame. "Years and years. Oh," she admitted, "that feels good."

A few minutes later, she amended it to, "Really, really good."

And then, "Fabulous."

"Fabulous? No, that's Ray in his red lace panties."

She sputtered the sip of wine she'd been trying to savor. "You...are a bad, bad man. And now I've got wine all over my shirt."

"We'll just have to take that off you and get it into the wash."

SOPHIE MOUETTE

Before she could protest—and she didn't want to protest, except didn't they need to plan and strategize, and figure out what to do next for Ray and/or Sandrine?—he'd slipped his hands under the lower edge of her tank top and started lifting it over her head.

Well, it would be a shame to have it get stained; it was one of her favorite shirts.

And if the best place to soak the stain out was in the bathroom sink, and the bathroom just happened to be connected to the bedroom, that was pure chance, right?

So maybe there was no such excuse for the bra to follow the shirt. Or the skirt. Or certainly not the underpants. But you couldn't be too careful. Red wine stains just didn't come out, everyone knew that, and the wine might have splattered farther than she thought.

Brand laid her facedown on the bed. Went over to the dresser. She turned her head, curious, watched as he lit a few candles and dug something she couldn't see out of the dresser.

Oooh, toys? She felt a surge of excitement, anticipation. What in the world was he up to?

She smelled lavender and herbs. Then his oil-slicked hands began moving over her body, not in that toe-curling way she'd come to know and love, but soothing her into a dream state, soothing the knots in her muscles.

She vaguely wondered how he was getting to the tangles in her brain as well, when his hands were on her back. But it was working. He worked in near-silence, and that was just what she needed, the quiet as calming as the massage itself.

When her back was no longer cobbled together out of rocks and steel cables, his hands slipped lower, gripping and caressing her butt. Sensuous, but not actually sexual, which she would have expected if she'd thought about it: wonderful and relaxing and melty, with a few less relaxing moments when he dug in a bit. No one normally described her as a tight-ass, but tonight, apparently, it fit. Weird.

It was a good sensation, but parts of her thought that maybe something else was in order to finish the relaxation process.

She arched her spine, purred. Parted her legs in a not-too-subtle hint. Which he didn't take.

Not right away.

Not until he'd worked his sensual way down her legs, stroking the insides of her thighs tenderly, but also paying special attention to her calves and her feet.

God, her feet. It shouldn't feel so good to have her feet rubbed. She didn't realize how abused her feet were, but she did spend a lot of time standing and really, she ought to get back to wearing more sensible shoes. (But it was hard to put on comfy but unbelievably ugly chef's clogs when she knew Brand might just make an appearance in the kitchen.)

When he finished her feet, he retraced his path.

With his tongue and teeth involved this time. Sensation flowed behind his touch, more like water than fire, spreading and swirling and washing away what remained of her tension and replacing it with a better kind of tension.

And this time, when she opened her legs, he took the hint.

Reached down, stroked and circled.

It had all been so mellow, so gentle, that she thought she was just getting started, but as he touched her, started stroking her lips, she shuddered and bucked. Oh my God. How had she gotten so wet? *When* had she gotten so wet?

Then again, she thought as sensations started swirling through her body, as her inner muscles began to twitch, as she opened herself more to Brand's caress—who cared? All that mattered was that she was here.

So good. So sweet. So what she needed.

Usually her orgasms were deliciously violent things. This one washed over her tenderly, slow, but deep shudders that made her sob. It actually brought tears to her eyes with the sweet relief, so she was grateful beyond belief for being facedown. She wasn't sure she could explain it to Brand in her current melted state, explain that there was nothing wrong and everything right, and that was why she was crying a little.

Definitely a chick thing. Although oddly enough, she thought Ray might understand.

And just when she thought she'd recovered, it happened again.

Another deep-rooted, brain-melting orgasm. Another bout of curiously happy tears.

Damn, where was all this emotion coming from?

Luckily, the shuddering of the happy/helpless sobs seemed to blend with the shuddering of the orgasm, and then Brand got distracted by getting his own clothes off and finding a condom (and about damn time) so she could take a second to sniffle and wipe her eyes on the sheet.

Rolling over seemed quite beyond her, and hiding her face still seemed comforting, so she spread her legs even further, tried to accommodate him that way. The head of his cock ran over her lips, and she clenched again, and made a little noise that turned into a larger noise as he found the right angle to enter her. He leaned forwards, his body pressing against her back, and began to stroke in and out with excruciating, beautiful slowness.

It was too much. Too beautiful and too tender, and she was going to start crying again, and then she'd have to explain herself and she didn't know if she could.

His lips pressed against the back of her neck, and that was it. That was too much. This wasn't just mind-boggling sex, this was something even more intimate than that, and really, all she could handle right now was mind-boggling sex.

"Back's tightening up," she lied. "Gotta move. Maybe try doggy style or something."

Brand, being Brand, shifted a little so she could.

She rocked back onto her knees, tried to push herself up.

Her arms refused to hold her up.

Must be the angle.

She tried again. Nope. Every time she'd straighten her arms, the muscles just went all noodly and she collapsed again. Oh, those stupid weights.

The strange feeling, the mixture of intensity and fear, got lost in a wave of embarrassment.

And determination.

She tried one more time.

No go.

Then she tried to push back onto his cock, and winced involuntarily as she stretched her poor, sore, rubbery arms out.

"Why don't we just try something different?" Brand suggested, then rolled her over, her jellylike muscles only partly cooperating.

Thank goodness for candlelight. He probably couldn't see that her face was a little red, or figure out that some of it wasn't just from embarrassment.

Then he drove into her and she lost embarrassment, lost the tears, lost anything like thought in the volcanic explosion that seemed to be going on where their bodies joined. If, earlier, things had gotten a little alarmingly intimate and tender, this was rough-and-ready sex at its best, hard and fast and furious, and she could tell Brand was building towards his own climax.

She wrapped her arms (sore as they were, she didn't care at that point) around him and held on for dear life, and the sun and moon exploded behind her eyelids.

For a brief time, everything was right in Chloe's world.

Until she decided to let go of Brand so they could both shift into more comfortable positions—and every muscle in her arms, including some she hadn't known she had, decided this was the perfect minute to go into spasm.

As he worked his massage magic on *this* little problem, Brand got treated to Chloe's full repertoire of multilingual foul language, including a few incredibly rude Laotian phrases (picked up from Crazy Uncle Pete) that she saved for really special occasions.

Chapter 25

"Are you sure this is a good idea?" Brand asked as Chloe bustled into the room, her arms laden with a blender and a brimming ice bucket, a plastic bag of drink umbrellas clutched in her teeth. The side table already boasted glasses, tequila, margarita mix, and coarsely ground salt.

She dropped the paper umbrellas on the table. "Absolutely. How can Ray express his inner diva without the proper accessories?"

The main bedroom suite in the mansion boasted his-and-hers dressing rooms, each large enough to park a Hummer in. Ray's seemed especially spacious because he didn't have many clothes—at least, not compared to Sandrine. Chloe had taken a deliciously guilty peek into Sandrine's dressing room. The actress could have clothed—and shoed—half of Los Angeles.

By contrast, most of Ray's shoes were for various sports and martial arts. Except for the size-thirteen pumps from that one movie. He'd dug them out from wherever he'd hidden them. He was currently standing on a chair wearing just the heels and a pair of boxer shorts, while Luanna fluttered around with a tape measure, stopping occasionally to make notes on her clipboard.

"Dennis Rodman," Chloe said, pouring margarita mix into the blender. "There's a role model for you. Nobody questions his masculinity, do they?"

"I can't pull off the pink hair, though," Ray said ruefully.

"It's not the details, it's the attitude!" Chloe said.

"Hey!" Luanna said. "It is *so* about the details! Otherwise my job here is useless."

"Well, that's true," Chloe conceded. "First the details, then the attitude to go along with them."

She hadn't had much luck finding decent women's clothing in Ray's size, but it hadn't been much of a mental leap for her and Luanna to come up with the idea of just going ahead and *making* him some. After all, clothing design was Luanna's specialty. It helped keep things private, too—nobody had any reason to think Luanna's latest trip to the Fabric District in LA was for anything other than work.

So, armed with bolts of chiffon and brocade and a lovely, fine silk-linen blend, they were ready to transform Ray into Raylene. Or whatever.

The timing was perfect. Chloe's horoscope had even mentioned "timing is everything," so maybe there was something to astrology after all. Sandrine was off at a photo shoot, which would take all afternoon, between the makeup and the set-up and the wardrobe and the actual picture-taking. She wouldn't be home for hours yet. Olive was with her, as usual.

Ideally, once Ray had the chance to get used to wearing the new clothes, he'd figure out a way to broach the subject with Sandrine.

"Excellent," Luanna was saying. "I was pretty damn close with my estimates of your measurements, if I do say so myself. The first mockup won't need much alteration."

Chloe went back down to the kitchen to get the mini corndogs and jalapeño poppers out of the oven—hey, Sandrine wasn't around, and she loved the idea of turning this into a little party. It had been *fun* making corndogs from scratch.

Back upstairs, she set the trays on another table, next to the plates and napkins and the chips and clam dip.

"Planning to feed an army?" Brand asked.

She swatted him lightly on the arm, then leaned in to kiss him to show she wasn't really mad. "I can't sew, so this is the best way I can contribute. What's your excuse for being here?"

He pulled her down onto his lap, and she yelped and giggled in surprise. "I'm starting to think my job is to keep an eye on you," he said. "I let you out of my sight for a few minutes, and you and Luanna concoct this grand scheme."

She briefly considered smacking him, but then he nuzzled the sensitive skin behind her right ear, and she couldn't keep herself from wriggling with delight and the first hints of arousal.

"Keep that up, and we're going to have to leave," he growled. She could feel him growing thick beneath her thighs.

"You started it," she said cheekily, kissing him on the nose before he let her up.

"Here, put this on," Luanna said to Ray. He obediently slipped the mockup of the dress over his head. It had no fastenings, so it gapped in the back where the zipper would be, but the hem brushed his calves and the high vee neckline would flatter him.

His face was impassive, but Chloe could see the spark in his brown eyes.

"Brand, come over here and make yourself useful," Luanna said.

Brand sighed and got out of the chair. Chloe busied herself with adding the tequila and ice to the blender, munching on a jalapeño popper as she worked the controls. She dipped glasses into the salt, poured in the slushy drink, added umbrellas, and turned to pass out the drinks.

"Thanks," Luanna said absently after she pulled the pins out of her mouth and stuck them in the pincushion strapped to her left wrist.

Chloe handed Ray the other glass and went back for her own. She didn't give one to Brand, because he had his hands full at the moment. Luanna had him standing with different fabric draped on his arms, holding them up against Ray as she instructed.

"What do you think, Chloe?" she asked. Chloe went to her side, and they both cocked their heads to the left, squinted, and sipped their drinks. God, the margarita tasted good. The day was warm and she had to restrain herself from gulping the drink and getting one of those awful cold headaches.

"The peacock blue satin, don't you think?" she said to Luanna.

"That's exactly what I was thinking," Luanna said.

"So is Evenrude," Brand muttered.

Chloe nodded, put down her drink, and started making up plates for everybody. Luanna stuck more pins into her mouth and went up to Ray to adjust something on the mockup. Brand stood with his arms outstretched, rolling his eyes.

"Yoo-hoo, Ray sweetie!" a voice trilled.

They all froze, a bizarre tableau, terror in their eyes.

Oh, yeah. "Timing" covered really, really terrible timing too.

Slowly, Chloe set down the hors d'oeuvres. Maybe, just maybe, she could head Sandrine off at the pass and come up with some excuse to keep her out of the room while everyone else escaped. Except there was only one door. And they were on the second floor, so they couldn't escape out the window, not even Ray because of the dress and heels. She backed towards the door. The rest of them stared at her, still unmoving.

No, they were staring past her. Too late. Chloe slowly turned her head.

Sandrine's face was so white, Chloe thought the woman was going to pass out. Her perfect lips were shaped in a shocked O as those unrivalled turquoise eyes took in the scene before her.

"Sands..." Ray said.

A strange keening noise emanated from Sandrine's mouth. Louder and louder and higher and higher, until Evenrude, all the way back at the cottage, surely began to whine and cover her ears with her paws.

Then she turned and fled.

The other three were still standing as if Sandrine had been Medusa and they'd been turned to stone.

"Oh. Crap." Brand said.

Chloe didn't stop to think. She headed after Sandrine.

This was all her idea, all her fault (if you thought of it as something blameworthy, which she really didn't), and it was up to her to fix it.

She came skidding into the vast living room to find Sandrine behind the mahogany bar. Her back was to Chloe as she shoved bottles around.

"Tequila. Dammit. Where the hell's the tequila?"

"It's upstairs," Chloe said helpfully, before she realized how saying that was only going to make things that more awful. "I, um, could go get it for you," she offered weakly.

"Screw it," Sandrine said, grabbing another bottle off the shelf and removing the top with such a vicious twist that Chloe rubbed her own neck, happy she was still standing across the room and out of range.

Sandrine guzzled vodka straight from the bottle, slammed it down on the bar, reached above her head, pulled a couple of glasses from the rack.

Oh good, maybe she was going to slow down and actually drink from—

Chloe ducked as a glass went sailing across the room and smashed on a marble-topped coffee table. In actuality, the glass went nowhere near her, but she was glad her reflexes were still sharp. And that Sandrine wasn't actively targeting her.

"Where's Olive?" Chloe asked, desperate. Sandrine's assistant knew Sandrine far better than Chloe did. Olive would have all sorts of helpful suggestions for how to deal with this.

"She's getting the zebra," Sandrine said, as if it were the most natural statement in the world.

Chloe opened her mouth to ask, and then just decided not to.

Sandrine found the rum and had that open on the bar, too. Chloe shuddered. This could only end in tears, and a hangover she wouldn't wish on her worst enemy. As crazy as Sandrine was, and as much as she made Chloe's life hell sometimes, Chloe didn't wish that on her.

With a sigh and a square of her shoulders, she dove into the fray.

Thankfully Sandrine threw only two more glasses; by the time Chloe got to her, she was shredding cocktail napkins and snapping those little plastic skewers you stick into olives and pearl onions.

At least she wasn't stabbing anyone with them.

Sandrine reached for the vodka and Chloe slid it out of her reach. Sandrine glared at her, and it took everything Chloe had not to recoil, because it was the look Sandrine had perfected in *Silk and Suede* when she'd played an assassin.

Chloe gave Sandrine her sternest look, the one she used with her brothers when they were being particularly difficult and pig-headed and trying to protect her from something she was perfectly capable of dealing with.

There was a lot of bravado involved, but hopefully she could fake it long enough to get the booze away from Sandrine, or Sandrine away from the booze. Or at least away from the breakable objects that, when flung with any amount of force, could crack open Chloe's head.

Sandrine, never taking her eyes from Chloe, slowly reached her hand towards the bottle of rum.

Chloe, never taking her eyes from Sandrine, moved just a tiny bit faster.

Their hands clenched on the bottle. Sandrine gave a little tug. Chloe held firm.

Deadlock.

"I could fire you," Sandrine said, her voice low and deadly.

It wasn't the firing Chloe was worried about. It would suck, but she could deal with it. It was the implied "and destroy your career" that loomed over her head like Damocles' sword.

But this wasn't about her. It was about Sandrine, and Ray, and even Brand and Luanna.

"Sandrine," she said. "I know things looked weird upstairs. I can explain. In fact, I'd really like to talk to you about it."

Sandrine waited a beat, then gave the bottle a sharp yank.

Her obvious intent had been to wait until Chloe was distracted. But Chloe had five older brothers, and knew that you never, ever let down your guard. Her grip on the rum never faltered, and the bottle moved barely an inch in Sandrine's direction before it resettled back in its original spot.

Sandrine's icy stare never wavered. But Chloe swore, just for a milli-second, that she saw Sandrine's lower lip tremble.

Brand's words came back to her: "She's never figured out how to make Sands and Sandrine into one person."

For all her bravado, for all her power in Hollywood, for all her movie roles and incredible, almost superhuman talent, Sandrine Moss was completely out of her comfort zone and experience, and she didn't have a clue how to handle it.

Chloe had to reach Sandra Mossiman, somewhere deep inside there. How *Sybil* was that?

"Sandrine," she said again, "I know this is weird. I know you're completely freaked out. I would be, too. But I think I can explain, if you'll just let me."

Was it her imagination, or did Sandrine just give her the tiniest of nods?

"I know it's scary and strange," she went on. "But I also know that Ray loves you, and so does Brand, and neither of them would do anything to hurt you. Let's just talk about it, okay?"

Definitely a little bob of the head this time. Good.

"Alcohol won't solve anything," Chloe said, keeping her voice soothing and low, as if she were trying to calm a spooked animal. "Neither will throwing things—although I totally understand why that feels good. Come into the kitchen. I'll make us something to eat, and we'll talk, okay?"

Sandrine seemed to be considering. She looked at the rum, back at Chloe.

"We'll have a glass of wine, how about that?" Chloe said. Wine was far less toxic than Bacardi 151 straight from the bottle. She'd learned that in college.

Sandrine hadn't gone to college, so maybe she'd missed that important life lesson.

Sandrine relinquished her grip on the rum. Chloe put the cap back on it and put it away, along with the vodka.

"Come on," she said. She put an arm around Sandrine's slender shoulders and led her towards the kitchen.

Out of the corner of her eye, she saw movement in the far doorway. She glanced back to see Brand looking in. A moment later, Ray's and Luanna's heads popped into view. From what she could see, it looked as though Ray was wearing a T-shirt again. Good.

Still, she knew Sandrine wasn't ready to talk to anyone else. Chloe had only just gotten her calmed down, and anything could set her off again. The last thing she needed was to see Ray, and remember what she'd just seen Ray wearing. She was guaranteed to go ballistic.

Get them out of here, she mouthed at Brand, waving her hand in a shooing motion.

He looked a little scowly at being shooed, but she waved her hand in an elaborate pattern to explain that she had it all under control, Sandrine was fine, and she'd take care of everything and talk to him later, okay?

Thankfully, he nodded, although she couldn't quite interpret his complex hand-waving response. She didn't have time to follow up, though, because she and Sandrine were already heading through the kitchen door.

"Sit," she said, pointing.

To her amazement, Sandrine obligingly sat. It didn't escape Chloe's notice or her sense of irony that Sandrine chose the same bar stool Ray had been sitting on a few days before when they'd had their heart-to-heart.

She went to the fridge and found an open bottle of Chardonnay; nothing terribly expensive or exciting, but one she kept there for splashing into sauces (and for an occasional nip, not that she'd admit that to anyone).

She poured two glasses of wine, then found a bottle of the expensive imported water Sandrine preferred. Twisting the cap off, she put the bottle and one glass in front of Sandrine.

"Take sips from both," she said. "You can have another glass of wine after you've finished the water."

She turned away so Sandrine wouldn't see her take a hefty swallow of her own wine. Dutch courage. Besides, Sandrine had already done multiple shots of both vodka *and* rum; she was way ahead of Chloe.

Now. Comfort food. That was something she could do. She ran through the various options—mashed potatoes and gravy, lasagna, kale and sausage soup—and discarded each one for various reasons: didn't have the ingredients, didn't have the time, didn't think everyone necessarily considered that to be comfort food, exactly.

Then she landed on that staple, that old favorite, that perfect balance of warmth and texture and taste.

Macaroni and cheese.

Chapter 26

"Okay," she said cheerfully, to keep Sandrine from slipping away, either mentally or emotionally. "Let me get some food started, and then we'll have a great girly chat and get this all sorted out."

She started pulling out ingredients and running the water to boil the pasta. She didn't have time to bake a full casserole, but she could improvise. Whip up a cheesy-creamy-full-of-gooey-goodness sauce that she could mix in with the macaroni.

A small sound alerted her to a big problem. She looked over. Fat tears spilled down Sandrine's ski-slope cheekbones as she cupped her wine glass in both delicate hands and stared into the liquid as if it were an oracle. Another tiny sob hitched in her throat.

"Oh, Sandrine." For the second time, Chloe went around the island and gave somebody a comforting hug. "It's okay, really."

"I don't under...what did I do...Ray..."

Chloe dug a tissue out of her pocket and handed it to her. "First of all, you didn't do anything."

"But Ray..."

"Ray likes to wear women's clothes," Chloe said as matter-of-factly as she could. "Once in a while, in the privacy of his own home. He likes the way they feel."

Now Sandrine started to wail again. "I can't believe he's gay! How could I not see that?"

"He's not gay." Chloe had to raise her voice a little to get through. "Sandrine, Ray is *not* gay."

The keening stopped. "Then why does he like to wear women's clothing? Oh my God, does he want to *be* a woman?"

"Nope," Chloe said. She stretched across the counter and snagged her own glass of wine. She needed it. "He likes the feel of silk and satin and stockings, and being pampered. That's all. That's it."

"I don't get it," Sandrine said.

Chloe patted her on the back and went to dump the macaroni in the now-boiling water. "Neither does he, really." She'd had some time to think about it all, and do a little research, so she was more prepared this time than she had been with Ray. "Think about *The Scarlet Pimpernel*. Any version, although I don't know about you, but I'm partial to the one from 1982."

Sandrine's eyes briefly unfocused, then refocused. "Okay."

"That was an era when men could wear all sorts of lace and flounces, and wigs if they couldn't grow their hair long. Nobody thought twice about it—it was just the fashion. Men were allowed to primp just as much as women were."

As she spoke, she cut cheddar and fresh parmesan and asiago into big chunks and fed them into the food processor. Between whirs of the machine, she went on,

"Some men still like that, even though society and current fashion think it's not okay."

"Hm." Sandrine thought about that. "So, it's like *Priscilla, Queen of the Desert*?"

"Well, I don't think Ray's interested in being a drag queen per se," Chloe said. "This is something that's private for him."

"But how could I not have *known*?"

Chloe dumped the cheese in a pan, added milk and a touch of flour, and set it simmering over a low heat. "He's only just figuring it out himself. He hasn't been actually…doing it for very long."

Sandrine's lower lip trembled. "You all knew."

"We were worried that something else might be going on, actually," Chloe admitted. "We wanted to find out what was really happening, so if it was bad, we could protect you."

As the words left Chloe's mouth, she thought about how foreign they seemed to her. If she found out her friends were keeping something from her because they were trying to protect her, she'd flay the skin off their living bodies. Slowly.

Sandrine had finished her wine *and* her water. She held out her wine glass, and Chloe filled it, as well as her own. When had her own gotten empty, anyway? Come to think of it, she *was* feeling a little light-headed. Not that that was a bad thing…

She set the macaroni and cheese in front of Sandrine.

Sandrine stared at the contents of the bowl for a long moment. "I can't eat this," she said finally, just as she said every third or fourth night.

"Yes, you can," Chloe said firmly. "This is comfort food. Comfort food has no calories when you're in a crisis and you need comfort. Eat."

Hesitant, Sandrine poked her fork into a single piece of macaroni and brought it to her lips. She swallowed. Ate another piece. Another. Moments later, she was loading up her fork, her eyes closed as she savored every mouthful.

Chloe's insides squee'ed with satisfaction.

"Ray loves you," she said again, because it was really, really important. If Sandrine heard nothing else, she had to hear—and internalize—this. "He's wanted to tell you, but wasn't sure how, because he was still trying to understand it himself. We thought that if he had the opportunity to wear a few more clothes, he'd be more comfortable, and he'd be able to explain it better to you."

Sandrine processed that. A tiny furrow appeared between her eyebrows. "He hasn't borrowed any of my clothes, has he? Because they're *designer*, and if he rips something, I'll have to kill him."

Chloe stared at her. Sandrine looked up at her under lowered lashes, and suddenly Chloe saw the wicked glint in those Mediterranean-blue eyes.

Chloe snorted. Sandrine fought back a grin, and failed miserably.

The next thing she knew, they were both howling with laughter, so hard that Chloe almost couldn't pour the rest of the wine into their glasses.

"You know what we need?" Sandrine asked.

"What's that?"

"Ice cream with hot fudge sauce. You can do that, right?"

There it was—the spark of the old Sandrine.

Well, the old Sandrine, but pleasantly tipsy and a hell of a lot more fun to hang out with.

"Oh honey," Chloe said, "I will make you the best hot fudge sauce this side of Willy Wonka's Chocolate Factory, and then you and I are going to have a nice long girl talk."

*

Brand cautiously pushed the door to the kitchen open, just a crack. No flung knives imbedded themselves in the door frame, so he opened the door a little wider and dared to stick his head around it.

Empty. Pots and dishes were stacked haphazardly in the sink, and the center island seemed to have grated bits of cheese and some dark, gooey substance. He stepped closer and chanced a whiff. Chocolate. Hot fudge sauce, from the texture.

Hot fudge? That hadn't passed Sandrine's lips since she had her first snarky magazine comment about her weight when she was all of fourteen years old. (He'd wanted to find that reporter and rip his eyeballs out. Thanks for supporting yet another teenage girl's messed-up body image and eating disorder, asshole.)

This didn't bode well.

And where the hell had they gone?

He went back out into the living room. Ray and Luanna lurked by the patio door, waiting to hear if it was safe to come in. Luanna had taken the bottle of tequila with her when they'd fled the house earlier. (It was all he could do at the time to keep her from bringing the blender container of margaritas, too.)

She still had the tequila bottle now, her hand clutching the neck of it. There was maybe one mouthful of amber liquid left in the bottom. She and Ray had had just too much fun passing that bottle back and forth.

Luanna was definitely worse for the wear; Ray's body mass had kept him from getting much more than slightly sozzled.

"I found chocolate on the counter," Brand reported.

Ray's eyes grew wide. "Uh oh," he said in a voice that implied the only thing worse would be finding blood on the counter.

"Where are they?" Luanna demanded.

"They could be anywhere," Brand said. "All we know is that the front gate hasn't been opened. So let's think logically."

"Logic'ly," Luanna agreed, nodding seriously. "I'm going to check the bathroom."

"Why would they be in the bathroom?" Brand asked.

"Dunno. I just have to pee." She wandered off.

"I think we should check the bedroom," Ray said.

"She'd return to the scene of the crime?" Brand said, but then he realized Ray was right. "Of course. She always retreats there when she's upset."

As they got to the top of the stairs, Brand heard voices. "They're up here," he said, relieved.

"You go first," Ray said. "I'll watch your back, in case there's an ambush."

As they got closer, Brand was gratified to hear laughter. Granted, it was broken by a hitch of a sob, but at least nobody was weeping or screaming, and there was a distinct lack of breakable objects being smashed.

He heard Chloe say something, and then there were peals of mirth. Okay, that was good…he hoped.

He found them curled up on Sandrine's massive swan-shaped bed, lounging on the astonishing number of pillows. Bowls with the remains of melted ice cream and hot fudge sauce teetered dangerously on the imported black silk jacquard bedspread as Sandrine leaned over to grab a bottle of wine from the nightstand and refill their glasses. They had their heads together like old chums sharing confidences.

They were wearing tiaras.

"Everything okay in here?" he asked.

They looked up. "Hi, sweetie," they said in unison. They looked at each other and dissolved into giggles again.

"Everything's great," Chloe said when she recovered. "How're you guys doing?"

"Well, I've got someone here to see Sandrine…"

Ray peeked around the corner, a hangdog expression on his face.

Sandrine flew out of bed and leapt into Ray's arms, wrapping her arms and legs around him and babbling about loving him and being sorry she got scared and wouldn't he please just try to explain things to her and wasn't Chloe lovely for making her the most yummy hot fudge sauce?

Brand held out a hand to Chloe, who climbed off the bed herself, a little unsteadily. She set the ice cream bowls on the dresser, and together they crept out of the room, closing the door behind them.

"What in the world is going on here?" Olive demanded.

They jumped, Brand feeling guilty even though he was pretty sure he hadn't done anything wrong.

Olive had Luanna with her. Luanna no longer had the tequila bottle, and she *did* look a little guilty.

"Luanna has been trying to tell me something about Ray's dress, and I'm afraid I just don't understand," the assistant said. "Could somebody please explain it to me?"

Brand, Chloe, and Luanna all tried, interrupting each other and finishing each other's sentences. Finally Olive interrupted them.

"Are you saying Ray's a *cross-dresser*?" she said.

"Yes," they all said at the same time.

Olive looked from one to the other, blinking as she apparently processed this new information. Brand had no idea what she was thinking, or how she would react. She was always just so efficient and controlled and organized.

"Ray Stark is a cross-dresser," she repeated.

They nodded.

Olive burst out laughing. She laughed so hard she had to prop herself up against the wall, gasping for air.

"Well," she said finally, still chuckling, "*there's* something I didn't see coming." She reached into her pocket for her phone. "I suppose he'll want a bigger dressing room now."

*

Chloe and Brand strolled across the lawn. They'd left Luanna collapsed in a lounge chair by the pool, sipping a bottle of water and dozing. Off to their right, a peacock unfurled his tail and strutted. It was a good thing Evenrude wasn't there to see it, or she'd have near to swooned.

"Thank you for taking care of Sands," Brand said.

Chloe waved her hand to dismiss his gratitude. The motion caused her to weave slightly. She wasn't drunk, but the wine had certainly gone to her head. Belatedly she remembered the hors d'oeuvres and blender and margarita glasses she'd left in Ray's dressing room. It took everything in her power not to turn around to go clean everything up. Sandrine and Ray might be…busy, and she didn't want to interrupt them.

Good God, no.

"I'm glad I could help," she said. "I knew it must have been a horrible shock for her—no matter how open-minded you are, you're bound to be blindsided by something like that. Once she stopped throwing glassware and chugging vodka like a Russian housewife, she was fine."

"Well, I really appreciate," Brand said. "She's my sister, and…."

"And it was my responsibility since I was the one who organized the ball-gown-fitting party." Chloe frowned. "That reminds me, I have to call my parents." She unclipped her phone from her belt.

"How did we get from enabling Ray's new hobby to your parents?" Brand wondered.

"Sister—brothers—parents," Chloe explained. "Try to keep up, would you? Mom, hi! Yeah, it's been a really busy day. Um, I can't really talk about some of it…. Because you'd tell Betsy Ferriera, and she'd sell the story to the highest bidder. Oh yes, you know full well she would. Anyway, I made some hors d'oeuvres and margaritas, and tonight's buffalo filet mignon. Yeah, she eats red meat. At least trendy, very low-fat red meat. Ooh, tomorrow I'll be making Grandma's seafood stew for dinner. Only with about an eighth of the olive oil."

"Tell them I said hi," Brand said, pitching his voice a little louder than necessary. She glared at him, and he grinned evilly.

"What? Oh, that was just Brand. Remember, I told you about him. Sandrine's brother. No, he's a CGI designer. I have no idea." She covered the phone with her hand. "Brand, what does CGI stand for? He says 'computer generated images,' Dad. You know, special effects. No, he didn't work on *Star Wars*…. He's too young to have worked on *Star Wars*. About my age… You haven't worked on any of the newer *Star Wars* movies, have you, hon?"

She rolled her eyes and made the universal blah-blah-blah gesture to let Brand know that her parents were rattling on and on and on. Every once in a while, she opened her mouth to say something, but she couldn't get a word in edgewise.

No matter how much she loved her family members, she occasionally wanted to beat them about the head and shoulders with a large wet fish.

After what seemed like hours, but was probably less than a minute in real, not-waiting-for-someone time, Chloe exclaimed, "A date? Oh…*that* kind of date!" She laughed, or maybe choked on one of those things you just couldn't say to your parents, even when they deserved it. "Jeez, Mom, slow down! You are so jumping the gun here. This is a really, really new relationship. Okay, I've got to go. I love you, too. Bye."

She thumbed off her phone and tucked it away before she realized that Brand had stopped walking and was staring at her with a really, really strange expression on his face.

"What? What's wrong?"

"Did you just tell your parents we're in a relationship?"

Chapter 27

*C*hloe thought she'd pretty much sobered up—half a vat of super-rich fudge sauce could counter a lot more booze than she'd actually had—but the grounds tilted and righted themselves as if she were channeling Luanna post–tequila binge.

What had she done now?

Mac-and-cheese, ice cream with hot fudge sauce, and several glasses of Chardonnay churned together in Chloe's stomach, along with the dregs of a margarita and snacks from the sewing party, which seemed to have been in another lifetime. "Re…relationship?" she managed to get out.

Was he mad? Oh God, please don't let him be mad. Sometimes guys went ballistic over the R word. She didn't even dare to look at him just yet. "Did I say that?"

Then she shut her mouth abruptly, because keeping your mouth firmly shut When Food Fought Back seemed like a good plan. Never mind that if she kept her lips buttoned, she couldn't say anything else that got her in trouble.

"You said it, all right." Brand's voice was frighteningly neutral.

Okay, so she'd said it. But for heaven's sake, her parents were just asking about potential wedding dates, and she had to say something to deflect that little misunderstanding without saying "Oh, we're just friends," because that was a lie, and while you certainly didn't need to tell your parents everything, outright lying to them was bad. Plus she'd been distracted and not precisely at her sober and level-headed best and she hadn't meant to say it, so Brand wasn't supposed to *hear* it.

Wouldn't it have been worse if he'd heard her say they were just friends?

And what was he doing listening to her private conversations with her mom and dad anyway?

Inner Chloe pointed out that she had called her parents with Brand walking right next to her. She mentally whacked the Inner Chloe in the kneecaps with a cast iron frying pan and moved on.

It was more than bad enough her mom had heard it, because now Mom and Aunt Rosa would be prying for information. Her brothers, too, especially Carl and Craig, who thought they were subtle and stealthy, like ninja. (Ninja rhinos, maybe, but they had their uses. Right now she wished she had her very own ninja rhino brother bodyguard to get her out of this, even if it meant she had to tell them everything. Then again, if she could tell anyone everything, it really ought to be Brand, but too much of what was going on between them was still hazy in her head.)

She stopped moving, ran her hands through her hair, and discovered she was still wearing one of Sandrine's tiaras. She pulled it off and stared at it for a moment.

Then she sat down on the crushed-shell-and-gravel path because the next bench looked too far away and gravity was no longer her friend and the world seemed really weighty all of a sudden.

"Relationship?" Brand reminded her, sitting down next to her as if it were the most normal thing in the world. She finally dared to look at him. He didn't seem angry, just confused, but it looked like it might be a good kind of confused, like he'd learned he had a winning lottery ticket but was now waiting to hear whether he'd won five hundred dollars or five million and what the loopholes were.

Better than mad, but it still made her nervous. He looked so…hopeful. That meant he had expectations, and that could be good or really, really bad, because…well, she supposed she had some, too, because people always have expectations or at least dreams, but damned if she'd thought them through yet enough to talk about them. She'd been too damn busy to think about anything much beyond *this is fun* and *he's really, really nice* where Brand was concerned, and *Let's keep having fun* might fall crashingly flat.

"Relationships? Oh, *that's* what we were talking about!" she said, desperately perky, her face plastered with what she knew was a fake smile. He made a noise that combined annoyance and reluctant amusement and she added, "Hey, it would work if your sister tried it."

That made him break a tentative smile. "Only because she probably *would* have forgotten. I don't buy it from you, not even tipsy and on the world's biggest sugar buzz."

"Damn." She snapped her fingers, did a *gee-shucks* face. "Can't blame me for trying."

"Well…it does make me wonder what you're trying to avoid talking about." He sounded way more serious than she liked. "And we really do need to discuss this."

The worst words ever to pass a lover's lips: "We need to talk." Okay, so he'd paraphrased it a bit. That was still what he meant, and it was still really, really bad.

The fact that he was right and they did need to sort a few things out didn't make it any better. Worse, in fact. This kind of talk led to hurt feelings as often as not—even if you figured you were starting on the same page.

"This is a scary talk, Brand. Plus I've spent so much time lately trying to straighten out Sandrine and Ray's relationship that I haven't had any brain cells to spare for you and me." She paused, took a deep breath, wished for another drink, less for the booze than for something to do with her hands. "Can we go back to the gatehouse?" she finally said. "I think better in the kitchen."

"You could eat now?"

"Hell no, but I can always cook. You might get hungry later—you didn't join in on the ice cream orgy…"

"I didn't get a tiara, either."

Wordlessly she held out the one she'd just untangled from her hair. He raised an eyebrow. Okay, not so much with the levity attempts right now.

So they walked in silence back to the gatehouse.

Actually, she walked. Brand tromped. Tromped like a man with a purpose and...well, if he'd been a girl, she'd have thought he tromped like someone having a hissy fit, but guys didn't have hissy fits, did they?

When they got there, she headed straight for Brand's little kitchen. It was a pretty minimal one, and even with her intervention, the supplies were low. Some cringe-inducing TV dinners and a single packet of microwave popcorn, well past its expiration date. Pasta and a few fixings. A lot of half-full condiments. A few odd bits of surprisingly good cheese. And hot dogs. *Hot dogs.* Why was she dating this man again? Oh, that's right. Sweet, funny, and genuinely nice—and he was utterly hot in the sack.

But his refrigerator and pantry still scared her. With luck, he could be trained to keep basic groceries on hand....

And in that way lay madness. She firmly set those thoughts aside as she grabbed a jar of crushed garlic, a lonely tomato, capers (she didn't know why the capers were there, and she didn't want to know, but at least they were still fresh), and the last bits of a bottle of olive oil, and began to construct a makeshift pasta sauce.

"Need a..." Brand cut himself off at her glare, amended it to, "Let me know if you need help finding anything. I actually do have some kitchen tools, though they're probably not up to your standard."

"He can be taught!" She smiled when she said it, not just to soften the edge, but also to celebrate it to herself. It had been a serious concern.

Then she organized the ingredients, considered her plan of attack— not that there was really so much to consider with a throw-together plan like this—and began the process of reducing the tomato to chunks.

Brand was pacing, looking like he really wanted to say something, and maybe not so much that he wanted to say something in particular, but anything, anything to break the silence, which was getting pretty oppressive even to Chloe, but she wanted to make sure she had what she was going to say straight in her head.

About the same time she was satisfied with the size of the tomato chunks, she decided she was satisfied with her prepared opening gambit. "We have a relationship, I guess. I'm just not sure what that relationship is."

"And that would be why we're having this…conversation that we're not really having yet." Brand was speaking slowly and carefully, with this undertone of martyred patience, like you would to a not-too-swift small child, or to Sandrine on a particularly ditzy day. He stopped pacing and ventured a smile, then sat down on a bar stool. He crossed his arms, leaned back against the counter, stretched his long legs out in front of him, sighed.

"So how about I get started? I like you, Chloe. I like you a lot. The whole thing's a little weird since you're working for Sandrine, and we've both been crazy-busy, and…" He stifled a laugh. "Well, then we got distracted with the whole my-future-brother-in-law-is-a-cross-dresser thing, but overall…"

Overall *what*? she wanted to scream. Preferably while brandishing the chef's knife.

The silence loomed between them like a monster from a 1950s B movie, funny and scary at the same time.

Chapter 28

"So overall," Brand repeated, "I like the idea that we have a relationship. Not in the 'let's get married right now' sense...."

"That was what I was trying to tell my mom when I...when I said it." Why couldn't she call this discussion off until she had a chance to rehearse with Luanna and could sound coherent? "But there's something more going on than the whole wild weasel sex thing, isn't there?"

"You don't sound very happy about it." He got off the bar stool and moved so he was hovering near her, like he wanted to touch her but was afraid she'd bite or something.

"Don't be scared," she said. "I'll put the knife down. It's pretty dull anyway—you really should get better knives, Brand. These are such crap they're not even worth trying to sharpen; you'd be better off with a nice set of..." She caught herself. "Avoiding the point again, aren't I?"

Now that she was safely disarmed, he came up behind her and slipped his arms around her waist. She leaned back for a few seconds, enjoying the solid feel of him, the warmth of his chest and the lean strength of his arms.

That was Brand, all right: solid. Which was good and bad, because she wouldn't want to be involved with a flaky guy with no sense of responsibility, but she wasn't about to put everything on his shoulders (although they were very fine shoulders, mind you) and it seemed that sometimes—maybe even a lot of sometimes—he wanted her to.

"So...where was I? 'More than sex'?" She wriggled her butt against his crotch, hoping to distract him back to the wild weasel sex theme because she knew exactly what was going on there and it didn't stir up the parts of her hindbrain that hadn't really bought into the career-first plan. Although it would have to be slow, decorous weasel sex right now because her tummy was still not happy with her.

Brand clasped her hips, pressed against her. She felt interesting things start to happen back there, and interesting things happening in her own body in response. Maybe her ploy was working and they could get back onto familiar, comfortable territory.

Brand stepped back. Damn his willpower.

She turned around, and couldn't resist a glance at his crotch. Okay, he might have willpower, but the flesh was definitely weak. That made her feel better, because it would be a shame to be the only one with the *wanting to jump someone at inappropriate times* problem.

Okay, she couldn't avoid this anymore. "I really, really like you, Brand," she said, forcing the words out at triple time. "And the more time we spend together, I'm seeing I really, really like you out of bed. But I'm not sure where this is going. I'm not sure where I want it to go. I'm working for your sister for about four more months, and then I don't know where I'll end up. It's been hard finding a job in LA, although I'm really, really going to try...."

"I might know some people...." Brand said.

"No!" she said, more vehemently than she intended. "No, but thank you," she amended. She took a deep breath. "All my life people have been trying to take care of me. Like just after I got back from Paris, and got a job in Boston, and Luanna and I were looking for an apartment together. We found one we really liked, but we didn't have good credit yet, and our application was denied. I was telling my family about it, and how we were going to have to settle for one in an iffy part of Mission Hill...and the next thing we knew, our application for the first place was accepted. I was so crazy-busy that I didn't realize until a few weeks later that Carl knew the owner and had convinced him rent to us in exchange for setting him up with my cousin Marina."

"Did you kill him?" Brand asked, his face deadly serious.

"Dude, I need to show you pictures of my brothers sometime. Carl is the largest person I'd ever seen before I met Ray. There was no violence." She chuckled, the memory still painfully funny even years later. "I snuck into his place and switched the sugar and the salt and replaced all his coffee with the nastiest cheap decaf I could find. And as it turned out, he'd had someone promising spend the night and served him salty, sawdust-flavored coffee. Didn't find that part out for a few years."

"Remind me never to get you mad at me."

"Don't get me mad at you."

Then the moment for humor passed and they stared at each other for another long, uncomfortable silence. "So anyway," Chloe said, desperately wishing to sink through the floor, "yeah, I plan to stay in LA when the contract's up, but I've got to go where the right job is, and if that's in Vancouver, well, I hear British Columbia's really pretty."

"It's really *wet*."

"It rains a lot in New England, too. I'd cope." Had she missed some undertone there, some don't-go thing, which might be a little more commitment than she was ready to think about, but face it, was the kind of thing that made a girl all fluttery inside even if it wasn't sensible? Or was he just saying that, to a Southern California boy, the Pacific Northwest had a definite downside?

"Anyway, Vancouver's just the first place that popped into my head. It wasn't the point, which is that it's hard to make plans or commitments when things are still so up in the air for me. I could end up anywhere in a few months—and your work's here. So for now we just have to take things day by day and see what happens."

Brand took off his glasses and squeezed the bridge of his nose. Chloe bit her lip. She wanted to take back everything she'd said and tell the little white lies he'd probably rather hear about her definitely staying in the area, no matter what. Because the fact was, she liked LA and she liked him, and if it worked that way, it would be ideal. But the truth was better, right?

"Okay," he said finally, replacing his glasses. "So the long view of where are we going with this is 'who the hell knows.' Short-term?"

Chloe screwed up her courage. She had an answer to this one, at least a partial one, but she wasn't sure he'd like it. "You need to stop trying to take care of me so much. If you think about fixing something for me, do me a favor and don't."

"What about your car?"

She sighed. "You asked me first, and it was in your area of expertise. I would've had to hire somebody anyway. If you'd just taken it to a shop and paid for it…"

"I understand what you're saying, but…it's what I do when I…when I care about someone." She had the feeling he'd almost said something else, something stronger.

"I know." She kissed his shoulder. "And it's a sweet impulse to do nice things for me, but at least talk to me about it first. Treats like back rubs and the occasional good bottle of wine are great, but sometimes you go overboard and make me feel like you think I *need* to be taken care of."

Brand laughed ruefully. "Force of habit, I guess, after years of dealing with my sister."

That was another thing. She hadn't meant to bring it up now, but it fit and besides, if she put it off, she might lose her nerve. "I don't think your sister needs as much babying as you think, either. She's pretty tough underneath all the flakiness."

"You saw how she was today when she found out about Ray. She was breaking the Waterford!"

"Well, that's a little different, don'tcha think?" She put her hands on her hips and glared. "I think a girl's entitled to get hysterical under those circumstances. If I walked in and found you parading around in an evening gown, I'd freak, and I'm semi-broken-in to weirdness between my gay brother and my drag queen friend. She calmed down pretty quickly once she realized Ray wasn't going anywhere."

Brand looked like he was ready to interject something, but she kept on talking. This was an important point, something Brand needed to understand, not just for his relationship with his sister, but for any chance of a relationship with her. "What *really* bothered her was that everyone else knew and was trying to protect her. If she can handle her fiancé being a cross-dresser without doing anything worse than throwing things, I think she can handle her big brother having a life of his own."

He raked his hands through his hair. "Did I ever tell you about my college experience? I went to Cornell for all of a month. Loved it. I was in a great program, I was making friends who had normal lives and had no idea who my sister was. Life was good. And then I had to come home because Sands started crying one day and couldn't stop. Once I got here, I realized I should just transfer to UCLA and save myself a lot of flying."

"I understand why you worry about her so much." Chloe put her arm around him. "That must have been an awful time for her, dealing with your parents' deaths and the pressures of Hollywood. It's no wonder she had a breakdown." Then she stepped away so she could look Brand in the eye. She had to crane her neck a bit, but eye contact was important when dealing with emotional males. "But she's not that screwed-up teenager anymore. She's more sensitive than most people, but that's partly because you shelter her so damn much that every little thing's a big shock! You've got to back off a little and let her grow."

"Are you saying I'm smothering her? I'm just trying to be a good brother...."

He looked so stricken that she gave him another big hug. "I know. Trust me, I understand both sides. I've got five wonderful big brothers who I adore, remember? And who I had to move to LA to escape so I could, oh, have a life? Which is why I twitch when you start coddling me...or even your sister."

He had the grace to look shamefaced. "Well, yeah. Maybe I do go overboard. But she's not like you. You're obviously capable of taking care of yourself, and she forgets what day of the week it is."

Chloe laughed. "She doesn't need to remember. That's what calendars and iPhone apps are for. And Olive. Your sister's not stupid, she's not a child, and she may be crazy, but she's genius crazy, not needs-medication crazy. She doesn't need to be hovered over and protected from things. Give it some thought, anyway. No one likes to be treated like they're too fragile or too dumb to handle things. For that matter, we should probably come right out and say we're dating. She's gotta know, but actually telling her is part of that whole not-overprotecting-her thing."

He pursed his lips and furrowed his brow in an utterly adorable way, but he didn't answer right away. Nervous, Chloe slid the chunked tomatoes into a somewhat battered pot with the capers and garlic and oil.

Finally, he said, "You know, we've really worked through a lot tonight, and it feels great. But I don't think we're going to resolve all of this now. This is big stuff, gotta-think-it-through stuff."

"Yeah." And what did that mean, exactly? Could be good, could be bad. Could be exactly what it sounded like.

"And you may do your best thinking in the kitchen, but I do mine in the shower." He stretched like a languid cat, pulling his shirt over his head to reveal those yummy, sleek, swimmer's muscles.

At the door of the kitchen, he stopped, turned, and flashed her that wickedly naughty grin of his, the one that had the power to immediately make her panties wet. "You're welcome to join me, of course."

And then pulled his shorts off.

She turned the stove off.

The hell with dinner. Neither of them were hungry, anyway.

At least not for food.

Chapter 29

Nurturing a relationship was hard when you were almost too busy to see each other.

Brand's latest project was still giving him some late nights and calling him away on the weekends, and along with the day-to-day mayhem of Chez Sandrine, Chloe had already started planning and organizing for the star's upcoming Birthday Party Extravaganza.

To snatch a little time together, Brand walked to the main house with Evenrude one evening to meet Chloe after she finished cleaning up the dinner detritus. It was one of those little things about him that charmed her, dammit.

Okay, two things: That he'd want to walk with her, and that he'd think to bring the dog.

They strolled along the crushed-shell-and-gravel walkway near the courtyard patio where Sandrine and Ray had eaten dinner. The pair still sat there, their heads close in conversation. Chloe and Brand might have walked by unnoticed if Evenrude hadn't whuffed at something unseen in the night.

"Chloe, Brand." Sandrine's greeting was casual, but she waved her hand in an imperious fashion that implied that they were still expected to enter her presence without question or hesitation.

Beside her, Brand stiffened. Chloe wanted to kick him in the shins and tell him to lighten up.

On the other hand, things had been decidedly tense when Chloe had served dinner. It hadn't seemed directed at her, but neither Sandrine nor Ray had eaten much (not that that was unusual for Sandrine), and they'd fallen silent when Chloe had approached the table, and Ray had seemed kind of sad.

Was this about the birthday party? Sandrine (via Olive) had given her almost a whole month's notice for this one—largely because if there was one date Sandrine never forgot, it was that of her own birthday, and she hadn't reached the age when it was something she needed to lie about or avoid by lying in bed all day with a soothing lavender eye mask and a Xanax blotting out the world.

No, "birthday" meant "a day that's all about me, me, me," to Sandrine, and *that* meant a massively huge party. And since she had such a fabulous personal chef, there was no need to rent a swanky restaurant or the top half of a Vegas casino for the bash.

"Hey, sis," Brand said, leaning down to give his sister a quick kiss. He and Ray bumped fists.

It was a little weird to be invited to sit at the table where she'd recently served food as an employee, but Chloe was kind of getting used to the dichotomy of being Sandrine's employee as well as something of a friend.

Scary, but true.

They settled into wrought-iron chairs padded with cushions that were changed for each season. Chloe wondered if she should wrap the end of Evenrude's leash to the chair, but the dog still had some energy and wasn't ready to sit still.

"Will you be good?" she asked.

Evenrude blinked her liquid dark eyes in utter innocence. If she'd had hands, she would have adjusted her invisible halo.

Chloe sighed, knowing she was a sucker, and unclipped the leash from the dog's collar. Evenrude took a couple of steps, sniffed something, and looked back over her shoulder as if to say "See, I'm just going right over here; it's not far…"

"We've been talking," Sandrine said, "and we're concerned about something."

"I really don't think it will be a problem," Ray said, and Sandrine shot him a look that clearly indicated that this was the source of their disagreement and he was wrong and should stop saying that.

Chloe was vaguely surprised Ray was still trying to express his opinion. She probably would have caved under Sandrine's "don't contradict me" weight long ago.

Ray sighed, and Chloe's heart went out to him. He and Sandrine were obviously at an impasse.

"Let's start from the beginning," Chloe said, "and hear all sides."

"I support Ray in his decision," Sandrine said. "I'm not sure I understand it completely, but I'm trying, and he's been very patient with me through this." She placed her slender hand over Ray's large one and smiled at him.

Aw. Sandrine and Ray were so in love. Chloe was impressed at how well they were working through this crisis, through what would have easily been a relationship-killer for most couples.

Why couldn't she and Brand manage that? Without the cross-dressing and the crazy diets, of course.

They had settled into a weird holding pattern. Where they were was fine enough, but they couldn't seem to move forwards, even though Chloe for one had the feeling she'd like to, and she wanted to believe Brand felt the same way.

"*É o que é*," as her grandmother used to say. "It is what it is." Meaning, if you don't like it, either fix it or accept it.

For once in her life, Chloe didn't have a clue how to fix it.

She liked Brand. A lot. Had it been anyone else being such a control freak, she would have dumped them and moved on. But she didn't want to dump Brand and move on. She still wanted to give things a chance, to see where they could go.

Right now, however, this wasn't about them.

"But I'm scared," Sandrine said, and her lower lip trembled. "I'm scared of what will happen if somebody finds out. If his secret gets out, we'll both be laughing stocks and our careers will be ruined, and I don't know what we'll do!" Her voice rose in speed and pitch as she grew more agitated.

"We'll sue their asses from here to next Tuesday, that's what we'll do," Brand said firmly. "Slander, libel, whatever. It's none of their goddamn business!"

"It's not slander—or libel, I can never remember which is which," Chloe said, "if it's true."

"But they'll imply—or maybe outright claim—that Ray is gay," Brand said. "And they'll do computer-generated pictures of him in dresses, and it *will* harm his career. We can sue for loss of income, all that kind of thing. But first we should up the security, both on the estate and off. Hire extra guards to keep an eye out for paparazzi…."

"Hold on, hold on," Chloe interrupted. "We can't necessarily just throw money and lawyers at this thing. That's defensive and reactive. We need to be proactive." Just like her horoscope had said about attracting more flies with honey. Although she'd never understood why you wanted to attract flies anyway.

She turned to Ray. "I hope this isn't too personal, but is the cross-dressing something you want to do in public, or just in the privacy of your own home?"

"Just at home, definitely," he said. "It's not an exhibitionism thing."

He'd been reading the literature she'd tracked down. Good for him.

"Not even, um, panties under regular clothes?" she asked.

He flushed and looked away. "Okay, maybe sometimes."

"See?" Sandrine said. "What if someone sees that?"

"Don't be embarrassed," Chloe said to Ray. To Sandrine, she added, "That's a good question. How about this: Just always remember to use a stall so it's not obvious.

"Meanwhile," she said to both of them, "make sure you really trust your staff, anyone who comes into the house. If there's a question, you can always say the clothes are for a role of Ray's. Or, better yet, keep them somewhere private, locked up, where nobody else has access."

"That makes a lot of sense," Ray said. Sandrine pursed her lips, apparently still not quite convinced.

"But what if someone finds out?" she repeated.

"I just think we can't worry about that right now," Chloe soothed. "After all, look how long it took us to find out, and we're the ones closest to Ray. I think you have to trust him, and trust yourself. If something does get out, well, we'll deal with that *if* it happens. A lot of celebrities have weathered scandals and come out the other side. I'm willing to bet a lot of people would be impressed that you and Ray have such a strong, trusting, accepting relationship."

"Really?" Sandrine's smile was hesitant, hopeful.

"Really," Chloe said.

"You know," Sandrine said, "I've had my eye on a really pretty antique armoire. We could get it fitted with a lock..."

"Good idea," Chloe said, feeling awfully pleased with herself.

"Thanks, Chloe," Ray said. "You're a peach."

"Uh oh," Brand murmured.

They all turned and followed his gaze.

"Oh, Evenrude," Chloe whispered. There was no way she could get to the dog in time.

Unnoticed by the rest of them, one of the peacocks had landed on the low wall, less than two feet high, that edged the patio. Because it was in the dark shadows near a tree, the peacock had apparently thought himself safe, and now his head was tucked down as he slumbered...

...entirely unaware of the curious, love-struck dog creeping up behind him.

How a short, stubby Welsh corgi could turn herself into a silent, slinking, stalking machine that would put a Navy Seal to shame, Chloe couldn't fathom. Maybe she should get Evenrude an agent and send her out on acting calls.

Evenrude reached the wall. Her tail waving slowly, she gazed up at the peacock with great devotion, then did what any self-respecting dog would do when attempting to woo a first date.

She stuck her cold, wet nose in the approximate area of the peacock's unsuspecting butt.

The detonation that occurred rivaled anything Brand's CGI expertise could have created. In a flurry of startled indignation, the peacock exploded outwards and upwards, puffing out to three times its size. Evenrude shot backwards, completely unprepared for this sort of violent reaction.

Trailing feathers and righteous offense, the peacock fluttered up into the tree and glared balefully down at Evenrude, who whined and wagged her tail so hard the lower half of her body shook, eternally hopeful for a reconciliation.

The peacock shook itself in a combination of "I meant to do that" and "you are beneath me" attitude, and tucked its head back down.

"The course of true love never did run smooth," Sandrine quoted.

"I think we can all learn something from this," Brand said, getting the leash from Chloe and clipping it on a disappointed but undaunted Evenrude. "You've got to fight for what you believe in."

Chloe wondered if that was directed at her, although it could have been as pointed at Sandrine and Ray, too. Good lord, she felt like she was trapped in some wacky nighttime soap opera. *As the Fruit Bat Turns* or *The Young and the Peacock* or something. All they needed now was an illegitimate love child and someone waking from a coma after seventeen years (which was three and a half weeks in TV time).

"Oh, Chloe, wait!" Sandrine said. "I almost forgot to tell you. Remember when we talked about DesJardins in Paris? I just heard Monsieur DesJardins is going to be opening DesJardins LA next month! Isn't that exciting?"

"So soon? That's really interesting," Chloe said, feeling entirely out of the loop with the foodie world. All her issues of *Cooks Illustrated*, *Bon Appétit*, and *Food and Wine* were piling up because she didn't have time to read them, and the only food blogs she'd looked at had been devoted to raw foods and Zones and other weird diets, because it wasn't like Sandrine ever ate anything *normal*.

"I can't wait to try it out," Sandrine said. "Anyway, good night, you two."

Chloe and Brand waved as they walked away. Evenrude resisted slightly at first, unwilling to be taken from her heart's desire, but then she gave up and trotted along at Chloe's side, secure in the knowledge that if she absolutely must be parted from her true love right now, at least there was kibble waiting at home.

"Wow, DesJardins," Chloe said with a sigh. "Even though he was so mean to me in Paris, I've always wanted to work with him again. Talk about a dream job—and right here in LA. It's too bad he'll be hiring before I'm available.

"Oh well." She shrugged. "*É o que é.* I'll put feelers out later, and see what happens. For now..." and she slipped her free hand into Brand's, curling her fingers around his "...I just want to curl up with you and have wild weasel sex until we're too tired to move."

"As long as you don't stick your cold, wet nose in my butt, I'm game," Brand said.

Evenrude sighed.

Chapter 30

"Sandrine and Ray are even more sickeningly cute together than they were before…." Brand gestured vaguely. "You know. Everything."

He was doing his best not to define "everything" because, much as he loved his brother-in-law-to-be, nothing would deflate his cock's current state of happy anticipation, brought on by Chloe saying the magic words *wild weasel sex*, than thinking too hard about Ray's unusual habits. Best to pretend that his sister and her sweetie had had a fight about something normal, like Ray spending too much time watching NASCAR or ogling a trashy-sexy Kardashian clone a little too obviously.

Of course, Brand's traitorous brain suggested, if Ray had been staring at a Kardashian clone, he'd been wondering where she got her boots and if they came in larger sizes.

Mr. Happy wilted a bit at the thought. Then Chloe slipped her hand into his front pocket for a subtle caress, and all was well in his world—or at least his underwear—again.

"They're doing great," Chloe agreed. "Every time I see them together, they're all snuggly and smoochy. But at the moment I'm more interested in getting snuggly with you." Her small, sure hand, working inside his pocket, found a very interesting area to stroke, one that made it clear she meant naked and snuggly, and probably hot and sweaty.

He'd been starting to ponder something that had seemed important for a few seconds, but suddenly nothing was more important than getting Chloe into bed—or at least into a relatively private place with a sturdy surface to lie on or lean against.

Wherever they were ending up, the first order of business was to feed Evenrude, so the first sturdy indoor surface they saw was the couch in Chloe's living room. "I don't think we've done it here yet," he said, trying to sound casual and knowing he'd failed.

Luckily they were two great minds with a single horny thought. "And Luanna's out tonight. One of her co-workers is having a party and she's going to crash there." Being the responsible soul she was, she gave Brand the kind of kiss that set a man's shorts on fire, then cooed, "Come on, Evenrude. Dinner."

Which would have bugged Bran a little except she was stripping off her shirt as she said it. She was wearing a bright green bra that put her already gorgeous tits on a platter.

The cottage was pretty small, but Brand hadn't thought it was even possible to get into the kitchen in three-point-two seconds, let alone get there, feed a hungry mutt, and get back, managing to shed her pants and shoes on the way.

The panties matched the bra. And they were satin and lace and cut so just the bottom curve of her ass peeked out, which was even sexier than a thong because it almost looked like she might not know how much she was showing off. Except, of course, she made a point of letting him see her butt, which meant she knew exactly how much showed and how much was suggested and how much he'd like it.

He wanted to take a little bite of that smooth olive butt cheek, wanted it like it was actually as delicious as it looked and he was starving.

So he did.

Chloe shrieked and swatted at him. "Stop..." she started, but Brand kissed and licked the spot he'd just nipped, and kissed and licked down her thigh, and she never finished her sentence.

Then he caught her around the hips and spun her around and continued kissing through the hot satin. He breathed deep, inhaling the scent of aroused woman, stronger than the faint cooking aromas that were equally a part of Chloe, caught on her clothes and skin from her day's work. "You smell good," he whispered.

She sighed and chuckled, an incredibly erotic sound.

"And those panties are sexy, but they have to go." He curled his fingers into the panties and pulled them off with her eager cooperation.

"Bra needs to go too." It was front-hook. He was thankful for that because he was too eager to do the suave one-handed unhooking thing behind her back, and besides, he just loved the way her breasts popped out when he opened the front hook as if they were happy to be free. He nuzzled first one and then the other, sucked one plump nipple into his mouth. Chloe wrapped one leg around him, pressing her wet little pussy against his thigh—he could feel the heat through his jeans, if not the actual wetness yet. His cock strained against denim that felt like a steel prison. Her breasts were heaven. Her hands, that sexy way she rubbed against him, no reason to be shy because they both admitted they needed each other that much. It was hard to make himself take one hand off her breasts, but he did because the rest of her was just as amazing and needed his touch. He stroked down her back, cupped her ass, then dipped between her legs from behind, touching her slickness.

Slippery fire.

Knowing he was getting her this hot made him feel as powerful as Superman, except Superman was clean-cut and goody-goody. Right now he felt anything but that, and with all his blood rushing to his dick, he couldn't be bothered to think of a studly superhero who actually had fun with hot babes instead of just rescuing them.

"Need you naked." Chloe reached for his zipper.

It was easier and faster to undress himself, Brand reflected, but infinitely more fun when Chloe did it, when she unzipped the jeans and wriggled them over his hips and helped him step out of them, when she pulled his shirt over his head.

And oh God, when she stroked his cock through his underwear, when she put her lips on him through damp cotton, his underwear suddenly felt like a vise because he needed it gone so badly...

Which she seemed in no hurry to do. She'd been in a great hurry to get naked, but now she was teasing him, licking and teasing, but without moving the damn underwear. Brand wanted to protest, but that would have meant actually scraping together enough brain cells to say something sensible.

Besides, it felt so damn good. Teasing, frustrating, but so incredibly good. He wanted her to move on to a full-out blow job, or let him slide inside her, but to get there she'd have to be out of contact with him for a few seconds and he didn't want that. A real dilemma.

Finally she relented and eased his underwear down. With one hand stroking his dick, Chloe led him to the couch, sat him down, and knelt between his open legs.

He'd pictured a different scene when he'd eagerly imagined a random sturdy surface: Chloe bent over, her cute little ass sticking out, him slamming into her from behind. Instead he found himself sprawling back, at the mercy of her talented hands and clever lips and talented tongue.

She sucked him in and her mouth was nuclear hot and her tongue swirled on him. One hand cupped his balls, caressed them, occasionally ran short, neat fingernails over them, making him shudder with need. She wasn't going for speed, but for depth, taking him in to the root, slowly and sensuously backing off, licking around his head, then doing it again.

It was delicious.

It was amazing.

It was... "too much. Too much. I don't want to come in your mouth." He laughed. He couldn't help it. Right now, everything was bright and wonderful. "Okay, I do, but I also want to come inside you, with your arms around me and you coming too. And if you don't stop..."

"I want you in me," Chloe said, "but not yet," and sucked some more. Just when Brand thought he was going to explode, Chloe backed off.

"Condom...back left pocket." Okay, maybe it was tacky to carry them any time he thought he might see Chloe, but with their crazy schedules, he always wanted to be prepared in case they could grab some private time.

She tore it open, and together, they rolled it onto his cock. He was going to offer the option of heading to the bedroom, but she was straddling his lap before he had a chance to speak. Chloe grasped his cock with that strong, sure little hand of hers and eased down onto it.

He grasped her very graspable, curvy hips and helped her move, but she set the rhythm, riding him hard, then slowing down and grinding her clit against his pubic bone, then riding hard again. She felt like hot, grasping heaven around him, and based on the noises she was making, he must feel just as good to her. Her eyes screwed shut, her face red, her lips swollen from sucking him, her hair a wild nimbus of curls, she looked more beautiful than he'd ever seen her—but didn't he think that every time he saw her like this, or just maybe every time he saw her after they'd been apart for a while?

That sounded suspiciously emotional, and it could have been scary, but it was hard to be scared when he felt so good, and besides, Chloe really *was* all that.

He moved one hand between their bodies, found her slick, swollen clit, and began to stroke. Her pussy tightened, and she swiveled her hips in just the right way that he couldn't hold back any longer.

He took over the rhythm from her, and she didn't argue, and things got very intense and noisy enough that Evenrude, alarmed from doggy dreams, started yapping.

After they collapsed in a sated heap, he had enough wits to put out his hand and let Evenrude slide her head under for a reassuring scritch. Mollified, she hopped up on the other end of the sofa, and he and Chloe detangled and staggered to the bedroom, where Chloe curled up on him and promptly fell into the sleep of the well-fucked.

Brand edged towards dozing off, but uneasy thoughts he couldn't pin down kept him from quite getting there.

Something about his sister.

But Sands was doing great. She and Ray had gotten through a pretty major crisis and they seemed stronger than ever for it. Ray was good for her. Hell, Chloe was good for her; Chloe, not Brand, had been the one to diffuse this particular bomb.

Maybe that was what was bothering him?

That was just plain dumb...but he thought it might have some truth to it.

That didn't make it any less dumb. Sandrine would always be his baby sister and he'd always be protective of her, but if Chloe was right and Sands was stronger than he realized—and it looked like Chloe might be right— that was a good thing. It was one thing to take care of your little sister because you loved her, but it was good if she didn't actually *need* so much care, and if she had other people she could lean on when things got rough.

Definitely a good thing.

So why did he feel a little sad?

"Because you're an asshole," he muttered to himself, and snuggled closer to Chloe. If an armful of warm woman who smelled like recently shared sex didn't shake him out of his weird mood, nothing would.

Chapter 31

The screenwriter for Brand's current project was having too much fun playing with science fiction clichés, and the wicked Rugulator warlord's lines were getting stuck in his head, apt to pop out at the least appropriate times possible.

All day, for instance Brand had been having a hard time not calling Chloe, cackling maniacally and saying "My evil plan is coming together" in a tinny Rugulator voice before hanging up. (A dumb line, but with Alan Rickman voicing it in the movie, it would probably be brilliant. Brand, however, was less Alan Rickman than Jordan from Concepts in his acting abilities, and he knew he'd sound like a dork.)

And while it might be funny to start the conversation like that, he wanted a slightly less geeky way to tell Chloe the good news that he'd figured out a way to bring her amazing culinary skills to the attention of Gerard DesJardins and get her the job she deserved.

Just sending a résumé wouldn't do the trick. DesJardins had to taste her food and be wowed. And Brand had figured out just the way to do it.

This wasn't fixing anything, just like she'd told him not to. He wasn't going anywhere near her kitchen, physically or metaphorically. He was just…facilitating. Setting up a situation where the right people would be in the right place at the right time. It would be up to Chloe to do her magic, the thing she was brilliant at doing.

(Well, she was brilliant at any number of things. His cock twitched in remembered admiration of several of them. But in this case, he meant cooking.)

Now…how to tell Chloe?

His vision of the big reveal involved champagne and a beautiful dinner, but realistically she'd end up cooking the beautiful dinner herself if, in fact, they could manage to eat dinner together at all. He'd worked late every night that week and had lost a few hours of a perfectly good Saturday morning he could have spent with Chloe to Rugulator crises. And Chloe's Saturday nights usually ended up consumed by Sandrine, although he couldn't remember if his sister was entertaining tonight.

But at least he had a chance to pick up a bottle of champagne (already chilled) on the way home.

The words were bubbling up inside him as he drove home. He rehearsed different phrasings in his head.

I have great news?

How would you like *not* to deal with my sister's diets du jour and Ray's fashion faux pas anymore?

Or how about this one: Our troubles are over?

Yeah, he kind of liked the ring of that one.

A bit melodramatic, but it would get her attention. And damn it, with all the drama he had to put up with, didn't he deserve a chance to be dramatic himself, even just joking around?

Then, while Chloe stood there flabbergasted and curious, he'd explain. Or maybe while she lay there, because he couldn't help but imagine the conversation taking place between rounds one and two of hot, sweaty sex.

Dammit, why did the big reveal always go so easily in the movies?

*

He found her sitting on the little patio of the guest house, staring into space and absently petting Evenrude. (The dog was blissful, her stumpy tail wagging, but she still seemed to have one ear cocked and one eye open

SOPHIE MOUETTE

for peacocks. Poor Evenrude.) Chloe looked drained, and glancing over her shoulder at the empty dish in front of her, he saw she'd been eating mac-and-cheese.

Remembering the last time he'd seen mac-and-cheese in her general vicinity, he shuddered inwardly. She'd had a salad with it, though so things weren't an absolute disaster. (She'd explained the whole Chloe Comfort-Food Scale after the day of mac-and-cheese and tiaras. Apparently you don't eat vegetables when your life is really falling apart, except maybe in the form of tomato sauce on pizza or in lasagna. Or mashed potatoes, but he guessed things hadn't descended to that level.)

He snuck up behind her, planted a kiss on top of her curly head, then snaked the champagne bottle around to the table in front of her.

She made a small happy noise, but not happy enough. It was nice champagne, not the Dom Pérignon his sister bought, but good enough that it ought to draw a squee of interest, especially when it was just a random Saturday afternoon with no obvious reason for champagne involvement.

Instead, she sighed.

"What's my sister up to now?" he asked. "Do I need to talk to her? Can't let one of my favorite women get away making the other miserable."

"It's food-related and I've got it under control," Chloe said, leaning back against him. "Besides, I think it's one of those things you would have fixed, like, ten years ago if it was fixable. Or her therapist would have. Or the two of you tag-teaming her. I think it's just one of those places where Sandrine is permanently broken and unfortunately I have to deal with it."

"Uh-oh. At least tell me and get it out of your system."

Chloe threw her hands up in the air and flailed them around, narrowly missing smacking him. "She gained a pound and a half! She can't possibly start shooting her new movie like this! In fact, she may have to give up acting altogether because she refuses to be stuck with fat-chick roles! She can't go out in public because someone might take a picture and then she'd be mocked in the press! And it's all my fault! Didn't I tell her comfort food had no calories if you're upset enough you really need it? How dare I lie to her?"

The slightly psychotic voice wasn't spot-on Sandrine, but close enough he'd have been able to figure it out even if he'd had no idea who "she" was.

"She was serious, like that pound and a half was ruining her life, and seriously mad at me, like I'd put a gun to her head and made her eat. Do you remember any guns being involved, Brand? Because I don't. Just a spoon and a big hot fudge sundae."

"I'm only an ignorant male, but I can't see where gaining a pound and a half is such a tragedy when you're a size 2…."

"Size 0, but who's counting? I think it's worse for skinny women. For me, a pound and a half is no big deal, but Sandrine…that's like *Evenrude* gaining a pound and a half, because there's so little there to start with." She rumpled the corgi's black and tan coat.

Evenrude, Brand thought, had actually lost a little weight over the past couple of months, maybe the mythical pound and a half his sister swore she'd gained. (Where did Sandrine think it was hiding, anyway? Her hair?) Must be all the exercise 'Rude got stalking the peacocks.

Chloe sighed, went from patting the dog to patting the champagne. "I don't know what the occasion is, but this was a brilliant idea. I really, really needed a pick-me-up and I'm all out of chocolate and don't have the energy to go out for more. She said she's back on the raw foods diet since she's sooooo faaaat now, and so I started replanning all the menus for the week. That one's no fun at all for me—how much can I do that's interesting, except maybe a nice ceviche or carpaccio, and she doesn't really *like* raw meat and hasn't been eating fish? Plus I end up making at least two dinners because Ray needs, oh, protein and carbs and more calories than a rabbit needs to sustain life.

"And then she went to a meeting with her agent and came back saying he said she looked great as always, but could she try to gain a few pounds for the new movie because it's Victorian and they want a more voluptuous look. Then she asked me to make seafood fettuccine Alfredo for dinner because she loved it and hadn't let herself enjoy it for ages and whee, now she had a good excuse. And of course I'd redone all the menus for the raw foods diet, *and* I haven't ordered any seafood in ages since the last I knew, she wasn't eating it. Whole big runaround. Again. Gah."

She heaved a sigh, leaned back against him, looked up, smiled a little. "Sorry. Ranting again. Your sister means well in her own space-muffin way." She made the universal *cuckoo for Cocoa Puffs* spinning-her-hand-next-to-her-ear gesture. He'd never heard *space muffin* before, but it described Sandrine to a T. Fruits and nuts and a lot of star-studded vacuum.

"And then, after playing the cosmic muffin," Chloe added, "she asked me if I knew anything about Victorian eating habits—asked some really detailed, smart questions about what a fancy Victorian dinner would be like and what foods were and weren't available, because there was a banquet scene in the script but she couldn't imagine herself into the setting, whatever that means. Then she asked if I could make a couple of Victorian-style meals to help her get into the mood for the part. Which Ray will love because they were really big on meat and potatoes and dessert and booze if I'm remembering my culinary history classes correctly. But does she always get so deep into her roles?"

"Just be glad she's not playing an assassin this time." Brand shuddered. Chloe thought it was best not to ask.

"I've gotten to care about her," Chloe said. "But working for her is making me old and grumpy before my time. And alcoholic. And I don't mean as in simply drinking too much, I mean as in I'm drinking so much my bloodstream is turning into an alcohol stream."

Well, that sounded like his opening. "What if I told you that you might not have to work for Sandrine much longer?"

"I'd say you're forgetting those Rugulator time machines you're designing only work in the movie. But if you figure out a way to get the time-travel thing to work for real, I think I could find some fun ways to show my appreciation. Especially if it could make our nights off longer, too." She turned and wrapped her arms around him, pressing her body against him until he almost lost track of what he was going to say because of the far more immediately entertaining possibilities it brought to mind.

She looked up, stretched a bit to kiss him.

Best idea he'd heard in a while. He met her halfway.

Her lips were soft and yielding and opened for him, her tongue danced with his, and she stretched up onto her tiptoes so she could reach better. He thought about scooping her up into his arms—he was no Ray, but Chloe was pretty scoopable, at least over short distances—carrying her into the cottage, and seeing how many ways he could take her mind off her troubles. (It might embarrass Luanna a little if she was home, but hey, Luanna was a big girl. She could cope.)

No, Chloe was seriously down and needed a glimmer of hope before she'd probably even be interested in making the beast with two backs. He'd tell her the good news first.

They heard a noise in the distance—maybe Ray out for a run, maybe a gardener, maybe just a peacock. Almost certainly not Sandrine, who rarely ventured outside in daylight lest damaging UV rays instantly age her skin. But they were both still aware of it.

Yes, he'd definitely tell her now. Dammit, he wanted to be able to give his girl-friend, his lover, his whatever-she-was and whatever-he-hoped-she-would-be, a hug and a kiss when he wanted to and not worry about making Chloe look unprofessional or causing Sandrine to worry she was being deserted.

"It's not a time machine," he said, feeling so proud that if he'd had a peacock's tail, he'd have fanned it, "but it's almost as good. I got Sandrine to invite Gerard DesJardins to her birthday party."

Chloe took another step back. Blinked twice, in a very considering way. He couldn't really tell what was happening with her body language, and that kind of scared him.

She looked like she might be shaking, but that could mean anything from "I'm so excited I can't contain myself" to "Gerard DesJardins is a scary rude Frenchman even if he is a genius and I'm having flashbacks" to "Can we go inside and get back to the necking, please? We stopped just when things were getting interesting."

"You did *what*?" she finally said.

"Got him invited to the party. Sandrine ran into him at an art gallery opening and was bragging on her wonderful personal chef whom he'd helped train and you know Sandrine...she was teasing him that you might be better than he was and he said he was looking for culinary rock stars—his words, which she quoted in this spot-on old French guy accent—and he might just have to steal you away. So when she told me the story, I convinced her to invite him."

"You did what?" Chloe repeated. "Aside from the sheer weirdness of Sandrine being cute at Monsieur DesJardins and him playing along—because the man may be French, but he's not the type to soften for a pretty face—I'm not believing I heard what I think I just heard."

Brand started getting more excited on her behalf. "This is perfect! His assistant's assistant's assistant might not recognize your name on a résumé, but once he actually tastes your cooking and sees how well you work under pressure, he'd be crazy not to consider you. I've eaten in some of the best restaurants in the country, thanks to Sandrine, and you're easily in their league. And once he spends any time with my beloved sister, Monsieur DesJardins will know how well you can handle stressful situations."

"You. Did. *What?*" she repeated yet again, and it finally registered in a way that the other times hadn't. This time she also crossed her arms on her chest and glared.

"I...uh... Oh, shit." Brand's stomach did some kind of elaborate snow-boarding move involving a 360-degree turn and a back flip. He recognized that posture. That posture meant a fight was coming, like a deadly avalanche he couldn't outrun, and for the life of him he couldn't see why.

Okay, he could maybe guess why. But it still didn't make sense to him.

"What made you think it was a good idea to poke your nose into my career, Brand? I'm perfectly capable of getting a job on my own, especially now that I can put on my résumé that I worked for Sandrine Moss so I have LA experience and know what Hollywood people expect. I know you're trying to help, but I don't need help. You didn't even ask me what I thought about it."

Well, no. He hadn't. "I wanted to surprise you," he muttered, suspecting it sounded pretty lame, even though it was true. Maybe especially because it was true, because now he realized it had been a bad idea. A good bad idea, but nevertheless a bad idea if it got her this mad.

"Did it ever occur to you that maybe I had a plan myself to get his attention when I was actually, oh, available to work for him?"

"Do you?"

"I've been working on it." That would be a *no*, he suspected, but he wasn't about to mention it to her right now. As it was, she looked like a small, cute, curvy dragon, steam all but coming out her nostrils. Any misstep on his part might cause her to sprout wings and actually breathe fire.

Being flamed for no reason—damn it, it *was* a good idea, even if maybe surprising her wasn't—was bad enough. Being literally incinerated wasn't going to work for him at all.

"Besides, you seem to have forgotten one important little detail," she went on. "He's opening next month, and I'm still under contract to your sister. I'm good. I know I'm good. But I'm not good enough to hold up opening your restaurant for. Especially not if your name is Gerard DesJardins and you're opening your LA restaurant so your regular customers don't have to fly their private jets over to Paris for dinner."

Luckily, Brand had thought about that—and had managed to phrase the question so his sister thought the solution was her own brilliant idea. "Sandrine thinks it might be good mutual PR if he hired the chef she 'discovered.'" He made air quotes, hoping that made it clear that he knew it was all Chloe's talent, not Sandrine's impulsive decision to hire her, that mattered. "They'll get name-dropped in connection with each other for a while and they'll both get more press. And you'd be able to get out of your contract and get out of here."

Which was really the point. Why couldn't she see that once they got her out of here, she'd enjoy her work much more? And they could relax and be open and see where this sort-of-a-relationship might go if they could really give it a chance?

"I signed a six-month contract, Brand. Amazing as it seems, I've been here roughly three. I have a responsibility to fulfill it."

"Sandrine basically blackmailed you…."

She snorted in what he suspected was self-disgust. "Yeah, she did, but it's still my signature on the stupid thing. It's not just a responsibility to her and Ray, although I honestly don't want to leave them in the lurch. It's a responsibility to myself, a matter of honor. Did you really think I was the kind of person who wouldn't keep my word?"

Brand blinked. Tried to think of a response. Failed. "Honor" wasn't a word he'd heard a lot in Hollywood, except in movie scripts. Not that some people weren't perfectly honorable—it just wasn't something you talked about.

One more thing to admire about her, except, of course, that it was currently blowing up in his face.

"I…I'm sorry," he finally said. "I didn't mean it that way. God, this is not going right. Not even a little right. I didn't mean any kind of slight on your character. I was just…."

"Just trying to help, I know. Well, I don't need help, Brand. I've already got brothers, and even they know better than to muck around with my work."

"But I thought if—"

She cut him off again. "They get their grubby little fingers in every other part of my life, sure, but they trust me to manage my own career. They know I'm good enough to make it on my own, and even when I was just getting started and Dad and Carl could have called in some favors at some of the big restaurants in Providence, they didn't. I'd appreciate the same courtesy from you."

He opened his mouth to try to explain, to try to make it clear (why couldn't she see it? It was so obvious!) that this was only somewhat about her career, and certainly not about him thinking she wasn't good enough or smart enough or anything enough to make it on her own. This was, as much as anything, because Hollywood relationships were stressful enough without the added weirdness of her working for his sister and them living in the same place but not exactly together. The fact that it was an amazing job opportunity was just the frosting on the cake.

The words were right there. He thought he could make her understand.

But even before he could get out the starting "Chloe," she turned and started to walk away, dragging Evenrude behind her.

The dog sat down, clearly not interested in going inside when her beloved peacocks could be just about to round the corner and profess their undying love for her. Chloe shrugged as if to say *Fine. Be that way.* and literally dragged the dog, letting her butt skid along the flagstones until she gave up and started trotting to catch up.

"Where are you going?" he asked.

"Inside. Away from you. I need some time to think, Brand, because if we try to keep talking right now I may tell you to get out of my life if you can't stop interfering with it, and I don't want to do that. At least not unless I'm sure I really, really mean it."

The cottage door slammed.

She'd left the champagne behind, and for a second, Brand contemplated taking it back.

But that seemed rude, since it had been a gift for her. And besides, champagne was for celebrating with someone you loved, not for solitary trying-to-figure-out-if-you'd-just-been-dumped, and if so, why.

He set it gently on the stoop and headed back to his own house.

*

The bottle of tequila was calling Brand's name.

He told it to shut up.

Brand, Brand, have a drink, it repeated its vaguely Mexican-accented siren song. *You know you want to.*

Well dammit, of course he wanted to. When faced with a relationship crisis, real men employed tequila. A lot of tequila. He had Ray Stark's example to prove it. (Never mind that Ray had been wearing a dress for at least part of the time. He could still be a role model of American masculinity. Chloe said so.)

The problem with tequila was that he knew it would just make him crankier. Not to mention totally robbing him of any ability to figure out what he'd done wrong, if he'd done anything wrong, and what he might do to fix it.

He'd spent a good chunk of the afternoon trying to figure it out, alternately brooding and swimming. The swimming worked him out of wallowing in utter self-pity and through the stage of being mad at Chloe for being mad at him. He was pretty proud of himself, actually, that he'd managed not stay for more than a few minutes in the blaming-his-sister stage. Okay, it helped that the only thing that even his most pissy, irrational, protective-of-Chloe self could pin on Sands was throwing a little more stress into the mix that maybe caused Chloe to get madder faster.

He'd worked on to the kicking-himself stage before he decided he wasn't getting anywhere on his own.

Distraction might help.

Maybe he'd call Ray. And see if he'd bring more tequila.

Chapter 32

"Yoo-hoo! We're here!"

Sandrine swept into the guest cottage, clutching a bottle of high-end tequila and being trailed by Olive. Ray staggered in just behind them, carrying a large trunk. A *Coach* trunk. Chloe hadn't known Coach made trunks, but what did she know? She couldn't afford a Coach wallet.

"Hey," Chloe said to Ray. "This is a *girls'* night. Not that you don't dress like us sometimes, but you still have the wrong equipment."

"I'll be out of your way in a minute," he promised. He set the trunk down on the living room coffee table with a thunk. "I wouldn't dream of crashing the party. Besides, Brand and I have a date to watch action films, drink beer, burp, and scratch ourselves. You know, a guys' night."

"As long as it doesn't involve strippers," Sandrine said, her tone so menacing that Chloe retreated to the kitchen to check on the goat-cheese rounds toasting in the oven.

"Damn," she heard Ray said amiably. "I'd better call Brand and tell him to cancel Suzie's Floozies. Bye, girls."

Olive followed Chloe into the kitchen. "I brought spinach-artichoke dip. Is that okay?"

"That's great!" Chloe said, even though it was weird that Olive seemed to be kowtowing to *her*. "There's a serving bowl in there." She pointed to a cupboard with her toe.

Soon they were all ensconced in the living room, margaritas in hand and plates of food in their laps. Sandrine flung open the trunk.

"Tiaras for everyone!" she said, passing them out.

"What's the rest of all that?" Luanna asked, her radar obviously honing in on the bright fabrics.

"Oh, some clothes and stuff I never wear anymore," Sandrine said. "I thought it might be fun to try stuff on."

Luanna looked down at her voluptuous figure and sighed. "Probably nothing's going to fit me."

Sandrine's eyes sparkled. "There are sho-oes."

"Shoes?!" Chloe and Luanna dove for the trunk.

Most of the clothes didn't fit Chloe, either, but a few of the more diaphanous tops and looser outerwear worked pretty well. Even though there was nothing more than a poncho and some shoes that Luanna could wear, she was the most enthusiastic because she recognized the designers and appreciated the quality and design.

Olive was mostly quiet, wearing a tiara with dignity and occasionally letting loose with an uncharacteristic giggle.

Of course, it went all downhill from there, with Chloe and Luanna running to their bedrooms and hauling out clothes for Sandrine and Olive (who could fit in a few of Luanna's things) to try on. At some point there was dancing. Plus Chloe kept busy blending more margaritas and bringing out more munchies, prompting Olive to question whether there was some sort of portal in the kitchen out of which Chloe kept pulling the food.

Olive was definitely more fun after a couple of margaritas.

"Tonight, forget your cares and relax with friends," her horoscope had said. "What could possibly go wrong?"

It had seemed like good advice at the time. She should have known better.

They started watching *Breakfast at Tiffany's*, but since they'd all seen it before, they started talking halfway through and never really got back to it. But it got them talking about relationships…

…the *last* thing Chloe wanted to think about, much less talk about.

Damn Brand's stubborn pig-headedness. Damn his "but I want to make it all better" attitude, which really translated to "I don't think you're capable of handling things yourself, so I'll just swoop in and take care of you."

It was amazing he hadn't patted her and said, "Don't you worry your little head about it, pretty lady."

That gave her a mental image of Brand in a cowboy outfit, and she had to admit, the chaps were awfully hot.

Wait, wasn't she mad at him? She squinted at her margarita glass. How many of these damn things had she had, anyway?

"Well, there's nothing I can say about relationships," Luanna was saying. "It's been so long since I was in one, I barely remember that I'm supposed to hide when I'm shaving my legs or peeing."

Sandrine shook some salt onto her hand, licked it, and took a shot directly from the bottle of tequila. She followed it with a dainty sip from the dregs of her margarita.

"Ray and I are doing really well," she said. "I've decided I just don't care about his proc—procill—prociv—thing with women's panties. I mean, I care, but just because I care about him. If it makes him happy, then I'm happy. Right?"

"Good for you," Chloe said. "That's a very healthy attitude."

"Olive, what about you?" Luanna asked. She had an ability to be pushy but not sound pushy because of her soft Southern accent or something. "Spill the beans."

Olive smiled. "I prefer to be a woman of mystery." Then she hiccupped, ruining her stately air.

"Okay, so Chloe, it's up to you," Luanna said. "What's the latest with you and Hunky Pool Boy/Bartender?"

"Luanna!" Chloe hissed, gesturing at Sandrine. "Not appropriate."

"Oh honey, that's okay," Sandrine said, waving a slender hand. "I haven't seen Brand so happy in a long time. You guys must be great together."

"Um," Chloe said. "Um. I…Is it really okay to talk about it? Because Brand kind of wants to keep it really low-key and not obvious."

"Yeah, what is it with that?" Sandrine asked. "Does he think I'm going to scare all his girlfriends away? Am I really that scary? I mean, it's not like I'm some shotgun-toting protective father."

"In Louisiana, we have our own shotguns," Luanna commented to no one in particular.

"Well…" Chloe was almost tipsy enough to say that Sandrine had apparently sabotaged some of Brand's prior relationships. Almost. Not quite. And the picture of Sandrine with a shotgun was more than a little bit scary. Especially considering what Brand had said about her really getting into the assassin role.

What was even scarier was that Sandrine seemed to read her mind. "Oh, did he say something about Heidi and Nadia? I don't do that anymore." She waved her hand dismissively. (It would have looked positively elegant if it wasn't the hand holding her glass, which dripped onto the carpet.) "Besides, Nadia wasn't right for him, and Heidi was just plain evil. But…" She gestured again with the glass. "You're cool. And you're both kind of glowing, which I like. Only not so much tonight."

It was Chloe's turn to do a tequila shot. She winced as the liquor burned its way down her gullet.

"He's driving me crazy," she admitted. It probably was a really, really bad idea to badmouth Brand in front of his sister, who had the potential to flip into fruit bat mode at any second (although she'd been a lot of fun tonight so far), but the tequila had loosened her tongue. She felt the need to vent, and where better to vent at a girls' night, surrounded by sympathetic girls who'd hold your hand and lie to you that it would all get better?

"First of all, it's the whole 'don't upset Sandrine' thing." She held out a hand to Sandrine. "Please don't be angry. He worries about you. He doesn't want to do anything to upset you."

Sandrine clutched her head in her hands, pulling at her hair in a dramatic gesture Chloe was sure she'd seen her do in *Princess of Nowhere*. "*When* is he going to stop treating me with kid gloves? I'm not fourteen anymore!"

"He loves you, dear," Olive said, patting Sandrine on the arm. "We all treat you with kid gloves because we love you."

Sandrine half-glared, half-smiled-fondly at her. "But I pay you exorbitant amounts of money to treat me with kid gloves. Brand's my brother. It's different. It's starting to drive me crazy."

"He's not much different than my brothers," Chloe said. "Imagine if there were five of Brand, all trying to take care of you."

"Ooh, five of Brand!" Luanna said. "Enough to share!"

Without missing a beat, Chloe reached out and smacked her friend on the arm.

"You said 'first of all,'" Olive pointed out. She paused to suck on a wedge of lime. (Olive doing tequila shots was a little disturbing in itself, but Chloe was too wibbly to really care anymore. Plus there was the fact that Olive had invaded her kitchen and cut up limes. Chloe decided not to stress about it.) "What's the next thing?"

"You've been really cranky lately," Luanna chimed in. "It's been obvious something's wrong."

"Oh, *thanks*," Chloe said. She put a note of sarcasm in her voice (well, she tried to, anyway), but inside she felt awfully guilty. The last thing she wanted to do was let her personal problems affect her friendships.

"Spill," Sandrine said, pressing a shot glass into her hand.

Chloe obligingly went for the salt and then knocked back the tequila, her eyes watering by the time she reached for the lime. "He's too fucking controlling," she said. Wow, did that really come out of her mouth?

"Brand?" Luanna said. "He seems so mellow."

"Oh, he's totally pulling the He-Man thing," Chloe complained. "Okay, it's one thing if he keeps leaping up to get me another bottle of water or a washcloth to—er, nevermind. It's entirely another for him to start trying to dictate how I handle my career. That's totally off-limits, and he should know that. I don't try to mess with his job, do I?"

There was a moment of silence, broken only by Bowling for Soup's "1985" on the stereo. Olive bounced quietly to the beat.

Then Sandrine said in a small voice, "Oh. This is about Gerard DesJardins, isn't it?"

Miserably, Chloe nodded.

"He's only doing it because he loves you," Sandrine said.

Love. Chloe snorted tequila up her nose. Holy crap it burned. It was astonishing just how much that hurt. Her sinuses would never, ever be the same.

"She's right," Luanna said.

"It's so obvious," Olive said.

"My family loves me," Chloe said, grasping for some level of normality in a world gone wildly mad, "and they know better than to mess with my career."

"Your family has had the benefit of years of experience with you," Luanna said. "Brand's still new at this. He's just trying to make you happy. I think it's sweet."

"It's just one person to add to the guest list," Sandrine said. "It's so not a big deal."

Sandrine was missing the point, but Chloe thought it was best not to point that out. Just as not mentioning that Sandrine could lose her as her personal chef was the wisest course of action by far. She clasped her suddenly cold hands together.

"He still stepped way over the line," she said.

"People in love do stupid things," Olive said. She curled up in the easy chair, cradling the bottle of tequila, although it didn't look like she was still drinking. "He's messing up, you've got to talk to him about it."

"But he's so irrational when I talk to him!" Chloe protested.

He really wasn't, that evil voice in her head pointed out. He usually tried to be very calm and logical and rational, and she was the one who got a little bent out of shape.

That wasn't the problem, though. Well, it was part of the problem.

The biggest problem was that she was pretty sure she loved him, too.

Meep.

Oh crap, where did come from?

It took everything in Chloe's power to resist the urge to run into the other room and hide under the bed. Of course. She got so worked up about Brand trying to be over-helpful because she cared about him so much.

No, admit it. Say the words.

Because she loved him.

If she loved him, then his make-everything-better attitude was scarier to the nth power. She loved her family, but she'd moved across the country to get away from them, to live her own life and not have them trying to meddle in everything (except her career) in an innocent and loving attempt to "help."

She couldn't have Brand as a large, permanent fixture in her life if he was going to spend all his time sheltering her and taking care of her just like her family tried to do. Like he did to Sandrine.

"Chloe, you okay?" Luanna asked. "You've turned kind of green."

"If I say something, do you all swear it won't leave this room?" Chloe asked.

They all nodded, hands on hearts.

"I love Brand, too," she said, and burst into tears.

Chapter 33

The next thing she knew, there was an arm around her and a hand patting her knee and a bowl of Godiva Belgian dark chocolate ice cream being pressed into her grasp along with a wad of tissues. It was kind of weird, everyone diving in to do something for her and making her feel useless. She was too tipsy to protest.

She'd point it out to them later.

"I don't want to love him," she said. "I don't want him to love me. This can never work out. He's doing exactly what my family did that made me move out here. I love them, but I can't live near them. How could I possibly live with Brand?"

"One day at a time, dear," Olive said. "You find a balance. Relationships are about compromise."

"There are always bumpy patches," Sandrine said. "You have to step back and figure out what's really important. If you really love him, you can work through just about anything. Look at Ray and me. We're role models. You said so yourself."

Chloe was kind of amazed at just how much she'd said had actually sunk in for Sandrine.

"I guess it seems really, really insurmountable," she said. "Opposites attracting is only supposed to happen in movies."

"Oh, I'm not so sure about that," Luanna said. "Look at my parents."

Well, she did have a point there. Luanna's mother was a flamboyant, Southern-to-the-core Sweet Potato Queen, whereas her father was a soft-spoken, genteel Louisiana gentleman. It worked, as near as anybody could tell—they'd been married thirty years, at any rate.

Chloe wiped her eyes and ate a big spoonful of astonishingly good ice cream. "I guess I don't understand how it could work, but it's not like we're making plans for the future. If he backs off and lets me *have* a future and get my career in order the way I want to, I guess we can worry about it then. The kitchen's off-limits when it comes to my job. That's non-negotiable."

"I'm sure you'll be able to work it out," Luanna said. "You're the mistress of fixing things."

Maybe. This was going to be a tough one.

"Ooh, look!" Sandrine said, grabbing for the remote so she could un-mute the TV. "*Love in a Bubble*. My hair is just so cute in this one!"

Chloe retreated to the bathroom to clean up and take care of an over-abundance of margaritas and tequila in her bladder. She splashed cool water on her face, and stared at her reflection in the mirror. She didn't *look* any different, which seemed impossible considering how completely different she felt.

Love. It had snuck up on her under the weirdest of circumstances, blindsiding her when she was in the middle of dealing with work and Sandrine and Ray and Evenrude. No wonder she hadn't seen it coming.

Wonderingly, she traced her forefinger across her lower lip.

She was in love. As scary as it was, it felt pretty amazing.

She had a feeling she was still going to have an awful lot of sleepless nights over it, though.

*

"So they're having girls' night? Why does this scare me so much?" Brand shuddered theatrically, imagining the margarita-sodden conversations that must be taking place at the guest cottage.

Ray laughed, his deep basso rumble practically shaking the house. "My girlfriend who is also your sister is getting drunk with your girlfriend who is your sister's personal chef, and for some reason Olive is involved. If this doesn't terrify you beyond all reason, you are a braver man than I am."

"And Luanna's there, too, who knows all your deep dark secrets—including your measurements."

Ray's brown eyes went wide. "The horror. The horror," he said, doing a credible impression of Marlon Brando in *Apocalypse Now* that probably would have surprised his agent.

After a millisecond, Brand asked the question that was really on his mind. "What do you suppose they're talking about over there, anyway?" Okay, that wasn't the real question. The real question was *Think they're over there ripping me a new one?*, but that would require too much explanation.

"Clothes, probably. Sandrine was cleaning her closet. None of her stuff fits me," Ray added wistfully, "but sometimes she lets me pet it."

That was a bit of a conversation-stopper as far as Brand was concerned, so he did what any right-thinking American male would do. "Beer or tequila?"

"Are we gonna watch a movie with explosions and belch like I told the girls, or is it my turn to listen while someone else spills his guts? You didn't sound so great when you called, and Chloe seemed a little off, too. That's gotta be why they're doing girls' night."

Brand thought about lying, but realized there wasn't much point. Ray was pretty damn sharp—which was probably what allowed him to handle Sandrine's mercurial moods. "I think we're looking at explosions and belching while I decide if I can talk about it. Today got weird, Ray. I can't decide if she's crazy or I am."

"Both," Ray said, nodding sagely.

"Yeah, we probably both are."

"I was thinking more of both beer *and* tequila, but that, too."

Ray flopped onto the sofa, taking up more of the big black beast than anyone had a right to, his long legs extending most of the way across the room. Brand sprawled in the lounger. For close to two hours, they fast-forwarded through to the good scenes (that is, the car chases, shoot-outs, fight scenes, and hot special effects, with occasional pauses for topless women) in several favorite films. The companionable silence was broken only by Brand explaining how some neat CGI moment was done or Ray trying to figure out the stunts.

And, of course, by "Pass the tequila."

Brand wasn't drinking all that much, just maintaining a light buzz that took the edge off his misery, but the cool, hoppy beer and the bite of the tequila tasted really good. Ray seemed completely unaffected, but that didn't mean he hadn't been drinking, just that he was an unnaturally large man with a superhuman metabolism.

And possibly fuchsia satin panties, Brand's hindbrain thought wickedly. His forebrain hadn't had enough to drink yet to really handle that thought.

Finally Brand couldn't stand it anymore. "Chloe's mad at me. Really mad. And I was just trying to do something nice for her."

"Safer to wrestle tigers, man. What did you do?" Ray handed him the tequila without being asked.

Pretty harsh, considering Ray *had* wrestled a tiger in *East Meets West* and still had some scars to prove it.

"She really wants to work for Gerard DesJardins, and thanks to Sandrine, I was able to give her a chance to show her stuff to him and now she's ready to kill me. No offense to you and Sandrine, but she never really wanted to be a personal chef. Not even to you guys." (Probably especially not to them, but he wasn't about to say that.)

"None taken, man. She deserves to cook for a bigger audience. I'd have done it if I'd thought of it. So that's a problem why?"

"Says I'm interfering with her life too much, being too controlling. She pretty much said I was treating her like I do Sandrine, and like her big brothers treat her." His thoughts took a tangent. "Do you think I overprotect Sandrine, Ray? Chloe thinks I do."

Ray didn't answer immediately, which was pretty much an answer in itself. Something else to consider once he'd solved the more critical problem of Chloe having an urge to make Rocky Mountain oysters with some of his favorite body parts.

What Ray actually said was, "Gotta watch the brotherly tendencies. I've seen how Chloe looks at you, and it's not the way you look at a big brother, so don't act like one."

"I was hoping you'd say she was being unreasonable."

Ray shrugged, which was kind of like seeing a mountain shrug. "I wasn't there. Don't know what you said, don't know what she said. But she's not like Sandrine. Sandrine needs protection." He screwed up his face thoughtfully. "Maybe not as much as you and I think—she's been dealing really well with…uh, with me. But Chloe's like a rock. Really stable and grounded and independent and all that stuff Sandrine isn't. She's like my mom." A slight pause. "Only a lot cuter."

"Watch it," Brand growled with mock menace, and threw a couch cushion.

"If I didn't think she was cuter than my mom, you'd worry." Ray deflected the cushion as if he were batting away an annoying gnat.

"So yeah," he went on—this was a lot of talking for Ray, and Brand was surprised—"I see where you messed up. Guys like you and me, we want to do nice things for people we care about, but we've gotta back off sometimes. I've learned not to try to take care of my mom too much, even though I have more money than I know what to do with and she hasn't had the easiest life. And I know better than to mess with Sandrine's work, and she *likes* other people taking care of stuff for her, which Chloe doesn't. And I know you're smarter than me. So why the dumbness?"

That, *that* was the question. "I thought she'd like the opportunity. I thought she'd like a chance to… Oh shit."

Again, Ray handed him the tequila without being asked.

"I don't think she got the point. I don't think I *made* the point, so of course she didn't get it. It's not about her career at all. I can see why she thought so, but what I really wanted was to make it so we didn't have to tiptoe around Sandrine." He took a huge slug of tequila, shuddering as the spirit rampaged through him.

"So stop tiptoeing. You know Sandrine loves a good love story."

He'd never thought of it that way. "Although it's not exactly a…oh shit, shit, shit. It is. I think I love her, and I just managed to push *all* her buttons including the big red Nuclear Detonation one. She's going to fucking kill me."

"Man," Ray rumbled pityingly, "you really screwed the pooch on this one."

Chapter 34

" The choices that frighten you are probably the right ones." That was what today's horoscope said. It went on after that, but Chloe pretty much threw the paper across the room after that line, deciding that her head hurt too much already without spooky synchronicity involving the damn astrology column.

Now, making brunch, she was wondering if she should read the rest. Astrology was utter nonsense, but if some weird chance made the tag line that spot-on, maybe it would have some useful advice.

"Morning," Brand said from the kitchen door, sounding very, very tentative.

It was more like afternoon than morning, but everyone in the household (with the exception of Ray, who seemed none the worse for wear) had been moving slowly and speaking more softly than usual, and no one had gotten up on time to actually see much of morning. Chloe couldn't imagine why. Not.

"Get out of my kitchen," she said, but without any real conviction. "Can't you see I'm trying to work around here?"

She turned her back on him, returned to chopping vegetables for the frittata. (If Sandrine's beauty and talent weren't enough of a genetic gift, she could apparently wake up from a night of injudicious snacking and serious drinking a little weary and headachy, but able to eat.)

Chloe couldn't say the same. A few extra hours of sleep, a lot of water, some orange juice, and a lot of ibuprofen had helped, but the lingering headache was adding to her grumpiness, and having to look at food wasn't doing much to add to her overall level of joy.

But mostly what was making her grumpy was that she wanted to put down her knife, throw her arms around Brand, and start apologizing.

And dammit, she hadn't even done anything wrong.

Okay, maybe she'd overreacted. Wouldn't be the first time; she'd bitten her brothers' heads off more than once, not to mention her poor dad, who'd been a bit shocked to learn she even knew some of those words, in either English *or* Portuguese.

But that had been different. Family was family. You might blow up at each other—hell, that was pretty much guaranteed—but you'd always forgive each other.

No saying whether that would work with a newish, still tentative boyfriend-relationship-thing.

And besides, it was really his fault. Wasn't it? He'd crossed a line that any smart, modern man should know better than to cross.

But she loved him. And she had reason to believe that he loved her. Didn't that mean something?

Yes: that he was even more likely to try to take care of her in pushing-around sorts of ways and she might even let him get away with it if she wasn't careful. Bad, bad, bad.

He was still there. She knew it. She could feel his gaze boring into her back like a corkscrew into a cork.

It was going to distract her if she didn't do something. Make her likely to cut herself or set the place on fire. She sighed inwardly.

Fine, she'd talk to him.

But she wouldn't relent. He'd been out of line.

She remembered to put the knife down before she wheeled around. No use scaring him. "Okay, what do you want?"

He looked down, shuffled his feet, did that whole embarrassed junior-high boy thing. It went straight to her heart.

Then he looked up, looked her in the eyes, and that look went straight to her groin. God, he had the most beautiful eyes—the little glasses enhanced them somehow—and they were looking at her with...well, regret and concern and caring at least. Maybe love, like the girls had said. And even with all the bad, crazy stuff, more than a hint of lust.

"Chloe...I was way out of line."

"Funny, I'd been thinking that myself." Her voice sounded as sharp as her knife, but still part of her just wanted to whimper at him.

"You know I...I really like you. I know it's been making you a little nutty that I didn't want Sandrine to know things were getting more serious...."

She couldn't help smiling at that. "Silly Brand. She already knew. We talked about that last night."

He got a very special look on his face. *Poleaxed* was the phrase that came to mind. He was a little green around the gills anyway, and that revelation made him look far, far worse.

"You were right."

"What was that?" Oh, she'd heard him just fine. She just wanted to hear him repeat it.

"You were right about that. And I was an idiot. I thought that helping you make the contact with Gerard DesJardins would get you out of the contract sooner so you'd have the job you really wanted and we could..." He took a deep breath. "We could date like normal people and see where this went. I thought you'd like that."

"I like the *idea*." More than she really wanted to admit, because if they got a chance to date like normal people, he'd have even more opportunities to play Cowboy He-Man, and if things got really serious, having it all go to hell would hurt a lot more. "But you went behind my back, set everything up for me, like I was...like I was too much of a bimbo to get my own job. At least," she amended, "that's how it makes me feel, although I'm sure you didn't mean it that way. Don't you get that?"

He looked down. Looked away. Looked back again. "I do now. And let me say right now, I know you're not my sister, I know you're incredibly competent, and I know you're more than capable of finding a job on your own. I just thought we had a way to make this contact for you and it would be a good thing for you. For both of us. I was thinking about us, not your job *per se*. But I can see why it came off wrong. God, I'm dumb."

"Yeah, you are. But you're cute." She got a bottle of water out of the fridge, slid it across the island, a peace offering.

"And it was a good idea, just crappy execution," she went on. "If you'd come to me after you'd gotten this little brainstorm and asked what I thought, it would have been different. I'm not sure I'd have gone for it, but I'd have been fine with discussing it. After all, I'd still be doing the *work* to impress him. Although there's still the problem of the contract…."

"Maybe you could have figured out something clever if we'd talked about it instead of me just springing it on you. Maybe," he added nervously, "you still can. Because he's said he's coming to the party, and you're going to wow him even if you're not doing it to try to get a job. So you might as well be prepared for the best."

An unexpected smell infiltrated her distracted and slightly foggy brain. "Oh crap! The onions!" She wheeled around, darted to the cook top, rescued the onions just before they crossed the line from thoroughly caramelized to burned.

"See, this is why business and pleasure don't mix. I'm not going to wow anyone if I do stuff like that."

"Pleasure? I thought we were fighting."

She surveyed the condition of the olive oil in the pan, then scraped the onions into a bowl. "We're making up, silly. I understand what you meant to do, and you understand why I got pissed. But we have to save the good parts of making up until later. Now get out of my kitchen, please." She made a shooing gesture, but smiled while she did it.

He blew her a kiss and obeyed.

Once he was out of sight, she let herself sag against the counter.

Had she forgiven him too easily? Had he really gotten the point?

No way to tell, because unfortunately she couldn't read minds.

Her choices were to dump him and run screaming, or to give him another chance and hope he figured things out.

Only it wasn't really a choice, because as soon as he'd come into the kitchen, looking so regretful and so damn gorgeous, she'd known she'd give him another chance.

She loved him. It terrified her, but it also gave her a warm glow, kind of like tequila only without the side effects.

Okay, maybe with some of the side effects. Love made you brave. It also made you dizzy and stupid.

Only time would tell which she was being.

But by God, even if it didn't work and it blew up in their faces eventually, they might as well enjoy the ride.

Starting with the make-up sex....

*

Several hours later, Brand opened his door to find Chloe, freshly showered, wearing a bright red halter-neck sundress that hugged her curves, and obviously feeling calmer and healthier than she had been earlier.

"Hi?" he said gingerly. No visible weapons, and she couldn't have hidden much in that dress, unless she had a tiny dart gun strapped to her inner thigh under the swirly skirt, like Sandrine in *Silk and Suede*. Things were probably better, then.

"Hi." A smile that looked about as tentative as he felt. "Friends?"

"We always have been." More than that, he wanted to say. A lot more than that. But it seemed premature if he and Chloe were still misunderstanding each other as badly as they had been. You could be crazy about someone and still not able to make it work. "We just had a fight. I even admit I goofed."

"Well, since you'll admit that.... I'll admit I over-reacted just a little."

She looked so cute, both proud and sheepish, and that lipstick-red dress did amazing things for her cleavage. He wanted to...well, all sorts of things came to mind, most of which started with slowly removing the dress, and a few of which involved working around it.

"Is it time for the good part of making up yet?" he asked, with what he hoped was a roguish grin. Some part of his brain suggested that maybe they should talk more. The rest of his brain, not to mention the rest of his body, shouted it down. They'd gotten the basic problem worked out, and beating a dead horse tended to spiral into the really stupid kind of fight where neither of you even knew why you were arguing anymore. Besides sometimes it was easier to show how you felt than to say it. Right?

"I thought you'd never ask," she answered, sashaying past him into the house. Once inside, she turned with a twirl of skirt and admitted, "I'm glad you did because I really, really wanted to, but I didn't have the guts once I actually got here. I could joke in the kitchen where it's safe, but here…."

He considered saying "shut up," but decided that just kissing her senseless was a better approach.

Brand closed the door, then wrapped around her.

She was small, but so solid, so warm, so real, and after a few seconds' hesitation, as if she were trying to decide if it was really a good plan, her lips opened under his. Her tongue darted into his mouth to dance with his.

The sensation went straight to his cock, as if her mouth were there as well as pressed against his lips. He hardened, swelling against his jeans in a way he hadn't from mere kissing since he was a teenager.

Except with Chloe. She did it for him in ways that he couldn't explain, only appreciate.

Damn, he was going to make things work with Chloe if it killed them both. There were a whole lot of fine reasons for that, but the way she kissed was definitely on the list.

As was the way she moved against him.

The sounds she made deep in her throat.

Her soft, silken skin.

Her breasts.

Did it make him a pig if untying the halter neck of her dress and baring those beautiful breasts with their puckered mocha nipples made him feel like the king of the world?

Did he care if it did make him a pig? No, not really. Not when he got to bend down and cup both delicious mounds and take one nipple into his mouth, and make her moan as he suckled one nipple and then the other. For a while, she just enjoyed, throwing her head back, making wonderful noises that urged him on, twining her fingers in his hair to show her appreciation.

Then she let go of him.

He didn't hear a zipper—he was just a little distracted—but he felt a *shoosh* of fabric.

Reluctant as he was to let go of her breast, other parts of Chloe merited careful attention as well. He snaked one hand down her side, reached around to cup her ass.

Naked.

"No panties? Now *that's* a pleasant surprise."

"I...uh..." She giggled. "Just seemed like it would be fun for a change. Got a real kick out of waving to your sister as I passed the house and thinking 'I have no underwear on and I'm going to visit your brother.'"

He looked up and found she was blushing. And, as he quickly discovered, very slick and squirmy under his questing fingers.

A couple of his actress/model flings had gone commando on a regular basis, usually with skirts so short they were more like wide belts, and that had been fun in a sort of sleazy way. He couldn't lie to himself and say that getting a glimpse of snatch at a totally inappropriate time wasn't hot.

But it never seemed to do a hell of a lot for *them*. It was just one of the things you did if you were a certain type of young, cute female celebrity: flash the photographers while getting out of a limo, get trashed and kiss another girl in public, have a fling with Brand Mossiman.

This was much hotter, because Chloe was having fun with it, getting turned on, *feeling* naughty instead of acting it.

And boy, was she feeling naughty. She seemed to suck his fingers inside her, and her hips rocked back and forth, and the noises she was making were erotic music, nonsensical and yet lyrical.

It wasn't easy to get down to his knees without breaking contact, but somehow he managed. (He sent a silent thank-you to Ray for convincing him to take up t'ai chi. He'd never be a martial artist, but at least he was pretty flexible and had decent balance.)

She was sweet and salty at the same time, and as soon as he began to lick, his fingers still inside her, her babbling music increased in volume and pitch. "Delicious," he murmured, letting his lips and tongue move against her.

She cupped the back of his head with one hand, gripped the other into his shoulder as she growled, "God, Brand." With encouragement like that, he got even more inspired, stroking inside her, swirling his tongue around her clit.

He felt her start to tense and clench an instant before she groaned, "I...I love...oh my God." Her body arched backwards and shook. The hot walls of her sex clenched his fingers so hard it almost hurt, her fingers dug in to his scalp, and he had to wrap his other arm around her to hold her up as she dissolved.

They hadn't even made it out of the doorway.

Maybe it was about time to. He scooped her up in his arms. She protested that she could walk, but he told her he didn't care, and stopped and kissed her until she stopped protesting.

Had she said what he'd thought she'd said?

More to the point, did she actually mean it? Had she been trying to say she loved *him*, or what he was *doing*?

Probably the latter. But that didn't mean that hearing those words from her lips, even incoherently, wasn't pretty damn sweet.

Chapter 35

"Now that's the right way to take care of a woman," Chloe purred once he got them both settled on the bed after taking a few seconds to shuck his own clothes at record speed. "You can spoil me *that* way any time."

She rolled over, straddling his hips. "Except right now. Now it's my turn to spoil you."

She began kissing her way down his chest. His belly. Nibbled his hip bones.

She'd wanted to do this anyway. She loved the way Brand's cock felt in her mouth, hard and velvety and tasting a little like brie but mostly like delicious man, and she hadn't indulged either herself or him that way nearly often enough lately.

Now, though, she had an added incentive. It might distract him from what had slipped out her mouth at a moment when her brain was between her legs and those parts of her refused to tell a lie.

And certainly, if her mouth was full, she couldn't say anything else honest but spectacularly ill-advised, or at least ill-timed.

Don't think about that. Think about Brand's body, the heat of him, his warm, spicy smell, the way his skin tasted as she nibbled and licked all around his straining cock without actually touching it. She could see a tempting diamond-glinting drop oozing out of the slit of his cock-head, but she resisted, for now, the urge to lick it off. A little more teasing, a little more kissing—he'd done this to her any number of times, but before, she'd been inclined to dive right in when it was her turn to play. She definitely got the appeal of it from this end, though, the power inherent in holding him off, pushing his pleasure to another level.

"Chloe…" He didn't ask for anything, didn't try to move her hands or her head, but that one word was weighted with begging.

She looked up, smiled with as much sexy evil as she could muster, and whispered throatily, "Yes? Want something?" before going on with what she'd been doing. (She'd never tell him that she'd kind of channeled Sandrine in *Coveting Thy Neighbor's Wife*, because that would be really, really squicky from his point of view, but she'd seen that movie long before she'd met Brand and it had worked its way into her brain.)

Finally, when she deemed he'd been teased enough, when his body was straining and her own body was slick and open again, needy enough that she was half-tempted just to climb on and ride him into the sunset, she moved in.

His balls were heavy and musky and they moved, crinkling under her tongue, as if they had a life of their own. She licked at them until he made a strange, strangled noise, took them gently into her mouth. God he was delicious! She wanted to tell him that, but she couldn't really talk, wouldn't trust herself to talk even if she freed up her tongue, so she let her actions speak for her.

She released his balls, licked her way up his cock as if he were a lollipop made for adults, not corn syrup and artificial fruit flavors, but something far tastier and more sophisticated.

Tasted the sweet, salty droplets at the head, teasing that tiny opening with her tongue until he groaned and grabbed her hair.

Yeah…that was it. He was a little crazy now, a little out of control. The part of Caveman Brand that she liked.

Only then did she take him deep in her mouth, tasting him all over her tongue, even deep in her throat, where she knew damn well there shouldn't be any taste buds but apparently there were at times like this.

His hips moved, thrusting him deeper into her mouth. Then he pulled back with an obvious effort, muttered something that might have been "Sorry."

"I'm not," she purred, letting the words vibrate around his cock.

And he got the point. Thank God he got the point, because she didn't think she was enough in her right mind to say what she wanted.

After that, things got even crazier, in the best possible way. She was slurping him like he was a treat so tasty she didn't care about manners, and he was bucking and making animal noises, and a couple of times his cock thrusting into her mouth as she moved up and down it came close to being too much but it wasn't.

And when he finally arched up and exploded into her mouth, roaring something that might have been her name or might have just been a primal scream, she squeezed her thighs together and, to her astonishment, came herself.

They didn't exactly fall asleep after that, just lay there, stunned and happy and, at least in Chloe's case, smug. Brand, after a while, got up to pee and turned on the stereo while he was at it, so they lay in a cradle of music. Brand had pretty wide ranging taste in music and once in a while the stuff that came out of his speakers made her teeth itch (angry German industrial was not sex music, not unless you were into far more leather than she and Brand were), but this time it was flamenco guitar, passionate and calming at the same time. It worked.

They didn't talk for a long time, at least not about anything sensible, although there was a brief discussion, for reasons that she couldn't possibly explain with anything except "sex-scrambled brains," about whether Bugs Bunny was an actual cross-dresser or just someone who liked fucking with people's heads. Their conclusion was to ask Ray sometime when he was very, very relaxed. Tequila might have to be employed.

Finally Brand glanced at the clock. "Don't you have to go start dinner?" he asked, pulling her closer as he said it.

She snuggled against him. "Didn't I tell you? They're out tonight. Vin Diesel's hosting bowling night. Or maybe games night. Something that was leaving your sister totally mystified about what to wear, anyway. I think she was going to call Luanna for advice."

Of course Brand laughed, and of course she laughed with him. Once they were able to control themselves, though, he said, "Good. Because if you'd had to work I would had to let go of you, and I can think of better things for you to do right now than make dinner."

She wanted to protest that she really *liked* making dinner, but he proceeded to demonstrate, and she totally forgot what she meant to complain about.

*

Chloe had thought nothing could top the mayhem of the first dinner party she'd catered for Sandrine.

She soon found out she just how amazingly, completely, utterly wrong she could be.

Oh, this time she'd had a month to prepare, to consider recipes and set up a schedule for the day, and she even had an assistant in the form of Lance, and there would be actual waiters and waitresses to circulate the food and staff the stations around the living room.

But this time, she also had to contend with the nerves about Gerard DesJardins being out there, tasting her food. Analyzing and critiquing her creations. Possibly, without even knowing it, affecting her career and the rest of her life.

She'd thought *that* was the worst of her worries. Once again, she was utterly mistaken.

The night before the party, she lingered in the kitchen after she finished making dinner, just making sure (again) that everything was ready. She was reading over her notes one more time, reviewing the plan of attack (she had everything broken down into fifteen-minute segments of what to do when) and practicing the anti-stress breathing exercises Luanna had taught her, when her cell phone rang.

Her heart slammed in her chest when she saw the number. If Carl was calling her at this time of night—after midnight in Rhode Island—then something must be horribly wrong.

She thumbed the button to answer the call. "What's wrong?"

"Hey, Munchkin, I wasn't sure if you'd be awake." He sounded a little groggy, and she let the accursed nickname slide.

"Are you okay?" she demanded.

"I'm fine. Just sleepy. I just... Look, Chloe, don't be mad. Mom and Dad wanted to keep this a surprise, but I'm started feeling a little guilty and..."

"Carl," she said in her most menacing tone.

He obviously recognized it, and its meaning—*Don't mess with me*—because he said, "Sorry. I'm calling because we're about to leave for the airport. We're coming to see you. Mom, Dad, Curt, Craig, Casey, Corey, and me. Oh, and Aunt Rosa, too. Like she'd let us go without her. And Joanie. Uncle Pete's doing really well—some new doctor at the VA got him on meds that actually work—so she figured she should get away while the getting was good."

Chloe wanted to scream, but the sound stuck in her throat, so all she could manage was a croaked, "*What?*"

"I'm e-mailing you our itinerary," he said. "I'm not sure how we're getting to your place yet, though. I think we land at five-something."

"You're coming here," Chloe said, because she still couldn't process it. Surely she was hearing him wrong? "Tomorrow."

"Yeppers. Well, today for us. Mom and Dad want to meet this boyfriend of yours you've been so secretive about."

Oh holy mother of... Chloe, very softly, swore a string of Portuguese curses that would have made her grandmother's hair curl if she were still alive. Her hair was probably curling in her grave. It had been a wig for the final years of her life anyway, so it might not have decomposed...

"Munchkin, I'm sorry I waited so long to tell you. I really feel bad. Like I said, Mom and Dad wanted it to be a surprise. But they think you're some hotshot celebrity cook now, and that you'll have a place to put us all up, and...."

Brand walked into the kitchen at that point, and she must have had a stricken, I'm-going-to-pass-out look on her face, because he rushed to her side and grabbed her free hand.

"Carl, I—"

"Shit, Mom's coming. I have to go. See you tomorrow—er, today." He was gone.

"What is it?" Brand asked. "Are you okay?"

No, she really, really wasn't okay. She wanted to scream. She wanted to fling her beloved Henckel boning knife so it stuck in the wall with a satisfying *thunk*. Her horoscope that morning had said "That which does not kill us, makes us stronger," and she wanted to go find the astrologer who wrote it and hurt him or her very, very badly. Repeatedly.

"I have to talk to Sandrine," she said, and headed out of the kitchen.

Brand followed her, for once not trying to get more information so he could figure out how to fix things. Dimly, she appreciated that. She'd thank him later.

If she survived that long.

Sandrine and Ray were in the media room, which was like a smaller, more intimate and cozy version of the size-of-a-small-movie-theatre screening room (if a room big enough to house a 50-inch flat HDTV could be called "intimate" or "cozy"). Sandrine was barefoot, her delicate feet (with shell-pink nail-polished toes) propped up on the coffee table in a relaxed, casual way the public never saw. Ray hit the Pause button when Chloe and Brand entered.

"Okay, um, I have a problem," Chloe said. "I just found out my entire family is flying in tomorrow, and I—"

"Your family! How wonderful!" Sandrine squealed.

Chloe blinked. What? No, no, Sandrine was supposed to say they'd have to stay at a hotel because Chloe would be busy with the party, and then Chloe would ask Sandrine for an advance on her paycheck, because although Sandrine paid really well, Chloe wasn't sure she had enough socked away to put her entire family up at the Hollywood Ramada Inn, much less a real hotel.

This didn't bode well....

"I can't wait to meet them," Sandrine burbled on. "Olive? Olive! Come here and write down these names and add them to the guest list."

Olive appeared out of nowhere, which Chloe found extremely disconcerting. The assistant even had her iPad in hand.

No, this was very bad. Astonishingly, mind-bogglingly bad. She couldn't have her family at Sandrine's birthday party. That way lay madness. Mom and Aunt Rosa and Carl and probably Corey and Joanie would be all over the kitchen, which was only marginally better than them swarming all over the living room and patio and "mingling" with the guests while Dad and the rest of her brothers cornered Brand and demanded to know what his intentions were with their little girl.

She opened her mouth to say how bad it would be, but Sandrine's bright eyes and big, genuine-looking smile stopped her.

Sandrine believed in family. Brand was all she had left, and they were devoted to each other. Their parents had died young, and that had scarred both of them.

If Chloe said she didn't want to see her family, neither Sandrine nor Brand would understand.

She swore again, but only in her mind, not aloud.

She was doomed.

Chapter 36

"No, Evenrude, you can't come with me," Chloe said to the hopeful dog the next morning. "You know you're not allowed in the kitchen." Evenrude leaned against her leg. Chloe sighed. "I know we might pass the peacocks on the way over, but I'm sorry, it's just not possible. Ask Luanna when she wakes up."

It was far too early in the morning, but Chloe hadn't been able to sleep. She'd done a good job of falling asleep last night (maybe there was something to Luanna's breathing exercises after all), but when she'd bolted awake at dawn, she knew her slumber was a thing of the past.

She might as well get a head start on the food.

She entered the kitchen quietly, put headphones in, turned her iPod on, selected her Cooking playlist. Normally she'd blast the music to keep her going, but it seemed far too early for that, even though Ray and Sandrine (and, she was pretty sure, Olive) slept on the far side of the huge house. Although Ray was probably awake and working out already, the freak.

Then, just to convince herself it wasn't just a nightmare, she went to the computer and looked again at the itinerary Carl had sent her.

Yup. Montiero, party of eight, and one stray Texeira, arriving at LAX at 4:45 PM—even earlier than Carl had thought. After two connecting flights with long layovers. She could almost feel sorry for them. Right now they should be wandering around the St. Louis airport, probably wondering where all the Dunkin' Donuts were and afraid to try alien coffee from a company not based in New England.

Good God, it wasn't a nightmare. Okay, it *was* a nightmare, and a hell of lot worse than the one about having to pass calculus to get her culinary arts degree. But it was undeniably real.

She closed the file abruptly. No time to think about that now. Focus on food.

What could she get off her checklist now? The fish and the bulk of the produce would arrive around eight, but she could start the goat-cheese filling for the heirloom miniature tomatoes and put the baby lamb chops in to marinate. Maybe make the herb-scented pasta for the various ravioli—lobster, exotic mushroom, fresh ricotta (which she'd started two days ago) and herbs.

Or she could reduce several huge pork tenderloins to dainty, bite-sized pieces for the tropical kebabs.

Yeah, that was the place to start. She'd had that job reserved for Lance, but he wouldn't be here until ten, and it wasn't like there was any lack of stuff for him to do. And hacking into meat sounded cathartic as well as useful.

She hauled the first twenty-pound slab of pork out of the refrigerator, slammed it onto the cutting board, reached for her cleaver.

Her parents—her whole damn family—would be here in a matter of hours. Twittering and fussing and trying to help her cook things they'd never heard of, let alone made before, and harassing Brand, and generally acting like her family at their best and worst.

Today. On what was probably the single most important and challenging day of her career.

She loved them. Oh, she loved them all to pieces.

But she figured she could be forgiven for the occasional flash of hacking *them* to pieces as she reduced the pork to manageable chunks.

É o que é. But that didn't mean you had to *like* it.

*

"You may be wondering why I called you all here," Brand said, pacing back and forth in his living room. Sandrine and Ray, holding hands, sat on his leather sofa. He refused to think about what he and Chloe had done on that sofa. Not now, anyway. He had to concentrate. To their right, Luanna lounged in an easy chair and Olive stood at attention beside a flip chart.

"Chloe's entire family is coming to visit—tonight," he said. "Sandrine has invited them to the party, which is very sweet."

Sandrine beamed. Brand decided not to add the part about how what she'd done was an incredibly bad idea.

"But Chloe is going to be busy in the kitchen with the party food, and it's especially important that she shine, because of Monsieur DesJardins," he went on. They all knew it, but when you were rallying the troops, you gave them everything you had. He'd worked on enough space battle movies to know that. "So it's our job—all of our jobs—" and he pointed to each one of them in turn "—to keep her family out of her hair so she can do her job, and do it well. Sandrine, I know it's your birthday, but we need your help, too."

Sandrine waved a hand. "Darling, I *adore* Chloe. I was the one who invited Monsieur DesJardins, remember, so he could see how fabulous she is. I'll do whatever you need."

Of course Sandrine had forgotten it was Brand's idea to invite Monsieur DesJardins. He was used to that.

"First, Luanna's going to give you a rundown of the people who are coming, and what to expect."

Luanna snapped to attention. "Chloe's entire family are dolls," she said. "They're totally sweet. But they're very…intense. A big loud Portuguese family. They love Chloe, but they're also kind of possessive of her. So we'll have to be subtle, and if we tell them anything, it's that it's best for Chloe to have some alone time in the kitchen. Olive?"

Olive turned the first sheet of the flip chart and pointed her pen at the photo of a late-middle-aged couple, their dark hair frosting at the temples, laugh-crinkles at the corner of their eyes. They had their arms tight around each other as they smiled into the camera.

Brand's stomach twisted. He could see Chloe in her parents' features. Suddenly he wanted to be middle-aged with her, still kissing her like it was their first time and making their passel of kids groan and hide their eyes.

He was meddling, he knew. He was doing exactly what Chloe hated, exactly what she'd railed about at him. He was running the very strong risk of pissing her off in a big way.

He was running the very strong risk of losing her for good.

He'd tossed and turned last night, thinking about that. But the conclusion he'd come to was so crystalline clear that it had taken his breath away: He loved Chloe, and he wanted the best for her. If that was corralling her family away from the kitchen so she could make the most brilliant food of her career and blow the socks of some snarky French guy, then this was all worth it.

Losing her would hurt like the seven layers of hell, but it would be worth it.

"Chloe's parents, Adelina and Mário," Luanna said. "They run a traditional Portuguese restaurant in Galilee, Rhode Island, that Adelina's grandfather started. Adelina's always encouraged Chloe to be independent, but Chloe is still her little girl. Mário's the same way, really. Brand, you'll have to tread carefully with them—you're schtupping their baby, and they're coming out here to make sure you're worthy of her."

Brand tried very hard not to feel terrified about that.

Olive flipped the chart to the next page. It contained a series of five photographs, all of handsome, olive-skinned men with glossy black hair. Their captions showed they ranged in age from thirty-seven to twenty-nine.

"Carl, Curt, Craig, Casey, and Corey," Luanna said. "Chloe's brothers. You probably don't need to worry about which one is which, although it might help to remember that Curt and Casey are married and Carl is the gay one. I believe Chloe said that either Craig or Casey had a poster of Sandrine in his bedroom when he was growing up."

Ray frowned. Luanna reached over and patted him on the knee. "They're no competition for you," she assured him. "On the other hand, I think Brand might be Carl's type."

"That's just wrong," Brand said. They all stared at him, and he added, "Because I'm schtupping his sister, I mean. Otherwise, it's rather flattering."

"As you probably know, they're very protective of their baby sister as well," Luanna said. "Chloe can stand up to them, but…we just need to keep them occupied so they don't gang up on her."

She indicated that Olive should move on. "Chloe's Aunt Rosa. Mário's sister. She's very…enthusiastic. Like Mário and Adelina, she's never been outside of New England, and barely outside Rhode Island. They think Providence is a slightly overwhelming metropolis."

Next picture up was mostly a mass of long, curly dark hair and a sliver of serious but not unattractive female face. "Joanie is Adelina's brother Pete's daughter. She's the fundraising office manager at a little Catholic college in Newport, and apparently scares the nuns with her efficiency. Crazy as this all is, I'm glad she was able to get away. Uncle Pete has health problems and she spends a lot of time taking care of him."

Brand took over then. "Ray, you're in charge of the brothers. They're guys; they like action movies. Tell them hair-raising tales of life on the set, near accidents, that sort of thing. Sandrine, you turn your Charm Factor to extra-high and don't let Mário out of your clutches until it's safe." The pair nodded.

"Luanna, you said Aunt Rosa is all about the Hollywood gossip, right?" At Luanna's agreement, he added, "Can you handle her? Tell her all about who's wearing what, and go from there? Also, Carl may gravitate over to you; as long as you can keep him occupied, that's fine. Oh, Sandrine, if Craig or Casey glom onto you, you know how to deal with them. Olive…"

"If you don't have another plan for me, I'll take the efficient, nun-scaring one. I like her already."

"Just what I was going to suggest," he said. To everyone, he noted, "Olive's arranged a limousine to bring the clan from the airport, and she'll be there to meet them. Hopefully that experience will have them all in a good mood by the time they arrive."

"What about you?" Sandrine asked.

Brand squared his shoulders, hoping the confident stance would give him actual confidence. Or at least let him fake it well enough. "I'll be squiring around Chloe's mother," he said, "trying to convince her I'm not the worst thing that ever happened to her daughter."

*

Chloe checked the clock around four, mostly to see how they were doing on their various timetables and checklists, and realized she hadn't had time to fret about her family in several hours.

Mostly because she'd been fretting about too many other things.

The lobster for the lobster ravioli hadn't been lively when it arrived—lobster simply wasn't fit to eat if it wasn't merely alive, but lively right up until it was cooked, and Carl would slay her even before Monsieur DesJardins got around to it if she hadn't sent it back with a snippy note—so she'd had to punt with scallop ravioli instead. She and Lance both agreed the new effort had turned out well, but last-minute menu changes weren't anyone's friend.

Neither was discovering that Lance, good as he was, didn't recognize fennel when he saw it and had slivered it into a slaw along with the jicama and napa cabbage. (Fortunately the result, though unexpected, was yummy, but then she'd lost Lance temporarily to an emergency fennel run, since she really, really needed it for another dish.)

And worst of all, the cakes hadn't arrived yet.

She'd *hated* the idea of ordering anything, especially something as critical as the cakes, but had finally convinced herself that getting something gorgeous from Hollywood's hottest bakery was a good plan. Cake-Decorating 211 had been her weakest course at school, and when the birthday cake (one of three identical ones—this was a big party and she wanted to make sure that everyone got a chance to see The Birthday Cake in its full glory) was likely to end up on *Entertainment Tonight*, photogenic was at least as important as delicious. And now the cake delivery wasn't here, even though it was supposed to arrive by three according to her timetable.

"Lance," she barked. "Call the bakery again. Make death threats if necessary."

She considered the bottle of inexpensive chardonnay stashed in the fridge. One glass wouldn't hurt, would it? It was just following in the grand tradition of Julia Child, who was, after all, a world-famous chef from Boston (if not from Galilee, Rhode Island). And it might mellow her enough that she wouldn't kill the cake delivery guy *or* her parents.

She'd just about talked herself into it when they buzzed her from the gate. Too early for her family. The cakes at last?

No, just the last of the flowers, which should have been Olive's problem, but Olive, bless her heart, had gone to LAX to greet Chloe's family. Chloe managed to direct the florist to someone from the housekeeping staff, who were, of course, out in force and supplemented with a few extras hired to make sure the house was killer-spectacular-showplace gorgeous.

Then she went back to panicking. And sautéing, because there wasn't time to waste on panicking all by itself, however tempting the thought was.

The wine would have to wait.

*

After three more increasingly strident calls, the bakery finally admitted that they were, in fact, running late, but not disastrously so. The cakes were done and decorated and gorgeous. They'd actually e-mailed a picture to prove it, but of course Chloe hadn't had time to check her e-mail. (Or pee and get a little fresh air, for that matter, and if she'd had a few minutes to spare, either of those would have seemed a lot more critical.) The cakes were en route and should arrive shortly.

But they weren't there yet, and it was just before six. Okay, okay, guests not due to arrive until seven, but there was still a lot to do, including the clam cakes. (They'd had the bright idea of setting up a station where Lance could cook them while people watched, which would make life easier, but she still had to get the initial batch ready.) And her family would be descending at any minute. The last thing she needed was to worry about the...

"Chloe, we're here!"

...cakes.

Shit.

Chapter 37

Olive threw open the kitchen door and hundreds of Montieros... okay, just eight plus one Texeira...streamed in. Corey, Craig, and Casey were all carrying enormous bakery boxes. "Hope you don't mind," Casey said, "but we ran into this poor delivery guy driving around the estate looking lost and your friend Olive said it would be easier if we just collected them."

"Set them down..." she gestured towards the one free space on the counter. "Gently. You don't want to know how much those cakes cost."

And those were the last words she managed to get out before she was engulfed in a mob of family.

A lot of her well-earned irritation vanished in the face of the stream of hugs and kisses and the realization that, while their timing couldn't have been worse if they'd *planned* to pick the worst possible time, she had missed them all terribly, even Aunt Rosa. They were all bleary-eyed from traveling, and her mother and Aunt Rosa couldn't stop exclaiming over really being in Sandrine Moss's house and wasn't the kitchen amazing, and the guys were all over being in a stretch Hummer limo, and Casey had already stolen a spring roll right from under her nose, and Joanie had already glanced at her checklists and commented that the cake had been really late and did she need a hand with organizing the waiters or anything (oh, bless Joanie!), and her dad, after glancing at Lance suspiciously a few times, finally asked if that was her "young man" because if he was, he looked too young for her.

And she still loved them.

Even if she had to correct them about Lance immediately. Bad enough if they started interrogating Brand, who was at least polite and mature. Lance's veneer of civilization was pretty thin and she was sure it wouldn't stand up to her whole family asking prying questions. (Her own didn't half the time.)

"No, no, that's my sous-chef! Lance, meet my family."

"Awesome! All the way from the East Coast for the big occasion!" Predictably, his eyes and his rakish smile were fixed on Joanie, who was almost twice his age, but the closest thing to an eligible female in the area. (To Chloe's surprise and amusement, her very, very serious older cousin flushed and grinned back at him, not flirting back, exactly, but appreciating the attention. Boy had a gift—and not just with food.)

Just when she thought she was going to have to start spraying them with the fire extinguisher to get them calmed down, Luanna stuck her head into the kitchen. "Hi, everyone!"

Mom was the first to recognize the voice and exclaim, "Luanna, honey!" but Craig was the first to get across the crowded kitchen to give her a hug. (He'd always had a little crush on Luanna; unfortunately he was the short brother and Luanna liked her guys tall.)

"Olive had the driver bring your stuff to our house for now. I figured you all might want to take showers after that long flight, and then Brand and I will show you around a bit before it gets too crowded with guests."

"Brand?" Chloe swore her mom's ears perked up, just like Evenrude hearing a peacock in the distance. "The mysterious Brand?"

"The mysterious and very *cute* Brand" was Carl's commentary, because the man in question was hovering in the kitchen door, over Luanna's head.

He waved at Chloe.

The entire family (and Lance, who must be almost as fried as Chloe) waved back.

"A shower? That sounds like heaven!" Aunt Rosa said. "Especially in that bathroom—you know, the one from *People*'s Houses of the Stars issue."

"I think Sandrine's using that one now," Luanna said quickly. "Ours isn't quite as elegant, but I hear they used to house the Rat Pack in the guest house in the sixties, back when Shirley MacLaine owned the estate, because they'd make too much trouble in the main house. In fact, I've heard all sorts of great stories about the guest house before it became our little home. I'll tell you on the way over." The part about the Rat Pack was a total lie as far as Chloe knew, but it got Aunt Rosa's attention.

Between the offer of showers and, she figured, curiosity about Brand, the kitchen cleared so fast it made Chloe's head spin.

"That's all your family?" Lance asked, awe in his voice.

"Yes as in they're all related to me. No as in that's not all of them. Not hardly. Uncle Carmine and Aunt Ellie are busy catching the last tourists before the Shore Shack closes for the season and Uncle Pete hates to fly." In fact, he hid under the nearest piece of furniture when a plane flew over the house, but Lance didn't need to know that. "Curt's wife Maria stayed home with the kids. They have a four-year-old and twin babies, all boys, who are the cutest things in Rhode Island, and thank God they stayed there. Plus there's Casey's wife Tammy, who's like eight months pregnant and probably didn't want to travel, and Carl's boyfriend Nick. And various other cousins and whatnot."

"Big family."

"No kidding."

"Your sister…"

"Cousin…"

"Whatever. She'd be real pretty if she smiled more often and wore something cute and bright instead of all that grey."

"She's too old for you," she said instinctively. Not that Lance wasn't right about Joanie, who spent way too much time around nuns for her fashion sense not to have suffered. But Joanie was Joanie and Lance was Lance, and there were concepts she just couldn't admit into her brain.

Lance shrugged and then grinned. "We're all on earth for a reason, Chloe. Mine is to make women happy."

"So make me happy. Shut up and finish the sauce for the Thai rolls, then start garnishing the fruit-tart trays."

*

Everything seemed to be going extremely well.

Which meant, Brand was convinced, that disaster lurked around the corner.

"Is everything all right, dear?" Adelina asked.

He winced. Chloe's mother was scarily psychic or something.

"I just want to make sure everyone is having a good time," he said, patting her hand in what he hoped was a reassuring, I-won't-malign-your-daughter's-good-name kind of way.

"Oh, that's so sweet!" Adelina said, beaming at him.

Brand suppressed a sigh of relief, because she'd probably pick up on that, too. So far, he was doing okay with Adelina, which was part of his problem—he was sure she was going to catch him unawares in a dark corner and threaten his manhood. If she had half the feistiness of Chloe, she would, and he was pretty sure Chloe had gotten all her feistiness from her mother.

He viewed the scene before him. The party was in full swing, the living room, patio, and God knew what other rooms packed with party goers. To his amazement, nobody seemed miffed that they weren't all the primary object of Sandrine's attention.

Then again, Sandrine seemed to be using Chloe's father as a *prop*.

"Yes, he came all the way from Rhode Island—can you *imagine!*—for my birthday," she cooed at a well-known director.

Mário apparently had given up trying to interject an explanation about how he was here visiting his daughter, really, and simply smiled and nodded. Brand was fine ignoring the fact that the older man occasionally cast a glance at Sandrine's cleavage. There wasn't much there, but it was well-celebrated, and the man wasn't *dead*.

Luanna was also doing a bang-up job with Aunt Rosa, circulating her through the crowd and, when Brand chanced to overhear, dropping little juicy tidbits of gossip. Judging from her goofy smile and bright eyes, Aunt Rosa was in hog heaven.

The champagne flute in her hand, always filled, probably helped with that. Thankfully, Chloe's family had no issue with alcohol. (And thankfully Sandrine had hired real bartenders for this party.)

Through the open patio doors he could see Ray leading at least four of Chloe's brothers through a series of t'ai chi exercises, a crowd of people watching with great interest. As long as Ray didn't flash anything untoward, they were all fine there.

Oh, crap. *Not* all was right in the state of Denmark. Somehow Olive had lost her grip on Joanie, and Chloe's cousin was over by the clam cakes station talking to Lance.

If "talking to" involved Lance's hand on her arm, that was. Joanie had cleaned up nice, borrowing one of Luanna's Luscious Couture outfits. The fuchsia top was the most color she'd probably worn in years, given what Chloe had told him about her cousin, and the way the folds fell revealed curves without being risqué. There was a sparkle in her eye that hadn't been there earlier, and she was leaning in to laugh at something Lance had said.

Brand was a guy. He knew that didn't bode well.

He turned to Adelina, trying to formulate an excuse for heading in that direction, when he saw Olive swoop down like a great horned owl and usher Joanie away before she agreed to something she'd regret later.

Okay, good. Everything was going fine, and—

Oh, crap again. The door to the kitchen had swung open, and Chloe was standing there, surveying the crowd.

Her hair was tousled, her face flushed from the heat of the kitchen and the fact that she hadn't stopped *going* since early morning. Her apron was stained.

His heart twisted. She was the most beautiful thing he'd ever seen.

In a room full of Hollywood elite, he had eyes only for her.

It was, he realized, because she was in her element. She was doing what she loved. She fairly vibrated with joy, despite all the stress and mayhem and combined insanity of a Hollywood party, Sandrine (who had her own personal level of wacky), and the presence of Monsieur DesJardins.

She caught his eyes, and he smiled, and she smiled back. Then her brow furrowed, and she made a motion that clearly indicated that she required his attendance in the kitchen.

He patted Adelina's hand. "Why don't you get us some of those clam cakes?" he asked. "You can tell me whether they live up to the Shore Shack's reputation. I'll be right back."

He waited until she'd turned away before he made a beeline for the kitchen. If she saw where he was going, she'd certainly follow...

The slim hope he'd harbored that Chloe would be contemplating a quickie, or at least some festive necking, vanished when she grabbed him by the shirt. Thank God she didn't have a knife in her other hand.

"What are you doing with my mother?" she demanded. "You're freaking me out."

Brand carefully peeled her fingers, one at a time, from their grip on his shirt. "I'm keeping her out of the kitchen so you can do your job. Deal with it, okay? Just work with me here."

She opened her mouth to protest, but he forestalled her words by distracting her with a searing kiss that certainly distracted *him*. He pulled away, and thought about programming code for a moment so he'd be able to return to her mother's presence.

"I'm clearing the way so you can do what you do best," he said. "Now, keep on doing it."

He walked out the door, feeling his hands shake just a little bit, not from desire, but from concern. Chloe could come flying out from the kitchen and jump him, pummeling him for daring to interfere.

Or she could just stay in there and decide he'd crossed an uncrossable line, and never speak to him again.

Across the room, he saw the short, quiveringly taut bundle of Gallic energy that was Monsieur DesJardins take a bite of scallop ravioli, and blink in impressed surprise at the rest of the morsel on his fork.

And he was reminded that this was all worth it.

Chapter 38

*H*ow…how…how *dare* he! Ooh!

Chloe knew better than to smash any of Sandrine's crockery, and as much as she sometimes wanted to, she'd never really risk harming one of the expensive knives by throwing it. Kicking something would just hurt. So she stomped around the vast kitchen island. Twice—once in each direction. Then, only then, did she feel marginally calmer.

What kind of macho bullshit had that been? "Deal with it," he'd said. Oh, she was going to deal with it, all right…

She almost stomped right out the kitchen door, but two things brought her up short: the presence of Monsieur DesJardins (not to mention half of Hollywood, and if she couldn't get a job with Monsieur DesJardins, it would be best not to make a scene in front of anybody who was anybody, because she'd need a job somewhere at some point), and the fact that she'd been about to go out there to see if Lance needed more clams, which it looked like he did.

Opening and chopping the clams calmed her. She didn't realize it at first; only after she finished did she notice she'd gone into her zone.

And nobody had interrupted her.

After her family had trooped en masse out of the kitchen earlier, she kept twitching, expecting any number of them to come bursting back through the door. But they hadn't, and she'd started to relax, stopped being so jumpy.

Now, coming out of the Cooking Zone, comprehension sank into her brain.

"I'm keeping her out of the kitchen so you can do your job," Brand had said.

Chloe picked up the pan of clams and nudged open the swinging door with her hip. She walked with measured steps to the clam cakes station, in part to keep from bumping into any guests (or to have the time to move out of the way if they rebounded towards her—it was apparently a good party), but also so she could surreptitiously scan the area.

Brand was squiring her mother around as if she were a queen. Sandrine was draped over her father, who was laughing. *Laughing!* Joanie was deep in discussion with Olive, but that wasn't too surprising, given all they had in common.

"Excuse me," Chloe said, easing her way past the women crowded around the clam cakes station. They were all giggling in an alarming fashion at something Lance had said. Chloe handed off the tray and backed away. The women were, she noted, the same Playboy types who'd been hitting on Brand at the last party....

She chanced making a circuitous pass around the room, ostensibly to check all the food stations, but in reality to see where the hell the rest of her family was.

Out on the patio, her brothers (including Carl, for an entirely different reason from the rest of them) were hanging on to Ray's every word. And Aunt Rosa looked to be in hog heaven, deep in discussion with Luanna and Hilary Swank, who also just happened to be wearing a Luscious Couture creation.

They were all taking care of her family. Her boyfriend, her friends—hell, even her bosses.

She was sure Brand had put them up to this.

But she couldn't bring herself to be angry at him.

Oh, she felt guilty that Sandrine was squiring her father around rather than enjoying her own party...but Sandrine still looked awfully happy, her eyes bright and her smile quick and, as near as Chloe could tell, truly genuine.

She looked over at Brand, where he was waiting on the bar line with her mother and apparently listening to some tale of hers.

Her heart did some sort of weird flip. Now she knew what sautéing vegetables felt like when she tossed them.

Just then, he looked up and saw her watching. His smile was tentative. She smiled back, nodding and hoping he could tell she wasn't angry.

His smile grew, and he blew her a kiss behind her mother's back. Her heart shimmied again. God, but he was cute, with his cheeky grin and those glinting eyes behind those little glasses, and that hair she just loved to run her hands through, and...

She was pretty sure she was in deep, deep trouble.

She was going to be in deeper trouble if she didn't get her ass back into the kitchen and save the next round of baby lamb chops.

She had her hand on the kitchen door when a voice said, "Mademoiselle Montiero?"

She froze. That voice had haunted her nightmares for several years after her Paris internship.

If you'd asked her three seconds earlier, she'd have said she knew all about utter career-related panic after working for Sandrine.

Oh no, she'd known nothing. Suddenly, she understood the sensations behind expressions like "heart in your throat" and "cold sweat" much better than she'd ever wanted to.

"Monsieur DesJardins," she said, turning and smiling at him. If she'd learned anything from this experience, it was how to smile like you meant it. Thank you, Sandrine Moss. "How lovely to see you again."

His brow furrowed slightly, his jowls vibrating as he thought. "Ah yes. I thought your name sounded familiar. You are the head chef here?"

Head kitchen lackey and keeper of the asylum seemed more liked it. "Yes."

"You made the pork tenderloin, the little kebabs? What is that spice combination?"

Once again, Chloe kicked into foodie mode. "Kefir lime, galangal, basil, and lemon thyme. All in a base of pineapple and mango juice, with a dash of peri-peri sauce, which is African by way of Portugal."

"Ah. Very inventive." He paused, and she was sure he was about to clarify that "inventive" meant "what kind of a flaming idiot would put *basil* with *fruit juice* and *African spices*, and pour it over a perfectly good pork tenderloin?" But then he actually said, "You've come a long way since you interned with me in Paris, Mademoiselle Montiero. I'm impressed. And those clam cakes with romesco sauce? Delightful."

And then he smiled.

In the time she'd worked with him, she'd never seen him smile, or even gotten the impression he could. She'd figured his smile muscles were atrophied. It was a very French smile—world-weary and affable and roguish all at once—and it made his round, sallow face with its ridiculous penciled-in mustache look…well, not attractive, but less like a cartoon version of an irascible French chef and more like a human being.

"Thank you," Chloe said. It came out more like a squeak, but at least she'd managed words. She was pretty proud of herself for managing words.

"Come by next week, and we'll discuss the terms of your position," he said.

This time, she didn't manage words. But her bunny-in-headlights expression apparently was in a universal language.

"You cook well and you can handle *les types folles de Hollywood*. I want you at DesJardins LA," he said patiently. Well, about as patient as a slight roll of his eyes and shake of his head conveyed. His expression was something along the lines of *it's a good thing you can cook, because you're not all that quick.*

Then he walked away, leaving her dumbfounded and slack-jawed, and still with sorbets and homemade chocolate ice cream she had to plate and garnish before they melted, because Sandrine had requested cake *and* ice cream in the classic kid's-birthday-party tradition.

*

It was over, or at least winding down. The kitchen still bustled with the cleaning-up and putting-away stage of party crazies, but Chloe was delighted to oversee *that* stage while Lance and the housekeeper did the actual work. The Hired Housekeeping Minions were already gone, but thanks to actually having Hired Minions this time, cleanup had been happening in stages; the kitchen, while a disaster area, didn't look as though someone should put up a wall of sandbags and call in the National Guard.

Most of the guests were gone or at least making their final goodbyes, although Chloe couldn't help wondering if they ever found visitors napping on one of the benches in the cactus garden, or wandering dazedly around the maze, the morning after one of these affairs. The estate was so huge, and some of the guests had been…so appreciative of the fine bartenders and the excellent selection of champagnes that she wouldn't be particularly surprised.

She'd have to deal with her family, but now that she'd survived the party, that sounded almost fun. Okay, maybe not exactly *fun*, but certainly not as dreadful as it had looked at this time yesterday.

Except for her sudden panic that she didn't know where they were all going to stay. How could she have forgotten to deal with that?

She just hoped the ever-organized Olive, or maybe Joanie (hardly a world traveler, but at least she'd left New England before, if only to go to a Catholic colleges' conference in DC) had thought to make reservations somewhere. Otherwise, the cottage would get awfully crowded, although Brand could probably pile some of her brothers into the gatehouse.

Tomorrow, after she'd rested—assuming they didn't decide to exercise the inalienable right of East Coast visitors to California and wake up at the first blush of dawn, expecting to be taken to the corner of Hollywood and Vine—it would actually be nice to spend some time catching up.

Although she wasn't looking forwards to ducking the inevitable questions about Brand. Largely because she didn't know how to answer them. That was another thing she had to wrap her brain around.

And sometime before or after *that*, she'd have to deal mentally with Monsieur DesJardins' offer. Which was more like an order, but that was about what she'd expect from an arrogant Frenchman who'd known her only as a homesick, slapdash, terrified twenty-year-old.

Then again, he probably treated everyone that way. Even his grandmother.

Damn, she wanted that job. Wanted it so badly she could taste it like slightly burnt caramel, sweet and bitter at the same time. But she simply could not, would not, break her contract.

"Hey," Lance said, "what should I do with the romesco sauce? More to the point, could I take some home? There's a lot left."

She was about to say "no problem" when Sandrine burst into the kitchen in a cloud of diaphanous silk chiffon, brandishing a sheaf of papers. "I've been talking to Gerard," she exclaimed (sounding remarkably like her *Princess of Nowhere* character when she learned the truth about her parentage). "Chloe, congratulations! I just *knew* you'd knock his socks off!"

Oh *no*. Sandrine wasn't supposed to know. Now everything was about as awkward has it could possibly be.

"Thank you," she said. "He won't be able to keep the job open until I'm done here, but at least I should be able to work my way in later..."

"Don't be ridiculous," Sandrine said. "Go."

How did this woman always manage to make her feel like the room was spinning? "Oh, no, I can't. I signed a contract with you, and I intend—"

Sandrine rolled her eyes and gave a theatrical sigh. "*Fine*. You're fired."

Chapter 39

*C*hloe, jaw dropping, felt like she'd just been slapped with a very large, very dead haddock.

It must have shown on her face, because Sandrine immediately added, "Of course I mean that in a good and positive way, if that's what it takes to release you from the contract. Poof! All gone! No more contract between you and that wonderful job! You can go whenever Gerard's ready for you to start. It's been fabulous having you here, and I'll miss you terribly and so will Ray, but it will give us an excuse to go out to DesJardins LA all the time, right?"

Chloe's overloaded brain got stuck on the fact that Sandrine called Monsieur DesJardins "Gerard"—she couldn't imagine Madame DesJardins, or even his mother, doing that—so she was caught by surprise when Sandrine threw her arms around her and gushed, "Chloe, sweetie, I am so happy for you! I just knew inviting Gerard was a great idea." Sandrine's many wispy layers of silk (shading from grey-blue to turquoise) wafted up with the movement and tried to cling to Chloe's clothes.

Chloe took a deep breath and didn't say anything about it having been Brand's idea.

Through the enveloping folds of fabric, she said, "But…are you sure? I don't know when he wants me to start, and it'll take time to find the right person for this job and I don't want to leave you in the lurch if…"

Sandrine stepped back and laughed that scarily beautiful, bell-like laugh of hers. "Oh, I've already figured that out. Lance, come here."

Lance, who'd been studiously pouring romesco sauce into a Tupperware container, looked up, startled by the imperious tone. He set the sauce down, wiped his hands on his apron, and walked over, his eyes guarded.

"You," Sandrine said. "You can be my new chef. I'll have Olive write up the contract in the morning."

Chloe considered hugging him, then decided he'd enjoy it *way* too much. She extended her hand instead. He hesitated, still shell-shocked, and then shook it a little too enthusiastically.

"Lance, congratulations. You'll do a great job. And I'll leave you notes and some of their favorite recipes."

She meant it about the great job. Lance might not have a ton of experience, but he had a real passion for food, an ability to cope with the unexpected, and a combination of charm and good-humored calm that would probably work well dealing with Sandrine's eccentricities.

In other words, he was young and adaptable.

"Well, then, that's settled!" Sandrine exclaimed. "And by the way, while I hope you'll be around a few days next week to help with the transition, you're off for the next two days so you can spend time with your family. You know, your dad's a real sweetie, Chloe. He's so proud of you. Of your brothers, too, but especially of you. I like your mom, too, but your dad's really special. And you should go tell them the good news and have a drink with them."

For a second, her beautiful turquoise eyes looked soft and misty. "This whole thing is like a fairy tale. Fate led you and Brand together at the AAMies, and then you came to work for me, and now your career is taking off.... I want to find a screenwriter to write your story!"

Chloe blinked, unable to take all of that in. Before she could speak, Sandrine refocused and smiled.

It was a very mischievous smile, the kind that set off a few alarm bells in Chloe's head.

"But first," she said, stepping to the stove, "let's get rid of this nasty old contract of yours!"

She turned the gas burner on to the highest setting, dramatically thrust the contract into the flame. Unfortunately, it was the special burner for the wok, and its highest setting was scary-high, kind of like the speakers that went to eleven.

The paper caught with an audible *whuff*, flaring up so suddenly that Sandrine shrieked and dropped it on the floor...

Too close to her long, floaty silk skirt.

Chloe and Lance didn't even have time to signal each other. Chloe, who was closer to Sandrine, dove in and started beating on the paper and the skirt with the damp dish towel she'd been clutching. Lance's reaction timing was even better. Before Chloe knew what was happening, he had the fire extinguisher in his hands and was spraying the burning paper, Sandrine, and Chloe indiscriminately with cold white foam.

It was over in seconds, leaving Sandrine—damp and foamy around the ankles, but unharmed except for some charred bits at the bottom of her dress—gaping, apparently uncertain whether to laugh or cry or maybe both.

"You okay?" Lance said, and Sandrine nodded.

"I think you might be able to fix the dress," Chloe said gingerly. "It only got a little bit of the hem, and it's a funky ragged hem anyway, so Luanna could probably make it look as good as new. But I'm afraid your shoes..."

"Last year's," Sandrine said briskly, kicking them off and punting them towards the trash as if they hadn't probably cost as much as Chloe's parents' mortgage payment. "Let's go share the good news with your family." She looked down at her dress. "On second thought, why don't you do that? I can't be seen like this. I'll take the back stairs."

As she was leaving, Lance called out, "Ms. Moss? I may not get a chance to talk to you again tonight. Do you know what you want for lunch tomorrow?"

"Salmon, or maybe tuna, and artichokes," she said grandly. "I'm in an artichoke mood. But only if they're okay for the Blood Type Diet. I was talking with Victoria Beckham tonight and she swears it's the best thing that ever happened to her skin, so I've got to try it, so if that's not right for my blood type, figure out something kind of like salmon and artichokes...only not. You know."

"Um, okay," Lance said. His voice was light, but Chloe heard an undercurrent of tension, as if he was keeping a valiant grip on his patience. She was familiar with that. "What's your blood type?"

"It's some vowel. O or A or E, I think." Sandrine waved a hand dismissively. "Ask Olive. She'll know."

And she was off in a swirl of damp, charred silk, still somehow managing to look elegant.

*

Of course, extricating herself from the kitchen wasn't quite as simple as Sandrine thought: there was still cleanup to finish, as well as cleaning fire-extinguisher foam off herself, and some good advice to impart to Lance, who at least, unlike her, had some idea of the madness he was getting himself into. ("Be good to Olive like you'd be good to a smart older sister who has something on you" figured prominently.)

By the time she managed to get out of the kitchen, the house was curiously quiet, except for Sandrine explaining to a couple of lingering guests that she'd suddenly become bored with her dress and wanted to put on something more comfortable and after all, it *was* her birthday. (Everyone was too polite to note that it was after midnight and, therefore, actually no longer her birthday.) Ray was none too subtly encouraging the rest of the stragglers to leave.

Brand was the first to reach her. "Success?" he asked.

"Success!" she said, still a little dazed. "Brand...I...Monsieur DesJardins... He offered me a job!"

"Of course he did. Because you deserve it." Then he put his arms around her, drew her close.

Kissed her decisively.

It wasn't a ten-minute, dancing-tongues, preliminary-to-tearing-off-clothes kiss, but it wasn't a peck, either. A definite boyfriend kiss, one that wasn't afraid to show he meant it.

"You do realize," a dry voice—Curt's, or was it Craig's?—said when he released her, "that we know Ray Stark's your future brother-in-law and all that, but if you hurt our sister, we'll still need to kill you."

"Duh. It's part of the brother package," Brand said affably.

And then Chloe and Brand were engulfed by family, all talking at once. Some asked about this new job; some (particularly her mom) asked about Brand, who was standing right there and blushing; Aunt Rosa bubbled about all the celebrities she'd met; and even Joanie, usually the quiet one, managed to say, "I can't believe how *nice* everyone's been. I mean, I know Luanna's nice, but everyone's been so great, even Sandrine and Ray, and they're famous. And your friend Olive is like a goddess. I want to be her when I grow up."

As she tried to answer nine questions at once, Chloe saw first her mother, and then her father, try and fail to disguise massive yawns. Aunt Rosa was struck next, and didn't even try.

"I haven't been up this late since the night you were born," her father finally said. "I don't understand you night owls. Olive said the limo would be waiting for us whenever we were ready to leave. We're ready." He said it in a tone that made all five brothers—and Chloe—stand up a little straighter.

"Where are you staying?" Chloe asked. She reminded herself to get flowers for Olive for dealing with their reservations.

"Cat and Marmot," her aunt said, her giggle betraying a little too much champagne. "Isn't it funny, naming a hotel after animals?"

"You mean Château Marmont?" Chloe said, her heart racing in financial panic. "You do know that's kind of expensive, don't you?" To put it mildly. That was the kind of place that foreign stars stayed while visiting Hollywood. There was no way her family could afford it—flying out here alone had put a major dent in their budget—and while her credit card limit might stretch to cover the gap, it would take forever to pay it off. What had Olive been thinking?

Sandrine—now a Hepburnesque vision in tailored burgundy linen slacks and a crisp white blouse with oversized cuffs—swept over at that point. "Isn't it delightful, Chloe? Some Bollywood power couple and their entourage got delayed leaving India because of monsoons, and there were last-minute openings at Château Marmont. I thought it would be such a nice treat for your family. I thought about the Standard or the Four Seasons, but it's their first time in Hollywood and I wanted to give them the best." Then she leaned over and stage-whispered, "My treat, and don't argue. The least I could do for such sweet people." She winked at Mário, who actually *blushed*.

Chloe's jaw dropped. She considered arguing, considered trying to squeeze them all into the guest house.

Then she melted. Sandrine really did have a good heart—and the way the actress was smiling mistily at her family, Chloe kind of understood her generosity. She'd never gotten a chance to spoil her own parents, so she was getting a kick out of spoiling Chloe's.

"We'll see you for brunch tomorrow, though, you and Brand," her father said. It wasn't a question. He put his arm around Chloe's mom. They both beamed at her and Brand, then at Sandrine, and then turned and beamed at each other.

She nodded. "At Château Marmont? It's kind of…"

"Once in a lifetime, and worth it for a splurge," her father said firmly. "Your friend Olive made us reservations at eleven, and remind me tomorrow morning when I start to go into sticker shock that I said it would be worth it just this once. The rest of the trip, we'll go budget, but tomorrow's brunch…."

"We'll split it."

"We'll talk about it tomorrow. We have a lot of things to talk about tomorrow," he added, mock-sternly, winking first at her and then at Brand.

Mom yawned again and said, "We shouldn't keep the car waiting too long, Mário. I'm sure the driver would like to go home."

In her usual unnerving manner, Olive seemed to materialize as soon as they started to organize themselves to head out. With her was a man whom Chloe first assumed had to be the driver, although he looked more like a male model: about her age or a little younger, tall, lean, and tasty, with amazing cheekbones and skin the color of really good dark chocolate.

But he was dressed way too well to be the driver. Fashion was Luanna's thing, not hers, but that suit screamed *unbelievably expensive.*

"Right this way," Olive said, starting to herd the Montieros out.

At that point, Chloe noticed the handsome man had his hand on the small of her back in a casually proprietary way.

He whispered something in Olive's ear and Olive…. Olive stopped in her tracks and giggled. She looked like she was blushing, although it was hard to tell with her dark complexion.

"Silly me! It's been such a crazy day I almost forgot. Sandrine, Brand, Chloe, everyone, please meet my husband, Antony Randall Duhenes III."

"As in the heir to Duhenes Industries?" Aunt Rosa blurted out. Trust Aunt Rosa to have read about Olive's husband in some gossip magazine.

Mrs. Montiero took her sister-in-law's arm gently but decisively. "Let's give Chloe and her friends some time to themselves, Rosa. It's been a very busy day for them. Car's that way, right?" She led Rosa out and the rest of the family followed like ducklings in their wake.

Olive and Antony were about two steps behind the crew, but obviously not with them. Lost in their own little world, in fact.

Chloe turned to Brand. "Olive's married to Duhenes Industries? And she works *here*?" She blurted it out before she remembered Sandrine was standing right next to her. But Sandrine wasn't paying any attention, because Ray was murmuring in her ear about some birthday present he had for her upstairs.

Sandrine turned from Ray long enough to smile at Chloe, Brand, and Luanna before waving towards the door and blatantly faking a yawn. "Well, it's been a long day for everyone," she said, "and I think it's time to say good night and head up to bed." She leaned closer to Ray and all but purred.

Ray actually blushed a little before taking Sandrine's arm and wishing them all good night.

They could hear Sandrine's throaty chuckles and Ray's occasional basso rumbling long after they were out of sight.

"Nice to see that," Brand said. "Now it's time for us to follow their fine example."

"Her stuff's in the cabana," Luanna said to him. "Have fun, you two."

"My stuff...what?"

The past few months had been bizarre, no doubt about it. But tonight seemed to be surpassing *bizarre* at every turn. She was going to have to change her name to Alice because she'd obviously fallen down the rabbit hole.

Brand took her by the hand. His grip was warm, and his touch made her shiver, just like it had the first time they'd met and he'd pointed out the flour on her nose.

"You and I," he said, leading her outside, "have a date with the Jacuzzi. You don't work for Sandrine anymore, so there's no reason to hide. Luanna brought your bathing suit and stuff so you wouldn't have to go back to the cottage to change."

"Thank you," Chloe said to Luanna, who was heading in the same direction they were. "For everything. For making sure my family—"

"Y'all hush," Luanna said. "That was all Brand's doing. But listen to me: you always take care of us. It's okay to let us take care of you once in a while. Didn't you read your horoscope today? It said 'You'll get by with a little help from your friends.' You did a kick-ass job tonight, so go and be pampered." She kissed Chloe on the tip of her nose and headed into the darkness.

The one day Chloe hadn't bothered to the read the astrology section....

Chapter 40

Chloe came out of the cabana in her suit (a fun little leopard print tankini and high-cut bottoms) and slid up to her neck into the Jacuzzi where Brand was waiting for her. She sighed as jets hammered hot water into her aching lower back.

Brand pulled a bottle of champagne from an ice bucket and poured her a glass. Well, a plastic glass, she discovered. That made sense. She hated to think about broken glass in the Jacuzzi.

"To Chloe Montiero," Brand said over the sound of the waterfall that cascaded into the pool and the fountains that dotted the spa area, raising his own glass. "The newest chef at DesJardins LA and an all-around incredible cook who makes the best clam cakes this side of the Mississippi."

Chloe blushed, telling herself it was a flush from the steaming water, and took a sip. Mmm, icy cold and bubbly and so very crisp.

"To Brand Mossiman," she said. "Without whose support none of this would have been possible."

She'd actually taken another sip before she realized he wasn't drinking. In fact, he was just staring at her. What? Did she have flour on her nose? Would he be able to see it from over there, even, without his glasses?

"Do you mean that?" he asked cautiously.

Oh. That's right. He hadn't been privy to her kitchen revelation.

"Yes, I do," she told him. "I understand what you did and why you did it. There was no way I could have pulled off that party with my entire family underfoot, trying to 'help.'"

"I was a little worried…okay, more than a little…that you'd think I was interfering too much."

"For about two seconds. Then I realized what you were really doing, and why, and it made me all warm and fuzzy. I hate it when someone tries to take over what I'm doing, especially where my career's concerned. Probably always will. But I've got to admit that sometimes a little help, a little bit of being taken care of, is a good thing."

"I'm pretty sure I get the difference between helping and taking over," he said. "But just in case I get confused, you let me know, okay? For example, I'm going to give you a foot rub now. If you're okay with that, I mean."

Chloe smiled. She finished her champagne and half-slid, half-swam over to him. She floated onto his lap, her legs around his waist. He looked different without his glasses. More vulnerable somehow. Still just as sexy, though.

"I am totally okay with a foot rub," she said. She kissed him, loving the way his lips felt moving against hers, the way his hard chest felt beneath her searching hands.

"You keep that up," Brand said, gulping for air, "and I'm going to be way too distracted to be rubbing your feet. Elsewhere, maybe…"

She tugged at his lower lip with her teeth, then released him and drifted back across the bubbling tub. "Oh, I want that foot rub," she said. "You're not getting off that easy." She giggled. "Well, maybe you will."

"So you're getting used to this 'people taking care of you' thing?"

"I'm working on it," she said. "I can be kinda slow, though, so you might have to keep reminding me."

"Sweetie," he said, "I'd be happy to keep reminding you for as long as it takes."

"It could take some time," she warned.

He smiled, the corners of his eyes crinkling. "I'm in for the long haul, baby. I've got all the time in the world."

She was about to respond to that, because it made her kind of nervous but kind of fluttery-happy at the same time, but then he did something utterly luscious to the ball of her foot, and all she could do was lean her head back and moan in pure ecstasy.

"Dude!"

The voice startled her out of her consummate bliss, and she nearly slipped off the bench deeper into the tub.

"Nailing her in the hot tub, dude!" Lance smacked his palm in the air. "High five!"

"Can we *help* you?" Brand asked.

"Yeah, well, the night is young and all that sh…stuff. I heard voices and thought I'd ask if you guys might be up for some post-party partying. But it looks like you've got your own private party on." He took a few steps, then added brightly. "Think Luanna's still up?"

"Go home, Lance," Chloe said. "You've got a long day ahead of you tomorrow. In fact, working for Sandrine, you've got a long, hard life ahead of you. Trust me, you need all the sleep you can get."

"Who can sleep?" Lance asked. "I just helped cater a major Hollywood party and got hired to be a celebrity chef! I'm going clubbing, man! I am *golden!*"

"He does know 'celebrity chef' isn't the same thing as 'chef for a celebrity', right?" Brand asked as Lance bounded off into the darkness.

"Somehow, I wouldn't be surprised if Lance ended up with his own reality show someday," Chloe said. "Something involving cooking, scantily clad bimbos, and fire. Lots of fire."

Brand's roar of laughter provoked a nearby peacock into answering with an indignant shriek. A soft, canine woof responded in the distance, followed by Luanna's faint voice demanding "*Even*rude! Heel!"

"Ah, true love," Chloe exclaimed, clutching her hands together over her heart and batting her eyes like a heroine from a silent movie.

"About that…" Brand started to say.

Then he bobbed over and kissed her instead in a way that got the point across better than any words could have.

Screw foot rubs. Foot rubs could happen later. Tomorrow, even. Or the next day. Like Brand said, they had all the time in the world.

If the Jacuzzi hadn't already been hot and bubbling, this kiss would have made it steam.

Brand used the magical properties of water to pull her onto his lap, and she wrapped around him as she had before, loving the feel of his hard, lean, water-slicked body in the circle of her legs, his cock hardening as it pressed against her, the heat of his skin layered with the water.

His nipples crinkled beneath her fingers as she lavished attention on him, just enjoying the luxury of being outdoors, under the stars, unconcerned about affronting Sandrine or anyone else. (Not, she figured, that Sandrine was likely to be out and about, not from the way she and Ray had been chuckling about the "presents waiting upstairs" and all that happy, sensual laughter as they'd headed off.) She wiggled a little so she could lick at his nipple. Yum. A little chlorine-laced, but still, yum.

"Good idea," Brand murmured, and went to work on her tankini top. Within seconds, it was bobbing next to them in the burbling water.

She wriggled out of the bottoms, tossed them carelessly towards the tiles, where they landed with a wet *splosh*. So much for Luanna making sure she had her suit. That must have been a record for getting back out of it.

Brand followed her lead. Another low-flying swimsuit. Another *splat* somewhere off in the darkness. Thank goodness for the lights around the pool or they'd never find them until morning, and as much as Chloe liked the Jacuzzi, she didn't want to spend the entire rest of the night in it.

Then their naked bodies pressed together and Chloe decided she didn't care if the peacocks carried off her bikini bottoms to nest in. (Did they do that? Or maybe that was magpies?)

Brand's hands and lips and tongue tantalized her breasts, sending spikes of pleasure from her nipples down her body to her clit. Did the water temperature notch closer to the boiling point, or was that just her blood?

The water was warm, but his mouth, suckling on her sensitive nipple, was warmer, and the night air, soft on her damp skin, helped Brand tease the other nipple. The bit of champagne earlier was just enough to make her feel extra-sensitive and, well, bubbly, not that she needed the help, and she ground herself against him to try to anchor, try to keep from floating away, but of course that just flooded her with more sensation that made her feel more deliciously light-headed.

Brand moved one arm away. It didn't even occur to her to question why until she felt something hard press between their bodies—something even harder than Brand's by now very hard cock.

Something that started to dance across her clit in the most amazing way.

Trust a techie geek guy to find a really, really *good* waterproof vibe.

She wasn't sure whether to moan with pleasure or giggle, but when she opened her mouth, what came out was a bit of both.

"This acceptable spoiling?" he asked.

"God, yes." How could she be on fire like this when she was in the water? That really shouldn't work. Maybe it was something like a pressure cooker, because there was definitely pressure building, delicious, delirious pleasure, and like an unvented pressure cooker, she was pretty sure she was going to explode.

That, incoherent as it was, was the closest Chloe got to a coherent thought for a while, because Brand bit down on one nipple and pinched at the other. The sharper sensation on top of all the wonderful floaty ones she'd been feeling and the vibrator on her clit and the hard cock teasing at her slit was enough to push her over the edge.

She drove her fingernails into Brand's shoulders and cried out her pleasure, and for a little while everything got blurry in the best possible way.

"Hold this for a second," Brand said, closing her fingers around the vibrator. "I'll be right back."

"Where are you…" Oh. Yeah. Safe sex and all that good, responsible stuff.

She bobbed pleasantly in the warm water, letting the vibe tease around her clit, as Brand pulled himself half out of the tub just long enough to grab a condom. He settled back down on the edge of the tub to roll it on.

Chloe had a better idea. At least she hoped it was a better idea, because it was a new experiment for her, if not exactly a new idea. (Hey, she had an active imagination, and dating her last boyfriend had left her with a lot of time on her hands to consider all the interesting possibilities she wasn't getting up to).

"Allow me," she said and bobbed between his legs, bracing herself with one hand and using the vibrator to tease herself with the other. She bent down and closed her mouth over his partially condomed cock.

"Sweet Jesus," Brand sighed, thrusting his hips forwards to encourage her.

Latex and chlorine—not exactly likely to be the newest gourmet taste sensation.

Latex and chlorine and *Brand*, on the other hand…now *he* was a seasoning that made latex and chlorine taste delicious. Hard cock and hot flesh made hotter by the tub, and all right, maybe Chloe couldn't actually smell Brand's warm musk, just clean, Jacuzzi-marinated skin, but she knew what he smelled like, knew what he tasted like, and could imagine.

With her lips alone, and with all the grace she could muster, she rolled the condom down onto Brand's cock.

From her perspective, she felt clumsy, and it seemed to take a lot longer than it should have.

But Brand's expression, and the interesting noises he was making, told a different story altogether.

Once it was on, she grinned, licked her lips, and pushed back just enough that he could back into the tub near her. They twined together again, letting the water bear them up. Hands cupped under her ass, he lifted her onto him.

His cock slid in, inch by inch, millimeter by millimeter, making her crazier with each fraction, until he was firmly seated and she was deliciously full.

Then, because she was still holding the vibe and why not, she guided it, not to where Brand probably expected her to put it (she was getting plenty of sensation there already from the friction of their bodies), but to the sensitive spot at the base of his taut balls.

He made a strangled sound, muttered something that she thought translated to "Can't last long like that," and started kissing her, hard and deep and wild, as they moved together in the water. He filled her so completely, so perfectly, that she couldn't help rippling and clenching around him, and each ripple seemed to send flutters of joy right to her heart as well as through the obvious areas.

Where did she leave off and he start? She couldn't really tell at this point, and she didn't think it had ever felt quite like this before, and that had to mean something.

She was pretty sure what it was, too.

And stopped kissing him long enough to choke it out. "Brand, I... love you."

His smile could have lit up the city. "Love you, too. Been waiting to say it."

Then his face screwed up with ecstasy and he stopped talking, at least not in any known language.

He'd been right. It didn't take long, but that wasn't a problem because Chloe was right there with him as he exploded.

*

Hand in hand, clutching towels around them (they could collect the swimsuits tomorrow, but they weren't about to abandon the rest of the champagne), they headed towards the guest house ("I figured after a rough day, you'd want to sleep in your own bed, with your own stuff," Brand said, and she loved him just a little bit more), stopping periodically to neck. By a fountain. On a bench. In several random places, just because they could.

Outside the guest house, they stopped again, but before they kissed, something caught Chloe's eye.

She nudged Brand, pointed to the edge of the little patio.

Evenrude, her chain loosely on the ground, was curled up asleep on a lawn chair. One of the peacocks was comfortably settled next to her, head under its wing. Another stood guard on the back of the glider, turning his head to watch their approach.

"Let's not disturb the happy ending," Chloe whispered, drawing Brand towards the door.

"Happy endings are good," Brand said.

Happy endings…happily ever after… She stopped.

"Uh, Brand?"

In the glow of the light over the cottage door, she saw a flash of worry in his eyes. "Ye-es?"

"Sandrine said something earlier tonight," Chloe said slowly. "Maybe she'd had too much champagne and misspoke, but she said you and I met at the AAMies."

He smiled. "We did. I figured you didn't remember, because it was just for a second. You asked me for directions to the staging area."

And in a white hot rush of clarity, she remembered. "Omigod," she whispered. "That's right. That was *you.*"

"I felt awful afterwards," Brand admitted. "I went to find someone who knew, but then one of my team needed something, and by the time I got back, you were gone." He winced. "Probably already out on the red carpet with Ray. It was all my fault."

He looked so guilty and forlorn that she had to throw her arms around him. "No, no! I just took off after you turned around, I was so stressed and in a hurry. It's not as if you told me to go the wrong way."

She pulled back, stood on tiptoe, kissed him.

"Think about it this way," she said. "If I'd only waited for you to get the directions, I wouldn't have ended up on the red carpet, and none of this would have ever happened. We would never have met again."

He grinned that perfect grin of his, the one that made his eyes glow. Not glow like a CGI effect—glow like there was joy and love dancing behind his glasses. "So what you're saying is, if you'd accepted help from me…"

She laughed and cuffed him lightly on the arm. "Don't push your luck. Even if you are right."

Her laugh made Evenrude lift her head. She looked at Chloe and Brand, then at the peacocks, and settled back down. If there was such a thing as complete and utter doggy satisfaction with the world, Evenrude embodied it.

"Happy endings," Chloe murmured.

Brand slipped his arms around her waist. "Think we…?"

"Happy, absolutely. But no endings, not yet. We're just getting started."

Then she kissed him again.

And again.

And again.

sophie mouette

author of *Out of the Frying Pan*

love,

IN STITCHES

a hollywood spice novel

Want to know how Luanna finds her own Hollywood Spice romance?
Turn the page for a sneak preview of *Love, in Stitches*,
available now from your favorite retailers in print and ebook formats.

Chapter 1

*I*f Luanna Devenaux had known what kind of day she was going to have, she would have worn a different blouse.

More than a year in southern California and she still couldn't get a handle on the weather. She was a Southern girl born and bred, but even the South cooled down *some* in autumn and winter.

With the arid Santa Ana winds sucking the moisture out of her very eyeballs and nearly eighty degrees at 9 a.m., her choice of three-quarter sleeves and a rayon-linen blend that apparently had more rayon in it than she recalled meant she was sweating like a whore in church, as her daddy would say.

She sighed with relief when she stepped into Luscious Couture's blessed air conditioning and sighed again with sheer joy (and some astonishment) that, more than a year later, she had a fashion design job here.

The sound of Los Angeles traffic was replaced by the hubbub of the warehouse. The two-story industrial ceiling meant all the discussions the designers had about their ideas had to be at a higher volume or their words would be swallowed by the space. Plus Tad, one of the other junior designers, always insisted on having Pandora radio on his favorite station, an unsettling mix of modern pop, Mexican pop, and Asian pop, and they had to raise their voices over that as well.

Luanna loved it.

She loved the smell of fabric, draped across mannequins or on bolts along one wall: sweet silk and sheepy wool and crisp linen.

She loved the enormous mood board that took up much of another wall, a crazy collage of fabric swatches and color chips and sketches and inspirational pictures.

The announced colors for two years hence—because next year's designs were already being produced—were Directoire Blue, Seashell Pink, and Mirage Gray.

Luanna privately thought of them as Barbie's Eyeball Blue, Hoohah Pink, and Confederate Gray, because by God, that gray *was* the official true gray of the fine soldiers of the South.

So the pictures, torn out of magazines or printed off the Internet, included ocean and sky and cornflowers for the blue, seashells and babies' bottoms and cats' noses for the pink, industrial punk and old pewter dishes for the gray.

The whole place thrummed with a creative energy that jittered her up better than crack. Not that she'd ever tried crack—she just didn't think she'd ever need drugs as long as she could shoot this crackling artistic energy into her veins.

She dropped her purse in a bottom drawer of her drafting table/desk and wished, not for the first time, that the vending machine in the break room dispensed real honest-to-God sweet tea. Not that weak lemony swill every else thought constituted proper iced tea.

Still, that was the only thing she didn't love about working at Luscious.

Before she could sit down and review the sketches she'd done yesterday in preparation for a mockup today—yay for getting to do some hands-on sewing!—she heard her boss's voice cut through the hum of work.

"Luanna, may I see you in my office?"

The hum stopped as everyone else pretended to be focusing on work when they really wanted to hear the gossip.

Diane, Luanna's boss, stood on the metal catwalk that provided access to the offices lining the upper half of one wall. She'd had the sense to wear a sleeveless sheath dress in royal blue. With her spectacularly slim figure and jet-black hair, middle-aged Diane could've passed for half her age.

Luanna wanted to be Diane when she grew up. Only curvy and blond, because there wasn't much she could do about her curviness, and she *liked* being blond.

Without waiting for a response, Diane disappeared into her office. Luanna trudged up the metal staircase to the offices that lined the upper half of one wall. She might be in blissful air conditioning, but she was still wilted from the walk from the parking garage to the studio through the Santa Ana hellwinds.

Diane usually worked on the floor with the junior designers, but as a senior designer, she warranted an actual office, which she went into only when she needed to make a phone call or do some computer work.

Luanna knew she wasn't late, knew she'd gotten raves at her one-year review, so she was only mildly unsettled—until she stepped into the office and saw someone else there. That guy from HR. What was his name? Hernando? Something like that. All she knew was that she'd seen Tad and Hernando, who'd clearly had a little too much to drink, stumble out of the electrical closet at last year's holiday party looking adorably mussed.

It was never good to find HR waiting when you've been summoned to your boss's office.

Diane, now behind her chic black metal desk, said, "Close the door behind you, please."

Luanna mentally straightened her spine. Whatever it was, she was confident it would all get sorted out, so she fell back on her Southern politeness, which called for her to comment on the weather.

"Whoo!" she said, sitting down in the padded chair across from Diane. The office was so tiny that her knees knocked against the back of Diane's desk, and she could smell Hernando's too-sweet aftershave because he was so close to her that if he tripped, he'd be in her lap. "It's hotter than Satan's housecat out there, isn't it?"

Diane normally loved Luanna's "Southernisms," as she called them, but not this time.

Hernando didn't crack a smile. Dayum.

"Luanna," Diane said, "we've got a situation that needs addressing. I'm sure it's a misunderstanding, something we can get cleared up quickly, but I do need to remind you of the legal forms you signed when you came to work for Luscious Couture."

She put a hand on a green manila folder on her desk, which Luanna guessed was her employment file.

"Of course," Luanna said, remembering the confidentiality agreement and raft of other forms she'd run by her best friend Chloe Montiero's brother Curt the lawyer before signing. They'd all been pretty straightforward; nothing she'd had a problem with.

So what *was* the problem? Why did Diane sound as if she were reading from a script? They'd always gotten along well, Luanna thought.

"It's come to our attention that you might be doing some design work on the side," Diane said, "which would violate the noncompete clause you signed."

Luanna felt her stomach spin faster than a NASCAR crash.

Now she knew what this was about.

She wasn't, in fact, doing any wrong. She was sewing on the side, and it was for money, but it wasn't couture design.

And it wasn't anything she could ever, ever tell Diane, or anyone else.

She might've signed a confidentiality clause with Luscious Couture, but her oath to the famous and high-powered crossdressing men she made women's clothing for went deeper than legalese.

She'd made them a promise. She'd made her friend Ray Stark—beefy action hero Ray Stark—a promise. And Luanna Devenaux would sooner sell her momma to the devil than break her promises.

"Oh, no," she said truthfully, "I'm not working for any other designer or company. I just do a little sewing for friends, you know, for pin money, and because that's what you do for friends. My best friend, Chloe—she came out with me from Boston—just got engaged, and of course I told her I'd make her wedding dress. Probably the bridesmaids dresses, too, because Lord knows I don't want to be caught in one of those hideous off-the-rack monstrosities. But I've never used any supplies from here, or sewn for friends on company time."

She suspected she had crossed the line into "talking too much to cover up your hedging the truth." She suspected Diane knew it, too. Diane was no fool.

Hernando probably wasn't, either, except when he had too much to drink. But who didn't do foolish things then?

Diane drummed her manicured nails on the file folder, black flashing against the green. "Luscious has a very narrow view of what constitutes a noncompete violation. We're going to need to see everything you've made, and a list of who you've sewn anything for."

Luanna felt like that time the horse she'd been riding had bolted.

She hated that out-of-control feeling more than anything in the world.

Blinking her big baby blues sometimes worked with men, and some particularly inclined women—she hated stooping to that, but if it got her out of a parking ticket, so be it—but she knew it wouldn't work with Diane, who was married and straight as a road in Kansas, nor Hernando, because, office indiscretion with Tad, duh.

Stuck between a rock and a hard place, that's what she was.

Screwed was another way of putting it. Seriously screwed.

She licked lips gone as dry as her eyeballs in those hot, arid winds. "I'm afraid I can't do that," she said. She was about to say more but stopped. Every word she added would bring her closer to dropping a hint about *why* she couldn't say anything, about *whom* she couldn't say anything.

Slippery slope.

And Lord knew, slippery slopes always ended you up ass-first into a swamp, eye to eye with a hungry gator.

She tried again. "Diane, I can assure you—I can swear on a stack of bibles a mile high—that I'm not doing anything that violates any of the agreements I signed with Luscious. You know me, you've worked with me for more than a year now. I'm asking you to go on my word and my honor."

That was how the world should work, anyway.

Diane glanced at Hernando, then shook her head, and Luanna saw regret in her soon-to-be-former boss's eyes.

"I'm sorry, Luanna, I truly am," Diane said. "You're clearly a talented designer. But Luscious, like any professional designer, has to protect its brand, and we have no choice but to let you go, effective immediately."

No choice? Even when the bear had you backed up against the tree and your shotgun had jammed, there were options.

"A check to cover this pay period and any unused vacation days will be mailed to you within two weeks," Hernando said.

"Thank you," Luanna said, because she was raised to be polite and because she wasn't really listening anymore. Her brain was already trying to figure out how she and Evenrude, her Welsh corgi, would keep from starving.

Diane's words, "like any professional designer," were loaded ones. Getting fired from a couture firm—fashion was a cutthroat and yet tight industry—would make it difficult to get a new job. Luanna could spin her leaving any number of ways, and HR wouldn't be allowed to give specifics, but Hernando's tone of voice could convey everything.

Hernando was highly unlikely to sound perky when he confirmed the dates of her employment. Even if Tad was…

Nope, not gonna go there.

"And again, I'm sorry, but I'm required to say this," Diane went on. "You're still bound by the confidentiality clause. If any Luscious designs show up somewhere, you'll be prosecuted to the fullest extent of the law."

Luanna tamped down her panic, stood, and held out her hand. "I understand. Thank you, Diane. It's truly been a pleasure working with you."

Diane followed her out of the office and stood at the railing. Luanna made her way down the stairs, followed closely by Hernando. As he watched—and her colleagues all pretended not to watch—she got her big gooshy purse out of the drawer and dumped her personal belongings into it. The framed photo of Evenrude and her beloved peacocks. The Paula Deen bobblehead, a gift from Chloe. The packet of ramen, which would've made Chloe shudder if she knew.

It made Luanna shudder, in truth, but she believed in being prepared, and she never knew when she'd have to pull an all-nighter. Or when there'd be an earthquake, but if she were trapped by an earthquake, the microwave probably wouldn't work. She could crunch the noodles, though.

She hadn't really brought any other personal effects to her workspace because every inch had been taken up with sketches and fabric swatches and pens and pins.

She looked longingly at her most recent sketch, the one she'd planned to mock up today, and pressed her lips together to keep them from trembling. Then she squared her shoulders and left her dream job behind as she went back outside into the hellish heat to figure out how to get her ass out of the swamp before the alligator chomped on it.

*

The heat slowed Luanna's steps, like an inappropriate faux-fur stole edged with lead weights dragging her down. The fabric shops, their wares spilling out onto the sidewalk, pushed bolts of orange and black and skulls and spiderwebs.

Halloween might have been her favorite holiday when she was growing up—oh, the costume opportunities!—but in this heat, it seemed ridiculous.

As in, you had to trick-or-treat as a surfer or bronze-bikini Leia just to stay cool.

She tried to take a deep, calming breath in through her nose, then remembered why that wasn't the best of ideas.

This part of Los Angeles never smelled good. Even though the streets were wide—two lanes in each direction—cars always clogged the streets, and the tall buildings trapped the exhaust. Combined with something unidentifiable she didn't want to think about (it wasn't the cleanest section of town), there was always a funky cast to the air.

Luanna fought off her churning emotions by focusing on the next step: get to her car and crank the AC.

One thing at a time.

She was tempted to stop at Starbucks, a familiar one between the parking garage and Luscious Couture, but the usual barista didn't know how to make proper sweet tea, and technically Luanna couldn't even afford a bottle of water right now. Tap water for this girl, damn the contaminants, full steam ahead.

Tears prickled behind her eyes (where had she found the moisture?), but she fought them back, pressing her lips firmly together and straightening her back. Her parents wouldn't approve of her getting hysterical in public, though they'd have different reasons for it. Daddy would remind her that she'd made the honorable choice, even if it was hard, and that meant there was no point in crying. He'd also recommend a bourbon and branch water once she got home to make the hard choice easier to swallow.

She was more of a margarita girl herself, but the general principle was sound. It would be noon in Louisiana by the time she made it home.

Momma, on the other hand, was the queen of making scenes, but she'd point out that Luanna was in the middle of Los Angeles, surrounded by strangers; with no one to hug her or fuss over her distress, it wasn't worth ruining her makeup. (Not that Luanna ever wore Momma-level makeup, with mascara on the false eyelashes, but again, the principle was sound.)

And thinking of Momma brought the briefest of smiles. Luanna's mother was, under her fluffy, flamboyant, big-haired costume, one of the smartest and toughest people Luanna knew, but she was an old-school Southern belle and mostly used her brains to get Daddy and other men to do her bidding.

She reached the parking garage, trudged up the cement stairs to the roof. And that's when she started to crumble again.

The way the rooftop garage worked was that early arrivals (for example, employees) got boxed in by later arrivals (for example, shoppers looking for fabric bargains). So Luanna had to stand in the heat—the flaming ball of evil pounding down in the cloudless blue expanse of hell—while the attendant found her car, moved the one in front of it, moved hers to escape position, and returned with her keys.

Waiting screwed up the plan of *Get to her car and crank the AC.* Waiting gave her time to think.

This was a poor time to think. No good could come of it.

By the time the attendant rescued her car and handed her her keys, she was practicing every deep breathing exercise she knew and a couple she'd made up on the fly.

She slid into the front seat of her beloved hunter-green Mini, and when the air conditioning, ancient but loyal, kicked in, the tears threatened again.

Next step: drive home.

It would have been an easy step except for the blurring tears and overall distraction, which meant that as she eased the Mini down the tight, narrow turns of the garage, she might have just drifted the tiniest bit toward the center, and when the driver of the car zooming up the ramp leaned on their horn, she probably jerked to the right a little too suddenly.

The fender of her car slammed into the steel post looming out of the concrete, placed to point drivers down the ramp. She hadn't been going fast, but the sudden jolting stop still had a whiplash effect, and her head bounced off the headrest, making the world spin for a moment.

The crunching of metal made her stomach lurch.

The other driver zoomed past, and if Luanna hadn't been such a positive person, she was sure she would've seen the driver flashing her the bird.

Not terribly charitable, but maybe they were having a worse day than she was.

Luanna rested her forehead against the steering wheel. Not likely.

Especially not when she tried to drive away, and her wheels wouldn't turn.

Okay, this was now officially the Worst. Day. Ever.

Luanna decided to blame the blouse.

Chapter 2

*T*he only tiny positive factor to Luanna's day was that it was a Monday, which was Chloe's day off from the restaurant.

Hearing her best friend's voice on the phone saying of course she'll come and pick Luanna up, don't you worry, nearly sent Luanna into another bout of tears.

Chloe was there for her when the tow truck arrived and the driver had to hammer on the poor Mini to get the fender away from the tire so that the car could be coasted down the ramp to the truck outside.

In fact, Chloe was the one who stood at the curve in the ramp and directed cars so nobody had a head-on collision, while Luanna waited outside (in the shade of a shop awning, clutching the cold bottle of water Chloe had brought for her) for the tow truck.

And because Chloe was constitutionally incapable of not taking care of everyone around her, Chloe was also the one who insisted on stopping at the grocery store on the way home to pick up the fixings for margaritas (although she offered to get bourbon). Luanna stayed in the Nissan and indulged in a brief bout of weeping, partly in gratitude.

She was finished and powdering her nose by the time Chloe crossed the parking lot again. Chloe, her curly dark hair piled on her head, her short, curvy form poured into a sleeveless white-with-red-polka-dots sundress, was a force of nature, and Luanna adored her.

"When you called to say you were leaving work, I was afraid you were sick," Chloe admitted as she eased her new-to-her car onto the 405 freeway. She and Luanna had driven the Mini from Boston to Los Angeles, but now they both had to drive to work. (Well, until today, that was.) Traffic was moving, but a bit slow; lunchtime in Los Angeles, yippee. "I'm so glad you're not sick. Sandrine's been reading WebMD—God only knows why—and if she found out you were sick, you know she'd quarantine us. And then forget that she did it, knowing her."

That choked a laugh out of Luanna, because Chloe wasn't really exaggerating all that much. Sandrine Moss, on whose estate they lived, was what Chloe termed "fruit-bat crazy." (Although Chloe had been trying to break herself of that habit, because she was engaged to Sandrine's older brother, Brand Mossiman. While Brand might not disagree with the description, refraining was the polite thing to do.)

In truth, Sandrine was a sweetheart. A little nutty, sure, but deep down she had a heart of gold. When you were one of the highest-paid actresses in Hollywood, you had a right to be a little eccentric.

Luanna was from the South: eccentric was practically what you aspired to be.

She'd already told Chloe about being fired—Chloe also already knew about Ray's proclivities and Luanna's side job, although she didn't know the other men Luanna made women's wear for—and about how her car insurance would be shooting up thanks to her little fender bender.

"So how's your day been so far?" she asked, deflecting Chloe away from being sympathetic and helpful. Luanna didn't think she could take much more of that.

They were going slowly enough that Chloe could take her hands off the wheel and fling them into the air.

"Sandrine called at four a.m. because she forgot about the time difference, wanting to give some wedding suggestions." Chloe made a sound, something like a strangled moan. From that noise alone, Luanna figured Chloe might need the margaritas as much as she did.

"What now?" Luanna asked.

"She wanted to talk about the wedding theme," Chloe said, and Luanna was pretty sure her friend was clenching her teeth. "We haven't even decided whether to have it here or Rhode Island, but Sandrine's already talked to some friend of hers, Valerie, who's some sort of socialite party planner. There was talk of clowns." She drew in a deep breath through her nose. "I do not want clowns at my wedding. The idea of clowns at my wedding makes me want to elope."

"You don't have to have clowns at your wedding," Luanna said, projecting as much *soothing* as she could. "Sandrine will understand."

"Oh, I know she will, in the end," Chloe said. "I just wasn't ready for the clown suggestion at effing four in the morning. And I know I have an enormous family and all, but I guess I never thought my wedding would be so…enormous. Or complicated."

"Your wedding should be what you want it to be," Luanna said. "Big or small." Southern weddings tended to be complicated, and Luanna had to admit she loved the dramatic aspect of them, but that didn't mean it was what Chloe wanted.

More's the pity. Luanna was on Sandrine's side about this one.

Well, within reason. She was kind of horrified about clowns, too.

"You're right, of course." Chloe sighed, but she was smiling. "After that call, I had about five seconds when I thought about eloping to Vegas. We'd never do it—weddings should involve your families, and the estate really is a dream venue. It's just challenging at times."

"Darlin', just give me a heads-up if I have to make spangly Elvis jumpsuits for everybody," Luanna said.

Chloe snorted as she took the freeway exit. "It'll never happen. For one thing, I am way too short to rock an Elvis jumpsuit."

Now they were on the shaded, quiet streets of Beverly Hills, home to the stars who were Really Stars and had more money than sense.

They stopped at the ornate, twisty wrought-iron gates, and Luanna looked out at the tall, leafy, black cottonwood trees with their rough, gray bark, similar enough to the poplars of Louisiana that they made her a little homesick.

"Oh, dear sweet Lord in heaven," Luanna said.

Chloe punched in the gate code and pulled her head back in. "What's wrong?"

"I can*not* tell my parents about this. About any of this."

Chloe patted her hand and put the car in gear. "Don't worry, sweetheart. You'll have a new job before you know it."

"I don't want to think about it anymore," Luanna admitted. "Not for the rest of today, at least."

"Perfect," Chloe said. "We're going to have our own personal spa day." She pointed out the window at the Arabian Nights fantasy of the estate pool and cabana. "We'll lounge by the pool, sit in the hot tub, drink margaritas, and convince Lance to make us something spectacular and decadent to eat."

Actually, what sounded even better was stripping off all her sticky clothes and diving into the cool blue water of the pool. Except other people lived on the estate, so Luanna knew it behooved her to actually put on a bathing suit first.

"Didn't Lance ban you from the kitchen?" Luanna asked.

Chloe rolled her dark eyes. "It was a misunderstanding."

The whole reason they lived on the estate—Luanna still in the guest house, and Chloe recently almost-completely-moved into the gatehouse where Brand lived—was that Chloe had been Sandrine's personal chef.

Well, to be honest, Sandrine had kind of blackmailed Chloe into being her personal chef. Semantics.

But when Chloe got the chance at her dream job, working at M. DesJardins' new restaurant, Sandrine had graciously released her from her contract and promptly hired a startled Lance, who'd helped as a sous chef a couple of times.

Young Lance, still wet behind the ears, with his tattoos and piercings and bad-boy swaggering, hadn't seemed the type to put up with Sandrine's admittedly wacky eating habits (which changed on a near-daily basis), but he'd settled in surprisingly well.

It had just taken Chloe a little while to get used to the fact that Sandrine's kitchen was no longer "her" kitchen.

Still, Sandrine never minded when Lance made a little extra food for his friends, because they were her friends, too.

Luanna shook her head. Friends with *the* Sandrine Moss. Who would've thunk it?

If Sandrine weren't on location in Romania, she'd probably have joined them for drinks by the pool.

She would even have brought them all tiaras to wear. Sandrine did like her tiaras.

Chloe pulled up in front of the guest house. "Go change into something more comfortable. I'll do the same and be back in a few minutes."

"You know you still have clothes here, right?" Luanna said as she got out, her purse and the bag of margarita fixings in hand.

"Yeah, I know, I'm sorry. Thank God Brand and I are going to look for a bigger place after the wedding. This living in two places is driving me a little bonkers." Chloe sighed. "É *o que é.*"

It is what it is. Luanna had learned that much Portuguese because it was Chloe's mantra.

Chloe pulled away and Luanna bent to scritch Evenrude behind the ears. The corgi was on a long lead so she could get from the shaded, relatively cool patio around to the grassy area on the side of the cottage to do her business. The two estate peacocks, Brad and George, who had some sort of platonic ménage romance with Evenrude, dozed on the lawn chairs.

The guest cottage was about three times as big as the apartment Luanna and Chloe had shared when they first moved to LA, and it was a hell of a lot nicer, too. Luanna kicked off her shoes by the front door and let the gushy-soft hunter-green Berber carpet perform better pressure-point massage than any shiatsu master. She set the liquor store plastic bag on the coffee table—a faux-distressed off-white piece with a glass top that was the farthest from Luanna's style, but Sandrine had decorated—next to the cereal bowl she'd neglected to put away this morning.

She took two steps toward her small bedroom, one of two in the place (she'd turned Chloe's old room into a sewing studio), and stopped dead in her tracks, quivering like a hound dog who'd sniffed out a coon.

Sandrine might be a friend, but Luanna was living rent-free in her guest house, a situation that had come about when Chloe worked for Sandrine. Chloe no longer worked for Sandrine, and was planning to move off the estate entirely, which left Luanna with no real reason to be mooching off Sandrine.

So on top of everything else, she might have to find a place to live, too.

She swore she heard an audible *chomp* and a swish of air as the alligator just missed chowing down on her ass.

She turned back, twisted the top off the tequila, and took a long swig.

Then she peeled off her unlucky, sweaty, evil blouse and tossed it in the direction of the kitchen trash.

*

Several months later, things were not better.

Things were *dire*.

But it was New Year's Eve, and she was determined to enjoy it.

She got to the party late—it had been relatively cheaper to fly on New Year's Eve, so the shuttle from LAX dropped her off at the estate close to 11 p.m. She quickly dropped her bags in the guest house, refreshed her makeup, and slipped into a glittery silver, low-necked top that did wonders for her cleavage and clung to her curves. She paired it with black capri pants and silver slip-on ballet-type shoes, because the festivities were being held outside, around the pool area.

Just a casual get-together for Sandrine and Ray and fifty or so of their closest friends, although Brand had friends in the area, too, and Chloe had invited a few people from work.

Luanna would've mentioned it to some of her co-workers—if she'd had a job, that is.

She shook her head and flicked her fingers to release the negative energy.

New Year's Eve. A time for celebration. A time to reboot and start fresh, dammitall.

She stepped out onto the patio. Cool air brushed her bare arms, but there would be heat lamps around the pool, and body heat, and hot food and warming alcohol.

Evenrude gazed up at her with hopeful, liquid eyes, and she dropped to her knees to hug her stupid, lovable Welsh corgi.

"No, you can't come with me, darlin," she explained, scratching behind Evenrude's ears. "Too many people to trip over you—and we can't have you y'all getting loose again."

She tried not to feel guilty for being in Louisiana for the holidays when Evenrude decided to go frolicking with the peacocks…and forgot she couldn't fly like the peacocks, which meant she'd ended up in the cactus garden. As in, cactus spines in *her*. Chloe and Brand had rushed her to the emergency vet, and Evenrude was pretty much already all healed up.

Still, Luanna felt something awful for not being there.

"You celebrate here with Brad and George," she added.

Brad the peacock fanned out his tail upon hearing his name. George chose to scream, and Luanna screamed and fell back on her ass.

"Dammit, George." She stood up, checked to make sure her capris were fine. "I'll be bringing back a treat for Evenrude"—the corgi thumped her tail against the tile—"and Brad, but not for you, you loud bastard."

George made an annoyed clucking noise and fluttered up to the back of a lawn chair.

Luanna gave Evenrude one last affectionate rub and headed to the party.

The noise greeted her before anything else: a frothy champagne bubble of voices, the big-band swing music from an incredibly good sound system.

Then lights. Strings of fairy lights draped everywhere, creating a magical sparkle on the Arabian Nights fantasy of the cabana, all brightly colored tile and minarets.

She spotted Chloe and Brand, headed their way. Chloe squealed and ran up to hug her, almost knocking her off her feet. Chloe might be five-foot-nothing, but she made up for it with enthusiasm.

Brand had his cell phone to his ear, giving someone the gate code, so Chloe grabbed her arm and dragged her a few steps away.

"I'm *so* glad you're back," Chloe said. "How was Louisiana? How's your family?"

Luanna had promised herself she wouldn't complain, wouldn't even think about it all, not on New Year's Eve, but Chloe's take-care-of-everyone superpower loosened her tongue.

"Oh, dear Lord," she said. "We were all playing cribbage one night, and we'd all had one too many drinks—cribbage just isn't worth it without alcohol—and Grand-mère asked me how Luscious was, and I accidentally might have made some remark that might have led them to figure out I was no longer employed by that lofty establishment."

"What did you say?" Chloe asked, her brown eyes wide with sympathy.

"I said Luscious could kiss my fine Southern ass."

"Oh," Chloe said. "Oops."

"*Oops* is right." Luanna closed her eyes, trying not to remember everybody's faces. "So of course they spent the rest of the time trying to convince me to come home, that there were perfectly good design jobs in Baton Rouge. My family is exceptionally good at guilt."

"Yours and mine both, sister." Chloe hugged her again. "Come on, let's get you some champagne—although whisky is traditional on New Year's Eve, if you want something stronger. Are you hungry? There's a ton of food."

"I can manage to get myself food, darlin'." Luanna smiled, loving how much her friend loved to make everyone feel at home.

"I know, but I thought I'd check to make sure we weren't running out of—"

"You don't work here anymore," Luanna reminded her.

"But Lance—"

"I'll wager you dollars to doughnuts he's doing just fine. You go find your sweetie. It's bad luck if you miss kissing him at the stroke of midnight."

"Yeah, where did he go off to?" Chloe left in search of Brand.

Lance was, in fact, competently dealing with the buffet of food in the outdoor kitchen, which was almost the size of the guest house. Heated serving dishes lined up on white-cloth-covered tables, with cold food arranged on the granite prep space. Candles in punched-metal lanterns gave the covered area a cozy feel.

"Hey," Luanna said, grabbing a plate.

"Hey yourself, gorgeous," Lance said, winking. Flirting was like breathing for him, and Luanna was used to it. His spiky hair, normally bleach-tipped, glowed electric blue in the lantern-light. Apparently that was his idea of dressing to the party theme. He wore his usual tight jeans and T-shirt combo; Luanna doubted anyone would ever talk him into chef's whites.

Something smelled both delicious and familiar, making her stomach rumble even as it panged for the South she'd just left. "Hoppin' John!" she exclaimed, making a beeline for the pork, beans, and greens dish.

"Sandrine, via Olive, gave me a list of traditional New Year's Eve dishes from around the world," Lance said, mentioning Sandrine's extraordinarily efficient and unflappable personal assistant (she'd have to be, working for Sandrine, who changed plans faster than it took to drive a lap at Talladega). He pointed. "Hoppin' John and cornbread from the South. Fresh fruit is Mexican, although the pomegranate is...Turkish, I think. Noodles are an Asian custom, big surprise."

"What's this?" Luanna pointed her fork at something that did *not* smell good.

"Pickled herring," Lance said. "A tradition of people from the land of crazy."

Luanna filled her plate with the edible food, then snagged a glass of champagne. It was cool and tart and bubbly, and she wasn't at all surprised to need a second glass almost immediately. Wisely, she then went in search of a place to eat that wasn't next to the champagne fountain.

She found herself smiling again. The food was tasty, the mood was infectious, and the champagne helped numb the nagging worry in her belly.

Fact was, she still hadn't found a job. Her car insurance had gone up, only for her car to be pronounced unfixable. (Brand, who fixed classic cars as a hobby, said the suspension was borked. Well, he'd used a more technical term, but the bottom line was that fixing the Mini would cost well more than the car was worth.) Chloe said she didn't need to be paid back for Evenrude's emergency vet, because Evenrude was practically her dog, too, but Luanna's parents had taught her never to owe money to friends. Speaking of parents, she'd racked up her credit card flying home for the holidays.

None of the design firms had openings. Or it was possible Hernando from HR was adopting a frosty tone when anyone called about a reference. Fact was, she didn't *have* any good current references, because Luscious had been her first real design job. Her favorite professor had retired to a small village in Italy and was hard to get hold of.

She'd even applied for a spot on *Project Runway*, but hadn't heard back from them. Yet. There was always hope.

A busboy swept away her plate and cutlery, and she went back for a third glass of champagne—this one she intended to save for midnight, which she was pretty sure would be soon. She'd left her phone in the guest house, and there were no clocks out here in fantasy pool land.

Rank the positives, that's what her daddy would say. Okay. She was healthy, her family was healthy, Evenrude had recovered. She had never been convicted of a felony. She had all her own teeth. And…

And oh, my goodness gracious, but that was a fine specimen of manhood also reaching for champagne.

Acknowledgements

Chloe may prefer to cook alone, and writing itself is a solitary practice, but in the end, it's a collaborative process. Many talented and committed people helped shepherd this book to completion, adding their own spices to the pot.

A brief encounter in Hollywood provided the spark of an idea that became *Out of the Frying Pan* (Sandrine's shenanigans are purely fiction, though); thank you to my friends who hosted the party!

My beta readers—Kelly Harmon, Leslie Walker, and Terry Mixon—read a rough draft and gave insightful comments on how to make it shine. Hugs!

Colleen Kuehne worked her copyediting magic to put the final sparkle on the manuscript (any remaining mistakes are entirely mine), and her embedded comments never failed to make me laugh. Thanks for being a fan!

Allyson Longueira patiently listened while I flailed around trying to describe what the cover needed to convey ("Funny! But also sexy! And…!"), ignored me, and designed something I never would have considered. And she was right. I mean, just *look* at that cover!

A brief encounter in Hollywood provided the spark of an idea that became the Hollywood Spice series (Sandrine's shenanigans are purely fiction, though); thank you to my friends who hosted the party years ago.

And to Sophie fans everywhere: thank you for hopping aboard the Hollywood Spice train(wreck)!

About the Author

Author of the steamy 4-star (*Romantic Times*) novel *Cat Scratch Fever*; the sexy paranormal romp *Possessed, Undressed, and in a Mess*; and more, Sophie Mouette is the brainchild of two widely published authors of erotica, romance, and speculative fiction. Her popular short erotic fiction has appeared in anthologies from Avon Books, Cleis Press, and Circlet Press.

The two halves of Sophie—Dayle A. Dermatis (aka Andrea Dale) and Teresa Noelle Roberts—met more than two decades ago at a writers' conference. Talking nonstop, they closed down the hotel bar and went somewhere else to keep on talking. Although they've always lived on opposite sides of the country (and for a few years, on opposite sides of the Atlantic), they've remained very close friends, and it was only natural that they should start writing together as well.

Visit SophieMouette.com for more information.

www.ingramcontent.com/pod-product-compliance
Lightning Source LLC
Chambersburg PA
CBHW030932260626
47169CB00002B/439